CASTLE
BAREBANE

CASTLE BAREBANE

JOAN AIKEN

THE VIKING PRESS NEW YORK

This ae night, this ae night
  Every night and alle
Fire and sleet and candle-light
  And Christ receive thy soule. . . .

If ever thou gavest hosen and shoon
  Every night and alle
Sit thee down and put them on
  And Christ receive thy soule

If hosen and shoon thou ne'er gav'st nane
  Every night and alle
The whins shall prick thee to the bare bane
  And Christ receive thy soule

This ae night, this ae night
  Every night and alle
Fire and sleet and candle-light
  And Christ receive thy soule.

Lyke-Wake Ballad

CASTLE
BAREBANE

CHAPTER 1

THE planning of her wardrobe and the subject of clothes had never, for Valla Montgomery, occupied more than a tiny, unregarded corner of her mind. Since completing her education she had bought the garments that seemed most practical and durable, warm in winter, cool in summer, and that was the end of the matter, so far as she was concerned. Fashion was of no interest to her, except in the professional sphere. Occasionally her father might admire a cut or a colour: "You remind me of your dear grandmother in that"; occasionally, glancing in her glass as she swiftly pinned on her hat before darting off to some appointment, she had been visited by the fleeting notion that she could, without exaggeration, be called a handsome girl. But as for clothes—of what importance were they? So long as they fitted, and did not outrageously offend decency, what difference could be made by the trivial details of material, trimmings, flouncing—what importance could these things possibly have?

Now, suddenly glancing round her in a panic, at the evening party with dancing which was being given by his family to celebrate the announcement of her engagement to Benet Allerton, Valla discovered that she had been wrong all her life, and that she had reached a complete culmination of wrongness at the present juncture.

"What should I wear?" she had asked Benet—she had at least possessed that much sense—and he had gaily answered, "Oh, full rig, sweetheart; dress right up to the hilt. All the old things will have dug out their Cluny and Valenciennes for the occasion, I daresay."

She had really meant to go to a dressmaker. But the three previous weeks had been unusually busy; two of her colleagues had been away, and there had been a congressional election, an agricultural convention, and a complicated scandal regarding the new city gas supply. She had never found time. And it wasn't, after all, as if she did not possess an evening toilette: she had one all-purpose dress for wearing to the various after-dark events—hospital galas, charity concerts, political buffet suppers—fashionable affairs which were considered the province of a lady reporter. The dress was made of dark grey velvet, a good fit but very plainly cut with hardly any bustle so that, if necessary (as it frequently had been) she could wear it under a thick, inconspicuous traveling coat and could ride without too much remark in train or streetcar or hackney cab. The dress was a good dependable dress which had stood her in excellent stead on plenty of occasions; it was comfortable and suited her. With its high, plain collar against her too-long neck, and the dark, silvery folds of the skirt falling composedly around her, she felt exactly herself, armed, cap-à-pie, ready to meet all comers.

Or had until this evening.

On the day before the party she had known a half-hour's uncertainty. Perhaps the dress was a fraction severe? Should she consult Benet's mother? His sister Delia? But they were such a silly pair; she had no faith in their judgment. Acting on a hasty impulse, she had run from the office of the *New York Inquirer* over to Fifth Avenue and bought a couple of yards of wide lemon-yellow moiré ribbon, which, that evening, she had sewed around under the collar and allowed to hang loose in two fishtails down the back of the dress. Now she wished that she had not done so. In her mind's eye she saw the two pale-yellow streamers flowing behind her like the decorations of some farmhorse groomed for a fair. Had she, indeed, caught a whisper, faint, behind somebody's fan, as she stood near the top of the stairs, "My dear! She looks exactly like a Percheron! Big as one, too."

It was of course bad luck that Benet's mother and sister, receiving guests at the stairhead, should be, unlike him, both so small: vivacious little plump ladies, the pair of them, their hair done in clusters like bunches of grapes, their lace tuckers pouting above tight, well-packed satin, their fat little feet on stilted heels among forests of petticoats incapable of carrying them at more than a toddle. Valla towered over them. One stride, and she was half way across the first reception room with its white marble Italian mantel and rosy flock wallpaper.

She stepped back uncertainly and caught the whisper once more.

"Who is she?"

"My darling, nobody! Her father was one of those newspaper people—edited the *Philadelphia Weekly Interviewer* or some such thing—and then I believe *Pargeter's Review*—dead, now, I think, luckily. No, no other family. Just as well for the Allertons."

"Poor things!"

"They seem to be putting a brave face on it."

"But it must really—" The fan obscured the rest of the sentence.

Valla had a fan of her own; a big, beautiful one, made from eagles' feathers. Benet had given it to her, together with her irreproachable fifteen-button kid gloves. She slowly wafted it, twice, to cool the angry sting of her cheek, and then held it as a barrier between her and the intrusive whispers; she would not yield them the advantage of glancing in their direction.

Everybody else was wearing silk or satin, tulle or damask; in the triple series of rooms leading to the Allertons' big second-floor ballroom—which was a sign of their eminent respectability and well-foundness, for what other New York family in these times could afford to keep a room of that size unused and shut up for three hundred and sixty-three days in the year?—the dresses shimmered and glimmered, catching the light from the newfangled gas chandeliers, and returning it in soft mistinesses and uncertainties; the women all rustled, the numerous layers of their silk underskirts keeping up a constant susurrus as they swished about. Only Valla, solitary in the crowd, stood tall and soundless, a dark poplar amid a froth of mimosa blossom, an obelisk surrounded by a flock of hummingbirds; it might be comic if it were not so dreadful.

Now Benet was bringing up two more ladies to be introduced.

"Valla dear—my cousins Mrs. and Miss Chauncey—Adelaide and Maria."

A tall hostility in feuille-morte taffeta, immensely flounced, with cascades of black lace, and a slighter, thinner hostility in a gauzy Directoire web of no doubt ancestral embroidered India mull, with crystal-spangled feathers in her piled hair. Their four eyes pierced Valla like hatpins. *What* has Benet let himself in for, said their combined stare; how could the Allertons have allowed it to happen?

"So happy to make your acquaintance, Miss—"

"Montgomery," Benet reminded his cousin.

"Montgomery, of course—" but there was a hint of doubt in her tone as if she were audibly wondering how much right Valla had to such a respectable-sounding name. "And is this your first visit to New York, Miss Montgomery?"

"Oh, no indeed." Val tried to keep her own rather deep voice quite colourless, without any touch of either defensiveness or irony. "In fact I was born here; I've lived in New York most of my life."

"Really? How very interesting." *Are you sure?* the tone suggested. For if you were in New York, in whatever bohemian or unfashionable corner, somewhere up north of Fortieth Street, I suppose, how is it that my vigilant hawk's eye never spotted you going about your lower-class concerns? Everything that happens in New York is known to me.

"But you and Benet did not meet here, I believe?"

"No, Cousin Adelaide, we met in Chicago," Benet said easily. "When I was defending in that Cottonmaster Trust case."

"Oh indeed." Mrs. Chauncey's manner dismissed any part of the United States west of Washington. "Do your family reside in Chicago then, my dear?"

"No." Valla could hardly believe that Benet's second cousin was not well informed already about the Montgomery background but she obliged with what was evidently the required answer. "I was working in Chicago at the time when I met Benet, writing a series of articles about women in industry for the *New York Inquirer.*"

"Oh dear me," Mrs. Chauncey said. "I *see.* How *very* interesting. It is really remarkable—is it not—the things that young women do nowadays. The *Inquirer*—just fancy—of course we don't see it—only the *Times*—but I understand it is a very good sort of paper. Come, Maria, we must pay our respects to Cousin Benjamin Babcock. So glad to have made your acquaintance, Miss Montgomery."

Inclining her plumed head briefly to Val, she twitched the arm of her child, who was showing a tendency to regard Benet's fiancée with large-eyed astonishment, almost bordering on respect. They moved away—a guinea fowl with duckling in tow.

Val smiled ruefully at Benet.

"I've made a terrible mistake, haven't I? I'm dressed all wrong for this occasion."

"You look beautiful," said Benet loyally. "To me, whatever you wear seems right on you. Everyone else looks overdressed and fussy."

A surge of warm feeling for him refreshed her sinking spirits. What a comfort he was, what a support in the midst of this fashionable idiocy.

Though she was bound to admit, studying him with detachment, that he himself presented as fashionable an appearance as any of the men present, from his patent leathers to his impeccable waistcoat. But there was so much more to Benet than mere fashion. He was large and calm—massively built even, overtopping the tall Valla—but nevertheless light on his feet, with an athlete's economy of movement. Not that he was lazy: his observant grey eye went everywhere, watching and recording. In that he certainly resembled his cousin Adelaide. But in all other particulars, how different! Benet's fresh-coloured, clean-featured, clean-shaven face instilled observers with immediate confidence; his expression was invariably urbane, good-humoured, and receptive; nothing ever seemed to disturb his air of cheerful equanimity. Though he was nobody's fool; the wide thoughtful brow under his beautifully cut thick brown hair gave true indication of an alert, well-stocked mind. He was certainly not handsome, but there was something so wholesome and attractive about his air and appearance that whenever she saw him anew, Valla was reinforced all over again in the certainty of her good fortune in having secured his regard.

Now he tucked his warm, firm hand comfortably under her grey-velvet elbow.

"Don't worry. You look distinguished, my dear. All the other women seem like dressed-up fashion models."

Valla knew sadly that this was not so.

"Every one of those dresses comes from Paris. I didn't work on the Butterick's Pattern page for six months without learning the difference between Fifth Avenue and the Rue de la Paix. Look, that's a Doucet."

A white-silk dress went dipping past them, its purity offset by one broad black diagonal satin stripe, swept up to an elaborately swathed series of overlappings and flounces at the rear, culminating in a big black bow.

"Cousin Lydia Babcock," he said indifferently. "The silliest woman in New York."

"And look at your grandmother in her black damask and Venetian point—if I'd had any intelligence I'd have asked her advice."

"You'd never have been able to get at her. She keeps herself shut in that castle of hers like the Old Man of the Mountains. Come and talk to her. And meet Cousin James Dexter."

He took Val's kid-gloved hand in his and led her through two more of the drawing rooms, one sea-green, one white-and-gilt, to where old Mrs. Allerton sat in state. A spare middle-aged man stood easily at her elbow.

Fully aware that this pair were the arbiters of opinion for the whole clan, Val accompanied Benet with feelings of trepidation mingled with annoyance. Why had she been fool enough to let herself in for this ordeal?

Why could not the engagement have been announced in some less formal way? She guessed this large party was the Allertons' banner of defiance. But why should I, she thought rebelliously, have to be nailed to their social mast?

She had not met Benet's grandmother before. Old Mrs. Allerton practically never descended on New York, but remained in stately isolation at Bridgewater, the family house on the Hudson. Cousin James, on the contrary, was a New Yorker to the ends of his elegant fingernails; witty, discreet, suave, erudite, and unmarried, he graced every dinner party in the select circles of society between Gramercy Park and Washington Square; but he had been away on a seven-months' European tour, and this was the first engagement he had accepted since his return; indeed the ball had been deferred until Cousin James could be there to give it the accolade of his presence.

Benet made the introductions with formal politeness and then stood lightly holding Val's arm, with the intention, she knew, of instilling confidence in her by his touch.

Old Mrs. Allerton's complexion was soft and unhealthy-looking, like bread dough, and the flat lappets of her hair, under the magnificent widow's lace, might have been a wig, so dry and strawlike did they look. But her eye was sharp and raking as a fisherman's knife, and her voice was startlingly deep and harsh.

"Valhalla—what kind of a name is that, pray?"

"My mother gave it to me," Val said mildly. "I understand she was going through a romantic enthusiasm for Norse mythology at the time. But my father shortened it to Valla."

"Well, young lady—I hear you write for the newspapers, isn't that it? One of these clever young women who aren't satisfied to stay home and see to the housekeeping—eh? Isn't that so? But how did Benet ever become involved with you, may I ask? Benet's not clever." She darted a needle glance at him.

"Oh, but he is," protested Val. "He's a very clever lawyer. Have you never heard him in court, Mrs. Allerton?"

Benet's grandmother completely ignored this remark; Val was at once made to feel that she had been unsuitably forward, even impertinent.

"How do you think you'll ever manage to settle down in this family, pray? None of the Allertons or the Chaunceys or Babcocks can be called clever; not the least bit of brain among them. The Dexters—well, now, it's true *they* know enough to come in out of the rain, eh, James?"

She turned from Val to the elderly man beside her. Mrs. Allerton was like, Val thought, a stout, diminutive owl, encased in her whaleboned damask, crested with cream-coloured lace. Huge sparkling watery diamonds added handsomely to her air of authority. Her small firm mouth and chin were supported on concentric ramparts of subsidiary chins; her small bright eyes, like those of some predator, glanced this way and that without registering favour or disfavour. But when she turned to James Dexter, the rigid line of her mouth eased fractionally into what might have been taken for a smile. Mr. Dexter received her pleasantry with an imperturbable air.

"I am gratified that you consider me clever, my dear Sarah," he said calmly. But he smiled at Val, who smiled immediately, warmly, in return. Her smile was quenched at once, however, when she met the eyes of the old lady; their cold and steady scrutiny did not soften; Val felt as if an icy wall of rebuff and exclusion would forever stand between her and any contact with Benet's grandmother.

"The Chaunceys and Babcocks and Allertons never had any time for writing or poetry or any of those fancy activities," old Mrs. Allerton continued. "No, no, we don't go in for that sort of thing."

"Mightn't have done any harm if you had," Val thought to herself but she had the good sense to remain silent.

"Mmm, your father, now—he edited a newspaper—was that it?"

"Indeed he did, and very well too," James Dexter put in. "He was a great and distinguished journalist. I met him several times, Miss Montgomery, and formed the very highest opinion of him. We have had some extremely interesting discussions. I was grieved when I heard of his death. A year ago, was it?"

"Two years." Turning gratefully to Cousin James, Val felt the warmth of tears in her eyes, and opened them wide, to let the tears drain back into their sockets. She would sooner be boiled in oil than betray weakness in front of that old bird of prey.

"Dear, how time flies. You must miss your father very much; he will have been a tremendous example to you."

"Oh, he *was*—"

"I wish I had met him." Coming from another man, these words might have sounded perfunctory; coming from Benet they were the warm and exact truth. Val smiled into his eyes.

"And your mother, child?" the corncrake voice of Mrs. Allerton struck in. "Beyond having an enthusiasm for Norse mythology—what about her? Is she in Chicago still?"

"No, she died seven years ago—before my father," Val explained. She did not feel the need to elaborate on this point; to reveal that in fact her parents had not lived together for eight years before her mother's death;

Benet's family had already found enough to deprecate in her history and circumstances without adding that to the score.

"Mercy, child—if she died when you were fourteen, who's been looking after you all this time?"

No wonder you turn up to your engagement party so unsuitably dressed, the pale old eyes conveyed.

"Oh, I had an English governess—Miss Chumley."

"Chumley, Chumley, humph—I think I recall the name. Didn't she teach the Agnew girls at one time?"

Val didn't know about that. "She is retired now. My father left her a house on Twenty-third Street. She gives a few French lessons, just to keep herself from becoming bored. I am staying with her at present."

"And you have nobody else? No other relatives?" No one of a more respectable kind to provide you with a bit of background and countenance— no one but an ex-governess? the eyes suggested.

"I have an elder half-brother, Nils; but he lives in England. I have not seen him for several years."

"In England? What's his profession, child?"

Val was tempted to reply, He lives on his wits, which would, she was fairly certain, have been a fair statement of the case in regard to her brother Nils.

"He began training as a doctor," she temporised. "At least he was doing so when I saw him last. But I believe that lately he has taken to medical journalism."

"Indeed. *All* your family are literary, then."

It seemed evident from Mrs. Allerton's tone that, in her view, doctors were barely gentlemen, and medical journalists were a totally unknown and unacceptable breed of creature. A kind of wintry gloom began to augment the previous chill of her manner, as if no more were to be hoped from this contact; she looked restlessly about her.

"Sarah," said Cousin James, "I can see Alma Warren trying to catch your eye; she is dying to tell you how well young Sam is doing at Harvard, poor thing, which means that he has not yet actually been expelled for gambling and playing the fool; she has had so little to rejoice over since Edward died. Shall I go and fetch her?"

"Do, James; they will be dancing presently and it will be impossible to hear anything at all. Well, Miss—Montgomery, it has been interesting to meet you. But you shouldn't be lodging with a governess on Twenty-third Street, you know; good gracious, you might as well be at an hotel. I'll ask my niece Amy Chauncey to call and see you; you'd be much better staying with her in Gramercy Park. She has three girls, so she can tell you how to go on."

"Thank you, ma'am—" Val was going, politely and firmly, to decline this suggestion, but old Mrs. Allerton had already turned away and was absorbed in conversation with the tiny sallow vivacious Mrs. Warren, whose white lacy widow's cap hardly accorded with a very dashing low-necked toilette—a Worth dress of lemon-yellow satin embroidered with iridescent beads.

Val exhaled a long, soft sigh, stepping aside with Benet.

"Oh dear! I don't think I made a great hit with your granny."

"Oh, you never can tell with her. She has that dry way—but if there's one thing she respects, it's spunk. She always—"

"Benet!" called the harsh old voice. "Benet, come here a minute. I want you to give Alma some advice about her house at Newport; what's the good of having a lawyer in the family if you don't make use of him?" she added with dry jocosity to the energetically nodding Mrs. Warren.

Benet gave Val's arm a quick squeeze and reluctantly moved back to his grandmother.

This arrangement left Val rather conspicuously alone at the end of the ballroom. She drew a deep breath and looked calmly about her.

The Allertons' ballroom was of handsome and spacious dimensions; when all the double doors of the three anterooms were flung open, as now, the vista seemed immense. Gleams from the lustres along the walls and the gas chandeliers overhead were flung back from the glossy parquet in a confusing shimmer, disseminated and broken by the waft of full gauzy skirts and the come-and-go of black trousered legs. The centrally heated rooms were spiced with scents of hot wax and tulle, hair pomade, and the peppery sweetness from the groves of ferns and exotics which embowered the stairs and reception rooms. There were flowers in the younger girls' hair, too: wreaths of rosebuds and forget-me-nots and forced apple blossom were fashionable that fall; while the coiffures of the older ladies, of course, flashed with diamond aigrettes and spangled feathers. With an effort Val refrained from raising a cautious hand to her own unadorned pile of *cendré*-fair hair, to make sure no wisp was out of place. Looking with dispassionate attention at all this radiance, ostensibly assembled in her own honour, she amused herself by trying to assess how much actual cash it might represent—thirty thousand dollars, forty? The mentality was quite outside her comprehension that could lay out so much money on a single evening and consider the outlay hardly more than she might the purchase of a peach from a sidewalk vendor.

I don't like it, she thought soberly. How much I would prefer it if

Benet's family were poor—Irish immigrants—Polish—anything but what they are.

"Ah now—this is too bad—" said a gentle voice at her elbow. "But we all have to make allowances for my cousin Sarah, you know; she is over ninety and has had her own way for so long."

"I think she is a very remarkable old lady," Val said, smiling at the spare, white-haired, beautifully turned-out Mr. Dexter, who stood beside her. "It's no wonder the whole family hold her in such reverence."

"But still she shouldn't have called Benet away from you just now. The belle of the ball ought not to have been left high and dry."

"But you have kindly come to my rescue so I haven't been. In any case I am not the belle of this ball, Mr. Dexter; I'm not equipped to be that, I'm afraid."

"Come, come, my dear; I have too much respect for Benet to allow any disparagement of his taste; he goes for distinguished beauty, not fuss and furbelows, and I applaud his choice."

"Thank you, Mr. Dexter; you are very kind; but I can't keep up this kind of conversation, you know," Valla said seriously. "I really am not used to compliments and flirtations."

"Sensible young lady! You have used your time to better advantage, and Benet is the gainer."

He nodded amiably to her, his narrow, lined face expressing nothing but friendliness; nevertheless she suspected that under his air of sympathy and encouragement, he was thinking: dull, provincial, too straitlaced, no party manners, what in the world can Benet see in her? How will she ever fit into this milieu?

It was true that Mr. Dexter had heaved an inward sigh, reflecting, Oh dear me, how this girl will encourage the latent Puritan which is already there in Benet; it's not surprising that they took to one another.

Despite the sigh, he did not dislike the tall girl in her severe dark velvet, whose hair, though abundant, was far too plainly dressed and too ash-pale in colour to be esteemed in New York in the eighties; whose complexion, at variance with the blond hair, was disastrously tanned; her face indeed was almost brown. It was plain to Mr. Dexter's eye that unlike the daughters of his friends round about, who carefully shrouded their porcelain skins under shetland or barège veils all through the summer, Miss Montgomery had never given her complexion a thought, except to keep it washed. Even the straight nose and regular features could not atone for that skin. How could the fastidious Benet have singled her out in the first place?

But the eyes—yes, Mr. Dexter had to admit that the eyes were very fine;

her best feature; huge, and of a brilliant, Scandinavian sea-blue, their piercing gaze gave him the same sense of exhilaration and danger as might a plunge into the ice-cold Atlantic—not that Mr. Dexter would ever contemplate such a plunge. Her chin was round and firm—very firm; the set of mouth, chin, and jaw suggested a strong will and a very considerable degree of faith in her own point of view. Mr. Dexter sighed again.

"Tell me more about your brother my dear—is he living in London?" By asking this, his main aim was to put her at ease; he had observed the rigid clasp of her fingers on the plumed fan, and the muscular tension at the corners of her mouth as she looked, rather forlornly, toward Benet, still in dutiful conference with his grandmother and the talkative Mrs. Warren. Another member had now joined their group: a short, dark, sallow girl with a pronounced resemblance to Mrs. Warren. She was beautifully dressed in voluminous billows of tea-rose pink silk, veiled by exquisite lace; but the choiceness of her costume appeared to give the young lady little satisfaction, for her head drooped dispiritedly over the posy of tight pink rosebuds she carried. Just occasionally she darted a furtive, wistful glance at Benet, who, apart from a kind smile as she joined them, had paid her no further attention.

"Oh—my brother." Valla firmly turned her attention back to Mr. Dexter —who was being very nice to her after all. "Well, I should explain that he is my half-brother really, six years older than I. My mother, you see, was married before, but her first husband died. He was half Norwegian, a professor of medicine at Cambridge, England."

"And your mother was English?"

"No, she was Norwegian."

"So that accounts for your sea queen's looks, my dear. Does your brother resemble you?"

"Yes, we are quite alike," Val said, bypassing Mr. Dexter's gallantry. "Nils takes after my mother—he is tall and fair and has a long nose." She smiled faintly, thinking of her brother's rather absurd clown's face on top of his beanpole height.

"And has your brother ever visited America?"

"Oh, yes. When my parents were first married. They met in England, you see, when my father was over there writing a series of articles on English universities. My mother came back to live in New York and she brought Nils with her. His own father had died when Nils was only two, of some disease that he caught in the laboratory. But then—but later on, Nils went back to England to be educated there."

"You must have missed him very much."

"Yes, I couldn't understand it at first—why he should have to go and I should have to stay."

Unbidden, a scene rose before her inner eye: a bleak wintry scene, the hideous, refuse-covered, snow-covered wharves west of Murray Street, the piles and piles of her mother's baggage, wooden trunks and leather cases, bandboxes and hatboxes, wraps and baskets and strapped-up steamer rugs; her mother, swanlike and elegant in a black velvet polonaise glittering with jet buttons and a vivid green muff, directing the porters, well in control of the operation. And Nils, even at twelve outstandingly tall, fair, and conspicuous, even at twelve indifferent to the cold, or the attention of strangers, or any ordinary human emotions, hanging over the ship's rail, waving his fur cap, calling, "Back to England, hooray, hooray! Goodbye to horrible New York and I hope I never see it again as long as I live!"

Nils her childhood's god, and devil.

Earlier he had reduced his little sister to tears by saying teasingly, "*You're* too small to come on the packet. *You're* just a nuisance. Nobody wants *you*. *You* have to stay here with boring old Chum. Boo-hoo, little Miss Blubbercheeks. You can take *that* to remember me by—it'll have to last for years and years, so I'll make it a good one," and he had given her arm such a savage pinch that the bruise had lasted for three weeks. Not surprisingly she had burst into tears and Nils had then knelt down by her and put his arms round her solicitously—at which sight Aunt Ellen Montgomery, there to see off her sister-in-law and give the parting an air of respectability, had said, "Oh, dear, brother, can it be right to part those poor children? See how the little thing feels it. Bad enough to lose her mother, but her brother too—"

"What can I do, Ellen?" her father said.

Friends and neighbours were told that Mrs. Montgomery was going to Europe for her health and would presently return. Val remembered her father coming to her room that night; they were living in the house on Twenty-third Street then. He sat on her bed, close and comforting, with his arm round her, and said, "Don't cry, pet; you and I will have to look after each other now."

Of course Val had sobbed, "Mama—Mama!" in a luxury of grief. But even then she had been clearly aware that she would far rather remain with her big, ugly, kind, capable father, who always kept his promises, who was there when he said he would be; who, when at home, however busy, always contrived a portion of time to play with her or read to her. Whereas Mama, fair and beautiful as the gilt angel on the Christmas tree, had a peevish, unpredictable temper. Plenty of slaps had come Val's way, generally for her carelessness in crumpling or tearing some elegant flounce or lace trimming as she ran hopefully to climb on her mother's lap.

"Get away, you're disgusting—you have egg on your tucker. Don't touch my dress, your fingers are sticky. Mind, child, you are creasing my silk. Sit *still*—look what your little kicking feet have done. There—that's enough—run away to Tabitha—or Hannah—or Chloe," had been the constant refrain of Val's childhood. Mama's clothes, of course, were always wonderful; no wonder she did not want jammy fingers on them. It had been the era of crinolines; Val could remember one outfit in particular, a black alpaca skirt, looped up like curtains over a sea-blue serge underskirt, all worn under a wide-sleeved black poplin jacket with ruffled blue muslin undersleeves, a flat black hat and black-lace parasol; very Directoire, she later realised. The four-year-old Val had torn one of the blue-muslin ruffles and been banished to the nursery for a week in disgrace. What an immense amount of material there must have been in those huge ballooning skirts, she thought. No wonder Mama was nervous about my tearing her dresses.

And then Mama had sailed away to England in her tight-fitting black velvet and green muff.

"When will Nils and Mama come back?" Val had asked nightly for the first months. Her father, or Miss Chumley, or Tabitha, would give some vague answer. And by degrees Val gave up asking; by degrees the identities of her mother and brother became unreal and indistinct. One or two letters came from Mama, one or two cards, addressed to "Dear little Valla." But these, somehow, did not carry conviction, did not represent the reality that Val remembered; her mother had never addressed her thus in speech; in actual fact they had never held a conversation at all. Mrs. Montgomery was always too busy getting dressed for some social occasion. I wonder what? Val speculated vaguely now, looking round the Allerton ballroom. Nothing like this, certainly. As the wife of a newspaper editor, in either New York or Chicago, she would never be admitted to the best circles of polite society; the Allertons or Babcocks or Chaunceys wouldn't dream of opening their doors to her. I doubt if she could even get tickets to the Public Assemblies. Poor Mama! I daresay she would have given her ears to be standing where I am now. What an ambition! I doubt if anything else in my life would have earned her approval, but I'm sure my engagement to Benet would.

Whereas I can imagine Father's comment: "Do what you like, my dearest girl, I'm glad of anything that makes you happy, but are you really sure that this *will*?"

Am I really sure?

Guiltily aware that she had let her attention slip away from Mr. Dexter, Val turned her eyes back to him. He said, smiling, "I daresay you find this kind of thing rather a waste of time?"

"Oh—it isn't that exactly. I mean, I'm sure it is wonderful for people who have been brought up to it. It's just that I am not accustomed to—to such grandeur and formality."

Mr. Dexter nodded his silver head gently up and down.

"It's such a pretty spectacle," he said. "Isn't it? And yet there's a lot of discipline about it really. We all know the rules and abide by them; without question we adhere to a set of conventions which I suspect that you, my dear, think ridiculously rigid and arbitrary."

Val felt that she ought to protest; however, since in her heart she entirely agreed with his assertion she made no reply but bowed her head with a faint smile and wafted her fan to and fro. Glancing at her with a flash of respect, Mr. Dexter went on, "And the question I ask myself about you and Benet, in the most guarded possible terms, is this: who will give way?"

"Give way, Mr. Dexter? I'm not sure that I understand you."

"When you and Benet are married—will you be able to persuade him to abandon this kind of existence?"

"But why should I do any such thing?" Val asked with genuine surprise. "I wouldn't have the least intention of doing so. If he wants to go to balls—then of course he is fully at liberty to."

"But you, my dear, will not be accompanying him?"

"Who can tell?" Her faint smile reappeared. "Perhaps I shall acquire a taste for them."

"And the other thing I am wondering is," he pursued peacefully, with his absent gaze fixed on a glossy green orange tree in a gilt pot, "how you will react to the family's pressure to—er—make you conform to their way of life."

"What—exactly—do you mean by that?" she inquired with caution.

"Well, of course, you must be aware that you will be expected to give up your—your professional and journalistic activities? I fear such pursuits could not possibly be countenanced in Benet's wife."

For a moment or two Val gazed at him wide-eyed, really silenced. He returned her gaze calmly; there was still nothing but benevolence in the dry, spare, slightly lantern-jawed face under the smooth white thatch of hair.

"You must be joking, Mr. Dexter?" she said tentatively at length. "You can't really be serious?"

"Indeed I can, my dear child. Without the faintest shadow of doubt, if

—when you get married, one or the other of you will have to make a radical change in your way of life. You may, of course, insist on Benet's doing so; you have that privilege. And I am sure that he loves you enough to make any concessions you ask. But you will have to understand that if you make him do this, you will cut him off from his family. And that would make him wretchedly unhappy. You, on the other hand, my dear—and though I have every sympathy for your solitary position, I am sure you have the intelligence to see that it may in some ways be regarded as a *simplification* at this particular juncture—you have no family to tug you into a position of stress."

"But I *do* have a position—a career," burst out Val. She could hardly believe her ears.

Mr. Dexter's eyelids drooped over his mild eyes. He went on suavely, "We can therefore only trust to your generosity to spare Benet and allow yourself to be the one who makes the sacrifice."

"But Mr. Dexter—"

"I know—" he checked her with a soothing, uplifted hand. "Believe me, my dear young lady, I am fully in accord with your feelings about this. May I say that, in hoping you *are* to become part of our family, I look forward with the liveliest pleasure to what I trust will be a long friendship between us, for I suspect that you and I feel alike on a great many important—and perhaps also unimportant—issues. But, as one who has also suffered—in some slight degree—for the cause of family unity, I believed that perhaps I was best qualified to approach you in this way—now, rather than later—to save you, it might be, a few surprises, a certain amount of heartache in the early days of your married life."

The tone of warning was unmistakable.

"Thank you," she said mechanically. So much had been so swiftly laid down that she would have to ponder it later, in her bedroom, in the dark and silence, when all this light and music and nonsense had ended—she could not properly take it in at present.

Presently she said, "Benet hasn't suggested anything of the—he never spoke to me in this—"

"Ah, Benet loves you so much! And he has a nature that turns naturally to the sun; fortune has always smiled on Benet."

"You mean he doesn't like unpleasantness," said Val bluntly.

Down came Mr. Dexter's lids again.

"Did Benet ask you to say these things to me?"

"My dear! How should you think it? No indeed, Benet would never ask anyone else to undertake a difficult task that he should do himself. But he has so much to tackle at present—his own career, and all the family affairs that are laid at his door—as you saw just now; and he has had the care of his mother and sister since his father's death; it was a heavy burden for a young man and he has fulfilled his charge loyally and conscientiously."

I know it, Val thought. And that is one of the reasons why I love him. But is he *never* to be free of them all? She wondered what Mr. Dexter had suffered in the family cause, what had been his sacrifice? An unsuitable marriage? Some other relationship, abandoned under pain of family censure?

Suddenly she had had enough of Mr. Dexter and his suggestions; though she did believe that they were kindly meant. Her eyes strayed back to the group around old Mrs. Allerton. Surely Benet would soon be able to detach himself from them? The band, in its grotto of tree ferns and camellias, had begun to tune up; the long procession of arrivals, snaking in from the street and up the red-velvet staircase to where Benet's mother and sister were positioned, was beginning to dwindle; couples had started to cluster together and move out tentatively on to the dance floor.

"Tell me, Mr. Dexter," Val said, coolly changing the subject, "who is the dark young lady in the pretty pink dress, the one who is talking to Benet now?"

"Oh, my, my," he said. "How very bad of me not to tell you. Indeed, I had no notion that you had not met her before; I'm afraid that's how it is in these large families, where we've all known each other since we were in pinafores and tuckers—we take it for granted that you know us all. That is Benet's cousin Lottie Warren—Charlotte—Alma's daughter. Let me introduce you to her."

And he began to steer Val gently back toward Mrs. Allerton's group with one gloved hand guiding her elbow. Then, clasping it a fraction tighter, he delayed her a moment to murmur, "Perhaps I *should* just mention—everyone else has known it for so long that it has become another of those items about which the whole family is so well aware that we forget to tell outsiders—at *one* time there was a kind of boy-and-girl arrangement, just a family thing, you know, between Benet and Lottie. Cousins marry so very often among the Chaunceys and Allertons and Dexters that for several years it was quite expected—but of course there was nothing formal or *binding* about it; you have no reason to reproach yourself; I just explain in order to avoid any possible awkwardness for you later, you know."

So that, Val thought hollowly, that accounts for the poor girl's miserable expression. Possible awkwardness, indeed! No wonder that, while Mr. Dexter was talking to me, I thought I saw her ever so discreetly blot away what might have been a tear with the tip of a gloved finger.

Poor, poor Lottie. To have lost Benet—what in the world could make up for that?

She imagined, with a shudder like footsteps on her grave, how it would feel: the sun of his warmth gone out for ever.

"But hark," said Mr. Dexter, finger uplifted. "Do I hear them playing a minuet?"

He made another of his sudden checking movements. "Yes, I see it is to be one of those four-couple minuets—a most delightful dance! And—oh dear me—I observe that Benet has been obliged—instructed, should I perhaps say?—to lead out his cousin; perhaps old Mrs. Allerton has decided that to be his partner for the first dance might be—some consolation for her disappointment in other respects? Yes, they are going off together—so, if you will permit an elderly bachelor, may I offer myself for this one, my dear?"

Dumbly, Val allowed herself to be led to the centre of the floor.

It was a great honour, of course. She knew that. To be partnered by Mr. James Dexter, a most accomplished dancer, set the seal of society's approval on any young female. She only hoped that her own dancing would prove adequate.

Her mind, as a rule so alert, felt curiously numb and blank. What was she supposed to make of all this? Was it a kind of threat? She could only decide, as she had over Mr. Dexter's previous communications, that she must postpone making any judgment.

Later. I'll decide about it later. I must wait and see.

She did, though, glance once, almost shamefacedly, toward Benet, as if she had no right to try to catch his eye. But her care was wasted; his face, bent toward that of his partner, could not be seen; it was not possible to gauge his expression. That of Charlotte Warren was visible, though; a tremulous, almost incredulous rapture irradiated her small face; she was glowing, Val remarked with a mixture of compassion and amusement, like one of the new gas chandeliers. But there was a sting of pain in the observation.

All the fiddlers swept their bows up high, then brought them down with a flourish. The music began.

For Val, dutifully dancing, smiling, enduring a nonstop sequence of introductions to members of this huge family, answering the same questions over and over, struggling to keep her expression calm and pleasant, in the face of antagonism, veiled or fairly explicit, patronising remarks, polite snubs, supercilious or ignorant or prejudiced comments on her profession, the next few hours seemed interminable. Names and faces of what appeared to be an endless horde of Chaunceys, Allertons, Babcocks, Dexters became entangled in her memory; aunts, sisters, cousins, uncles and their wives, husbands and grown-up offspring came, spoke, and moved on, spoke and moved on.

Punch was presently dispensed, strictly nonalcoholic, for the benefit of the younger ladies present, and then, later, champagne. Supper was served in the conservatory.

Mr. Dexter took Val in to supper; sitting confidentially beside her on a gilt bamboo chair at a little table in a palm-shaded corner, he consumed terrapin soup, crab mayonnaise, duck, and ice cream; Val found that she had little appetite. She feared at first that he might revert to their former topic of conversation, but he did not. Instead he discussed the paintings of Millais and Rossetti, which he had lately seen in London, the writings of Ruskin, George Eliot's last novel, the meteoric rise of a new young politician, Nugent Reydon, who seemed likely to become the next English prime minister, and the poetry of Lord Tennyson and Mrs. Browning, both of whom Val thought greatly overrated. They also touched on a work which Val had read and Mr. Dexter had not—*A Vindication of the Rights of Woman,* by a writer called Mary Wollstonecraft. He had hardly heard of her.

"She died more than eighty years ago," said Val, "and yet her ideas are still revolutionary, a long way in advance of current opinion. She thought that men and women should be equal, that the marriage bond is unnecessary, but, if marriage takes place, then husbands and wives should be allowed their own friends, professions, and property, that they should be able to live together in a free relationship of unpossessive affection."

"My dear!" Mr. Dexter seemed startled to the roots of his being. "Do you share these views, may I ask?"

She said drily, "Perhaps! I can see they are impracticable in society as it is arranged now. But I think there is much to be said for them. Women should be allowed control of their own fortunes and lives. I fancy there is more enlightenment on these matters in England than in our country, progressive as we Americans think ourselves; what is your opinion, Mr. Dexter, you have just come back from England?"

"It is true," he said, "that English women go about more freely, unescorted, and enter more into public life than is encouraged in America at present. You speak as if you had been in England yourself?"

"I have," she said. "Several times. My father took me when I was in my teens, and I have been back since, writing a series of reports for the *Inquirer.*"

"You intrepid young lady! And did you travel about unescorted?"

"I'm afraid so." She smiled inwardly, thinking of streetcar rides, with carpetbag, to and from the steamer, of the London cab drivers and the underground railway system, and the shabby hotels. How different from the carefully chaperoned trips around Europe of girls such as Charlotte Warren, with their mothers and their maids, and the couriers who were paid to conduct them to all the correct works of art and the necessary viewpoints. "And I may say that I was never once molested or treated with any kind of incivility."

Mr. Dexter looked as if he thought it would be a brave man who attempted such behaviour. "But just the same, my dear child—my gracious me! Going unescorted about London! Why, did no one even mention—for instance—the terrible risks that are run by females in that area south of the Thames—"

"You mean those awful murders? The Bermondsey Beast? But *they* were all a particular class of women."

"I should not have alluded to it." Mr. Dexter looked as if he very much regretted having spoken. "It is not at all a proper topic for this kind of occasion. Tell me rather on what subjects you were reporting?"

"Oh—factory conditions, education, slum housing. Not very proper topics either, I'm afraid!"

With grace, Mr. Dexter intimated that he was unequipped to handle these subjects; he turned the conversation on to a comparison of English and American social manners and customs; Val obliged him by playing her part, and they tacitly agreed to eschew any other dangerously controversial areas.

But as he led her back toward the ballroom, where the cheerful notes of the Lancers were encouraging laggard eaters to abandon the supper tables, he sighed again, at the vista of inevitable frictions and hard choices which must, it seemed to him, lie ahead for Benet and this intelligent, awkward girl.

In place of the docile and acceptable sprat from his own pool, Benet had cast his line into the open sea and landed himself a dolphin. How could they possibly settle down together in peaceful conjugality?

It won't do, Mr. Dexter was thinking regretfully. No, it most definitely won't do.

As the night wore slowly on, Val began to feel more and more severed from Benet. During the various waltzes, polkas, gavottes, he was kept continuously busy leading out his aunts, nieces, in-laws, and cousins young and old. Val, for her part, danced with an interminable procession of male relations whom she mentally divided into two classes: those who were stiffly correct, obviously alarmed by her, and the others who, equally obviously, felt she might be fair game and would have made unsuitable advances had she given them the slightest blink of encouragement. To be on the safe side, she adopted the same glacial manner toward both groups. In the whole course of the evening she and Benet achieved only two dances together, a mazurka and a schottische; neither was conducive to intimate conversation. But twice more she noticed that Benet danced with his cousin Charlotte, and each time her downcast face became suddenly transformed, glowing out into animation as she lifted her eyes to her tall cousin.

"Too bad about that affair," Val heard Edith Calbert, one of Benet's cousins, murmur behind her fan, glancing significantly at the pair.

"What went wrong? I thought it was all fixed up."

"Oh, greedy Alma took the girl to London, hoping to hook an earl; didn't succeed; brought her back, by which time they found that Edward had left them without two dollars to rub together; Lottie needs a good *parti* even more now; but in the meantime Benet's eye had wandered elsewhere."

"And, my dear, look what he—"

Val moved away. It seemed she had been employing the same evasive technique for untold hours.

At last the long ordeal slowly began to wind down toward its conclusion. Farewells were said, the ladies once more picked their way upstairs with carefully held skirts to the bedrooms where, hours before, they had given their ringlets a last-minute tweak by the gas burners. Cloaks reclaimed, they descended. Family landaus and broughams clattered and battled their way over the cobbles to the red-covered steps. The guests ran out under the awning, clutching their furs round them, for a cool breeze blew and leaves scuttered on the sidewalk; summer had suddenly turned the corner toward fall.

Benet, overriding the protests of his mother—and of Val herself, who had intended to order one of Brown's coupés from the livery stable—had promised to drive Val home to Twenty-third Street in his brougham. Now she was glad of this, thankfully able to keep aloof from the gossiping swarm of ladies in the bedrooms engaged in comparisons of dance programmes and blistered heels. At least she need not suffer their inspection of her workaday plaid merino coat and beaver tippet. She remained with Benet's mother and sister, politely stifling yawns, until the last of the aunts and cousins had left. At last she was able to say her thanks and farewells to the Allerton ladies, who were drooping with sleep like small wax dolls left too near the fire.

"Good night, my dear—ahhhh!—I'm sure it all went very well—ah!—excuse me. Take good care of her, Benet. Don't be long, now. Doyle will be waiting to let you in."

He nodded, for once with a slight touch of impatience, refrained from pointing out that he had his own latchkey, and slammed the brougham's dark-blue polished door.

The drive from Washington Square to Twenty-third Street was a silent one. Val was tired and depressed. Not for the first time after exposure to the Allerton family she found herself wishing ardently for some kin of her own; how different it would have been if this return could have been made to sympathetic, exclaiming younger sisters, or a mother with whom she could have discussed the whole affair, or to her father's cool, detached, but friendly interest.

"I won't ask you in," she said, collecting her muff and fan from the cushions and preparing to alight.

He seemed cast down at this, as if he had really expected that she would. Absurd creature! It must be past three in the morning. But he said, sighing, "No, I suppose Miss Chumley would hardly approve."

"Indeed she would not." Val omitted to mention that Miss Chumley was out of town, visiting a married ex-pupil in Maryland; there was no need to scandalise the Allertons even further by letting them discover that for the last two weeks she had been housekeeping on her own, unchaperoned, in this shabby bohemian neighbourhood.

"I'll wait till old Chloe comes to let you in."

"Oh, mercy! She's been asleep for hours. I have a key; I told her not to wait up."

She slipped from the carriage at the foot of the six steps leading to the battered old brownstone with its peeling stucco.

Benet prepared to follow. Impatiently she gestured him not to but he ignored the gesture. For once, his pleasant face had lost its equable expression; he looked tired and perplexed, almost angry. Val determinedly kept her eyes on her muff, in the recesses of which she was hunting for her latchkey.

The big lopsided ailanthus tree growing at one side of the steps cast a fringed and jagged shadow over half the stoop. Val, on the second step, was suddenly glad of Benet's company, as, with a smothered gasp that was half a shriek, she stopped at the sight of a long, black-trousered leg extending from the tree's shadow.

"What the devil?" Benet exclaimed, coming up beside her.

A voice spoke from the darkness.

"Vallie? Is that you? What late hours you keep!"

Rising from the shadow like the serpent in the garden of Eden, a long, languid figure uncoiled itself and was revealed as an elegantly dressed young man, hatless, despite the cool of the night breeze, with a mop of pale straw-coloured hair and a long, smiling clown's face.

"Nils!"

He seemed so like an apparition in the bright moonlight, as if he had been summoned to the spot by some uncanny spell in answer to her wish for a member of her own family, that Val could hardly believe he was real. She felt like Faust. But he came stiffly down the steps, smiling still, and gave her a light kiss on the ear.

She grasped his arms, laughing with surprise and pleasure, looking up at him.

"It really *is* you! You've grown even taller! I thought you were a dream. But how in the wide world do you come to be here?"

"Off the steam packet from Liverpool, my angel. Waiting for you to come home and welcome me in. And a devilish long time you took about it. I'm half starved; they feed you like slave cargoes on those boats."

"There'll be something inside; Chloe always leaves me sandwiches when I'm late back. Wouldn't she let you in?"

"Not she! In spite of all my asservations that I was your kith and kin."

Then Val recollected Benet, who was still standing halfway up the steps with an expression of well-bred calm and detachment.

"Won't you introduce us?" he said.

"Oh, Benet! Forgive me! I was so surprised! I hadn't the least expectation—it's so long—Benet, this is my brother Nils—Nils Hansen, Benet Allerton. Nils, Benet and I have just become engaged to be married."

"Well, well! Is that so? Congratulations to the pair of you," drawled Nils, glancing carelessly from one to the other. "I've arrived at just the right time, then?" He smiled, grimaced—and then yawned widely. "I'm sorry, Val my dear, but if you've the key, I'm really a bit too tired just now for social stuff."

"Of course—you must be." She found the key at last. "Here."

Nils picked up a small Gladstone bag from the shadows where he had been sitting.

"Gracious, is that all you brought across the Atlantic?" Val asked, laughing. "How long do you plan to stay?"

"Oh, I've another bag, but I left it at the steamer office and walked. The street hasn't changed a bit, has it?" he said, fitting the key into the lock.

"How long is it since you were here—fifteen years? Have you brought Kirstie with you? And the children?"

"Good heavens, no! But it's partly about them that I've come. That's a long tale, though. I'll tell you later—"

He had opened the door and was moving through into the stuffy hallway in which the radiator from the hot-air furnace, installed by Mr. Montgomery shortly before his death, creaked and clanked and let out a dusty smell of warm metal.

"Phew! How well I remember that smell!" said Nils.

Val heard a slight sound behind and turned to see Benet's brougham roll off at a gentle trot. With a pang she realised that he had left without his usual goodnight kiss. Had he felt excluded by her brother's sudden arrival? Were his feelings hurt? Well, she would put everything right tomorrow. They had arranged to go for a walk in Central Park after lunch. And, in the meantime, how delightful to have Nils here, someone of her very own to confide in.

"Come along to the kitchen," she said. "We can talk there."

CHAPTER 2

SOMEHOW they had ended up in the garden. Late though it was when Val returned, she could not bear to remain in the house, which felt like a small stuffy box filled with darkness. Lured out by the freshness and brilliance of the night like swimmers who cannot bear to leave the water, they had wandered outside. In spite of her fatigue, and the hour or so that had passed since she left the ball, Val was still feverish, tight as a coiled spring; she felt restless and trapped, and knew that she would not be able to fall asleep for a long time yet.

The house on Twenty-third Street had a little paved court at the back, where Miss Chumley fostered nasturtiums in summer and tubs of roses and baytrees all the year round; a sooty lilac exuded fragrance in spring-time. The old wooden swing still stood in the middle, relic of Val's childhood.

"Will it bear me?" asked Nils.

"Goodness knows . . ."

She was pacing round the little yard, brushing the withered lilac leaves with her long velvet skirt.

Nils shrugged and folded his long length into the swing seat; lounging there, sandwich in hand, he idly kicked himself to and fro.

"But do you mean to tell me you hadn't considered all this before?" he asked.

They were discussing her engagement.

"Why in the world should I? No—it never even entered my head. Benet hasn't once suggested that I would be expected to give up my job when we married."

"Why didn't you ask him about it this morning? on the way home?"

"I—I couldn't."

"Perhaps he was being an ostrich about it all," Nils ruminated. "Didn't want to face what he knew his family would say." He skilfully stifled a yawn. "But if you had children, you'd *have* to stop working." He rested his head against the swing rope, turning his face up to look at the moon; the silvery light aureoled his blond hair giving him the appearance of some medieval saint strung up in a position of torment.

"Oh well, that's another matter. If I had children it would certainly be different. But I don't want children. I don't intend to have any, or not for a long time, anyway."

Unseen by Val, his brows shot up at this; his mouth turned down at the corners.

But all he said was, "Had you told Benet *that*?"

"We hadn't discussed it."

"You don't seem to have discussed much, my angel."

It was doing her good, this conversation with Nils; now she began to realise how much she needed to discuss. And he appeared really interested, asked questions, drew out the whole history of the evening from her, laughed appreciatively at her descriptions of Mr. Dexter, Mrs. Chauncey, old Mrs. Allerton, and the male cousins. Yet he was dispassionate, nonpartisan, seemed merely as if he were concerned to lay bare as many facts as possible and do justice to both sides with sleepy impartiality.

"Benet's mother and sister always quite civil to you?"

"Oh yes—they are rather stupid but kind—"

"Is he well off, Benet? What does he make a year?" And when Val told him the sum—which she had learned, not from Benet, but from a colleague, a law reporter on the *Inquirer*—"Is that all? But there's family money too, of course. Mind you, if *I* were in your shoes, I'd let my pride go hang, if somebody offered to support me in idleness! What a cursed stiff-necked girl you are, after all."

"You wouldn't really choose to do nothing—just live on someone else's money?" she said with real curiosity.

"Why not? If there was enough? What's so deuced elevating about having to work one's fingers to the bone, day in, day out?"

"I like my work," said Val. "I enjoy writing my stuff for the *Inquirer*. Some day I want to write a book, about social conditions."

"Yes, I remember you always were a restless little busy bustling inquisitive sort of creature," he said, yawning again. " 'Member that time you smelled smoke and came yelling down to old Abby, Tabby, whatever her name was, saying the house was on fire—"

"And it was you and three boys smoking Papa's cigars?" She chuckled. "*How* angry you were with me."

"Nothing like as angry as the governor . . . That was the last thrashing he gave me before Ma decided to leave him. Matter of fact," he said, "I'm in the journalism line of business myself now; devilish hard work it is, too, but at least it's quite entertaining, I'll say that, more gentlemanly and more perks than cutting up corpses, anyway."

"What *are* you doing now, Nils?"

It was never easy to get information from him, but, asking questions in her turn, Val gathered that Nils, who seemed from his school and college days to have acquired a circle of friends drawn from the topmost echelons of London society, now made his living by writing a kind of highly superior Notes-about-Town column for the London *Morning Post*.

"It ain't half bad," he said. "Of course, people pretend to turn their noses up at that kind of thing, but, bless you, they all read it before any other news, they're as pleased as punch when their own names are in; I get invited to so many houses that I can afford to pick and choose, too; needn't put in a Friday-to-Monday at home above three times a year, unless I want. It's wonderful how civil fellows are when they know you write for the papers."

"But what about Kirstie and the children? Do they come with you on these visits?"

"My dear girl! Don't be an ass. One can hardly take a parcel of squalling brats to houses like Chatsworth or Rosings. Kirstie would be all right on her own, of course, perfectly unexceptionable, but she don't care to leave the children; and we never seem able to keep a nursery maid for more than a month—she never seems to trust 'em. Besides, Kirstie ain't much for social flimflam."

"How *are* Kirstie and the children? Tell me about them."

"They're all right, I daresay," he said vaguely. "Funny little things. People say the boy's like me. I don't see it. I suppose the girl is like Kirstie."

He did not seem very interested in his offspring. Val supposed that many fathers were like this; hers had been a lucky exception.

She had never met her brother's children, or his wife, a young Scottish heiress whom Nils had encountered during the second year of his medical training at Edinburgh. It seemed possible that his courtship of this moneyed girl had been the cause for the premature termination of his studies. Val knew the bare bones of the matter, that they had married in the teeth of spirited opposition from Kirstie's family, had traveled in Europe for a year or so, spending lavishly, and had then settled in London. The picture of their life that she had formed was lacking in detail; her correspondence with Nils, though friendly enough, had been irregular, with long gaps; she really knew very little about what had happened to him, particularly in his childhood, after their early separation. To the day of his death her father had been extremely reticent on the subject of his estranged wife. Val knew that her mother had never remarried, and that Mr. Montgomery had always given her an allowance; but since she apparently kept up a stylish small house in Bruton Street with a carriage and a manservant, had a weekly salon, and paid regular visits to Deauville and Baden-Baden, it was to be assumed that she had acquired some additional source of revenue. It was all a region for speculation. After that wintry farewell at the wharfside, Val had never seen her mother again; the first visit to Europe with her father had been a year after Mrs. Montgomery's death. One of his purposes, Val knew, was to settle various monetary affairs which his wife had left in disorder. They had not seen Nils on that visit. He, having just come of age and inherited some money left him by his own father, was traveling with friends in Italy. However on a subsequent visit they had gone to Scotland, renewed acquaintance with him, and had some pleasant outings together in Edinburgh.

Val, impressed by her half-brother's easy charm and blond elegance, could not understand it when, after one of these occasions, Mr. Montgomery had sighed, and, half to himself, murmured, "Poor Nils; eh well, we'll see."

"How do you mean, Papa? Why poor Nils? What will we see?"

"I hope he has inherited more than cash from his father's side of the family, my pet."

To the sixteen-year-old Valla, Nils appeared to have everything: grace, assurance, knowledge of the world, wit, intelligence, and high spirits. If he could not be called handsome, at least, wherever he went, his long comic face and lint-fair mop of hair attracted people and amused them; he had friends all over Edinburgh.

But when she said this to her father he merely and with total irrelevance, remarked, "I'm glad you stayed with *me*, sweetheart."

"Oh, *so* am I, Papa." She gave him a hug. It had never occurred to her that there might have been any alternative. "Did Mama want me to go with her, then?" she asked in surprise.

But he evaded a direct reply, and said, "It was different for Nils, of course. He went off to school at once. And he was not my boy, after all. No—it wouldn't have done at all for you." He closed his lips firmly and would say no more on the subject, at that, or any later time.

Now—"Were you happy at school, Nils?" Val asked irrelevantly.

"God, *no!* It was a dismal hole—halfway between a prison and a barracks. And the food! Worse than you'd get in the workhouse. American boys would never endure what the English upper classes put their sons through. And of course all the other fellows laughed at me, at first, because they said I talked like a damned Yankee. But I soon got out of that. And one has to go to school, after all. That's where one makes friends and meets the fellows who are going to be useful later on. And my father had been to the place, and his father—so in the end they accepted me. I got into Pop, and all that. But it's long ago now. I'd almost forgotten about it."

"Shall you send little Pieter there?"

"Of course," he said indifferently.

"What about the girl—Jannie?"

"English girls don't go to school. Anyway girls don't need an education. Besides she's—not clever. She'll find a husband, I daresay. Kirstie's family might have come round by the time she grows up; there are a couple of flinty old aunts who could just as well do something for the child, when they've got over their spleen."

"What is Kirstie *like*, Nils?"

"What is she like?"

He looked at his sister blankly. His large, rather protuberant slate-blue eyes had a way of turning almost opaque when he was faced with a troublesome question; at the same time he had a trick of projecting his full lower lip away from his teeth and rubbing a hand over his chin. "Oh—it's a beastly bore trying to describe people. She's not a bad little thing, I suppose. A deal smaller than you—wouldn't come up to your shoulder. You've grown into a deuced fine girl, my love."

"Oh, never mind me! Is she dark or fair?"

"I suppose you'd call her fair. Ringlets. But it don't curl naturally—she has to put 'em in with crimping pins. I tell her she ought to rouge, too, but she won't. Her manners are on the retiring side; timid, you could say. Not much to say for herself in company. Though she has plenty of ideas of her own when she's by herself. More than one wants, 'n fact; she can be a beastly bore, sometimes, about ethics and principles and things; it's the Scotch in her. She don't go down too well in society, not lively enough. In the houses where I go you've got to hold your own. Now, *you'd* go down uncommon well, my angel."

"Oh, what nonsense, Nils! As if I'd be interested in that kind of life. I don't like fashionable circles any more than Kirstie does. New York society is quite bad enough."

"Bah—New York!" He dismissed it with a shrug. "Colonial—what can you expect? A lot of strait-laced, provincial tallow traders. London society is quite another thing, you'd find. Of *course* parties over here are a thundering bore. But in London, anything goes, if you're clever. The Prince of Wales has all manner of friends—actors, painters, bankers, jockeys—anybody who can talk well and has done something notable can get on."

"Have you met the Prince of Wales?" Val asked, curious in spite of herself.

"Lord, yes, over and over. He stays in people's houses, you know, for weekends, as informal as you please."

Much to her own surprise, Val found her curiosity pricked by his descriptions of London life. Not the grandeur; she told herself that she did not give a rap for people's riches, or for their family and aristocratic pretensions: what if they *could* trace ancestors back to the Norman Conquest? That proved nothing; anybody could do the same who took the trouble to search through town records; merely to have all your forbears listed said little, after all, as to their quality. But the greater freedom of thought in London's world, the respect for literature and the arts—that did attract her. She questioned Nils about Ruskin, Rossetti, Miss Nightingale, Herbert Spencer—disappointingly he had met none of them. But he had plenty of anecdotes about other prominent personalities—the Duke of Clarence, Mr. Joseph Chamberlain, Sir Charles Dilke, the Aylesford-Blandford scandal, the mysterious character known as "Sherry and Whiskers," Disraeli, Mrs. Langtry, Irving, Kendal—"a good-looking bounder"—Bancroft, and George Lewis—"the lawyer who has all the scandals of the rich up his shirt-sleeve."

"Well, perhaps I should like it," she conceded at length. "When Benet and I are married we plan to come to Europe, and I want to stay in London for several months, so you can introduce us to all your interesting acquaintances, Nils."

"Glad to, my love. But when *do* you plan to get married?"

"We haven't fixed on a definite date yet. I had thought perhaps some time next fall, about a year from now. But—well, lately I have begun to think perhaps it would be better to wait till the following spring . . ."

"In other words," said Nils—he spoke in his habitual soft lazy drawl, but the glance he threw her was very shrewd—"in other words, you ain't so sure, now, that you want to get hitched up at all, is that it?"

"Oh, I don't know, Nils! I do love Benet with all my heart—he's a good, sweet, intelligent, *valuable* person—but marriage seems such a ball and chain!"

"You're deuced right it is," he said with feeling.

"I just am not prepared to give up all my freedom in order to lead a stuffy conventional, aimless empty life with nothing in it but paying calls and leaving cards and giving dinner parties and going to the opera on Mondays and Fridays at the Assembly of Music."

"Why not Tuesdays and Wednesdays?"

"You must be joking! No person of fashion would be seen at the opera on Wednesday in New York; that's when you lend your box to your poor relations."

"Humph," said Nils. He gave her another long, considering look. "No, I can see that ain't the life for you."

"And I don't want our life to be one long wretched struggle, either."

"Between you and Benet, you mean?" said Nils, looking as if this were familiar territory.

"Between us both and his family."

"That's like us too," he said moodily, pushing the swing to and fro with his foot. "Kirstie's people—well, I won't bore you with all that tale. They are a set of nine-shillings-in-the-pound skinflints. But I tell you what it is, my love, you need more time to think about the whole business, and whether you're taking the right step. You need to get away. Why don't you come back to England with me, when I go, stay a few months with us, maybe six or seven, and see how you get on—see how you feel about Benet then?"

"Good heavens!" Val stared at him. "Go to England for *six months* on my own, just after we had become engaged? What do you think Benet's family would say to *that?*"

"They might be pleased as punch," he pointed out. "Anyway, nothing to cavil at: you stay with me and Kirstie—why not? Perfectly aboveboard. Your own family. Nothing to raise eyebrows over, surely?"

He gave her a cajoling smile, and she was strongly tempted. She said slowly, "I suppose not. Perhaps—I wonder what Benet would think?"

For some reason the image of Charlotte Warren came into her mind, standing beside Benet so dejectedly, in her exquisite pink balldress, casting those timid, forlorn looks at him. Val had little doubt that, once she herself was off the scene, away in England, there would be a concerted family drive to bring Charlotte and Benet back together again.

"Oh—the devil," said Nils, when she explained this. "*What* a pickle you are in. Well, look at it this way—if the fellow really loves you, they won't be able to budge him. For all you know, he might follow you to England—had you thought of that possibility? Then you could see each other on equal terms, without all his family sitting on your feet."

"That's true," she said, tempted by the thought, and then, after another moment, "In any case, perhaps poor Charlotte ought to have her chance—"

"My good girl, have you taken leave of your wits? Life's a *battle*—not some kind of chivalrous parlour game—you toss me the handkerchief, I toss it back to you! 'Pon my word, I begin to wonder if you really do love the fellow—do you or don't you? If you don't—and he don't—then you're well rid of each other."

Val felt, and stifled, a deep, dreadful, transfixing pang at the thought of Benet lost—of Benet's kindness and solicitude, his intelligence and un-selfishness, diverted away from her, back to poor little Lottie Warren. No, of course Nils was right; one could not dispose of people as if they were parcels. But Nils was right also—if she and Benet did not love each other enough—

"Oh, I don't know *what* to think." Looking at Nils she suddenly felt a strange qualm; the moon, shining full on him now, defined the long wandering nose, the full, flexible mouth, puckered up like a clown's at the corners, lower lip slightly projecting; the silver light just caught the tips of his almost white lashes, which gave a very curious and rather disquieting impression as if a pair of sightless eyes watched her from his smiling face. All at once she realised how exhausted she was; she pushed her hands backward through the carefully piled tower of her hair, hopelessly disarranging it.

"I'm too tired to talk any more. We must be mad, sitting out here till all hours like this. Listen—there's St. Peter's clock striking—five o'clock! Nearly time to get up!"

"My dear girl! What time do you rise, for heaven's sake?"

"Seven. Come along—I haven't even put sheets on your bed; I'll do it now. And I'll tell Chloe not to call you in the morning."

"When does your old Chumley get back?"

"Not for a couple of weeks yet. How long are you planning to stay, Nils?"

"Depends how my business goes."

He followed her in and stood soundlessly whistling, watching while she lit a lamp, carefully turned up the wick, and then replaced the glass chimney and the fringed shade.

"Nils, I'm truly ashamed of myself. Here I've been, pouring out all my woes, and you've told me nothing about what brought you over here."

"It'll keep," he said easily, following her up the Turkey-carpeted stairs. "Business dealings. I'll tell you tomorrow."

She led the way into the spare bedroom and pulled a white embroidered counterpane off the mahogany bedstead. As she swiftly tossed clean sheets over the mattress, and tucked them in, he put down his Gladstone bag on the rose-garlanded carpet and, without offering to assist her, stood with hands on hips looking round the room.

"Wasn't this where I used to sleep? It's been done over since, though. The wallpaper's different: very fancy."

It was a French one, imitation watered silk, with a valanced border and tassels.

Val pulled the curtains, layers of Nottingham lace, more layers of velvet.

"I daresay Step-papa was fairly well-fixed by the time he died? He gave Ma an allowance all along, didn't he? Did he leave *you* much, my love?"

"Very little," said Val cheerfully, taking a pile of blankets from the huge mahogany closet. "He told me why he wasn't going to; said he didn't want people marrying me for my cash. I didn't mind. He left a lot to endow a library in Marshfield, the town where he was born."

"I call that thundering mean!"

"No, why?"

"How much *have* you got?"

When she told him her income he whistled, and said, "No wonder you think Benet quite a catch! But what about this house? Ain't it yours?"

"It belongs to Chum for her life, on condition I can live in it. At her death it reverts to me—but that's a long way off."

"How peculiar," drawled Nils. "Was she his mistress, then?"

Val burst out laughing. "His *mistress*? Are you mad?" She thought of little brown Miss Chumley, tart as a hawthorn berry, dry as a pebble. "Don't you remember her? Father had the greatest respect for her. He used to consult her on legal affairs and points of literary style."

"Well then—"

"No, no." She wiped the tears of amusement from her eyes. "Did you think *that* was why Mama left him?"

"Well no, to tell the truth, I didn't; judging from the kind of life she led when she got to London, it was some little caper on *her* part that caused *him* to give her the push."

Val glanced at her brother speculatively and wondered what it had been like, living with their mother in London. She could without embarrassment ask him about his schooldays, but she found herself unable to put questions to him about conditions in Bruton Street, unless he volunteered any details. And she doubted if he would do that; he did not seem given to divulging unasked information about himself—or much, indeed, even when it was asked.

She wondered what had brought him to New York. Not given to sentimentality, she doubted if the ties of family affection had anything to do with his crossing the Atlantic—why, after all, should they, after fifteen years? She was certainly pleased to see him—delighted, at this juncture in her own affairs—but she did not pretend to herself that the fraternal tie was a very strong one.

Well—no doubt he would tell her when he was ready.

"I say," he said, glancing round the room which she had now made ready for him, "I don't suppose you'd have a drop of curaçoa about the house?"

"Mercy, no! Curaçoa? I've never even tasted it. There might be some madeira or burgundy in the dining-room closet—we don't drink much wine, Chum and I, when we're on our own."

"Sickly stuff," he said discontentedly. "Madeira! How you can. I thought Yankees drank spirits all the time. How about cherry brandy?"

She shook her head. "No, but now I come to think, there's probably some cognac. Chum likes to have a bottle in case of sickness."

He accompanied her to the dining room, where she found the brandy and was about to pour him a glassful.

"Give me the decanter," he suggested. "That'll save you coming up to the top floor again."

She had not been intending to, assuming that he would take his drink down stairs. But he walked off with the decanter before she could answer and called softly back over the banister, "Don't forget to tell that woman of yours not to wake me! And you think over what I've said. I believe a trip to England just now would solve a lot of your problems."

In spite of retiring so late, Val found it hard to get off to sleep and slept poorly when she did. Her mind was still running like a millrace: the lights and spangles, the satin trains, the fronds of fern and shining draperies of the ball floated and swirled inside her closed eyelids, inside her brain; she could hear old Mrs. Allerton saying, "How do you think you will ever settle down in this family?" And Mr. Dexter: "One or the other of you will have to make a radical change—we can only trust to your generosity to allow yourself to be the sacrifice."

Why must marriage involve a sacrifice? she cried now furiously and silently at the unheeding Mr. Dexter, asleep no doubt hours past in his tidy bachelor house over in Waverley Place. We are not a lot of ancient Greeks! I am not Iphigenia, and what is more, I don't intend to be. All right, he replied placidly out of his pillow, then you will make Benet wretchedly unhappy.

Val flung herself from side to side; she threw off the bedclothes and then pulled them back on again. At last she slept briefly and was prey to harried, frantic dreams. But the moon hardly seemed to have left her window when the sun burst in, for, sleeping at the back of the house, she preferred to let in the air, however smoke-laden, and never troubled to pull her chintz curtains. Sunlight fell in layers of dazzling silk on the new French wallpaper and woke her; she opened her eyes.

For a couple of moments she lay in a state of suspended awareness, vaguely conscious that something momentous had happened, or was about to, but unable to recall what it was. Her short sleep had been deep as death; awakening felt hard as birth.

Suddenly she remembered Nils. Her brother—how extraordinary! He lay in the room above—what a strange thing. And yet, how natural, after all; doubtless it had been thought peculiar enough by the Allertons, that interwoven, gregarious clan, that the link between her and Nils seemed so frail.

Attached to the thought of the Allertons came recollection of the ball: a prickly torment, like putting on a hair shirt. Later in the day she must pay a formal call on Benet's mother and sister to thank them and discuss it all in dismal detail. And soon, she supposed, letters of congratulation and engagement gifts would begin to arrive, and they must all be acknowledged and thanked for, a prospect that made her heart sink.

Why not come back to England with me? Nils had said it so lightly, and it had seemed an utterly impossible scheme, not to be thought of. But just the same, what temptation lay in the idea. Had he really meant it?

Val rolled over in bed and looked at the watch her father had given her for an eighteenth-birthday present; it hung by its velvet ribbon over the mahogany knob of her bed head.

Nine o'clock.

And she had three articles on school library facilities to finish and take round to the *Inquirer* offices by twelve.

She sprang out of bed with less than her usual bounding vitality—even though impelled by conscience-stricken haste—bathed, pulled on a faded old blue-poplin dress, and bundled up her hair. Fortunately the articles were half done, all they required were polishing and the addition of a final two paragraphs to each. Buttoning the crochet lace collar which Miss Chumley had kindly added to the dress to alleviate its plainness—and which Val was too kind to say she thought unbecoming and fussy—she ran softly downstairs.

Old Chloe was on the lookout, and came lumbering up to the dining room soon after with a huge breakfast on a tray—melon, rice griddle cakes and syrup, scrambled eggs, coffee.

"I can't possibly eat all that, Chloe; I don't have the time."

"Rubbish, Miss Val. You been dancing all night, you must be tired to your bones. You just eat it without arguing, I know you didn't get home till three, I heard you come in. Did you have a good time, now? And who was that talkin' with you out in the yard?"

"Don't worry, you won't have to tell Miss Chumley that I've been letting strangers into the house—not even Benet! It was my brother from England; he's up top, sleeping in the spare bedroom. Mind you don't disturb him; he just came off the boat last night."

"Oh, that one?" said Chloe. "So he really was your brother? He didn't look like no brother to me. He ain't a bit like you, Miss Val, bar the fairness. I didn't trust his looks, I can tell you that; brother or no, I wouldn't do no horse-trading with that one."

"Oh what stuff, Chloe; he's exactly like me," Val said, scooping out melon with one hand while she turned manuscript pages with the other.

"He is not so! You're too honest for your own good, you are. Anybody could make a fool outa you. Now you eat up those griddle cakes; I didn't cook them to have them go to waste."

"All right, Chloe—don't bully me. Go away and let me get on with this. I'll tell you all about the ball, cross my heart, when I've delivered these to the newspaper."

"I'll bet you was the best-lookin' there."

"No I wasn't—not by a long way," said Val shortly and returned to her rewriting, taking occasional forkfuls of griddle cake, while her coffee grew cold and the pages piled up round the table.

Immersed in her task, she was oblivious to the passage of time. When the front doorbell rang, two hours later, she did not even hear it; the first intimation she had of any arrival was voices just outside the dining-room door.

"Well, I'll tell her you're here, Mr. Allerton, but she's awful busy just now," Chloe was saying defensively, and then she heard Benet's voice,

"Oh, I think she'll have a minute or two for me, Chloe; after all, we are engaged now, you know!" and Benet walked into the room.

Rather startled, full of mixed feelings, among which joy did not predominate, Val stood up, scattering papers. He came round the table and kissed her.

"Good morning, my dearest! How did you sleep? Soundly, I hope, after all that dancing?"

"Like a top, thanks," she lied. "I hope you did too? But Benet, I thought it was this afternoon that we were to meet?"

She was very conscious, annoyingly so, of her faded dress, untidy hair, inky fingers, the relics of breakfast on the table; even more so of those final paragraphs still unwritten. Surreptitiously she pushed a couple of sheets over a patch of crumbs and glanced back at the sentence she had just begun. Half past eleven . . .

"Yes, my dear, I know; our walk in the park. But unfortunately I've been summoned to Boston to advise a client; old Pendleton thinks that I would be the best man for the job, curse him! So I have to catch the half-past two train. That's why I have come now, hoping I can persuade you to come out to lunch with me before I leave."

"Out to *lunch?*" she repeated in dismay.

"Yes, at the Amsterdam Hotel—properly chaperoned! With my cousins the Warrens, who are staying there—Lottie is so anxious to know you better."

"Benet, I'm afraid I can't possibly. For one thing I'm not suitably dressed; and I just haven't time; these reports I'm working on have to be round at the *Inquirer* by noon. Please give my apologies to your cousins. Another day, perhaps. I really am too busy right now."

He looked disconcerted and very much cast down at her decisive tone.

"Surely you can take a couple of hours, on the morning after you have announced your engagement? Lottie will be so disappointed! I'd not have thought it would make much difference if they had to wait for your little piece until this afternoon?"

"I'm afraid it does, Benet. They have to go to press," Val said patiently. "I'm very sorry."

"My cousins are outside in the brougham," he said. "Don't you think if they came in they could persuade you? Shall I call them?"

"Mercy, *no*, Benet! The room's in a mess, and so am I—"

For the first time in their relationship she felt exasperation with Benet, as he stood there so large and impervious to argument, his fresh kind face hurt and puzzled, wearing without any concealment its look of chagrin.

He said, "You see I'm going to have to stay in Boston for at least two weeks. If you don't come now, it's going to be such a long gap till I see you again, my dearest! There's a whole series of hearings scheduled, it may take even longer—"

"Oh, dear, that's too bad. I'm really sorry," she answered mechanically, thinking, How would *he* like it if *I* were to walk into his law office and expect him to drop whatever he was engaged on and come out with me on the spot? How lucky men are! They have so many strongholds they can retreat into—clubs and offices and libraries where women aren't allowed. Whereas anybody can stroll into any woman's room.

As if to give point to her thought, the door opened and her brother Nils ambled in.

He was unshaven, bleary-eyed and shock-headed. The silk dressing gown he wore was a handsome one, but it was frayed and soiled, and had plainly been subjected to years of wear. So had his carpet slippers.

"Oh, hallo, my dear, is that coffee I smell?" he said, yawning cavernously. He dumped the empty brandy decanter and glass on top of her pages of manuscript. "Brought these down," he pointed out virtuously. "Let's have a cup of that coffee, like a love, will you—doesn't matter if it's cold; I've a mouth like the Tyburn River this morning." Without waiting for permission he poured himself a cup of the cold coffee, and then, drinking it, noticed Benet for the first time.

"Hey there! Good morning!" he said sociably. "You're an early caller, ain't you? Well, well, I was in love myself once. Seems a long time ago now, though."

A somewhat awkward silence fell; Val felt like screaming at both of them to get out and leave her to work in peace.

"I was goin' to suggest that you and I go out presently and have a meal at some chophouse?" Nils said to Val, yawning again. "I daresay there are places where one can take a lady? Why don't we go out all three? Are you game?" he said to Benet.

Val said, "Thank you, Nils, but I'm afraid I can't. I've just been giving the same answer to Benet, who kindly invited me out to meet his cousins. I *have* to get this work delivered by twelve o'clock." Rather pointedly she glanced up at the ormolu clock on the marble mantel.

"Oh, deuce take it—women—they're always so cursedly full of their own affairs. They live in such a fuss and fluster!" Nils drawled good-humouredly. "Look at all this muddle—in the dining room, too. Where am I supposed to take my breakfast?" he said to Val, and to Benet, "Just you wait, my boy, till you've been married six years, like me; the varnish soon wears off, I can tell you."

"Chloe will bring you some breakfast in the drawing room," Val said, trying to choke down her irritation.

"Ne'mind, my dear—I'd as lief go out and stroll round town." He said to Benet, "Why don't you wait till I get myself dressed, and we'll go together, if Valla don't want to? You can show me a bit of the town, I daresay? I haven't been here since I was a whippersnapper. I expect there's places you could take me where it wouldn't do to have Valla with us."

"Another time I'll be happy to show you round," Benet replied, civilly but with a marked lack of enthusiasm in his tone. "Just at the moment, though, I have my cousins waiting for me in the carriage; I have delayed them too long already, I fear; I had better get back to them. Will you at least come and give them your explanation, my dear?" he said to Val.

She saw that she must and walked out reluctantly after him on to the porch. There were the Warren ladies, seated waiting in the brougham. Mrs. Warren wore black poplin trimmed with crimson velvet bands, and a huge black hat wreathed with crimson roses. Lottie was dressed in white; her small pale face looked anxiously out of a white-velvet cabriolet bonnet plumed with crystal-spangled feathers. Their gaze fastened rather blankly on Val; for a moment, she suspected, they thought she was the housemaid.

Val made her apologies stiffly and noticed an expression of hardly concealed satisfaction in Mrs. Warren's face as she did so. But Charlotte looked truly disappointed.

"Oh, *what* a pity," she said in a soft voice. "I had hoped to talk to you last night but there was never a chance—I would *so* much like to hear about your work, it must be *so* interesting." And she smiled up at Val appealingly.

But the appeal was lost on Val.

"The main thing about my work is that it must be done to time and not thrown aside at anybody's whim," she said shortly and saw Charlotte wince as if she had been struck.

Making her adieux, Val turned toward the house and found Benet still beside her.

"I'm very sorry about our walk in the park, my dear," he said, and she could tell from his low voice how true this was. "We must take it as soon as I get back. Two weeks without you is going to seem like an awfully long time."

Inconvenienced by finding her throat tight with tears, Val could only nod dumbly.

"At any rate," he added, pausing on the step and sounding more cheerful, "we shall have to see a lot of each other—almost too much, you may think—after I get back."

"Why so?" she managed to articulate.

"The calls. We'll be at it day after day for a couple of months."

"Calls?"

"On all my aunts and cousins—you know, we have to do the whole round of family visits, formally announcing our engagement to each lot, and inviting them all individually to the wedding. It's always done; I'm afraid we can't avoid it. Mother's making an alphabetical list, so nobody will be left out and have hurt feelings. At two a day, it'll take us quite two months."

"What about your work?" she said rather blankly.

"Oh—old Pendleton quite understands how it is—he'll let me have the time off. He's been through it himself. And, after all, he's a cousin too! But that's why I have to give in about this Boston business. Goodbye then, my dear."

He made as if to kiss her, but Val did not want to be kissed in front of the Warrens. She squeezed his hand and slipped swiftly back through the open door.

"Formal kind of a stiff fellow, ain't he," said Nils, who was standing in the hall. "Damned odd, all these social rigmaroles you have over here— just where you'd think things would be free and easy. I can quite see how you feel about it all. Still, he seems a decent cove enough, I don't mind going out with him sometime. It's as well he couldn't just now though: I quite forgot, I'm cleaned out. Not quite up to trap to borrow from your future brother-in-law on your first meeting. I wonder whether *you* can let me have fifty dollars, my dear, just for now?"

"Fifty dollars?" she said vaguely.

"Yes—or seventy-five if you can spare it—I've several introductions which I hope will soon jolly up my finances but just at the moment I'm as clean as a cow's whistle—had enough for my ticket on the boat and a few hands of cards on the way, and that was it. So I'd be greatly obliged—I need to prime the pump, don't you know."

"I'll see what I have."

She went to the bureau where she kept her money; meanwhile Nils rummaged discontentedly among the bottles in the sideboard, found the madeira, and poured himself a tumblerful.

"I'm afraid I've only forty-five dollars," Val said. "Will that do?"

"Have to, won't it?" he answered amiably, rolling up the bills and putting them in his dressing-gown pocket. "Thanks, Valla. I'll do as much for you, some time."

Val's eye wandered back to the clock; she must fit in a call at her bank on the way back from the *Inquirer,* and before going on to Mrs. Allerton's. Well, no walk in the park with Benet, that would save an hour.

"I know, I know, I'm keeping you from your work," said Nils. "I can take a hint! I'll make myself scarce. Got work to do myself, anyway. D'you know where I'll find the offices of a rag called the *Knuckle?*"

"I've never heard of it, I'm afraid," she said, surprised.

"No matter. Some cabman will know. I'll see you later on."

And with exaggerated care, finger on lip, he tiptoed from the room.

Instead of sensibly getting on with her work, Val laid her head down on the table and burst into tears.

And of course, exasperatingly Nils chose that moment to put his head back round the door.

"Can you tell me where's the best place to—*Hey!*" he exclaimed, on a long, drawling note of astonishment. "Hey—what the devil's all the row about?"

He came back into the room and stood, hands on hips, regarding her with comic wonder, his fair hair rumpled up like a jack-in-the-box. "What the deuce has upset you?" he repeated. "Not just because that fellow's gone to Boston for two weeks? You ain't so spoony that you can't bear to part for a fortnight?" She shook her head miserably. "Wish I may die if I know what's the matter! Was it something *I* did?"

The look in his large blue eyes was so naively anxious and puzzled that she had to laugh.

"No—no—I don't know! I'm just tired, that's all, after last night. And it's all a bit too much for me. The thought of those calls! And I daresay I am disappointed to miss my walk with Benet in the p-park." Her lip quivered again, childishly.

"Oh well, if *that's* all it is—" he said. "Didn't think a little thing like that would throw *you* off your perch, a big handsome sensible gal like you! But still, if that's all that needs mending, *I'll* take you in the park. Hey? How about it? I'll come and pick you up at your newspaper office— shall I? How'd that be? And then we'll have a pleasant stroll and you can tell me all your troubles—if there's any left—and I'll tell you all mine. Just like old times it'll be, hand in hand round the reservoir with our tops and hoops, you in your white-velvet bonnet with the pink and green trimmings, wanting to be carried piggyback. Well? What's the answer?"

"Thank you, Nils. Yes. That will be pleasant." She smiled faintly, blowing her nose, and he left again, waving a kiss from the doorway.

This time she settled resolutely to work and wrote fast and steadily, without pausing until she had finished.

But all the time, something fidgeted at the back of her mind, some small idea, just out of reach in the obscurity, that chimed, that echoed, that reminded her of something else. A likeness, a similarity, a kindred feeling. With what? What could it be? Her brother's remark about tops and hoops and piggybacks had set it off.

Fancy his remembering that white-velvet bonnet. It had been her best, her very best and favourite for years and years: white velvet, quilted over with strips of pink-and-green plaid.

As she scribbled the last sentences and her name, she thought, I was unkind to Lottie. Poor little thing. But how could one have a serious conversation with such a silly little babyish creature? Still, I shouldn't have snubbed her; it was bad manners. I could see that Benet didn't like it.

Bother him! He shouldn't have dragged me out on the porch in my dusty old dress.

As she hastily blocked her pages together and called to Chloe to look out for a cab, Val was still ransacking her mind for that teasing connection. "Hand in hand round the reservoir with our hoops."

Then, as she ran down the steps, buttoning her cloak with one hand, clutching muff and papers and umbrella with the other, it suddenly came to her.

Those cards from her mother in London addressed to "Dearest little Valla" signed, "hundreds of kisses, your loving Mother"—those curiously unreal cards, assuming a closeness that had never existed.

She had never walked in the park hand in hand with Nils; he had never spun tops with her or bowled hoops, or carried her piggyback. He had flatly refused to accompany her on such babyish airings; from the very first he had declared that walking in Central Park with one's small sister was only fit for muffs or milksops. Nils had always gone off with his own friends.

Nils did, however, turn up at the *Inquirer* offices, as he had promised, to take his sister to the park. He turned up early, in fact, half an hour before she had said she would be ready, and occupied the time until she was free by strolling round the office and, with his usual talent for bypassing barriers, making himself so generally agreeable that she saw her stock was rising with all her colleagues for having such a brother and felt quite ashamed of her previous, rather uncharitable thoughts about him. After all, people could have mistaken memories, couldn't they? And it was all so long ago.

"What a charming person your brother is, isn't he?" whispered Henrietta DeJong, who had recently been promoted to the fashion page after years of running the New England love stories. "Doesn't he look exactly like the hero of *The Mother's Reward*—Silas Sawyer, do you remember? The plain, fair, good young man who loved Thankful Page for seventeen installments in silence and finally got her when it was too late and she was dying of consumption?"

Val, scribbling corrections in the margin of a proof, suppressed a smile. Even after a mere twelve hours' reacquaintance Nils did not, to her sisterly eye, at all resemble the pure-hearted lovelorn young swain in question.

"He isn't my idea of a farmer," she said. "He works on a newspaper himself, as a matter of fact."

"*Does* he?" Henrietta glanced wistfully across the room to where Nils was deep in conversation with Henge Gruber, the feature-page editor.

While Val was in the editor's office, submitting her final corrections, Nils evidently made good use of his time, for she emerged to hear him promising Gruber an article on English country houses with knowledgeable sidelights on the owners.

And when Ted Towers, the editor, strolled out for a few minutes to have a word with his senior assistant, Nils murmured in his sister's ear, "Introduce me, there's an angel."

Not best pleased, she did so; but she was bound to admit that his behaviour with Ted was perfectly unassuming and correct; he said some polite things about the *Inquirer,* compared it with the *Morning Post,* and then turned the talk to a comparison of English and American politics; after a few minutes Val said that she was ready to go and steered her brother away.

"It never hurts," he said cheerfully as they gained the street.

"What doesn't?"

"Having a friend or two. Making oneself known."

"You are certainly expert at it," she remarked rather tartly.

He turned to look down at her, his long fair hair blowing out. He was hatless, as usual. "My dear Valla, if you haven't learned yet that you can't get on in journalism without plenty of push and selling yourself at the highest possible value—then you never *will* get on at it. Though you don't seem to be doing at all badly, for a girl," he added kindly. "I was talking to several people and reading some of your stuff on the spike, while you were in that fellow's office; they seem to think highly of you. And you've not a bad way of expressing yourself, by any means."

Raising her brows at this, she contented herself with a nod of acknowledgment, and was turning up a flight of steps when he stopped her.

"Hey—where are you flyin' off to now? I thought we were going to the Central Park."

"It's my bank—I'm just going to get some money."

"Oh," he said, "you don't have to do that; I can pay you back that forty dollars—right here, on the nail." Slightly to her surprise he pulled out a fistful of bills from his pocket and stuffed them into her muff. "Had a very successful lunch," he explained gaily. "Fixed up with the *Knuckle* to sell them my stuff at an excellent rate and handed over two articles on the spot, so, all in all, the day's not gone too badly. I'll take you out some-where tonight, shall I? What shall we do—Wallack's Theatre? I believe they have something by Ibsen. Would you like that? Or there's *La Dame aux Camélias?*"

"Thank you Nils; I'd like to go out with you," she said, touched and somewhat startled at this sudden transition from poverty to affluence. "But we'd never get into the *Dame aux Camélias*. It's Bernhardt. I'd like to go to the Ibsen, though."

"Thought that would be the sort of gloomy stuff that's just your ticket; I daresay it's all about women leavin' home and making things uncom-fortable for everyone," said Nils, grinning. He hailed a cab and told the driver to take them to the park. As they rode up Fifth Avenue, "Nils," said Val, "do tell me now, exactly, what you are doing over here?"

"Visiting you, of course, my dearest Sis! Going to give you a good time!"

"No, but seriously? It seems quite a professional trip?"

"Half and half," said Nils. "Always mix business with pleasure. That's how I have arranged my life, and I find it works out very well indeed. Pleasant visits to congenial hosts—write about 'em—everyone wants to read about 'em—everyone wants to be read about; so—everybody pleased. And *I'm* paid for doing what I enjoy."

"Did you come to America to arrange about those articles with the *Knuckle*? What *is* the *Knuckle*, anyway?"

"Oh," he said vaguely, "it's a kind of a men's magazine that gets read in bars and clubs and—and barbers' shops and so forth. Not very high-class but its politics are quite radical, which ought to please you. And they don't pay badly."

"Why didn't you just write to them from England?"

"A personal visit is worth twenty letters," he said. "Supposing I write and tell 'em what I can do—how do they know I'm telling the truth? Sup-pose I send 'em a sample of my stuff—what's to prevent 'em pirating it? That's done all the time. But if I appear in person and make a good impres-sion—d'you see?"

"What kind of articles are you selling them? Are they political?"

"No, they're just a series of pen portraits of well-known society personalities; same kind of thing that I've been doing in London, only longer."

"English personalities?"

"Certainly."

He paid off the driver and they alighted and strolled out of Fifty-ninth Street into the Mall, which was full of sauntering couples enjoying the late-summer sunshine.

"But who over here wants to read about English personalities?"

"Plenty of people, so long as what's written is lively and spicy enough! What they want is intimate details—whose bedroom is next to whom, in those big houseparties, and whose brougham is seen outside whose house late at night, and whose parents are convicts out in Van Dieman's Land, and who wins and loses in the baccarat games, all that kind of thing, which, luckily, I'm in an excellent position to provide."

Val glanced sideways at her half-brother. Strolling along with a smile on his long, good-natured, absurd face, his hands in his pockets, his untidy fair hair rising in a crest from his hatless head, he looked harmless and innocent as a newly fledged duckling. But was he really so?

"Have you written the articles already?"

"Some of 'em. I brought over a few samples to show and they've snapped 'em up. That's why I'm so flush." He slapped his pockets cheerfully.

"But what will the people themselves say? The ones that you have written about? Do they know? Will they mind?"

"To begin with, how will they ever know? The *Knuckle* doesn't come out in England."

"Well, but it might get back. And then what would they think of you?"

"Bless you, the articles won't have my name on 'em. They're going to be signed 'Hospes,' to give a nice refined classical touch. So no one's to know it's me."

Val walked for fifty yards in silence, her hands clasped inside her sealskin muff and her head, in its grey fur cap ornamented with a bird's wing, bent forward, silent and thoughtful.

At last, in a troubled voice, she said, "Nils?"

"Well?"

"Do you—do you really think that's a decent thing to do? Accept people's hospitality and then write scandal about them?"

"My dear Valla! I've told you before, you just can't get on in this profession unless you're prepared to be as tough as whipcord. It's just no manner of use entertaining these mawkish, squeamish, tender, middle-class kind of notions."

"But to do it about your *friends*—to exploit them like that—"

"Oh," he said quickly. "I wouldn't do it about my real friends. And, damn it, I only write what's common gossip anyway."

"Well I don't like it, just the same," said Val. "It's muckraking."

"One man's muck is another man's pigeon, my dear. Anyway, I daresay I shan't do it for ever—certainly don't intend to. Sometimes it can be risky, I don't deny. And I've plenty more ideas. For instance, a series of medical articles which I expect to pay *very* handsomely. If there's one thing that goes down well, it's illness—people love to read about 'em. 'Ailments of the Great'—you know the kind of thing. Mad Queens. Caesar's gout. Napoleon's epilepsy. Dementia praecox—is our prime minister suffering from it?"

"Good heavens," said Val, startled, "is he?"

"Not that I know of. But one can go on for ever at that sort of lark. How many members of Parliament are sane? Was Constance Kent mad? And then, of course, some day, Kirstie's old aunts will finally be gathered in to their fathers and I hope I'll be able to stop this sordid grubbing around altogether."

"Old aunts? Doesn't Kirstie have any parents?"

"No, they died out in India. Her father was some kind of a nabob. The aunts brought her up—real old pair of Gorgon spinsters they are. When they die, to the best of my knowledge, all their cash comes to Kirstie and a devilish great barracks of a place up in the wilds of Lammermuir called Ardnasomething. Castle Barebane, the locals call it—it's all falling to bits. So we can only hope the aunts will be gathered in quite soon; they're old and ugly and cantankerous enough, deuce knows! And confoundedly tight with their cash; won't lay out a penny, even to buy the children a Christmas gewgaw. Anyway one of the aunts, the older one, is always riding round the Arabian desert on a camel, wrapped up in a blanket; keeps a diary of her travels and hobnobs with sultans; so I daresay sooner or later she'll get desert fever—or some sheikh will lop off her head," Nils said hopefully. "I wrote a piece about her once for the *Post*—nothing much— but, deuce take it, the old girl went up like a rocket. Won't even bow to me in the street now—not that I care."

He screwed his head round to stare with interest at a very dashing black-haired girl in a dress of black-and-white-striped moiré with cherry piping. The fashionable crowd in the Mall was increasing.

"Oh dear," said Val, "there are the Chaunceys."

"Who are the Chaunceys, my love? Some more of Benet's tiresome connections?"

"Yes, his cousins; perhaps they won't see me."

But as they walked across into Fifth Avenue the old-fashioned yellow coach with fringed hammercloth rumbled to a stop beside them. Two ladies were in it, Mrs. Chauncey and her daughter; both were staring at Nils with frank curiosity.

"Good afternoon, Mrs. Chauncey," said Val politely, as they bowed. "This is my brother, Nils Hansen, from England."

Mrs. Chauncey, stately today in royal blue velvet and a bonnet to match trimmed with frosted grapes, glanced sideways with a sharp flash of interest at this piece of information; but it was plain that her raking scrutiny had immediately summed up the hatless Nils as wholly unsuitable company for her daughter; the greeting she gave him was brief and cool.

"Dear me, Miss Montgomery, what a pity your brother did not arrive in time for the party last night."

"Yes, wasn't it?" Val agreed, thinking how much easier to bear the evening would have been with Nils there to support her and share a joke from time to time. Or would it? Might she have found the tension exacerbated by uncertainty as to whether Nils was taking surreptitious notes about his fellow guests for future publication?

After a few commonplaces about the ball, the news of the day, and the weather, Mrs. Chauncey remarked, "And so I hear Benet is escorting the Warrens to Boston? Leaving this afternoon, is he not?"

Startled from her composure, Val said, "Is he? I mean—yes, I knew he was going to Boston, he called to tell me so this morning, but I—"

"Oh indeed, yes, he is to advise Cousin Alma about the sale of her house. They travel back with him. Such a worry for her, poor dear, after her husband's death. But Benet will see to it all. He is a dear, good fellow."

"Yes . . ." agreed Val rather wanly.

"Such a comfort to the family. Well, we must not keep the horses standing; it is quite cool today. Drive on, Thomas."

Mrs. Chauncey and her silent daughter inclined their heads again with distant politeness, and the yellow carriage moved off.

After a moment or two, Nils remarked, "Benet hadn't told you he was accompanying the Warrens to Boston? Isn't that rather peculiar?"

"Oh, I daresay he forgot, or didn't think it of importance . . . Or perhaps it was arranged after he saw me—" Her voice died away uncertainly.

Nils paused, and then said, "Valla, my dear, listen to me. What I'm going to tell you is entirely for your own sake—you know that?"

She nodded.

"You are *never* going to be happy in this set. It ain't right for you. It don't take half an eye to see that. They're all stuffy, snobbish, intolerant—I could see how that old b—that old hag was looking you up and down—and me too—as if we were something that had gone mildewy in her pantry. How can you endure such treatment? By God, when I compare it with my life in England—all my friends—"

"Oh—but when I've been married to Benet for a bit, and we've settled down, then they'll accept me."

Even to her own ears, Val's voice sounded singularly lacking in enthusiasm at this prospect.

"Accept you? They'll pulverise you. They'll put you through the grinder and roll you out and jump up and down on you before they are satisfied. And then they won't be. Because you'll always have a bit of spirit left. And if you haven't, what does that mean? That they've really done for you."

His lazy manner had left him. He spoke with unusual energy.

"I can't stand that butter-voiced supercilious set of people; I'd like to grind all their faces in muck."

"You really think I ought to break it off, Nils?"

They had turned away from Fifth Avenue again and were wandering through the hills and dells of the Ramble; Val prodded at the soft earth with the point of her umbrella, remembering with a kind of remote pain the times when she had come with her father to pick violets here. How easy and simple life had been in those days.

"Break it off?" Nils appeared to consider the question with care. "No, no I don't say you ought to do *that*; not yet, at any rate. Benet is a good fellow, you say; he certainly seems all right; I quite took to him, I must say; and there *is* the family money, that's not to be sneezed at; don't toss away your cheese for the moon. But do what I said before; come to England for a spell, look around there; maybe Benet will follow you; or maybe England will change your ideas a bit. You might even see someone you like better than Benet, who can say?"

"Oh, that would be too unprincipled—"

What did his words echo? My mind is full of loose ends, Val thought. Something somebody said last night at the ball. That cousin: "Greedy Alma took the girl to England, hoping for an earl . . . in the meantime, Benet's eye had wandered." That was a bit of irony, wasn't it? Everyone going off to England in search of better game, giving Benet time to think again. Maybe it would be better for him to think again. But I don't want anyone better than Benet. I love him with all my heart.

"Unprincipled? What nonsense you talk, my dear Valla. You're as bad as Kirstie. Now, you just forget all those highfalutin ideas and come back with me. Can't you get that Towers fellow to give you some assignment in England that would pay for the trip? Didn't you say he had before?"

"Yes, very likely I could, but—"

"Well, then! Ask him tomorrow. And—I was coming to this—"

Nils' authoritative manner suddenly changed to a more diffident one than he had shown hitherto. Val was not too preoccupied to be slightly amused at the contrast between his previous confident air and this unwonted anxiousness and humility. He paused, picking a plane leaf from the grass, and rolled it between his fingers. "You see—you could also do me and Kirstie a great kindness, if you'd care to."

He gave Val a slow, tentative, pleading look; the large blue eyes were guileless now, transparent.

"What is it, Nils?"

"Well—these aunts of Kirstie's have started kicking up a row; they really are the most beastly bore you can imagine! They have been putting ideas into Kirstie's head."

"What kind of ideas?"

"Well, they go trundling round to our house in Welbeck Street in their smelly old barouche, when I'm not there, and telling Kirstie that I neglect her, and all that kind of thing. Deuce take it, what am I *doing* all the time I'm away but making our living? But they won't see it. They say I never take Kirstie anywhere and it's a black shame, and she never gets a chance to go out or meet people—and a lot of bosh of that sort. It *is* bosh—as I've said, she don't care for society, you can't pry her away from those brats— and she's downright scared of mixing in a great rout of people. Rather like you, eh, Valla? I daresay you and Kirstie will get on very well."

"I daresay we should. But what is it you want me to do?"

"Well I've got a particular pal called Nugent Reydon; Lord Clanreydon, he is now, got made a baronet last year, for lending eighty thousand to the Prince of W., so the story goes."

"I've read about him," Val said. "Isn't there some mystery about him— he came from the colonies—Australia—very rich? Isn't there talk that he might be the next prime minister?"

"Yes, if the Whigs get back. That's the fellow; he keeps his origins dark —and who's to blame him? He's probably the son of an Irish weaver who got deported to New South Wales and made good; why should he have to acknowledge his scrubby kin to all the world? He keeps the best table in London—always cooks his ham in champagne—why should anybody need to know more than that?"

"Why indeed?" agreed Val gravely, reflecting that her brother did not seem to put these praiseworthy principles into effect while pursuing his profession. But he had said that he never wrote about his real friends; presumably Lord Clanreydon was one.

"What about him?"

"He has just got himself a new yacht; devilish neat job it is, cost a cool three-quarters million. Tiled bathrooms, carpets, curtains—everything done to a T."

"A *yacht?* How can it cost as much as that?"

"Steam yacht, of course," said her brother impatiently. "Now, the thing is, old Nuggie's collected together a very jolly sporting party, and he's invited us all for a two-month cruise in the Mediterranean, around Christmas. Fun, eh? All the best people are going—he's even asked the prince—"

"Gracious. Would the prince really go?"

"Not for Christmas. But he might slip away for a bit. He likes to get off, you know, *en garçon*, now and then; he travels around incog as Baron Renfrew; but anyway there would be *all* the swells."

"And so?" Val said, as her brother seemed slow in coming to the point. She lifted her watch on its ribbon; the afternoon was drawing on; soon she must go round to the Allerton house. And what, anyway, had Lord Clanreydon's new yacht to do with her?

"Well, Kirstie's old aunts are cutting up *really* rusty at the thought of my going off for two months; more or less urging the poor girl to get a divorce if I do any such thing—"

"You aren't serious?" She turned to look at him in astonishment. "*Divorce*, because you go on a two-month cruise?"

"Yes, ridiculous, ain't it? After all, it would be a professional trip for me; much as my name is worth, with the *Post*, to be on board. But the thing is, you see," Nils rolled his plane leaf in the other direction, and then impatiently threw it down, "the thing is, I'd got to know this gal, kind of a dancer, very jolly gal called Letty Pettigrew, and old Nuggie was going to ask her along, just for larks, and somehow the tabbies got wind of it. That's the worst of them," he burst out, "they're ancient, but they ain't out of touch, not a bit of it! They write letters to everyone, and everyone writes to them, and when they're in town they've got this great mouldy house in Grosvenor Square, and all the old sticks go to their soirées. And the gossip that gets passed around there makes my column seem like Little Miss Muffet, I can tell you! So, as I say, they cut up rusty, and I had to tell Letty P. that it was all U.P. with her coming on the cruise. But even *that* didn't satisfy the spiteful old hags; nothing would do for them but I should take Kirstie along. Or else, they say, I'd better decline the invitation. Decline! It would be professional suicide! Besides, I practically helped Nuggie *design* that yacht."

Reading between the lines of this artless history, Val began to feel intensely sorry for her sister-in-law. Poor Kirstie; either left alone at home, or taken as a matter of convenience and whitewashing—what humiliation, either way. But perhaps Kirstie had her own friends, diversions, compensations—how could one judge, from such a distance? What did Val know, after all, about the kind of life her brother and sister-in-law lived in fashionable London?

"Did Kirstie agree?"

"Well, I got her to consider it—matter of fact her doctor said it would be a very good thing for her, as she's not been a bit well lately; she had a low fever in the summer that's turned to a cough, and somehow she can't seem to pull herself out of it. The doctor said sea air and so on would be just the article."

"I expect it would," Val agreed. "Poor Kirstie."

"Ay, but here's the rub; she won't leave the children! You'd think after all this time she'd have found someone that she could trust with them, but no! All the gals that come to us get turned off after a month or so."

Val wondered fleetingly if the proclivities of Nils had anything to do with this phenomenon, and was confirmed in her hypothesis when he added, "All except one old trout who was as strict as a jailor and as ugly as sin, and I turned *her* off; couldn't stand the sight of her. If you ask me," he went on aggrievedly, "Kirstie's got a bee in her bonnet about those brats. She's reasonable enough on all other points, but when it comes to them, she won't listen to sense, you might as well waste your breath talking to the wall."

"Perhaps it's because she's not well?" suggested Val. "Ill people are often unreasonable."

But is it so unreasonable, she wondered, not to want to leave your children? It depends how long for, I suppose.

"Well, this all harks back to some affair about a year ago when I took her to the races—thought it'd be a treat for her, for heaven's sake!—and when we got home, Kirstie looked through the window as I was paying off the cab and saw the girl we had then—redheaded Irish colleen, that one was, pretty girl but a devil of a temper—Kirstie saw her give the little one, Jannie, a bit of a cuff on the head. *I've* never seen Kirstie so angry, she flew in like a tigress. Gave the girl her marching orders then and there, watched while she packed her box, and turned her off with a week's wages and no character."

"I expect I would have done the same."

"Oh, stuff!" said Nils. "You have to teach children to mind you, after all; spare the rod, and so forth. Still," he added, recollecting his mission,

"I can see that you and Kirstie would see eye to eye on that head, which brings me to what I want to ask: what she sent me to say: would *you* consider keeping an eye on the brats for us while Kirstie comes with me on the *Dragonfly*? There'd be a maid, too, of course, and cook, and so forth; all you'd have to do is *be* there, you know?"

A whole series of things immediately fell into place for Val. Her brother's airy and nonchalant manner of putting the request had not wholly disguised the eagerness he felt, and with which he now waited for her reply. She suspected that considerably more was at stake in his personal life than he had so far conveyed (or ever would convey, probably); it must be so, indeed, for him to have come all the way across the Atlantic to ask this favour. Well, true, he had also arranged the lucrative commission with the *Knuckle*; but still, despite his previous arguments, that could have been done by letter?

For that matter, why had he not written to Val to make his request? Because he mistrusted his epistolary powers of persuasion?

It certainly did seem quite a lot to ask, of somebody, moreover, to whom he had not written for two or three years. He had really come to America, she deduced, to look over the situation and come to a spot decision.

"But," she said, "Kirstie doesn't even know me. How can she be sure *I* wouldn't ill-treat the children? Haven't you any closer friends—somebody—"

"No. Not a soul."

"How about the old aunts?"

"Are you joking? They wouldn't be plagued with children Pieter and Jannie's age. *Do* say yes, Valla," he said coaxingly. "Think what fun it would be! You could come back with me on the boat—no end of larks—and then, you'd like our house, Welbeck Street ain't bad—we could give you introductions to our friends—you could go about a bit and see London—"

"I thought the idea was I should be with the children?"

"Well, that's only for two months, rot it; plenty of time after that. Besides, they ain't bad little things—you could take them out—in the park and so forth."

"Well . . ." said Val, "I'll think about it."

Indeed she was tempted. To look after her niece and nephew, for two months, after all, would be an unimpeachable excuse for temporarily quitting her own predicament; nobody, not Mrs. Allerton or Mr. Dexter, no Chauncey or Babcock, would be able to find fault with that. Val did not particularly like children—had had little contact with any, in fact—but two months was not long, she could accommodate to them for that length of time.

"When do you go back?" she said.

"Next week."

"Next week? I thought you were staying two or three weeks?"

"Not if it ain't needful," said Nils simply. "I've plenty of things to do back at home. And I daresay the old girls will be up in the boughs if I stay too long—think I'm taking out opera singers or something."

"But if I came with you next week—I don't know if Mr. Towers could spare me—Chum wouldn't be back from Maryland—"

"Oh, you'll find all these things can be arranged," he said easily. "I'll help—I'll run errands for you—what's a brother for, hang it?"

"And then," said Val—it was the whole heart and body of her argument, really, the prime cause of her reluctance—"I'd not have a chance to see Benet again; he wouldn't be back from Boston."

She glanced at her watch; by now he would be sitting on the Boston train, with Mrs. Warren and Charlotte.

"So much the better," said Nils callously. "It'll be a shock to him when he gets back; make him sit up and realise what he stands to lose. *Do* come, Valla; we'll give you a really rousing time in London before we go off. I'll introduce you to Nuggie Clanreydon for a start, and *he's* the most amazing fellow you ever met in your life. I swear there's nobody like him."

Val glanced at her brother, astonished; for a moment he looked quite unlike himself—or quite unlike any self that she had yet seen: with his face lifted to the wind, and a strange visionary gleam in his eye, he appeared to be remembering some experience whose nature she could not begin to guess at. Then he came back to earth and said, "Here—while I think of it—Kirstie gave me this to give you—been carrying it so long that it's got a bit rubbed."

He pulled from his waistcoat pocket a small piece of folded paper and handed it to Val, who unfolded it and stood still to read it.

The handwriting was shaky—either Kirstie had written it in haste, or her state of health was even worse than Nils had represented.

"Dear Val, if you do this I will bless you forever. I hope and pray that you will. I know the kind of person you are from your letters—I know I can trust you. The doctor says I need to go away. I know the children will be good with you, they have promised. Pieter can read now, he reads to Jannie. Be good to them—I know you will. Your loving sister, Kirstie."

An hour later, sitting in Mrs. Allerton's dark drawing room with its heavy red flock paper that effectively swallowed every scrap of light, Val was passionately envying Nils his freedom.

"Go calling on a pair of old tabbies? Not likely!" he said and strode blithely away down University Place. "I'll see you later—we'll dine somewhere before the theatre, hmm?"

The Allerton ladies, with a handsome mahogany worktable between them, were placidly stitching away at their tapestry: large pink cabbages, which formed, Val knew apprehensively, part of a set of twelve dining-room chair seats destined to be sat on by Benet and herself and their guests for the next thirty years; it was plain that only flood, fire, or some other act of God would be a sufficient cause for getting rid of them.

"Do you like the way your mother's house is furnished, Benet?" Val had once cautiously inquired, and he had replied, without much interest, "Why, yes, it's all right, I guess. Rather too many little tables to bump into, let's not have so many in our house, shall we? But otherwise there's nothing much wrong with it; the chairs are comfortable, that's the main thing; and I have enough bookcases in my study; I think it's rather affected and snobbish to be too particular about furnishings, don't you? Can't stand those de Kuypers, everlastingly importing cabinets from Italy and making such a precious fuss about Louis Quinze and Corinthian pilasters. Mother don't like my smoking in the drawing room, though; I hope *you* won't mind?"

In part, Val agreed with Benet; she too disliked aesthetic snobbery; but she did find the Allerton drawing room oppressive. Family portraits in heavy gold frames peered gloomily and severely down from the red walls; the subjects had a tendency to point an admonishing finger toward thick books or terrestrial globes, or to the sky, as if they exhorted: time is short, work apace. The dozens of small tables held lustre pots of immortelles—real flowers were seldom seen since Delia suffered from hay fever—silver-framed photographs, little silver nicknacks, and more thick volumes—views of Rome and the Rhine, Turner's *Rivers of France*, McDougall's *Waterfalls of Scotland*, Smith's *Châteaux of the Loire*. Why are rivers so respectable? Val wondered fleetingly and frivolously. Wholly uninterested in and suspicious of art, the Allerton ladies reserved their esteem for landscapes, and if the landscapes had running water in them, so much the better. Perhaps it was somehow connected with hygiene, Val decided, and wondered how many servant hours each day it took to maintain the drawing room in its state of aseptic dustlessness and order. No window was ever opened; no breath of the outside world was allowed to enter. In summer, striped awnings held the sun at bay; in winter, massive velvet draperies excluded snow and storm.

"And now, dear," said Mrs. Allerton, who had been in a state as near nervousness for the last ten minutes as her placid disposition would permit, embarking on abortive, distrait snippets of conversation, and then discarding them like unwanted shreds of embroidery silk, "Now, dear, there's just one—oh dear, here's Parker with the tea, perhaps I should—Delia, dear, will you pour out, I expect dear Valla would like a cup—it's always so difficult saying this kind of—thank you, my darling, just put it here, I will have a sip the minute I have finished this petal—you see, Valla dear, Benet's grandmother—though of course she very much *admires* the way you tackle your life so bravely and splendidly—what was that, Delia? Yes, a small piece of cake, thank you, my darling—well, as I expect you saw, Valla dear, old Mrs. Allerton has very decided *views.*"

"What is it that she doesn't like about me?" said Val, sitting very straight and upright.

"Oh, nothing, *nothing* of that kind at all!" Benet's mother was terribly flustered; her two little fat white hands flew up distractedly like butterflies. "No, no, she *likes* you, my dear, very much—of *course* she does—it is just that she *cannot* approve of your living alone the way you do—"

"Except that Miss Chumley is there too?" Val pointed out with restraint.

"Oh well—some person like that of course, Grandma Allerton would hardly—you see, in this family we do always—Benet's fiancée isn't just like any—if only your dear father were alive, I'm sure *he* would understand—it's not as if it were a case of—"

Unhelped by Val, who remained silently observing her during this recital, Mrs. Allerton distressfully proceeded, "So just before she went back to Bridgewater this morning she called on Cousin Amy Chauncey, who has sent round this letter for you—"

The letter from Cousin Amy was written in a thin spidery hand on paper stiff as whalebone, and the style had something of whalebone about it too; it invited Miss Montgomery to remove herself and her effects without delay from Twenty-third Street to Gramercy Park, where due to the departure of the family governess, the four girls' education now being completed, there was a vacant bedroom which Miss Montgomery would be welcome to avail herself of until the date of her wedding to dear Benet; and in the meantime Mrs. Chauncey would be happy to give Miss Montgomery the benefit of her advice and experience in all the realms where a young lady, lacking a family and mentors of her own, could derive profit from listening to the words of somebody well versed in the ways of society.

In other words, I'm to be completely made over, thought Val.

"Very kind of Mrs. Chauncey," she contented herself with saying, but a scarlet spot stood out on her pale cheek; Mrs. Allerton observed this with dismay.

"It isn't that Mrs. Allerton—well, you know, dear, she—it was just *little* things—like your dress—and the fact that—"

"I'll write a reply to Mrs. Chauncey as soon as I get home," Val said calmly, though her heart was hammering with rage.

"Oh, *do*, dear, that is perfectly—I'm sure you will really find Cousin Amy very very—she knows *all* the little ways of—and the girls, too, of course, dear, sweet creatures—you will soon feel at home there I am quite —and Benet will be so relieved—"

"You misunderstand me, Mrs. Allerton. I shall write to Mrs. Chauncey declining her kind offer."

Mrs. Allerton's mouth dropped open; her hands were suspended in mid-air.

"In fact I am setting sail for England next week with my brother; his wife is not at all well, and I have promised to go over and be with them for some months, perhaps a year," Val heard herself saying.

The house was silent when Val returned to it. No sign of Nils. She was disappointed—she had been longing to describe to him the expressions of utter disapproval and astonishment with which the Allerton ladies had greeted her bombshell.

"They could hardly have been more appalled if I had announced that I was going off to the sultan's harem in Constantinople," she had imagined herself saying to Nils—but she consoled herself by thinking that he must be back very soon if they were to dine before the theatre. Meantime she could have a leisurely bath and put on a more suitable dress. Her grey poplin would do.

She was fastening its dozens of tiny buttons when she saw the note on her dressing table.

"Dear Valla"—in Nils' scrawled handwriting—"very sorry couldn't stay but had news of crisis from Kirstie and must dash back if I can get today's boat to Southampton. Pity about our theatre party but I'll take you to Covent Garden instead! It is grand that you are coming—can't wait to tell Kirstie and see her face of joy. Cable which boat you are taking—I'll meet you at Southampton. Make it next week if you can. N."

Val could not make it next week. But sixteen days later, by dint of frantic work-filled days and many hasty arrangements, she was on the ocean. Benet was still detained in Boston; she had not seen him again.

CHAPTER 3

"Look, cheer up, that's the Isle of Wight," Val said to her companion.

"I couldn't cheer up if you told me it was the Isle of Elysium," he replied gloomily, dragging down the ear flaps of his traveling cap and sinking his head as far as it would go into his fur collar. He ignored the fog-shrouded, tree-girt, greenish wedge sliding by on their starboard bow, and added, "This has been without exception the most wretched trip of my life."

"Never mind, it will soon be over. A sailor told me that we should berth by four o'clock."

"It can't be too soon for me. If it hadn't been for you, Miss Montgomery, I doubt if I should have survived."

"Oh, come, Mr. Cusack! The ship's doctor would have pulled you through. They have their pride, after all."

It had certainly been a wretched trip, though, she was obliged to acknowledge. Autumn gales had dogged them all the way; the ship had suffered several mishaps, first boiler trouble, then screw trouble, and the passage had taken six days longer than expected. Although disappointed not to have the company of Nils on the trip, Val had several times reflected that in the circumstances she was possibly better on her own; she had vague recollections from childhood of Nils' inability to put up with any kind of sickness or discomfort; he might have proved a difficult fellow passenger. As it was she had shared a cabin with three older ladies who all took to their bunks as a matter of course on the first sign of bad weather and remained there throughout the voyage. Val had left them to the ministrations of the stewardess and spent her time mainly up on deck, wrapped in all the warmest garments she had brought with her. She was not precisely ill herself, though queasy a good deal of the time, but her spirits were as low as they could be; miserably uncertain as to whether she had made the right decision, homesick, missing Benet acutely, attacked, now, too, by considerable doubts as to the candour and reliability of Nils; she huddled against a pile of coiled rope, hour after hour, watching the heaving grey turtleback seas slide by, wondering dismally if she had made a horrible mistake.

"When did Nils go off, Chloe? Did he get a cable? What made him decide to leave?" she had asked.

"I never saw him get no cable, nor no letter either, Miss Val. He jes' came straight back at four o'clock, packed up his things, an' ask me to call him a cab."

The curl of Chloe's lip suggested that Nils had given her nothing for her trouble—and he had also forgotten to pay Val the rest of the money she had lent him; what he had tucked into her muff outside the *Inquirer* office proved to be only twenty dollars.

Still, perhaps he had had a cable from Kirstie addressed to the *Knuckle* office; or perhaps he had met someone he knew, who had brought tidings . . . It was useless to speculate, Val knew; she went on speculating. Her low state of mind was aggravated by hunger; she found it impossible to enter the stuffy, steamy dining room with its smells of greasy food and tobacco smoke.

But on the third day of the trip she had come across somebody in even worse case than herself: a tall, limp man in an astrakhan coat and cap, who seemed to be almost on the point of death from cold and sickness; Val had grabbed the skirts of his coat just as he appeared to be about to faint and pitch head first over the rail. She had summoned a steward and told him to take the man to his cabin.

"No—no—can't stand it down there—" gasped the sufferer, opening bloodshot brown eyes. "Must—stay—fresh air—" So, instead, Val had ordered the steward to bring up beef tea and brandy, and when the sick man—his name was Cusack, she learned from the steward—had taken a little of each, and was able, shivering, to climb onto his feet, she had walked him unremittingly round and round the deck, despite his groans and protests and demands to be left alone to die. At first he eyed Val with the utmost dislike and suffered her ministrations in silent hostility, but by the end of several days they had struck up a kind of relationship, based largely on noncommunication, as they paced unspeaking, hour after freezing hour, round the wet, cold, and cluttered deck, or shared beef tea and champagne in some semisheltered corner.

Mr. Cusack paid for the champagne.

"Better for the liver than brandy," he remarked with his usual brevity, throwing an empty Moët bottle over the side. Val gathered that he was rich. "What the deuce is the good of all one's cash if it can't save one from this kind of pitch-and-toss?" he remarked once, bitterly, as the ship clambered among waves the size of ten-storey houses. "Some day they'll have flying machines that will cross the Atlantic in twelve hours. But I'll be six foot under by then."

He certainly did not seem like a man who expected to live to a ripe old age. He was an extraordinary-looking individual—tall, cadaverously thin under all his wraps, hollow-cheeked, always shivering despite the fur-lined garments which seemed wholly ineffectual in protecting him from the chill sea air. Val found it quite hard to make a guess at his age; sometimes, drawn with cold, scowling with wretchedness, he could have been in his fifties, while at other moments, when a passing spark of interest in some external event lit up his expression, he might have passed for no more than thirty-eight or -nine. His hair, under the heavy fur traveling cap, was a dark Irish blue-black, and he had a big bony nose and forehead to match. His mouth was large, thin, mobile, and usually curved downward in utter disgust at his circumstances.

Val occasionally felt inclined to tease him, but forbore, because she was not certain whether seasickness was all that afflicted him, or if he suffered from some other more deep-seated complaint. His pallor at times was almost green. He had traveled widely in the tropics, she gathered. "Learned not to touch brandy when I was in India," he had remarked once; she wondered if he might have picked up some tropical disease when he was in that continent.

They had exchanged virtually no personal information. He knew that she was traveling to England to stay with her brother; she, that he was Irish-born of Scottish descent, that he lived in Edinburgh, and was traveling on to Scotland by sea.

"Mad thing to do," he morosely remarked. "And as for Edinburgh—might as well live in the northwest passage."

"I should think it is a little cold after India," Val remarked moderately, and earned a sharp, ironic glance. They walked on, falling into another of their prolonged, but not unfriendly, silences.

Their ship's arrival in the Solent had called out of him the only personal remark he had made on the whole trip.

"I don't think," he had observed dispassionately, looking with gloom at the grey, damp Hampshire coast, "I don't think that I have ever before spent ten days with a woman who did not ask me a single question."

"Then I had better not begin now," said Val.

She spoke rather absently. She was beginning to be consumed by a stupid anxiety—anxiety? at times it felt more like terror—about this whole English venture. Had Nils received her cable? Would he be there to meet her? Of course he would. Why should he not? He had promised. Promised? Would he be bound by his promise? But if he were not there? Then what was to stop her catching the boat train and traveling up to London by herself? She had been to England before, she had traveled by herself before. But she had not then arrived feeling so physically and emotionally depleted, at the end of such an uncomfortable and exhausting trip, after making a difficult and upsetting personal decision. Passionately she longed for Nils to be there on the dock, and Kirstie too; for a warm, loving family welcome.

Probably because she was low-spirited and worried, she had dreamed about her father on almost every night of the voyage, although nowadays, during her daytime existence, she did not consciously miss him. Every night she had talked to him, laughed with him, been comforted by his companionship; each morning she had woken to dried tears on her cheeks and the knowledge of loneliness.

"Look, there come the tugs," observed her companion. "It begins to look as if we shall make land after all."

"I had better go and collect my things," Val said, realising that all the other passengers were dashing about like possessed lemmings. People who had not shown their noses on deck for the whole voyage suddenly appeared; the air was full of excited joyful chatter.

"Go below? For your things? Do you have to? Won't someone bring them up?" Mr. Cusack seemed surprised.

"No—who? I haven't got much. I'll see you on the dock, I expect—" she said vaguely and hurried down the companionway. Her anxiety had turned to restlessness; she must be doing something, although no doubt it would be a long time yet before they docked. She found her cabin companions, up at last, feverishly bustling about and impeding one another, curling their hair, pinning their collars, putting on rouge to disguise the ill-effects of the trip. It was impossible to come near the tiny mirror; in any case, why bother? She was only being met by her brother, after all. Val pushed the last of her belongings into her two small bags and, grasping their handles firmly, walked up on deck. The docking had proceeded faster than she had expected; already the ship was alongside the wharf, edging in closer and closer. Hopefully she scanned the heads of the crowd on shore for a lint-white mop of hair standing higher than the rest.

But the crowd broke and flowed distractingly; no one kept still for a moment; it was impossible to pick out individuals.

Perhaps he would be waiting by the companionway.

At last the ship was made fast and instantly passengers began pouring ashore by two gangways. Val was swept off in the first wave and suddenly found herself on solid land, which seemed to rock underfoot more violently than the deck had done at its worst. She staggered and grabbed for a convenient upright post. A man laughed at her, not unkindly.

"Porter, lady?"

"No, thanks, I'm being met."

Escaping to the rear of the crowd she put down her bags and looked about her. A confusion of coaches and baggage carts were picking up the passengers and their bundles. No sign of Nils. But there was plenty of time. Quite two thirds of the passengers had still to disembark.

Among the cries of greeting and recognition, clamour of porters, and shouts of dockers unloading mail, she caught a familiar voice behind her.

"Ah, there you are, John-Jo—"

"Oh, Sir Marcus, you do look poorly. You should have taken me along to look after you, wasn't I after telling you so?"

"Nonsense, John-Jo, you would have been nothing but a nuisance. I managed very well."

Turning she saw her companion of the trip being greeted effusively by a little roly-poly man, apparently his servant, who relieved him of various wraps and a brief case, bobbing up and down with joy, and then rushing off with the things to an adjacent brougham. Val smiled involuntarily at the disparity between the two men. At that moment Cusack looked up and caught her eye. He gave some brief order to John-Jo, who immediately made off toward the ship. For a moment she lost sight of Cusack in the crowd, then she found him beside her.

"I began to fear I might not see you again," he said—she could only just hear his rather dry voice amid the cries of the crowd. "Here—"

He was proffering something small and white; even in the midst of her acute anxiety and suspense she was a little startled and entertained to see that it was a visiting card. Somehow their companionship had not seemed to be proceeding on the kind of level that accords with the exchange of cards; she would have been quite prepared to part from him without any of the conventional social usages; had, indeed, hardly expected to see him again. But she took the card with a murmur of thanks and tucked it into her muff.

"Being met by your brother?" she heard above the clamour. Although his voice was colourless, a certain air of concern was detectible in it. "Are you sure about that?"

"I daresay he's here somewhere," Val said hopefully, looking around. "And if he isn't, it doesn't matter. I have his address in London."

"Here we are, Sir Marcus." Little John-Jo the manservant had reappeared, staggering under three large leather portmanteaux and a thick fur steamer rug. "Now we're all Sir Garnet. You pop into the broo'm, sir, and I'll wrap you up snug. I've a fine room booked for you at the hotel."

"You're sure I can't drive you anywhere, Miss Montgomery?"

"No, no, thanks, really, I shall be quite all right." She was quite amazed at such thought and solicitude. "I hope you have a good journey to Scotland."

"Oh—yes," he said. "Thank you. Supposing that you should find your brother out of town, what then?"

"That's not very likely," said Val, "since he has a wife and it's for her sake I've come. But if he should be out of town, I shall stay at the Jersey Hotel in Tabernacle Street, near St. Paul's. I have stayed there before and it is very comfortable."

He gave a nod. "Oh yes—the Jersey—not a bad place. Well—if you are sure—"

"Yes, thank you. I'll really be quite all right."

Her wish to see Nils had suddenly become so intense that she longed to cut this conversation short; all she wanted to do was look about her, concentrate on scrutinising the shifting crowd. As if guessing her wish, Cusack said, "Well—goodbye, then—" gave her a brief, strange, difficult smile—his first, she afterward recalled, since the beginning of their acquaintance—and allowed himself to be steered away by John-Jo. Val instantly forgot him.

By now most of the passengers had disembarked, and a large proportion had already been driven away in various equipages or had left the dock for the railway station at the rear.

The area near the ship was fairly clear. She could not see Nils anywhere.

Buttonholing a passing porter, Val asked him when the boat train left.

"There's two, miss. One goes in five minutes, t'other in an hour."

Since it was plain that she could not expect to be united with Nils in time to catch the earlier train, Val resigned herself to wait and looked round for a seat. There was none. She changed some money, bought a newspaper at a stall, and found a pillar to lean against, where she could keep an eye on the thinning crowd, now mostly composed of stevedores unloading heavy baggage from the ship.

Still no sign of Nils.

After another half hour she decided to give him up, and made her way toward the station. By now dusk was falling and she felt weary, confused, hungry, and bitterly disappointed. It was foolish to have laid such store on being met. She might have known Nils would never do it. Go all the way to Southampton, when she could just as easily get on a train by herself? Benet would have, she thought. I've been spoiled by Benet, that's the truth. And, not for the first time, nor the last, she longed for his calm, warm, reliable presence.

There were plenty of porters free, now; she beckoned one and tipped him a shilling to find her a corner seat while she bought her train ticket. The second-class compartment was empty when he installed her in it and put her bags in the rack overhead, but it rapidly filled up. Two immensely fat old countrywomen installed themselves alongside and opposite Val, and immediately went on with a conversation that had obviously stood them in good stead all their lives.

"No, as I say, Mrs. Jennings, I like something substantial for my dinner, say some pea soup to begin with, then a biled leg of mutton with plenty of fat, with turnips and caper sauce, followed by tripe and onion and some nice suet dumplings as a finish."

"For my part, mum, I prefer something more tasty and flavoursome; now a well-cooked bullock's heart, followed by some liver and bacon and a dish of greens, then a jam bolster and a black pudding and some toasted cheese to top up with—"

Val felt all her queasiness of the voyage return. The engine let out a shriek and a series of diminishing puffs; the train jolted off into the dark. Val stared out at the black, rainy countryside. I am in England, she thought, but felt none of the romantic excitement of her previous visits.

"Excuse me, dear," said one of the old women kindly and leaned past Val to pull the red rep curtains, blocking out her view altogether. Val knew that it would be sensible to try and sleep, in order to reach London refreshed, but she was unable to lull her mind into somnolence. Mentally she began letters to Benet. "Dearest Benet, I love you with all my heart but I don't think I can stand the prospect of pink roses the size of footballs on our dining room chairs and having to call on your cousins every week."

"Dearest Benet, it would never have worked." "Dearest Benet, please come and see me in England. I need you so badly."

Sighing, she unfolded the *Morning Post* again and scanned its columns with an apathetic eye. She had bought it hoping to find the column that Nils wrote, but there was nothing by him on the Court and Society pages. She turned to Home News. Parliament was reassembling after the summer vacation, and Lord Clanreydon, the *enfant terrible* of the Whig party, had made an inflammatory speech about the Irish Question. A revival of *Ariel* at the Gaiety, with Meyer-Lutz's music, had been received by a rapturous audience. Miss Farren, wearing electrically lit wings, had danced exquisitely. The queen's dentist had been given a knighthood. The first lady to do so had climbed Ben Nevis. General William Booth, in a speech at Scarborough, had called on the police to lose no further time in tracking down the perpetrator of the dreadful Bermondsey murders, of which there had been two more last week after a long gap during which it had been hoped that the murderer had died or disappeared. The *Army and Navy Gazette* was recommending that all soldiers carry slippers.

Val turned to the editorial column which was speculating as to whether, if Lord Clanreydon headed a Liberal breakaway including Bright, Hartington, and Chamberlain, Mr. Gladstone might retire from public life (as he had once before) and a new Liberal party reassemble under Clanreydon's leadership . . .

Val must have slept, in the end. She woke with a jerk, stiff, cramped, and startled, as the train came to a grinding halt. Following the old ladies out she found herself in a bewildering chaos of crowds, gas lamps, steps, rails, balconies, luggage, and great choking clouds of sooty steam.

"Cab, lady?" A porter snatched at her bags. "This way. Jest you follow me."

She went dazedly after him through the turmoil and climbed with his assistance into a hansom.

"Where to, lady?"

"Welbeck Street—number twenty-three—"

Just giving the address imbued her with confidence. It sounded so respectable and established. The driver nodded and whipped up his horse; the cab rattled down the cobbled slope from Waterloo station. Evidently the bad weather of the voyage had now reached London: rain dashed against the cab's apron and rattled on the leather hood; hanging streetlamps swung wildly. I hope Nils and Kirstie are at home, sitting in front of a blazing fire, thought Val. Kirstie is sure to be in, anyway, because of the children. And they'll have had my cable, they'll be expecting me—won't they?

Now the cab was crossing a bridge; dangling reflections in the river broke and bounced as the gale thrashed the black, invisible water. "Is it far to Welbeck Street?" Val called up to the driver. "Matter o' fifteen minutes," he replied briefly.

His horse plunged on fast, as if hating the weather, and the journey was shorter than Val had expected; soon they were proceeding more slowly along a demure-looking street, while the driver studied the house numbers.

"'Ere, didn't you say twenty-three, lidy?" he asked aggrievedly.

"Yes, twenty-three." To reassure herself, Val pulled out her last letter from Nils, but she could not see the address in the dark. But in any case she knew it by heart.

"Yer must 'a got it wrong. Look, this 'ouse is empty. Sign up says For Sale," the driver pointed out. "Sure it ain't twenty-five? Or twenty-two?"

Val's heart fell horribly. "No, I'm certain," she answered the driver. "Twenty-three Welbeck Street is the address."

"Well, your parties must 'ave moved, then," he snapped. "See for yourself. Watcher going to do? You going to get out 'ere, or not?"

Val peered hopelessly at the house, which was dimly illuminated by a gas streetlight. As the driver had said, it was shuttered and unlit. An agent's For Sale notice was attached to the front railings. What could she do? Get out into the wet and dark? Hammer on the locked door? What would be the point of that? She imagined herself left in the wet, empty street with her bags, while the hansom clattered off into the dark. The idea was too dismaying to be entertained.

"No, I won't get out," she said. "Take me to the Jersey Hotel, in Tabernacle Street."

"Saved a deal o' trouble if you'd 'a said that fust off," grumbled the driver, turning his horse. "Right the other side o' town, that is, an' my nag's tired."

The cab slowly got under way again.

By the time they had reached the Jersey Hotel Val had acknowledged to herself that, from the very first, she had a premonitory feeling that something of this kind was going to happen. Why? She hardly knew. Somehow, among all the things that Nils had said, nothing, really, had given her any confidence. Now she admitted to herself that she had believed him only because she wanted to; she had come to England simply because she needed to escape from her own predicament. None of his airy promises had seemed valid to her. Indeed now, tired and discouraged as she was at present, Nils himself hardly seemed to have any reality; he seemed like some teasing marsh fairy, a will-o'-the-wisp that would dance away over the bog, pale hair flying, eyes bright with malice, leaving her far behind, up to her knees in mud and mire.

The light streaming out from the Jersey Hotel, however, looked homely and welcoming. She paid off the cab and found with relief that the hotel had a single room at a reasonable price. A porter led her upstairs. The interior was as she remembered it from a visit with her father—old-fashioned dark panelling, red carpets, lithographs on the walls. Comfortable smells of gravy, dusty carpet, brown sherry, and old polished wood.

"The dining room's down that way, miss, if you should be wanting supper."

Her bedroom was warm but small, with little more than a white-spread bed, washstand with jug and basin, a chair, and a small table.

"No, I'll just have some soup in my room," Val said. The bed drew her; she longed in every bone to throw herself on it and sleep and sleep.

Outside the curtained window she heard the solemn boom of St. Paul's clock striking ten.

Next morning, drinking the Jersey Hotel's excellent coffee, Val wondered what she should do. Where to begin?

A fair night's sleep had cleared her mind. Instead of the evening's phantasmagoric images, she was able to see that Nils had probably been summoned home by some financial crisis. He had plainly been pressed for money when he arrived in America; and perhaps he had not done as well there as he had hoped. And while he was away, perhaps Kirstie had been obliged to move out of their house; it was possible that they had written to Val about it and she had sailed before their letter arrived. So how would she find them? Through the house agent, presumably. She would have to go back to Welbeck Street.

Then it occurred to her that an even simpler source of information would be the offices of the *Morning Post* in Fleet Street, close at hand.

The *Morning Post* proved unable to help, however. Yes, Mr. Hansen was a contributor, but he did not belong to the regular staff, and, in any case, had taken a month's leave of absence which had been prolonged to six weeks, during which time there had been no word from him. The only address they had for him was the Welbeck Street one.

This was disappointing, but Val's doom-laden feelings of the evening before had lifted. The day helped to raise her spirits; it was a clear, pale, frosty autumn morning. With a feeling of adventure she walked the bustling streets, bought a map of London, and boarded a westbound horse bus, cheered by the thought of how scandalised Mrs. Chauncey and old Mrs. Allerton would be, could they see her now.

Welbeck Street, with a silvery sun dispersing the morning mist, looked clean and cheerful, quite different from the dark, lonely, wet, unwelcoming place it had seemed last night. Val walked along to number twenty-three and took note of the For Sale notice. The house agent's address was in a street she had noticed not far off, Stratford Place; she turned to go back there, but, before leaving, lingered a moment, studying the empty house, as if hoping it could tell her *why* its inmates had suddenly departed. There were evidences of a recent removal; straw, paper, string in the front area, and a flash of something pink—what was it that lay down there?

The area gate swung open; on a sudden impulse Val ran down the steps and picked up the pink object. It was a child's toy—a small painted wooden pig with black glossy patches and ears made from leather. She had sent it to Pieter herself, for his third birthday.

As she stood holding it in the gateway, staring at it rather blankly, a large horse-drawn removal van drew up outside the house and two aproned men jumped briskly down, and, consulting a paper, unlocked the front door, went into the house, and began to carry out various articles of furniture—bureaux, escritoires, armchairs, sofas, tables.

Embarrassed but resolute, Val approached the men and asked, "Can you tell me where the owners of this house are now?"

"Arr!" said one of the men, and winked at his mate. "That's a question, ennit? There's several as'ud like to know that, mum."

"Why?"

"Why, they shot the moon, don't you see? Flitted. Brushed off. Mizzled."

"That's why we're a-taking the sticks, see," said the other man. "Sold to pay the creditors. Ninepence in the pound. Our guvner's a debt collecter, see?"

Val thought she did see. It all sounded much as she had feared.

Greatly discouraged, she walked round to the house agents, Messrs. Boyce and Dobbie of Stratford Place. But their representative, a smooth young man in a pearl-grey waistcoat and rosebud buttonhole, was unable to help her. Yes, he understood that the tenants of Twenty-three Welbeck Street had left suddenly, owing six months' rent. No, he was afraid he had no further address for Mr. and Mrs. Hansen; he would be glad to know himself where they could be found, as his clients were naturally anxious to collect the outstanding moneys. He gave Val a cool, assessing glance, as if wondering what kind of a creditor she might be, and then turned over the pages of a huge ledger and addressed himself to an ostrich-plumed lady who was demanding to know the rent of a house in Grosvenor Square.

Grosvenor Square—that rang a bell in Val's mind. Something that Nils had said—what? Something that might give her a clue—a means of reaching him and Kirstie? Puzzling and pushing at this elusive memory, she walked southward toward the Green Park.

Fashionable London shone and sparkled in the frosty sunlight. Polished leather and metal reflected the pale light; jewels and enamels flashed in the Bond Street windows. Ladies in furs and plumes stepped out of jingling broughams and barouches. Men with canes and top hats and carnations strolled and puffed cigars. It was like New York—and yet, Val was forced to acknowledge, it was different: more sophisticated, more exciting. Yes, perhaps more wicked too. Who could tell what might go on at night in some of those little back streets?

Val passed a bank in Piccadilly, and that reminded her of another possible lead; her father had bequeathed a small legacy to Nils and in arranging for its transfer Val had learned the name of his bank, the London Cotton Bank, in Dover Place. Consulting her map, Val walked in that direction.

But the bank were as politely unhelpful as the house agents. No, Mr. Hansen had closed his account with them some months ago. No, they were afraid they had no present address for him—and if they had, it was totally against bank policy to divulge it.

"Even to his sister?" Val asked wistfully. The fatherly, grey-headed bank official shook his head.

"I'm very sorry," he repeated. The genuineness of his sympathy prompted her to ask, "You can't think of anywhere else I could inquire for him, can you?"

The grey-haired man became a little more human.

"Well, miss," he said confidentially, "I know Mr. Hansen used to be a member of the Beargarden Club for we had many cheques made out to it and—knowing these young gentlemen and the store they set by their clubs —it's possible he still goes there. But, of course, that's not a place where a young lady could go. You could address a letter to him there, though, miss, and I daresay they'd forward it."

"His club? Now that *is* an idea," said Val. "Why didn't I think of that myself? Thank you very much for suggesting it."

She beamed at the grey-haired man and hurried out of the bank.

Val knew all about the sanctity and privacy of men's clubs. Even in New York they were forbidden ground for females; and she knew that in London the restrictions were still more strictly observed. But just now she was not disposed to respect these arbitrary and one-sided taboos. They will just have to waive their absurd rules for once, she thought robustly.

"Can you take me to the Beargarden Club?" she asked a cab driver, beckoning him with her umbrella.

"Well, I could," he replied, chewing on a straw, "but fust off it would be a-cheating of you, and second it wouldn't be a bit of use."

"Why?" demanded Val, her spirits falling. Had the club, too, closed down?

"Well, for a start, it's just round the corner, in Stable Yard Road, and you could walk it yourself in five minutes. And second off, the Beargarden don't open till three in the afternoon. So it ain't a bit of good going there now."

"Oh," said Val. "Well, thank you."

"And third off," he said, looking at her severely, "the Beargarden ain't no place for a nice young lady like you, so I'm a-telling you, that's old enough to be your father."

"Thank you for that too," said Val, and smiled at him. "But I think I will have to go there just the same."

"Well then you best get some gentleman to go along of you," admonished the cab driver and whipped his horse off towards Piccadilly. He called back, "Otherwise you're likely to get more than you bargained for, and I ain't joking."

Val pulled up her watch on its neck ribbon and consulted it. Two o'clock. Her stomach might have told her, had she consulted that; she was ravenous. But there seemed to be no place in the vicinity where an unescorted lady could eat in comfort; the inns and chophouses round about were full of club-men and guards officers; eyeing the places through their plate-glass windows she thought they looked like more exclusive male preserves, full of smoke, loud laughter, sawdust, and stamping feet. Becoming very irritated, Val bought a meat-pie in a little shop off Shepherds' Market and ate it on a bench in the Green Park. In one respect, at least, New York was a far more civilised town.

The pie eaten, she amused herself by studying the shop windows in Bond Street, and the ladies who rode up and down it in their carriages. The fashions in dress here, she observed, were far more extreme than those in New York. She remembered hearing Benet say, with an indulgent chuckle, that his mother, grandmother, and several of his aunts, though they bought their clothes in Paris, generally kept them decently packed away in tissue paper for several years, until they could not be regarded as too *outré*, or indecently in the van of fashion; one old aunt, it was reported, had died leaving ten years' of unworn dresses laid up in trunks in her attic for a vanished future. It did not seem probable, thought Val, that such practices obtained in London. Casting her mind back to the Allertons' ball—how long ago that seemed!—she suddenly wondered if, after all, half the dresses there had not seemed over-frilly, rather provincial?

She looked at her watch again. Ten minutes to three. She might as well stroll down St. James', in the direction of Stable Yard Road.

The Beargarden Club, when she reached it, was an unassuming establishment, without any of the marble steps, urns, or Corinthian columns which embellished the larger, better-known clubs in St. James'. They, with their morning rooms, coffee rooms, and libraries full of newspapers, had been open and functioning for hours already, but the Beargarden was only now beginning to wake up. Crates of poultry and lobsters were being delivered down the area steps; a small, sleepy-looking page in a liver-coloured uniform, covered with a rash of buttons, was sweeping the steps; another was watering a couple of potted palms inside the open door.

Val walked boldly in.

"I'm looking for a Mr. Nils Hansen," she said to the larger of the two pages. "Can you tell me if he is here, or expected?"

The boy gaped at her. He was a sharp-looking, pasty-faced urchin, his hair so plastered with Rowlands Macassar Oil that it looked like over-cooked spinach.

"I—I dunno," he said at length.

"Well, will you find out, please?" she said crisply.

The boy retired to the back of the hall and summoned his mate by gestures. A lot of whispered confabulation went on, and some giggling; then both of them disappeared to lower regions.

Val stood waiting, feeling decidedly impatient, but also somewhat conspicuous in the small entrance hall, which had a marble floor and was furnished with a mahogany counter, a brass rail, and a rack for members' letters. Her eye roamed to the H section, but there was nothing in it. She moved closer to make certain, ignoring footsteps and voices growing louder in the entrance.

"Good gad!" exclaimed a voice close behind her shoulder. "What the deuce have we here? Don't tell me old Fenimore's breaking out and introducing Daughters of Joy into the club? Dunno what Fothers and Dolly Longstaffe will say, though; neither of 'em's much in the petticoat line. However—let's inspect the article—see if it's worth the row there's bound to be?"

A sudden jerk on her shoulder pulled Val round; she was startled at the strength of the grip, and even more when she saw the individual who had grasped her, for he was a pale, slight man, no taller than she was herself.

"Well, just look at that, will you, Grass, my dear fellow?" he drawled, coolly looking Val up and down. "They are making Daughters of Joy on a new model, what do you say? Not bad, quite handsome in fact, but a bit too starchy for my taste. However, let's see—" and, leaning forward, he pinched Val's cheek, looking into her eyes from a disconcertingly close range. His own eyes were extraordinary: pale-grey, and set at an angle far out from his nose. In their colour and slant they resembled a goat's eyes.

"Quite a good-looking strumpet, don't you think?" he remarked to his companion.

Val boxed his ears.

"Temper, temper," said the pale-faced man calmly, but a red weal had sprung up on his cheek and—if Val did not imagine it—matching red sparks burned in his eyes. The pupils had widened enormously so that the eyes all of a sudden looked very much darker. She had never seen such naked dislike as in the look he gave her.

"What a spitfire, eh, Grass? I say, I don't think *she'll* do for carrying in our devilled bones at two A.M. after a late sitting; she might pour the mustard sauce over old Fothers, if he got up to any of his larks. *Who* do you suppose she *is*, by the by?"

He continued to speak as if Val were deaf, or did not understand English. She, for her part, was speechless with rage, struggling to find a retort telling enough to put him in his place once and for all.

"Oh come on in, Nuggie," said his companion, a stocky, dark, bushy-bearded man. "Whoever she is, it ain't any of our business. Fenimore'll send her to the rightabout. Come along up." The dark man spoke nervously, in a low tone, as if he were afraid that an awkward scene must develop.

"Well, where is old Fenners?" drawled the pale man. "Deuce take it, can't he protect a fellow from being assaulted in his own club? I'll be obliged to resign if this kind of thing goes on."

"I beg your pardon," said Val icily—she had by now taken firm control of herself—"I called in here to inquire—"

"Here's Fenimore," said the bearded man in an undertone. "Now do come on, Nuggie, don't regard it—"

"No, I'm curious," said the man addressed as Nuggie. "Well, Fenimore, why aren't you at your post, man, eh? Look what happens—club members are subjected to all manner of annoyance in their own vestibule—"

An immensely fat, red-faced man had appeared panting up from the basement; he was still tying his cravat as he arrived at the desk. In spite of his girth he moved rapidly and was light on his feet; a pair of very sharp black eyes glanced rapidly from Val's stormy face to the pale man and back again.

"Miss, miss!" he exclaimed, laying a slightly sweaty hand on Val's arm and trying to urge her towards the street, "I am sorry, I am very sorry, but it is *absolutely* against the club rules for *any* ladies to come in here—any ladies at all! I must please ask you to leave directly, please, immediately!" There was a touch of foreign accent, Italian, possibly, in his voice; he spoke civilly enough but his eyes looked unfriendly; mentally Val put him down as somebody who might at once turn nasty if crossed.

"Look," she said calmly, standing still and resisting his efforts to shift her, "all I came here for was to ask if my brother is here, or if you can give me his address; what's wrong with that? If I can't ask a simple question and get a civil answer—"

"Without being outrageously insulted, eh?" suavely put in the pale-faced man. "*What* an upsetting thing to happen to a decent, respectable godfearing young lady who just *happened* to step inside the club—what an atrocity, eh, Grass? I've a good mind to write to *The Times* about it."

His ironic eyes met those of Val, who returned his stare coldly and said nothing.

The manager became even more flustered. "Very sorry, miss—er, madam —that's another club rule—very strict. We never divulge members' whereabouts to *anybody* who comes asking—"

"Particularly females, eh, Fenners?" drawled the pale-faced man. "Otherwise we'd have half the wives and sweethearts in London clamouring on the front doorstep, my love! We poor males have to defend ourselves *somehow* against the petticoat invasion—deuce take it, they're creeping in everywhere now. Next thing they'll be getting votes and sitting in the House—eh, Grass?"

"So you see, you'll have to leave, miss," said the manager. "I can't help you, I really can't help you."

"Listen," said Val, "I don't even know if my brother is a member here still, though I have reason to believe he was at one time. If he has left, surely your rule wouldn't apply? In that case you could give me his address?"

"If we had it," said the bearded man. "That seems fair enough, eh, Fenners? What's your—brother's—name, then, ma'am?"

A couple more men had by now lounged up the steps and stood watching; Val heard a smothered chuckle, and more tittering from the pages; she felt extremely uncomfortable in this all-male purlieu, and only too anxious to get away.

"His name is Mr. Nils Hansen," she said clearly. "I would be extremely grateful if anybody here can give me his address."

At the name Nils Hansen she felt a sudden extraordinarily intense change in the atmosphere; somebody in the group had reacted with extreme violence to the news of her relationship. She glanced from face to face but all were noncommittal; none of the men betrayed any overt interest.

"Hansen?" said one of the pair who had just come in. "Haven't seen him around lately, have we? Is he still a member?"

"I can tell you nothing—nothing," repeated the fat Fenimore. "And, now, miss, I must again ask you please to leave."

"If the young lady cared to write a letter care of here, it'd do no harm, eh, Fenners?" murmured the bearded man, who seemed anxious to placate all parties.

Val glanced at him sharply. She was on the point of saying, "Does that mean that he *is* still a member of this club?" when she caught the pale man's eye, still fixed on her in a scrutinising stare. She bit back the words and simply said, "Thank you. I'll do that," and, turning on her heel, she walked out of the lobby with her head high, feeling all their eyes on her back, hotly imagining the outburst of knowing jokes and laughter there would be as soon as she was a couple of yards along the pavement.

When rapid steps came after, apparently in pursuit of her, she did not turn her head, but walked fast and angrily toward St. James'.

"Miss! Er—Miss Hansen, is it? Er—excuse me!"

A new voice—not one of the three who had spoken. She turned slightly as the pursuer came alongside and saw that it was one of the two men who had come in during the scene. He was a tall, fair, fresh-faced, ingenuous-looking young man with a high cravat and the exaggeratedly upright bearing of a guards officer.

"Forgive me pushing my nose in—couldn't help overhea'ing—" he spoke with a slight lisp—"but if old Nils is weally lost to view, I can think of one person who might know where to find him."

"That's very kind of you," said Val. She was still angry enough not to be able to resist adding—"if you're sure I'm not a revengeful wife or rapacious creditor? I know how your club members have to be protected."

"Oh well—deuce take it—ve'y sowwy about all that fwacas—anyone can see you're his sister! I mean to say—spit image! Now—about this person—she ain't exactly top-drawer and I don't know if I'm doing w'ong in telling a nice young lady like you—but she's a deucid good-hearted gal—"

"Oh!" exclaimed Val on a long breath, suddenly enlightened. "Do you mean a dancer—what's her name—Hetty something?"

"Letty—Letty Pettigrew—that's the girl. Kindest c'eature that ever stepped. Devoted to old Nils, too. If he's anywhere—depend on it—she'll know. Not offended, I hope? Didn't do w'ong, did I?"

"Not a bit," said Val warmly. "I'm most grateful to you. Have you any notion where I can find—Miss Pettigrew?"

"Last I heard she was in something down at the Elephant and Castle Theatre. Not one o' the top-notchers—but—well, we all have to live, eh? Hope you find her—and your brother, Miss Hansen."

"Thank you," said Val. "You are very kind. My name is Montgomery, actually—I am Nils' half-sister." On an impulse she added, "I'm staying at the Jersey Hotel. If—if you should receive any news of Nils, I'd be even more grateful if you could let me know there, or ask him to get in touch with me. Could you do that? I'm really anxious about him. I came to London especially to see him—he invited me—and now, when I get here, I find he's—he's just gone. It's very upsetting—well, frightening, really."

"Oh, I wouldn't worry too much, ma'am," said the young man easily. "Old Nils may have the best of reasons for bobbing out of sight for a few months—even the starchiest of us have to do it at times, y'know. Anyway, if I do hear word, I'll let you know. Delighted to meet you." She smiled at him and he blinked, quite dazzled. "My name's Orville, by the way—er, card."

He handed Val a card and then, blushing pink all over his ingenuous face, made his escape back to the club.

Val, rather amused, glanced at the card. Lord Orville, it said, and gave the club address and a house in Somerset. Tucking it into her muff, Val was reminded for the first time of her fellow passenger on the ship; his card was in there too and she had never looked at it. She drew it out and read:

SIR MARCUS CUSACK
Editor: *Selkirk's Magazine*
Appin Court
Cockburn Street,
Edinburgh

CHAPTER 4

WHEN, at a late lunch next day, Val asked her table waiter at the Jersey about the Elephant and Castle Theatre, he primmed up his lips and said it was not one of the better houses.

"South o' the river, it is, miss; not a nice neighbourhood for a young lady to visit."

"What's the matter with it?" asked Val drily, reflecting that if, in her researches, she confined herself to the regions thought suitable for young ladies to visit, she was not likely to get very far.

"Well, the theatre itself ain't so bad; music-hall at the moment, miss, but not too low class—not that I've been to it meself; but the district ain't far from Bermondsey, and that's a part no young lady oughta go near."

"What happens in Bermondsey?"

"Why, ain't you heard o' the Bermondsey Beast, miss?"

"Oh yes—vaguely—"

But the old waiter insisted on telling her all over again, with gloomy relish, how during the past year a series of horrific murders had been committed, almost all in the Bermondsey area, all, apparently, by the same hand; neither the Bermondsey constabulary nor the metropolitan police had been able to catch the killer.

"Yes, there were reports about it in the American papers," Val said, hoping to stem the flood.

"Reports? There's been broadsheets, pamphlets, all sorts o' stuff published. All women of a bad sort, they are, what gets killed, miss; and they're done in in an 'orrible way, stabbed and then bits of 'em cut off."

"Well I won't go to Bermondsey," Val promised. "But I do want to get to the Elephant and Castle Theatre; there's somebody acting there who knows my brother, and I don't know how else to get in touch with her."

"Well, it ain't so far as the crow flies, miss, jest across Blackfriars Bridge; my advice to you is to get a respectable keb driver to take you there and ask him to wait for you till you've finished your business."

Well tipped, the old waiter promised to procure a cab driver of sufficient respectability and departed on this errand.

Val reflected that she would soon be short of money. The income her father had left her permitted her to live in moderate comfort in New York, where her accommodation was rent free and her funds were augmented by earnings from the *Inquirer*. But the fare to England had made a large hole in her savings, and unfortunately Ted Towers had not been very forthcoming with promises to pay for travel articles or more information about British social structure.

"You've done all that before," he pointed out. "Readers want something new. And James O'Brien is in London already, writing the same kind of thing. If you could go to France, now, or Scotland. Well, send me some pieces if you want to, and I'll see if I can use 'em. And, I tell you what: I'll give you a few addresses of editors you can call on in London; maybe you can pay your way by doing stuff for them: Impressions of an Americaine in Mayfair."

"I should think that's been done to death too," said Val, discouraged. However she had the addresses and had spent the latter part of yesterday afternoon and some of this morning going to see editors, with not very encouraging results. But her principal task, she still felt, must be to find Nils and Kirstie. The longer it took to locate them, the more deeply concerned she became; under all her actions and her impressions of London lay a pricking anxiety and a sense of urgency. For, surely, if all had been well with the pair, they could have found *some* means of getting in touch with her by now? Nils might have remembered the hotel, where Val had stayed before with her father. Or he might have arranged for a message to meet the ship when it docked?

And since he had not done that—arrived at this point, Val was suddenly overtaken by an alarming thought: suppose Nils had *never returned* to London? Then Kirstie and the children were on their own, perhaps completely without resources? No wonder they had been obliged to leave their house. From the various remarks about Kirstie that Nils had let fall—scrappy and incomplete though these were—Val had gathered an impression of a small, frail, timid creature, rather solitary, friendless, far from adequate to cope with such a situation.

And of course, if Nils were not back, Kirstie might very likely not know where to start looking for Val. Might not even have received her cable?

She pulled out Kirstie's little note and read it again. "I know I can trust you. . . . Be good to them—I know you will. Your loving sister."

Now it seemed a cry for help—a cry of despair.

But *was* Kirstie so completely friendless and solitary? She had some family still—her parents were dead, Nils had said, but there were—were there not?—two eccentric old aunts. Of course! And that was the source of the teasing memory that had assailed her in the house agents' office—"and when they're in town," Nils had said, "they've got this great mouldy house in Grosvenor Square."

Grosvenor Square—no distance away. The only difficulty was that Val did not remember ever having heard Kirstie's name before marriage. Nor had she any idea whether the aunts bore the same name. It would hardly be possible to call at every house in Grosvenor Square asking if two elderly Scottish ladies resided there whose niece, in opposition to their wishes, had married a man called Hansen?

At this moment Val's waiter reappeared, with the intelligence that a cab was waiting to take her to the Elephant and Castle Theatre. As she followed him to the lobby she asked him, "Is there any kind of directory of London that gives the names of the people who live in each house, by streets?"

"Yes, there is, miss," he surprised her by answering. "Kelly's Directory will tell you. O' course it doesn't list the poorer parts, like Spitalfields and Whitechapel, where folk lives twenty and thirty to a house, an' sleeps in shifts."

"Do they really?" asked Val, appalled.

"Lor' bless you, yes, miss. An' there's sailors and foreigners an' all sorts coming and going there. But up the West End, where the nobs live, that's all listed."

Val resolved to consult Kelly's Directory as soon as she returned. Indeed she would have sought out a copy straightaway if the cab had not been waiting.

The morning's fine promise had been belied as the day declined toward dusk. A thick, blanketing, icy fog had settled over the town. Cries of street vendors and newspaper boys wailed eerily through the gloom. Nothing of the river could be seen as they crossed Blackfriars Bridge; the cab seemed suspended in a strange grey-brown cloud, palely illuminated by gas lamps on either side, with the occasional splash of oars and mournful hoots from barges down below.

Val shivered. It was not difficult to believe the most horrific tales of the Bermondsey Beast in weather like this.

"Wait here, please," she said to the driver when they reached the Elephant and Castle Theatre. "I shan't be any longer than I can help."

Since she had not paid him, she felt fairly certain that he *would* wait, though he grumbled that it was a most awkward location; five or six roads met together here, and there was a constant jostle of vehicles, mostly market wagons. The theatre was not open for business yet, for it was still early in the evening, but Val found a side entrance and made her way determinedly down a narrow, precipitous flight of stairs. At the bottom her way was barred by an old charwoman with a bucket and broom and a severe cold.

"Nobody ain't allowed in 'ere," she snuffled. " 'Cept on business."

"Well I am on business," said Val. "And I want to see Miss Letty Pettigrew."

She had some visiting cards printed with her name and that of the *New York Inquirer*; she had had the forethought to provide herself with one of these, and she passed it over.

"Ho," said the charwoman, after she had read the card with mumbling slowness, shaping her lips silently over each syllable. "Well, you're lucky; Miss Pettigrew ain't hoften 'ere this early, but she 'appens to be re'earsing up on stage; re'earsing hof 'er new number she is, hat presink, so I dessay you can go hup." She gestured toward another flight of stairs which, Val found, led to the balcony. A piano was being thumped in the auditorium and on the bare dusty stage a buxom, untidy flaxen-headed girl was singing a song about how the boy she loved was up in the gallery, at the top of a pair of powerful but not very musical lungs.

"Not bad, darling," said the pianist, after five or six verses. "Soften it up a bit on verse five, can't you—just to show that you know the difference between piano and fortissimo, eh? Now I must be off—the landlord of the Royal Oak will murder me if I'm not there by seven."

"Miss Pettigrew, there's a newspaper lady 'ere wants to speak to you," said the charwoman appearing on stage with her mop. "She's up there in the circle."

"Well, tell her to come down to my dressing room," said Miss Pettigrew impatiently and disappeared into the wings.

Val made her way downstairs again, located a door on which "Pettigrew" was scribbled in chalk, and knocked. "Come in!" sang out the same powerful voice, and she walked into a room about eight feet by six, with one gaslight, a small coal fire, a shelf, a broken-backed chair, a powerful scent of violet powder, and a cracked mirror. A heap of soiled clothes lay in the corner, more clothes hung on hooks, and the shelf was covered in stumps of wig paste.

Miss Pettigrew was briskly hooking herself into a tarlatan ballet skirt which had seen better days.

"Give us a hand to do this up at the back, dear," she said, "I want to see if it still fits."

"It's a bit torn at the waist," Val said.

"Well, it'll have to do; can't expect new on the Elephant's screw."

Seen at close quarters Miss Pettigrew's air of a plump, good-natured, round-faced eighteen-year-old was replaced by a different impression; she looked older and harder, the lines round her eyes and at the corners of her mouth suggested that she was nearing her thirties, and a quarter inch of black was visible at the roots of the flaxen mop. A pair of shrewd eyes regarded Val.

"Well, what is it, dear? Are you really from the *New York Inquirer?*"

"Yes I am, but that's not what I'm here about," said Val frankly. "I've just come over from New York, I'm the sister of Nils Hansen, and I want to ask you if you know where he is?"

Letty Pettigrew had been leaning back negligently, resting her shoulder against the make-up shelf and balancing the broken chair on one of its legs; now she brought it down to earth with a crash.

"You're *Neal's* sister? Fancy that! I never knew he had any family—he always told me he was a poor lonesome orphan."

"I'm his half-sister; I live in New York."

"Well, well! Wonders will never cease! Now I come to think of it, you *do* have a look of Neal," said Miss Pettigrew. Her manner was not unfriendly, but there was something dry about her, as if she had long since discovered that a natural good humour was more than she could afford among the sharp practices of her world.

"Have you any idea where I can find Nils?" Deciding that complete candour was the best policy here, Val added, "He invited me to come over to London and stay in his house while he and his wife went on a cruise; but now I've arrived I find they've left their house and I haven't any new address for them."

As the words left her mouth she suddenly remembered that Miss Pettigrew was originally to have been a member of the cruise party; perhaps it was not the most tactful thing to have said.

Miss Pettigrew took it calmly enough, however.

"Oh, the *Dragonfly* cruise, yes; Nuggie Reydon's yacht."

"I suppose they haven't gone off on it already?" it suddenly occurred to Val to ask.

"No, last I heard the *Dragonfly* was at Tilbury fitting up; anyway my cousin saw Nuggie Reydon only last night, at Mereweather's in the Strand, with a party of swells."

"Is that Lord Clanreydon—the owner of the yacht?" Val asked, remembering some of the things Nils had said about his well-known friend. "What does he look like? Is he a thin, pale man with very odd eyes?"

"That's the one, dear," Miss Pettigrew nodded. "Odd eyes is right: looks as if his Ma had been friends with a goat. Oops! Pardon me."

"It must be the same man—I met him yesterday. But how peculiar," Val pondered. "He heard me say I was Nils' sister—he's a friend of Nils'—and yet he said nothing, when he knew I was looking for him."

But was it so peculiar? she wondered. Given the instant antipathy that had sprung up between her and the pale-faced man, why should he want to help her?

"He *is* a very queer cove, that Nuggie—a nasty one to cross, too. Clever —oh yes, I grant you that," said Miss Pettigrew. "He's a real dab at politics and speechmaking, Neal says; means to step into the G.O.M.'s shoes one o' these days; but just the same I'd never have close dealings with him if I could help it. I was just as glad not to go on his yacht, if the truth be told. But as to where Neal is—no, dear, I'm sorry; there I *can't* help you. Cross my heart, cut my throat, I'd tell you if I could. I reckon old Neal must have run into a spot of trouble, an' he's gone to ground till it blows over."

"Debt, you mean?"

"Maybe. Or maybe he cut a bit too near the bone with one o' those bits he writes for the papers. There's been newspaper writers got a taste o' the horsewhip, before now, when they wrote what someone didn't care for. Maybe there's some cove with his dander up, hunting round to give Neal a belting, an' he thinks it best to lie low for the time."

Val, too, had been reflecting along these lines. It did seem possible that his gossip-mongering in print had landed Nils in trouble. But—even so— wouldn't he have found some means of getting in touch with his sister?

Perhaps not. Perhaps he would be more likely to contact Miss Pettigrew.

"If you *do* hear anything from him, I'd be extremely grateful if you'd let me know," she said. "Or tell him I'm looking for him."

"All right, dear! You're not the only one as would like to know where Neal's got to, I can tell you that," Letty divulged. "There's my auntie Liza a-looking after those two brats of his; fit to be tied, she is, acos it was to be just two or three days, cash in advance, an' now nigh on a month has gone by, an' no more dibs, no word, and the kids is still there."

"What?"

"Didn't you know that, even?" Letty had been rather absent-mindedly painting her face; now she screwed her neck round and stared at Val, hare's-foot in hand. "Neal's kids—little Pieter and what'shername. They're at my auntie Liza's."

"But why?—Where is your aunt?" Val almost stammered in her astonishment.

"Islington."

"I don't understand!" said Val. "I thought Kirstie—my brother's wife—would never leave those children!"

The more she thought about this revelation, the more extraordinary it appeared to her.

"How did it happen?"

"Well," said Letty, "I daresay you didn't know my young cousin Mercy was housemaid at your brother's?"

"No, I didn't."

"I mentioned her to Neal a couple months ago an' they took her on," explained Letty. "Mercy wanted to go on the stage like me, but she got took bad with the smallpox, so she had to go into service instead; no stage manager 'ud look at her, her face is all pocked. So she's been obliging in Welbeck Street. Well, when Neal got back from America—this is what Mercy says, I was in a pier show at the time, Southend, cockles and mussels and mud—his wife had been poorly, an' had to go to the country for a rest. She'd bin worried with duns, too; Mercy said none o' the tradesmen's bills had been paid for ever so long, and Mercy only got her wages because she was my cousin an' I told Neal to see she did. So Neal says to Mercy, 'We're a-going to close the house up, do you know a decent woman as can look after the kids for a few days?' an' Mercy said her ma would oblige."

"Yes, I see," said Val, unravelling this slowly. "So Nils did come back from New York. And they left the children with your aunt and went off—when was this?"

"When I was in Southend. Three weeks ago—maybe more."

Immediately on Nils' return, then, Val deduced.

"And the children have been there ever since? And your aunt doesn't know where Nils and his wife went?"

"That's about it," said Letty, nodding, and then carefully holding her head still as she supplied herself with a pair of very improbable black eyebrows.

"Well then—good God—something, some accident must have happened to them!" Val was more and more dismayed. "From all he told me about her, I'm sure Kirstie would never leave her children so long with a stranger."

"There's naught amiss with my auntie Liza." Letty was rather affronted. "She's brought up five children and buried seven; she's a decent sort o' woman—runs a respectable clean lodging house in Islington."

"Of course," said Val hastily. "I'm sure she does—all I meant was—here, give me her address. I'm their aunt, after all; at least I can pay her what's owing."

And see that the children are being properly looked after, she mentally added.

Letty's face cleared. "Ah, that's not a bad notion," she owned. "To tell the truth, I ain't been up to Islington for a couple of weeks; Aunt Liza *was* after me a good deal—even had the crumb to suggest I might pay her a bit, as Neal's my pal. *I* reckon he an' his wife probably sloped off, to France, maybe, to lie low till times is better—but it *was* ha'penny dealing to leave the kids with Aunt for so long without paying. I'll have a word or two to say to Master Neal when he shows his face again. Mind you—that's always been his way: a three-and-sixpenny dinner at the Holborn Restaurant's plenty good enough for *him* when he takes a girl out—you'd never catch him laying out his dibs at the swell places farther west. And as for bringing a bottle of fizz when he comes to see a girl—Lord love you!"

"Well, I wish I'd thought to do that," said Val, digging out a couple of sovereigns. "But here—I hope you can send out and get something now—you've been very kind to tell me so much, it's been very helpful—"

"Bless you dear, I'd do as much any time. Ta, that's kind of you an' I'll drink your health in it—you really take the biscuit, even if you are a Juggins! See you sometime." With which obscure piece of theatrical slang, Miss Pettigrew turned round and applied herself to her make-up in good earnest.

Val left her and hurried back up the narrow stairs. The theatre was beginning to hum with activity—more actors were jostling their way down to the basement dressing rooms, a dolorous noise of orchestral tuning up could be heard from the pit, and a chocolate-, apple-, and shrimp-munching throng was beginning to file into the vestibule.

Outside, both Val's driver and his horse were becoming extremely restive.

"I could 'a hired myself fifteen times over while you was a-jawing in there," he grumbled. "Two shillin' a mile is bad enough, but one shillin' the half hour for staying still is enough to starve a man."

Val promised to pay him four times his fare and told him to drive back to the Jersey Hotel.

She was strongly tempted to go straight to Islington then and there, but second thoughts prevailed. The children would probably have been put to bed, hours before, and would be fast asleep. No sense in waking them up. And how could she tell what kind of treatment they were receiving unless she talked to them?

But she resolved that she would go to Islington the very first thing next morning.

CHAPTER 5

Next morning, while eating a rapid breakfast, Val cast her eye swiftly through the Grosvenor Square section of Kelly's Directory of London, and was somewhat unnerved to find that the only pair of ladies who appeared on the list as owning a house in that august area were the marchioness of Stroma and Lady Honoria Carsphairn, at number forty. Could they be Kirstie's aunts? They sounded Scottish enough, and aristocratic enough. No wonder they had not been enthusiastic about Kirstie's marriage to a medical student who had neither birth nor breeding nor much in the way of fortune to recommend him; nothing but a gentleman's education, an ability to mix with the right people, and a talent for writing newspaper paragraphs about them.

"Have I the courage to go and call on those ladies?" Val wondered. "Well at all events, I'll go to Islington first."

The morning, like the previous afternoon, was icy, dark, and foggy. Val wrapped up in her warmest cape, sealskin muff, scarf, and fur cap to go out in it—she had already discovered that the raw, damp London air could be quite as chilling as a far lower temperature in New York. She hailed a hansom, knowing as she did so that she must abandon this habit of traveling by cab. And in the next couple of days she must come to some decision about where and how she was to live, if she remained in London; it was far too expensive to stay at the Jersey Hotel for weeks on end. If she remained in London she must move into lodgings. Perhaps the best solution would be to rent rooms from Mrs. Eliza Pipkin in Islington, so as to be with the children? And that would ensure her getting into touch with Nils and Kirstie if—when they returned; obviously they would go straight to Islington. But I won't decide, thought Val, till I see what Mrs. Pipkin is like. Islington did not seem a very convenient locality, she reflected, as the hansom rumbled on in a northeasterly direction, up cobbled streets, across numerous squares, along wide, busy, shabby thoroughfares down which horse trams screeched and rattled. Islington seemed far, far removed from the elegance of Welbeck Street.

At last they arrived in front of a mean, black little house in a row of similar mean little houses. Val alighted and paid the driver half a crown. There was a rusty gate, a little garden before the house, full of wet sooty grass and frost-blackened geraniums, with a cinder path leading to an iron-grated door. A brass plate said Mrs. Eliza Pipkin, Lodgings. Val rang vigorously at the bell, and the door was opened by a pale, down-at-heel-looking girl, with her hair in rats'-tails, and very bad pockmarks all over her face. Assuming this to be the luckless Mercy, returned home from Welbeck Street, Val asked, "Is Mrs. Pipkin in? I'm—"

"I'm Mr. Hansen's sister," she was about to add, but the girl nervously inquired, "Was it about lodgings, miss?" just as a loud, furious voice broke out at the top of the stairs which led directly down to the front door.

"Oh, look what you've done now, you horrible, filthy little toad! If this happens *once* more, I'm not keeping you here another day, that I'm not! I'll have you taken away to the Union, I don't care who your mother or father is. Mother or father! Precious fine pair *they* are!"

There came, faint but distinct, the sound of a slap, and a low cry, followed by a muffled sobbing. A child's voice said, "Please don't—she can't help it—"

"I'll please don't you, Master Please Don't!"

"Mother!" called the girl sharply. "Mother, there's a lady here about the lodgings. What did you say your name was?" she asked Val.

"Miss Montgomery," said Val quietly.

"A Miss Montgorry about the lodgings, Mother!" called the girl.

"Tell the young lady I'll be down directly," said the voice from above, in quite a different tone. And it added in a fierce whisper, "Now, don't you move an inch from that spot, either of you, or I'll tan you alive!" A door slammed.

Quick footsteps rattled on the stairs, and a short, stout woman came into view. She had greyish brown hair and sharp grey eyes; her coarse skin was high-coloured, as if she were in a temper about something, with broken veins, and a thin-lipped, down-curving mouth revealed, when she smiled perfunctorily at Val, rather bad teeth. A kind of suppressed rage seemed to hang about her, in all her movements, as she looked at Val, at her daughter, about the shabby little front hall, and back up the drab-carpeted stairs.

"There's the first-floor room with piano, seven pun' the month with board," she said rapidly, "or one up on the top floor you could have for four. D'you want to see the rooms?"

"Yes, I'd like to," said Val. It was the first time in her life that she had not instantly divulged her purpose and identity, but she was quite unconscious of any change from her normal behaviour. Her attention was concentrated on the room upstairs from which the voices had come, and also on the arrival of a butcher's boy, who at that moment came whistling through the gate with a wooden tray full of skewered bits of meat.

"Mercy, show the young lady upstairs; I'll see to the boy," said Mrs. Pipkin sharply. "And tell her about the washing and coals."

Val allowed herself to be led up and shown a medium-sized room, containing a piano, a bed that pretended to be a sofa covered by a plush spread, and an aspidistra in a brass pot. Then she said that she would like to see the four-pound room, which was on the top floor, up more stairs covered with drugget, and which was so very small that it only just contained its narrow bed and washstand.

"You get a nice view from here," said Mercy hopefully. The view was certainly extensive: a whole grey hillside covered with terraces of other dismal little houses, their rows of chimneys all dribbling yellow smoke into the soupy atmosphere.

Val followed Mercy down again, making affirmative responses to the information that she was being given regarding laundry, coal, and hot suppers. On the first-floor landing, she said, "I believe I'd like to look in here again," and deliberately opened the door of a room they had not entered before.

"Oh, that's not it—" began Mercy, but Val had already walked through the door and was looking at the two children who were inside the room.

They were thin little creatures. The boy wore a shabby sailor suit. The girl—much smaller—was dressed only in a nightdress. Their hair was very fair, like Nils', their eyes slate-blue. They were extremely pale. The boy had an arm round his small sister, either for protection, or restraint, or to comfort himself; Val noticed the little bony hand, blueish against the yellowed flannel. Their faces were rather dirty, and the little girl's was smeared with tears. Also Val noticed fastidiously that they smelt unwashed—and that the girl's hair had not been brushed for days, by the look of it.

"Hullo," she said gently, crossing the room to where they huddled together in the corner. The four slate-blue eyes looked up at her warily, fearfully.

"Oh, miss, you've gone into the wrong room!" cried Mercy anxiously. "That's not the one—"

"It's all right, Mercy," said Val.

She noticed that the little girl sat on a damp patch on the bare wooden floor. Indeed the whole room smelt faintly of urine. Like a zoo, thought Val.

Mrs. Pipkin came rushing back up the stairs, her colour higher than ever.

"*That's* not the room, miss," she said sharply. "Mercy, what did you show the young lady in here for? That's a pair of young 'uns I'm looking arter to oblige someone—and enough trouble they've given me, dear knows —the room that's to let is *this* one; what'd you do a stupid thing like that for, Mercy? *You* keep still or I'll knock your teeth in," she threatened the children in a whisper, trying to urge Val out of the door with impatient jerks of her head.

Val had noticed how the children flinched when Mrs. Pipkin entered the room.

"I'm their aunt," she said clearly.

Mrs. Pipkin's jaw dropped. Her high colour faded. She looked, suddenly, both angry and uncertain; she began to gabble: "Why didn't you *tell* me, Mercy, that the lady was the children's aunt? I'm sorry, I'm sure, miss—I'd have had them ready if I'd a known you was coming, though Lord alone knows the inconvenience I've had with them, left with them a whole month and not a penny paid since the first, downright inconsiderate, if you'll pardon me, and the little girl's more than *anyone* could be expected to look after that wasn't related to her, she's dirty, miss, it's enough to break your heart keeping after her, in my opinion she's mental, not all there, I'll have to have compensation for the damage she's done. I'm a respectable woman and this is a clean house and if I'd known at the start how it was going to be I'd never have said yes, and supposed to come from a good home—good home indeed, it's downright disgraceful the way some people bring up their young ones if you ask me—"

She was working herself back into a rage again. Val cut her short.

"Will you pack the children's things, please?" she said. "And tell me how much is owed to you. I'll pay you immediately and take them away as soon as you can have them ready."

"Take them *away?*" demanded Mrs. Pipkin, indignantly, suddenly changing her tack. "'Ere, you can't do that! Their pa and ma left them with me; I undertook to look arter 'em, and 'ere they'll stay—'ow do I know you're who you say you are, anyways? There's plenty owing, which I'll be obliged if you *will* pay—and about time too—but as for taking them away, that's another kettle of fish! Why don't their pa come for them hisself?"

Ignoring this awkward question, Val said again, "How much is owing to you?"

"Fourteen pun' ten shilling!" said Mrs. Pipkin threateningly. "An' it should be more by rights, considering the 'orrible haggravation I've been subjected to—not an easy minnit 'av I hed wi' them young 'uns in the 'ouse."

"Then you should be relieved that I'm taking them away," said Val, taking her purse out of her muff. She counted out the money—it was dangerously close to all she had on her. "Now—please get their things together and wash their faces."

At sight of the money Mrs. Pipkin's expression had become less hostile, more cupidinous.

"That fourteen ten's only on account," she snapped. "There's demmiges to be took into consideration as well."

"You'll have to write to my brother's lawyers about that," said Val. "Now, where are their clothes?"

She looked about the room. It was bleak enough—bare boards, a cupboard, an iron bed in one corner, a cot in another, a chamberpot. Val crossed to the cupboard and opened it. But it was empty.

"They've only got one or two bits o' things," said Mrs. Pipkin defensively. "I've 'ad to wash for 'em every blessed day. There's some stuff out on the line now. Fetch it, Mercy."

"The little girl can't have come here in her nightgown," said Val. "Where are her other clothes? She must have a coat, a dress?"

The boy spoke up for the first time.

"We had some other things but she took them away," he said in a very quiet voice, each syllable precisely accented. A kind of flash transformed Mrs. Pipkin's face and Val moved forward protectively; she guessed at the courage it must have taken for the child to speak. But Mrs. Pipkin evidently thought better of her impulse; she muttered, "You can't believe anything they say, there's not a particle of truth in it. Anyhows, where are you takin' them?"

"I'm taking them to Mrs. Hansen's aunt, Lady Stroma, at her house in Grosvenor Square," Val said boldly.

The splendid address had its effect; Mrs. Pipkin became quite subdued.

"'Ere, Merce, why din't you tell me before that Mrs. H had some grand folks? We could a' writ to 'em—"

"I didn't know their name, Ma," Mercy muttered nervously. "The old lady did come a-calling onct, but she jest said, 'Tell Mrs. Hansen her aunt is here—'"

Val had had enough of Mrs. Pipkin and her daughter.

"Please hurry up and get the children ready," she said shortly. "I don't wish to wait here all day."

A self-conscious bustle ensued, with Mrs. Pipkin harrying Mercy. A basin of hot water was fetched up, the children's faces were scrubbed, a few items of clothing were packed into a canvas bag, and, after a longish pause, a serge sailor dress was brought and the little girl dressed in it. Val had noticed Mercy slip out of the front gate and round to the house next door during this interval and harboured a suspicion that the dress had been sold or bartered and was now being hastily retrieved. Mrs. Pipkin's mixture of aggression and defensiveness was not conducive to confidence; throughout the whole scene Val found herself continuously wondering: how could Kirstie, who loved her children so devotedly, and was so fanatically particular about not entrusting them to unreliable nursery maids— how *could* she have left them with a woman like this?

At last they were ready, their pallor enhanced by the scrubbing they had undergone. As a final sop they had each been given a slice of bread and butter and brown sugar.

"There!" said Mrs. Pipkin. "Now don't you go a-telling your ma and pa you din't have a nice time at ol' Mrs. Pipkin's!"

She tried to manipulate her face into an indulgent smile, but the effect was not convincing.

"As to that, I should think their looks will speak for themselves—they don't need to say anything," Val said curtly, closing the gate.

This enraged Mrs. Pipkin; she came rushing down the garden path, and the children instinctively clutched Val's hands.

"'Ere!" said Mrs. Pipkin furiously. "Arter all, 'ow do I know you aren't a kidnapper? I ought to 'ave the law on you."

"I wouldn't try that," said Val. "The police might be interested in finding out what you had done with all these children's belongings. Come along, Jannie and Pieter."

She led them along up the street at a brisk pace, thinking ruefully that this final scene must have looked ludicrous enough to any observer. In-

deed, a man in a Tom-and-Jerry hat and a blue cravat, who had been leaning against a gatepost a few houses farther along, eyed them curiously as
they passed, and then strolled after them.

"Where are you taking us?" the boy asked presently and then added, in
his quiet, precise manner, "*Are* you a kidnapper?"

"No I'm not," said Val shortly. "Mrs. Pipkin only said that to frighten
you. I'm your aunt Val."

"Oh," he said thoughtfully, and then, after a pause, "How do we know
that?"

"I suppose you'll have to take me on trust," Val said, rather nonplussed.
How old was he—five, six? Was this what all children were like?—so clear,
so logical? Then she recollected something. "Can you read?"

"Print, I can—not handwriting."

"You'd recognise handwriting, though, I should think? I have a letter
from your mother. I'll show it to you in the train."

There had been no possibility of finding a hansom in those parts; in any
case Val's store of ready cash was now so depleted that she feared she
might not have the fare. However, partly by luck, partly sense of direction, she had steered their course so that quite soon they arrived at King's
Cross station, where Val bought tickets for the Marylebone underground
railway. The children had not traveled on this before; their eyes widened
in fright as the train rattled them into a black, smoky tunnel, and the little
girl burst into wails.

"Oh heavens! Don't do that!" said Val. She felt, uncomfortably, that
people were staring at them. Wholly unused to the company of children,
she did not know what to do. If only she had some buns or lollipops to
give the howling Jannie. A penny? Doubtful if that would bring any consolation; rummaging rather hopelessly in the recesses of her muff she came
across a small object and pulled it out, puzzled, wondering what it could
be.

"Why, you've got Pig," said the boy. "*Look*, Jannie—it's Pig!—she
dropped him, when Papa was bringing us to Mrs. Pipkin's," he explained
seriously to Val, "and we thought we'd lost him for good."

The sight of Pig seemed to have a beneficent effect on little Jannie. She
clasped the wooden object tightly in one hand, while sucking the thumb
of the other, meanwhile leaning against her brother. No new tears rolled
down her pale cheeks. Val took this opportunity of showing Pieter his
mother's letter. She was not sure whether he was able to read the faint
scrawl, but at least he evidently recognised the signature at the end and
appeared reassured.

"Can you walk a bit farther?" Val asked, when they had reached Marylebone Station, and emerged above ground.

"How far?"

Val consulted her map again. "From here to Grosvenor Square. I should think it may take half an hour."

"I can," Pieter said. "But Jannie may get tired."

"Oh well, in that case I'll have to carry her."

"Why aren't you taking us back to our own house?" Pieter asked as they walked rather slowly down bustling Baker Street, Jannie clinging tightly to her brother's hand on one side and Val's on the other, flinching slightly as waggons and horse omnibuses flashed past.

"Because your mother and father aren't back yet."

"Oh." After a minute the boy added, "Where are they?"

Val had seen this coming. "I don't know, Pieter," she said. "I think they must still be traveling. Wasn't your mother supposed to go away for her health?"

"Yes, I think so," he answered doubtfully.

"I'm sure they'll be back soon."

She tried to make her voice as confident as possible, and he apparently accepted her assurance.

Presently Jannie's pace began to drag more and more.

"She's tired," Pieter said. He added explanatorily, "She's only little, you see."

Val picked up the child and settled her as comfortably as possible on her arm. Jannie was a frail, thin little creature—somewhere between two and three, Val would have guessed—but even the smallest three-year-old makes a surprisingly heavy burden after a short time. It was a relief when at last they reached the spaciousness and quiet of Grosvenor Square.

"Here," said Val, putting Jannie down by the garden in the centre, "I should think you could walk a few yards by now. Oh," she added in dismay, noticing a damp stain on her own coat sleeve, "You're wet!"

She knelt down and felt the child and discovered that, instead of proper underclothes, Jannie had on merely a sodden flannel napkin.

"No *wonder* she couldn't walk. Her legs are all chafed."

"I know. Mrs. Pipkin wouldn't give her proper drawers because she wet them such a lot. She's like that all the time now," said Pieter resignedly.

"But she must be about three? Surely she ought to have stopped wetting herself by now?" Val was extremely vague about when this should happen, but before the age of walking, surely?

"Yes she had stopped. But she started again, at Mrs. Pipkin's," said Pieter.

Val gave an impatient sigh, and then checked herself. It wasn't the child's fault, after all. But what a way to arrive at the mansion of an unknown marchioness who might not even, for sure, be Kirstie's aunt. If only the Jersey Hotel were a bit closer. But that was a good half hour's ride away, even if a cab had been in sight, which it was not, and even if Val had had enough money on her. Whereas number forty, Grosvenor Square was just across the road—a large, handsome house with a white-pillared porch.

"Come along children," said Val, sighing again. "We'll go and see if that's where your great-aunts live."

Holding their hands she crossed the street, entered the pillared porch, and put her finger firmly on the brass bell push.

CHAPTER 6

A FTER a short pause the door was flung open by a black-coated manservant. He gave no flicker of recognition at the sight of Pieter and Jannie but impassively inquired Val's name; just the same, from something in his demeanour, she felt instantly certain that he had seen the children before.

She gave him her card and asked if the marchioness of Stroma was at home.

"I will ascertain, ma'am, if you will be so good as to take a seat."

He spoke with a slight brogue; Val, unfamiliar with variations on the English accent, could not be certain if it were Scots, but it reminded her of the voices she had heard when in Edinburgh with her father.

"Can you tell Lady Stroma" (she hoped this was right) "that I am Mr. Nils Hansen's sister."

He went off with her card. Val sat down collectedly and looked round the hall, which was about the size of the whole ground floor in the Twenty-third Street house, floored with marble, and decorated with stags' antlers and numerous sharp-pointed and lethal-looking weapons. A banner hung in one corner.

The children remained very quiet and subdued beside her, but Pieter murmured, "That was great-aunt Louisa's buter. His name is Sutherland."

"Oh, so you *have* been here before?" Val was relieved.

"Yes, once we came to tea. But Jannie was sick on the rug."

"Her ladyship will see you, miss," said the butler returning. "Please to come this way."

They ascended a broad flight of marble stairs, Jannie with great difficulty, and were shown into a long, high, handsome room on the first floor. Two ladies were seated, very upright, on high-backed chairs at the far end of the room, below the marble bust of a Roman emperor which stood on a black column. It might well have portrayed an uncle or grandfather of the ladies; their physiognomy was markedly similar to that of the bust, particularly as to the arched nose, curved nostrils, and high, patrician expression; Val entertained a fleeting irreverent suspicion that the bust had been acquired because of the resemblance.

"Miss Montgomery, my lady," announced the butler.

"How do you do, Miss Montgomery," said the taller and more impressive of the ladies. "This is my sister Honoria."

Val made the journey down the room.

"How do you do, Lady Stroma, Lady Honoria. It is kind of you to receive me."

"And to what do we owe the honour of making your acquaintance, Miss Montgomery?" inquired Lady Stroma. She spoke in a high, dry voice, through her nostrils; it sounded, thought Val, like the honking of a flight of geese.

"Well—" said Val. "It's a long and quite complicated story. I wonder if, while I tell it, the children might—might perhaps go and play somewhere? Also, little Jannie has had a slight mishap and could do with some attention—"

"Tuts!" said Lady Stroma. "Sutherland—call Dundas!"

Nervously on the children's behalf, Val awaited the arrival of this person.

Dundas, when she appeared, looked, at first sight, alarming—she was a lady's maid in grey poplin and starched cambric, tall and severe as a grenadier—but when Lady Stroma said, "Take Miss Kirstie's children away and see to them, Dundas; the little girl requires changing," she exclaimed, "Och, maircy, the puir bairn! Here, come awa', Miss Jannie, till I sort you," in a voice as soft as a moorland mist, and the children went with her willingly enough.

While they were being ushered out, Val took covert stock of the ladies facing her.

Lady Stroma certainly appeared sufficiently formidable, with very black hair, just beginning to silver, a cold grey piercing eye, a thin, arched mouth, and deep incised lines running downward from her fastidiously dilated nostrils. Pride, said those nostrils. Pride, said the long, slender, bony hands, the immense diamond brooch, the waterfall of exquisite lace, the black draperies.

The younger sister, Lady Honoria, was less alarming. Her face, though aquiline, seemed cast in a softer mould, her lips were less resolute, and the grey brocade dress she wore owed more to fashion and femininity than did that of her sister. Her skin was pale as paper and she did not look well; a cough shook her at frequent intervals.

"Now, Miss Montgomery: how can we serve you?"

"First, Lady Stroma," said Val, "do you, by any chance, know where my brother and his wife—your niece—are at this moment?"

Lady Honoria looked extremely startled. Lady Stroma thinned her lips even more fastidiously.

"I understood that they were to go on some cruise with that politician person. Reydon—Clanreydon, he calls himself now—as if *he* had ever belonged to a clan! A plausible *parvenu* of the worst type—flashy, self-seeking, and a Whig, furthermore."

"My sister and I have always been Tories, naturally," murmured Lady Honoria.

"Are they not back from the cruise?" inquired Lady Stroma.

"They never seem to have set off on it," said Val. "But they *have* left their house in Welbeck Street and—and nobody seems to know where they are."

Briefly she explained the cause and circumstances of her own presence in London, and how she had discovered the children—passing rather hastily over the portion of the story relating to Miss Letty Pettigrew.

"And—and I can't describe to you, Lady Stroma how—how very unsuitable were the circumstances in which I found the children with this wretched woman in Islington."

"Well?" said Lady Stroma. "How do you propose that my sister and I should concern ourselves in this matter, Miss Montgomery?"

Her tone was most unpromising, but Val continued firmly.

"I am only in London for a short visit, Lady Stroma—indeed, I haven't funds to support myself here unless I am provided with somewhere to live and can acquire a few newspaper connections"—Lady Stroma's long lids came three-quarters of the way down over her chill grey eyes at this vulgar suggestion—"but you, I believe, are the children's nearest relatives on their mother's side—I was wondering if they could not stay with you—just until their parents reappear."

She tried to speak as if this were a reasonable and foregone conclusion, stifling her own growing doubts of such a lucky and simple solution to the problem.

"That is quite out of the question," said Lady Stroma instantly. "Why, pray, should *we* have them? I must tell you that we never made the slightest attempt to conceal our disapproval and displeasure at our niece's imprudent marriage, Miss Montgomery."

I'm sure you didn't, thought Val.

"You may be a very good sort of young lady yourself—we know nothing of you to the contrary—but there is no getting away from the fact that your brother is little better than an adventurer, and moreover keeps highly undesirable company, of the most flashy and meretricious kind. No, my niece has made her bed and she must lie on it; we have washed our hands of her affairs."

"But the children! Why visit your disapproval on *them?* These matters are no fault of theirs. And they are your kin, after all."

"There is something in what Miss Montgomery says, sister," put in Lady Honoria in her softer voice.

"They seem to be well-behaved, quiet little things," Val went on persuasively. "Could they not stay here just—just for the moment?"

"*Quite* impossible, Miss Montgomery." Oh, bother you, you old battle-axe! thought Val impatiently. But then Lady Stroma went on to explain, with a more natural and human manner than she had hitherto used, "In point of fact my sister and I leave England less than twenty-four hours from now; we are catching the London, Chatham, and Dover express sleeping car tomorrow morning at ten, traveling straight through to Nice, where my sister is to spend the winter, as she has delicate lungs, while I plan to travel on to Constantinople and the interior of Persia."

"Oh—I see." Val was very much dashed. Obviously it was out of the question that two highly-bred and elderly ladies should take the children along with them on such a trip. "I suppose the children couldn't remain here, in your house?"

"No, young lady. The house will be shut up. Our servants, of course, accompany us, and nobody will remain here except a caretaker."

"Oh dear."

"But what is to prevent *you*, Miss Montgomery, from remaining in London, hiring an establishment, and retaining the children with you until your brother returns?"

"I can't afford to hire a house, Lady Stroma." Down came the pale lids again. "And I have my living to earn. I don't really have time to look after the children." Val was slightly nettled at being thus relegated to the status of child-minder.

"Oh—I see—" Lady Stroma gazed vaguely down her high-bridged nose as if such a possibility were too bizarre to have occurred to her. "I see . . . How unfortunate."

A slightly uncomfortable pause ensued, which was broken by the arrival of yet another deferential, black-coated manservant, a spare, white-haired man who might, from his air of consequence, have been a steward. He coughed and murmured, "Ahem! I wouldnae have interrupted ye, mem, if it were not airrgent. It's with regairrd tae paiking up yer diaries. Shall ye be traivelling wi' the hale clamjamfrey o' them on camel back, or merely a selaiction?"

"Oh, a selection; but I must have at least forty; I will come and show you which. Excuse me, Miss Montgomery—"

Lady Stroma, rising, swept from the room, so much, in her draperies, re-sembling the black marble column that Val, despite a strenuous effort to do so, quite failed to picture her on camel back; imagination simply boggled at the task.

Lady Honoria, having ascertained that her sister was out of earshot, said hurriedly, in a low voice and a much more friendly manner than she had hitherto used, "I have read a number of your newspaper articles, Miss Montgomery, which Kirstie has kept and shown me on various occasions— I have so much admired your enterprising spirit and your superior literary style!"

This wholly unexpected commendation almost brought tears to Val's eyes. She returned Lady Honoria's timid smile with one of warm grati-tude.

"Why—why, thank you! I had no idea—" Fancy Kirstie having done such a thing—having taken the trouble to get hold of the newspapers—and they must have been mostly American ones—and saved up her articles! For the first time, Val had a sudden feeling of fellowship for her ghostly little sister-in-law.

She would have said more, but Lady Stroma sailed back, the affair of the diaries having been settled.

"Sister, I have had an idea," said Honoria, who seemed heartened by her brief exchange with Val. "Why should not the children go up to Ard-nacarrig? The air up there will be good for them, poor little pale things, much better than London, there would be old Elspie to look after them, just as she looked after Kirstie; Doctor Ramsay could keep an eye on them, and we can leave word for Kirstie that that is where they are to be found. Now, do you not think that an excellent plan?"

"It is not a bad notion," conceded Lady Stroma. "In fact, McPherson made exactly the same suggestion to me. Their board need not be a consideration at Ardnacarrig; there is plenty of bedding, the oat harvest has been a good one—" (Oats? thought Val. Anyone would believe the poor things were horses.) "and they need not be an added expense in fire and candles, for I daresay they would in general be out of doors, or in the same room as Elspie. And at least there would be healthy influences at Ardnacarrig to counteract the unwholesome environment in which they have hitherto been reared. Yes, I believe that will be the best plan. But you have overlooked one important detail, Honoria—how are they to be transported to Ardnacarrig? McPherson and Sutherland come with us to Nice, so do Dundas and the other servants—we can hardly require old Elspie to travel all the way south."

"Where is Ardnacarrig?" asked Val.

"It is our house in Scotland, Miss Montgomery."

Val had a sudden recollection of her brother: "They have a devilish great barracks of a place up in Lammermuir; when they die, all their cash comes to Kirstie . . ."

She had been walking with him in Central Park when he said that; what an infinite time and distance off that day seemed; worlds away. Astonished, Val realised that during the last twenty-four hours, she had hardly given Benet a thought, or any other member of the Allerton clan.

A house in Scotland. And somebody called old Elspie who would look after the children. That seemed like a perfect solution to the problem. They would be in the country—healthy, cared for—

"If it is only the question of escorting them up there, Lady Stroma, I could very well undertake that," she said. "I wouldn't have the least objection—in fact my American editor has suggested that I might go to Scotland. I could travel with them to your house and leave them with—"

"Elspie, our housekeeper, Kirstie's old nurse. If you can accompany them, Miss Montgomery, I believe that will do very well," said Lady Stroma. "Scotland will be good for the children. Perhaps, once they are there, Kirstie will allow them to remain. We *have* been concerned for them from time to time, I must confess."

Concealing her surprise at this admission, Val ventured, "The little boy resembles you, Lady Stroma. Have you noticed his hands? They are exactly like yours."

"Indeed? I had not observed it," said Lady Stroma loftily. But just the same she seemed gratified. Now she began to act like a general. She summoned McPherson once more.

"McPherson, I wish you to procure three tickets on the Caledonian Flyer from King's Cross tomorrow for this young lady and the two children."

Val interposed.

"It is exceedingly good of you to offer to procure my ticket, Lady Stroma, but that will not be necessary—I had not the least intention—"

Lady Stroma took no notice of this, and Lady Honoria murmured, "Pray do not regard it, Miss Montgomery! In point of fact, it will not cost us a penny! My sister and I are directors and chief shareholders of the London and Eastern Scottish Line; we can travel to Scotland for nothing as often as we please."

"Oh I see; in that case, I am very much obliged to you." Val was entertained by this confirmation of her feeling that the purchase of a rail ticket for a total stranger was quite outside the usual scope of Lady Stroma's generosity; for a lady who lived so handsomely, Kirstie's aunt seemed curiously parsimonious in some ways.

"Will tomorrow suit you, Miss Montgomery?" Lady Stroma added as an afterthought. Val said that it would suit very well. "Good. Telegraph Elspie at Ardnacarrig, McPherson, to expect Miss Montgomery with the children on the day after tomorrow. Also telegraph Robina Gourlay to have suitable accommodation prepared for them all tomorrow night. Mrs. Gourlay is a maid of ours now married and living in Edinburgh, Miss Montgomery; she will provide more suitable lodging than you would find at an hotel. Tell Robina also to arrange for Jock Kelso to come in with the coach and pick them up. Winter provisions may be obtained at the same time, so the trip will not be wasted."

"Thank you," said Val, slightly dazed at all this organisation. "You are very good." She wondered if the Stroma ladies also had shares in the General Post Office.

"Think nothing of it," said the marchioness, whose good offices seemed much more accessible provided that she, personally, were put to no trouble. "Now—where are you staying, Miss Montgomery?"

"At the Jersey Hotel."

"The Jersey—hm, you might do worse. It's respectable enough. McPherson will bring your tickets there presently. Put the children to bed early— they will need a good night's sleep before their journey."

Val could not help blenching a little at the thought of taking the children back to the Jersey Hotel. Still, there was no help for it. Since Lady Stroma was being so unexpectedly accommodating in the matter of tickets and arrangements, the least she could do was find them a hotel room for a night.

However at this moment the maid, Dundas, came in wearing an expression of extreme disapproval.

"If I might speak to you a moment, my lady—"

The burden of her communication was that when she had looked through their small bag of possession to find some clean underwear to put on little Jannie, she had been scandalised by their lack of proper clothes.

"And if, as I understand, you're planning tae send them up to Ardnacarrig, my lady, they've naething fit to wear! They'll need completely outfitting before they go. There's not a thing in the bag that would keep out the wind for five minutes."

"I have reason to believe," said Val, "that the woman they were lodged with sold most of their things, alleging that she had not been paid for their keep."

"Outrageous," muttered Lady Stroma. It was not apparent whether her stricture applied to Mrs. Pipkin or the lack of payment. "Well, Dundas? What do you suggest?"

"Well, my lady, there's Mrs. Ponsonby across the square—many's the time she's said to you that young Master Hugh and Miss Georgina grow as fast as mustardseed. I know for a fact she has some things of their laid away she was going to give me for my missionaries. With your permission I'll just step across and get them, and I daresay Phemie and I could alter enough to fit the children if they could stay here this afternoon, or better still, stop the night."

"But what about my sister's and my packing, Dundas? We leave at half-past nine sharp tomorrow, don't forget."

"Och, that's all taken care of, your leddyship; don't fret your head about that. Mrs. Carrig and I were just wondering how tae occupy the time."

So it was arranged that Pieter and Jannie were to stay on. Val was unfeignedly relieved. If she was to leave London so soon, she must draw out some more money from her dwindling funds; also she wished to call at two more of the addresses Ted Towers had given her. She was delighted that the children were disposed of for the rest of the day.

Arranging to return at eight o'clock the following morning, she said goodbye with repeated thanks to the marchioness and her sister.

"Think nothing of it," said Lady Stroma again. "I believe you to be a very good-hearted sort of gel, Miss Montgomery. If your half-brother had been more like you, I believe my niece's marriage would be a happier one. However—no use repining over that. I wish you good day."

On her way out, Val called in at the housekeeper's room and found

Pieter and Jannie half-buried among assorted clothes of every kind, suitable and unsuitable, which two or three maids were unpacking from a hamper amid laughter and chaff.

"Here—wouldn't this cut up lovely!"

"Doesn't she look a little duck in that?"

Jannie's pale little face peered out wonderingly from under the brim of a huge hat wreathed in ostrich plumes, and Val left the children with a lighter heart, promising to see them on the morrow, and feeling that at least they were in a more cheerful environment than Mrs. Pipkin's horrible upstairs room.

Toys, she thought. I'd better get them something—shouldn't think there'd be any toys at Ardnacarrig. But what should I buy?

Leaving the house, she looked round absently for a hansom, remembered that she had only a few pence in her purse, and started walking south toward Piccadilly. A lounging man in a Tom-and-Jerry hat and a blue choker pushed himself off the wall against which he had been leaning and followed her.

Val walked fast, preoccupied. She would have liked to ask Lady Stroma and her sister more about Nils and Kirstie—what they thought could have happened to her brother and his wife—but the aura of disapproval surrounding Nils was so strong that she had not had the heart. Besides, it seemed plain that Kirstie's aunts knew no more than she did herself; still, it would have been instructive to hear their views.

If only she knew some of their London friends!

Arriving at Piccadilly, she caught a bus back to her hotel, changed some money, and then walked down Ludgate Hill into Fleet Street.

The man in the blue choker was still behind her.

CHAPTER 7

VAL returned to the Jersey Hotel, after her editorial interviews, in a more sanguine frame of mind than she had known since her arrival in London. She ran up the wide, shallow stair to her bedroom, pulled off her walking boots, and sank onto the chair for a short spell of rest and reflection before she went down to dine.

An immense amount had been accomplished during the day, she felt with satisfaction. The children had been rescued—that was the most important achievement—and in a couple of days they would be secure and well cared for, in a peaceful, healthy environment, where they might recover from their unhappy experiences at Mrs. Pipkin's, and where they could remain until their parents reappeared.

Val thought that she was entitled to congratulate herself on the way in which she had dealt with Mrs. Pipkin—and, for that matter, with Lady Stroma. It had all passed off most successfully, she felt. She found it hard not to harbour some indignation against Nils and Kirstie—some scorn, even; scorn mixed with pity in Kirstie's case, of course, because it must be dreadful being married to Nils, but still!—what a shocking arrangement, to leave the children with such a woman. Anybody could see what she was like.

But then, Val remembered, Mrs. Pipkin had not actually mentioned Kirstie, possibly had not even met her; Kirstie might not have known what she was like. But if not, why not; where had Kirstie been? Surely she would have wanted to see the person who was to have charge of her children for so long a period? Had Kirstie—the idea now occurred to Val for the first time—had she, perhaps, been ill? Was that why Nils had been summoned home so hastily? Val now wished that she had had the presence of mind to question the doleful Mercy, but in front of Mrs. Pipkin she had been reluctant to. Could Kirstie be laid up on a sick bed somewhere, worried to death about her children, in financial straits, longing for news, while Nils had gone off on some business of his own?

It was too frustratingly exasperating not to be able to discover any link that would lead her to Nils and Kirstie. For one thing, Val longed to be able to say to them, "Don't worry about your children, set your minds at rest: these are the excellent arrangements that I have made for them!"

Still, sooner or later the parents must get in touch with Mrs. Pipkin—then they would be referred to the house in Grosvenor Square, where the caretaker would of course give the final and wholly satisfactory information that Pieter and Jannie were now at Ardnacarrig. Kirstie would be delighted by that news, surely; she must be glad to know that the children were safe in her own childhood home and that the breach with her family was somewhat mended. Even Nils must be pleased?—"mouldering old barracks somewhere in Lammermuir," Val heard in her mind's ear—but despite his sarcasm Nils had a very healthy respect for money and family property; if it was only for the superior status of their environment, he must surely be gratified to learn that his children had been transferred from Islington to Ardnacarrig.

And there, Val herself felt that she could leave them with an easy conscience. She certainly did not wish to be saddled with the poor little things for the rest of her visit to England, once they were in good hands. She had had two highly satisfactory interviews during the afternoon, with the editors of *Fireside Words*, and the *London Illustrated Weekly*; the former wanted a series of articles contrasting the lives of English and American women in various spheres, while the latter was prepared to pay quite well for a set of Scottish Impressions by a Yankee Lassie. With the money she received for these and the articles she planned to send Ted, Val thought that she might get by, at least for six months.

A satisfactory day, altogether.

Humming tunelessly she bathed her face and hands, shook herself into the grey poplin dress and fastened its myriad buttons, and was on the point of descending for an early dinner when a tap came at the door and a page boy handed in a card.

"The gentleman asks the favour of a word with you, miss."

"Where is he?" asked Val nervously.

LORD CLANREYDON said the card.

Could it be the man she had met at the Beargarden?

But what other could it be?

"He's waiting downstairs in the hall, miss. Shall I show him up?"

"No—not up here." All Val's feelings of self-congratulation and efficiency flew from her. She was near to panic at the thought of that strange, hostile, disrupting presence coming into her room. "Is there some room downstairs where I can see him?"

"There's the card room, miss. That's usually quiet at this time of the evening."

"Tell him I'll be down in ten minutes."

What could he have come for, Val wondered feverishly as, hair severely reswathed, and with a fortifying dab of Cologne behind each ear, she walked slowly, with all the aplomb she could muster, into the card room. Was he here to apologise? To bring some news of Nils, after all?

It was a relief to discover that the card room—a dingy, medium-sized, ill-lit place that smelt of snuff and had bad sporting prints on its brown walls —was not quite empty. An elderly lady was conducting a low-voiced, anxious discussion with somebody who looked like a lawyer at one of the little tables in a distant corner. Their presence was a reassurance.

Her own caller stood motionless by the window, staring out into the gas-lit fog. He stood in the posture of a man quite at ease, resigned to wait in patience for an unlimited length of time—but a nerve jumped in his cheek. At the sound of Val's step he turned slowly and greeted her with smooth politeness.

"Miss Montgomery. Very obliging of you to make time for me."

"How can I serve you, sir?" Val asked stiffly, with a manner modelled on that of Lady Stroma.

Yes, it was certainly the same man. He was now impeccably dressed for the evening; his tails were very black; his pumps were very polished; his necktie and gloves were dazzling white; his shirt studs were dull-red carbuncles; his hat, cloak, and cane lay on a chair. And his manner, as if in conformity with the change of attire, was now completely decorous and grave. He stood waiting for Val to be seated. Extraordinary creature—he *wasn't* going to apologise, or allude to their previous meeting—he was going to pretend that the incident at the Beargarden had never occurred!

Well, two could play at that game, Val thought.

In spite of his gravity and elegance, and his correct deportment, she felt even more nervous with him than she had the other day; rather less at ease, in fact, than she would had she found a cannibal waiting for her, with a pierced nose and necklace of skulls. He seemed not to belong to the same civilisation as herself; there was something about his whole presence which she found infinitely alien—profoundly unsettling and alarming. His strange green-grey eyes with their sidelong glance carried no expression that was recognisable to her. Nor did the slightly twitching mouth. When he smiled, she found the effect neither friendly nor reassuring; his face was no more adapted to convey reassurance than that of a wild beast. His voice, those high, grating tones that she remembered vividly, acted on her nerves like some inexplicable, disturbing noise heard at night; she longed for it to stop.

Yet his intention seemed conciliating.

"It was good of you to make time for me," he said again, and then, glancing round with visible dissatisfaction, "Is there nowhere we can be more private?"

"I prefer to conduct our conversation here, sir," Val replied coldly.

"Oh—very well." He glanced at the couple in the corner. "Point is—I have matters of a private nature to discuss."

Val remained silent. Lord Clanreydon gave her a long, assessing glance. Despite her resolve to remain unflustered, she felt the blood rise in her cheeks. However she met his eyes straightly. Having allowed the pause to draw out, he remarked in a cool tone, "After all, you are not much like your brother."

"I should be obliged, sir," said Val, "if you would be so good as to let me know what it is that you came here to discuss?"

She felt a burning resentment, besides apprehension, because she sensed that the control of the interview was slipping away from her. Doing her best to be firm, she went on, "Did you come here with some news of my brother, Lord Clanreydon?"

"No. On the contrary. Learning from my friend Orville that you were in town, and were hunting for your brother, I came to ask if you had succeeded in your quest. I gather that is not the case? You have had no news?"

It was hardly credible. He really did mean to pretend that the scene at the Beargarden had not taken place.

Well, Val certainly did not intend to give him any information. Certainly not about her discovery of the children. They were none of his business.

"No, I've heard nothing of Nils," she said. "I shall simply have to wait until he gets in touch with me. No doubt he will do so in his own time. But why are *you* so interested in his whereabouts, Lord Clanreydon? Are you a very close friend of my brother's, may I ask?"

He stood motionless, staring down, as if scrutinising the word *friend* with his pale eyes; then slapped it away.

"A friend? No. We have some common interests. Your brother has sometimes made himself useful to me in doing—research—of a kind that I have no longer time to carry out for myself."

Very much Val wondered what. Something of a discreditable kind, she suspected. But she was not going to give Lord Clanreydon the gratification of being asked and refusing to answer. She waited.

"Your brother was about to undertake such a piece of investigation—may indeed have commenced on it—when he—so unfortunately—became lost to view."

"And his wife?" Val coolly asked. "Did she help with this research?"

"Wife?" He looked blank.

"She has vanished also."

"Ah—" Lord Clanreydon inserted a monocle into his left eye. It did nothing for his appearance. "I was not aware of that. Odd—deuced odd." He pondered, absently turning a large onyx scarab ring on his thin finger.

"Your brother did not write to you in New York before you set sail for England, Miss Montgomery?"

"No he did not."

Val was more and more puzzled. The man who, two days ago, appeared to be unaware of her very existence, today displayed apparently detailed knowledge of her movements and history. "My brother has never been a particularly good correspondent."

"He did not leave any papers—reports—newspaper articles—in your charge? Or with anybody in New York that you know?"

"No he did not," Val said again shortly. It began to seem plain that Lord Clanreydon's concern arose not from any regard for Nils, but from an anxiety to lay his hands on those reports, whatever they might be. "Was that all you wished to ascertain? If so I am afraid, Lord Clanreydon, that I must now leave you. I have to—"

She had nothing in particular ahead of her, except to eat and pack her scanty belongings, but this interview was making her more and more uncomfortable. She felt strongly that what Lord Clanreydon actually expressed bore only the slightest relation to the real underlying reason for this call; his remarks had seemed casual, almost random. And his gaze, roaming coldly over her person, affected her as might the cold finger of some dead hand that idly touched her and then withdrew; it seemed not to care about her, yet she detested it.

"Oh pray don't go yet, Miss Montgomery," he drawled, his languid intonation contradicting the sense of the words. "Dear me, I was hoping that you'd favour me with your company for dinner."

"I am sorry; that is not in my power," Val replied politely. "I shall be occupied in packing for most of the evening. Thank you, but I must decline."

"Packing?" The grey-green eyes moved up. "You intend leaving town?"

Why had she given him that handle?

"Yes," she said reluctantly.

"Ah—you return to the States, Miss Montgomery?"

"No, sir."

"Might one inquire, then—where you are bound?"

Why can I never think of some plausible lie? Val demanded of herself furiously. It was her weakest social front—faced with this kind of situation she invariably lacked the presence of mind to invent a convincing story.

"I hardly see that it concerns you, sir," was the best that she could achieve. Which was useless, of course. His brows shot up.

"Of course it does not, dear lady." His tone expressed light surprise at her presumption. "But I daresay you would wish me to inform you, should I become acquainted as to your brother's location—or let him know where you can be found? And I can hardly do that without some direction."

Although this seemed reasonable enough, she found herself highly reluctant to give him any information about her plans.

"I am going to Scotland, sir," she explained unwillingly.

"Indeed? You have friends—relatives, there? May I be entrusted with an address which I can relay to your brother, should he return to town?"

"I believe that will not be necessary, sir, thank you. I am not—"

She came to a lame halt.

"Your brother had the direction already, of course," he filled in smoothly. "Ah—will you be going to Edinburgh? You have connections there?"

Without having the least intention of doing so, she found herself mentioning her professional plans and saying that she could be reached through *Selkirk's Magazine*.

The brows flicked up again.

"You—ah you, then, like your brother, occupy yourself with journalism, Miss Montgomery?"

"Since you appear to be so well-informed about me, sir, I wonder that you did not know that also," she could not resist commenting tartly.

This annoyed him; she noticed the twitch in his cheek again; his nostrils flattened as he drew a quick breath.

Used to his own way, Val thought; a spoilt man, possibly a dangerous man to displease. A vain man, too; in spite of his outrageous behaviour two days ago, he really hoped to charm me, and is angry that he has not succeeded. Could Nils have offended him in some way? Could *that* have been the reason for the flitting?

"You do me an injustice, madam," Lord Clanreydon said coolly. "I was, certainly, cognisant of the fact that Mr. Hansen had a half-sister in the United States, but that was the complete extent of my information—I was not honoured by any particulars as to your circumstances."

If he were angry with her, Val was equally so with herself. What folly, to provoke this man, one of her few possible links with Nils; and a man, too, of considerable power and position. His whole bearing demonstrated that, even if she had not known it already.

Adopting a milder tone she therefore said, "Yes, I am in the same profession as my brother. But my kind of writing is quite different from his. While I am in Scotland I plan to do a series of impressions of domestic life there, for a London journal."

"Indeed? Very clever of you," drawled Lord Clanreydon, evidently losing interest at once. He added as if on an afterthought, "Mrs. Hansen has some relatives up there, I believe? Where do they live?"

"Really?" Val parried. "Nils may have mentioned them, but I do not have their address."

For once she had achieved a neat, frosty half-truth and was pleased with herself until she noticed the slight sardonic smile, hardly more than a curl of the lip, with which it was received. "I have never met my sister-in-law," she added. "Are you acquainted with her, Lord Clanreydon?"

She glanced down at her watch, as she put the question, in a plain hint to him that her time was valuable; she badly wanted to terminate this queer, unprofitable, strained interview. Then, wondering at his silence, she glanced up again and surprised a very odd look indeed on her companion's face.

Occasionally during the past ten minutes—so completely at variance were his manner and bearing from his behaviour during their previous interview—wild irrational notions had come into her mind concerning impersonations—identical twins—*doppelgangers*—mysterious substitutions. But at this moment she was certain again that it was the same man. The dark restless light burned in his eye that she had noticed the other day after she slapped him, together with a mannerism that she had not consciously registered at the time but which now came back to her—a trick of staring at his hands which were outspread a foot apart, as if they held an invisible globe, a cushion of air between them.

What did he see in that globe of air?

"Eh?" he said, as if bringing his mind back from an immense distance. "Oh—your sister-in-law, Hansen's wife? No, I don't believe I've had the pleasure—May have met her at some big crush, possibly—I'm afraid I don't recall."

Val thought this unlikely, remembering Nils on the subject of Kirstie's antipathy to big parties.

"Now, if you'll excuse me, Lord Clanreydon, I have a great deal to do," she said, making a move to rise. His hand was instantly beneath her elbow, assisting her. It was startlingly cold; she felt the chill through her grey poplin sleeve. Partly because of that, partly from an almost physical repugnance, she flinched away from his touch, moving clumsily backward. He noticed this—as he did every nuance of behaviour, it seemed. The greenish eyes glanced ironically sideways; his lips curled. Awkward in her embarrassment, stumbling against the chair she had just quitted, Val dropped her knitted purse. A twist of paper in it came undone and a dozen marbles—blue, green, blood colour—rolled out on to the dusty Turkey carpet.

With little Pieter in mind she had impulsively bought them from a street vendor in Ludgate Hill.

"Ah—fond of marbles, Miss Montgomery?" inquired Lord Clanreydon, inspecting the rolling baubles with an air of mild surprise. He raised a pale finger and summoned a page. "Boy! The lady has dropped something."

"Hardly, sir," Val answered with equal calm. "I bought them—for a child of my acquaintance."

"Just so. Are you fond of children, then?"

That question at least Val could answer truthfully.

"No, sir. Not at all." She accepted the marbles back from the grinning page boy and poured them once more into her purse. "Good evening, Lord Clanreydon. It was kind of you to call."

"*Au revoir,* Miss Montgomery. So sorry you could not dine. Another time, I hope."

"Thank you, but it is unlikely. My plans are uncertain."

She flushed at the irony of his tone. Odious man! Why, at the outset, had she not made some round allusion to the previous meeting?

As she walked across the room and mounted the stairs, she could feel his measuring, calculating stare, sharp as a dart between her shoulderblades.

Regaining her room, she found that a cablegram had been laid on her table. It was from Benet, to whom she had telegraphed her address on arrival.

"I find your behaviour extraordinarily hasty, ill-timed, and thoughtless," he had wired, regardless of expense. "Please make arrangements to return without delay. Yours, Benet Allerton."

It was a chilling message to receive, particularly after such an uncomfortable meeting. It made her both depressed and angry.

She had intended to write Benet this evening, a long, lively, and loving letter about her adventure in London (well, perhaps omitting the Beargarden and Miss Letty Pettigrew); instead, sitting down, she dashed off a short note regretting that it was not in her power to accede to his request at present and explaining that she was on the point of departure to Scotland, where she could be contacted through *Selkirk's Magazine*.

Then, having given her visitor sufficient time to get away, she went down to dine.

"Warn't that Lord Clanreydon, that gentleman as I seed you with in the card room?" her elderly waiter inquired as she ate her roast mutton.

"Yes it was. Does he come here often?" asked Val.

"Lor' bless you, miss, never! The Jersey ain't his line—much too old-fashioned for a gent like him. That's why I were so surprised." The waiter's expression also suggested that a staid young lady such as Miss Montgomery was decidedly less scintillating than Lord Clanreydon's usual companions.

"Is he very well known?" Val inquired, helping herself to greens.

"Oh, very much, very much so indeed, miss. Quite a public figure, you could say. Friend of the P. of W., *and* half the cabinet, and a big sporting man—has his own runners in all the top races, and a yacht at Cowes; very popular, he is. You can't hardly pick up a picture paper without you find a sketch of him at the play or some nob's party."

The waiter wrapped his napkin round his arm and ambled away.

Val munched her tough mutton, wondering even more why this ornament of fashion and the sporting world should be so anxious to discover the whereabouts of Nils.

She walked upstairs, vaguely registering the presence of a shabby man conferring with the clerk at the desk. He wore something blue round his neck and looked like a messenger. His face seemed familiar; she wondered where she had seen him before.

Her mood of satisfaction had completely evaporated.

CHAPTER 8

THE journey north was a nightmare. Wholly unused to the company of children, Val had been prepared for it to prove difficult and tiresome, but her imagination had not supplied her with any details; her fears fell far short of the reality. She was not ready for the insatiable, voracious questions of Pieter, who behaved as if no adult had ever given him rational answers in his life before. "What makes the train go?" "How many people are there on it?" "Where does the driver live?" "When does he get his tea?" "Why are they driving those cows out of that field?" "Why are there sheep in *that* field?" "What will happen when we get to Edinburgh?" "And then?" "And then?" "And then?" If, stumped for an answer, she honestly said, "I don't know, Pieter," he instantly accepted the fact, but that did not stop him; he merely branched to another line of inquiry. "Why is it raining here and not over there?" "What makes the rainbow?" "I don't know everything in the *world*, Pieter." "Why not?" He was like a small relentless machine, frantic for knowledge.

But Pieter was easy, was child's play, compared with Jannie. Val had been utterly unprepared for the problems of dealing with Jannie's physical needs. To begin with, trains, it seemed, made her vomit. "Has she never been in one before?" asked Val, desperately mopping and dabbing. "I don't think so," said Pieter, "but going in a horse bus or a carriage always makes her sick, too." "I wish you'd told me before." "Why? What difference would it have made? She'd have been sick just the same," said Pieter reasonably. "Yes, but I wouldn't have let her drink all that lemonade."

Also, as Val had already discovered, Jannie's bladder was at present completely out of control, and her bowel functions in not much better shape.

"Did that happen since you were at Mrs. Pipkin's, too?" "Yes," said Pieter. "You see Mrs. Pipkin used to leave us alone in the dark, and that frightened Jannie, so she couldn't help going, and then Mrs. Pipkin used to hit her with a wet cloth, and that made her worse." Val had a pleasurable vision of herself pushing Mrs. Pipkin under a train. "She was a horrible woman, Pieter." "Yes. Shall we ever go back to her house?" he asked nervously, his knuckles clenched together with strain. "No. Not ever, *ever*, Pieter, I promise." "But are there other people like her?" How could one answer that? The world was full of cruel people, harsh, unjust, thoughtless, insensitive, brutal people. "Perhaps. But there are lots of kind people too. Let's think about them. Who's the nicest person you know?" "Look," he said, "we're coming to a station. You'd better get Jannie out, quick; she wants to go again."

From hard practice at Peterborough, Grantham, Doncaster, and York, Val had become adept at combing through the Colman's Mustard, *London News*, Tickets, Refreshments, or Parcels Office signs, as they slowed into a station, and finding Ladies; she was off the train like a fifty yards' sprinter, with Jannie, leaving Pieter to guard their places. Jannie was totally unused to public lavatories and let out ear-piercing screams at the first two, but her need was too great for even her acute degree of fear to hold her back.

In the train she was continually restless; not from naughtiness but, it seemed, from a congenital incapacity to remain in the same position for more than about thirty consecutive seconds; then she would squirm and wriggle into a new attitude. By the end of the journey Val's arms ached as if she had hauled a team of climbers up a mountain, due to the effort of trying to prevent Jannie from precipitating herself on to the filthy carriage floor.

Lady Stroma's providence, or McPherson's, had provided them with a tea basket, and Val was grateful for it not only because of the distraction it provided on the monotonous journey, but also because its napkins, towels, and receptacles were invaluable equipment in the desperate struggle to meet Jannie's physical contingencies. Val was not hungry herself. However she welcomed Pieter's suggestion that they should get off the train and go to the refreshment room at York, where the train stopped for half an hour. Val tipped the guard to watch over their seats—though it seemed unlikely that anyone would voluntarily choose to occupy their crumb-strewn, bedraggled, bepuddled corner.

York's refreshment room offered soup, fish, meat, pudding, cheese for two shillings and sixpence a head, all served in half an hour. "That's a penny's worth a minute," said Pieter, working it out. "Goodness, Pieter, you're quick at arithmetic." None of them wanted that. Val bought the children ices, and herself a brandy and soda, which cost a shilling; it was dear, but she needed it. Gulping it down, waiting for its restorative warmth, she remembered Nils, taking the brandy decanter up to his bedroom. Extraordinary to think that these were his children; they seemed in no way part of him.

Back in the train, Jannie suddenly fell into a deep and mercifully prolonged sleep, sucking her finger and clutching Pig against her flushed cheek. While she slept, Val was able to read aloud to Pieter in a low voice. She had cursed herself earlier because, though she had bought the children a swift and random selection of toys and games the previous day, these were all packed away in the luggage van among their baggage, inaccessible until they reached Edinburgh. However she had acquired two books of fairy tales at the York bookstall. It was no use reading while Jannie was awake; she paid not the slightest attention to the sound of the words, merely tried pertinaciously to turn over the pages, faster and faster, without waiting for the story.

Val was troubled about her.

All the other occupants of the carriage had got off at York. Perhaps York was their destination; or perhaps they had had enough of youthful company and had found places elsewhere on the train. At all events Val was able, thankfully, to stretch out Jannie's little warm, inert body along one seat, covered with a shawl, while she and Pieter sat softly reading aloud and conversing on the other side.

"Tell me, Pieter, why does Jannie talk so little?"

"I suppose she doesn't want to," he said, after thinking about it.

"I can't understand what she says very well."

In fact the child's communications, what few there were, consisted of curious gibberish words and incomprehensible grunts.

"Oh, you'll soon get to understand her," said Pieter confidently. "I can, and Mama can very well."

"What's the matter with her?" Val wanted to ask, but you cannot ask such a question of a child Pieter's age. It was plain though, even to Val, ignorant of children as she was, that all was not well with Jannie. Nils had started to say something about her and then stopped himself, Val now remembered, as if there were some defect, something unsatisfactory about her. Well, perhaps there would be an expert in Edinburgh whom it would be possible to consult. Medical opinion should certainly be sought, Val decided.

Meanwhile she read aloud to Pieter and was rewarded by his flushed, breathless, utterly concentrated, almost mesmerised attention. Never had she had such an audience. They raced through the Three Bears, Rumpelstiltskin, Cinderella, Hansel and Gretel, the Juniper Tree. At one point she thought Pieter had fallen asleep, but he was merely rereading the last page of Rumpelstiltskin very carefully over to himself, his lips moving softly as he mouthed the unfamiliar words.

"Was Rumpelstiltskin a wicked person?" he looked up to ask.

"I'm not sure, Pieter. What do you think?"

He thought about it carefully, and then said, "The queen shouldn't have done what he said."

"Agreed to his bargain, you mean?"

"Yes."

"But then the king would have cut off her head."

"Well, she shouldn't have married him if he said he was going to do that. Really," said Pieter, thinking it out, "it was all the fault of the mother, who said that lie about her in the first place," and Val marvelled again at the cool intelligence and logic of this pale, thin little boy who hardly came up to her elbow.

Jannie woke with a sudden clench and struggle, as if she were fighting her way out of a bad dream. Thinking it would help and distract the child, Val hoisted her up to look out of the window, but this was a disastrous blunder; they were just crossing the Tyne Bridge at Newcastle, Jannie looked out and, seeing nothing but water, burst into a convulsive series of high-pitched screams, arching her body back as if she were about to have a fit; it took the combined efforts of Pieter and Val to soothe her down. Pieter was touchingly good with his small sister, Val had already discovered: intuitively quick to grasp her needs, ingenious at amusing her, gentle and infinitely patient.

After Jannie had slowly recovered, by lengthy and protracted stages, from sobs to hiccups, from hiccups to silent trembling, they played games, endless games. Val taught Pieter naughts and crosses and, to her astonishment, he then taught it to Jannie, who grasped it instantly, and proved able to beat her brother three times out of five. So she can't be mentally defective—can she? thought Val. This was a fear that had troubled her several times before on the journey when Jannie, finger-sucking, eyes glazed, had seemed vacant, stupid, almost cretinous. But now, with bright eyes, face sparkling with wicked pleasure as she blocked her brother's row of crosses she looked, surely, bright as any child her age, if not brighter? She was a complete puzzle. She also, with the same easy rapidity, learned scissors-paper-stone, and greatly entertained an elderly Scottish farmer who had joined the train at Newcastle, by playing it with him and beating him six times running.

"Hech, sirs, the little lass is a fair caution!" he said.

At last, after what seemed like a lifetime in it, the train began to slow down, and the farmer told them that they were coming into Edinburgh. Dark had fallen long ago; now the lights of houses began to climb up hillsides on either side.

"Is Edinburgh like London?" Pieter asked.

"Not so big," Val said.

"Will Mama and Papa be there?"

"I don't know, Pieter. But if not, I hope they'll come soon."

"Will you stay with us till Mama and Papa *do* come?"

"I'm not sure," she said guiltily. For of course she intended to leave them with this Elspie; who sounded just the kind of reassuring, comfortable person to care for them faithfully until—until their circumstances improved; of course Val intended to make her escape as soon as she had settled the children. If she had known what caring for children entailed, she would never have accepted Nils' proposition in New York.

And (as Pieter would say) then what? wondered Val. What do I do with myself? One of these evenings I must write another letter to Benet.

"Want Mama! Want Mama!" wailed Jannie, and burst into a heartbreaking flood of tears.

"Oh, heavens! Don't do that *now!*" exclaimed Val, at the end of her tether. "Look! Look at the pretty lights! Look at all the other trains!" For they were now pulling in to Edinburgh station, granite-built and glass-roofed. "Look at all the horses, Jannie! Look at the man in the kilt."

But Jannie wept all the harder and would not be comforted. Weeping, she was lifted from the train by the kind farmer; weeping, she allowed herself to be led along by Pieter while Val wearily saw to their luggage; weeping still, she was hoisted into a cab.

"The lassie's tired, forbye," said the driver. "Ah, it's an awfu' long journey frae London. Where'll I be taking you, ma'am?"

And when Val told him it was number twenty-nine, Regent Terrace, he said comfortingly that it was no' sae far to go, and urged his horses out into the wet night. For it was raining in Scotland, as it had been raining in London that morning, though Val noticed, when they stopped in a quiet tree-lined road, after ten minutes' drive through the cobbled streets, that the rain was coming down in large lumps and showing a dismal tendency to turn to snow.

CHAPTER 9

VAL pulled her beaver collar tighter round her neck. The fine, gritty snow, blown on a piercing northeast wind, seemed able to penetrate the tiniest opening, and stung her skin like grapeshot. Ducking her head against the blast, she darted across Cockburn Street and plunged down a narrow steep wynd, which, a helpful man had told her, would bring her in due course to Appin Court where, at number seventeen, she would find the offices of *Selkirk's Magazine*.

In the shelter of the high buildings the wind was less ferocious but the light was correspondingly worse; although the hour could not be much after three in the afternoon, the alley was so confined, and the houses on either side so high—seven, eight, nine storeys, many of them, each floor extending out beyond the one below—that the footway was almost obscured in gloom. The cobbles were uncomfortably wet and slippery, too, half-buried in slush and dirt. Val picked her way as best she could, observing with a professional eye the damp, insanitary-looking brickwork, black with age and streaked with green, suggesting a constant seepage of water. Lines of dingy washing dangled from wall to wall overhead, heaps of rubbish often partially blocked the way. Skinny children lurked and stared in corners.

Edinburgh was depressing her. On her last visit she had thought it a grand city, handsome and windblown. But that had been a carefree summer week, spent sightseeing with her father. They had stayed at the Charlotte Hotel, dined out in elegant eating houses with Nils, and hired a carriage for jaunts to Stirling and the Lothians. She had hardly seen this face of the grim old town. But just the same it was here, she thought with a shiver; it was here waiting all the time. She was daunted by the prevailing blackness, the narrowness and height of the houses, jammed together like stalagmites; the reckless steepness and breakneck angles of the passageways, and the savagery of the climate. And, after all, this was autumn! How much worse could it become when true winter closed in? New York seemed a temperate, civilised, sybaritic place in comparison. Moreover, how did people ever learn to find their way about this mazelike wilderness?

Coming at last into Appin Court—a murky, cobbled rectangle about the size of a kitchen table, with black walls rising to seven-storey height on all sides—she stopped a moment to shake the snow off her muff and cap, then plunged into the entrance of number seventeen. A black unlit stone stair confronted her; she began to climb. Each landing was faintly illuminated by a grimy window, but since there were no numbers or names on the doors, and few people seemed to be behind them, or prepared to respond to knocks, Val soon began to wonder how she was ever going to achieve her objective. After fifteen steep flights, however, she found an open door and a sign that said *Selkirk's Magazine,* Editorial Offices. Inside the door lay a small dusty gaslit cubbyhole containing a table littered with papers and a dour-looking elderly clerk who asked her name and business.

When she had recovered her breath she said that she would be glad of a word with Sir Marcus Cusack. Hearing this the clerk informed her with evident satisfaction, "I doubt Sir Marcus'll no be in, the day. He sent word by his man that he was terrible bad wi' the gout."

"Oh dear." Val was acutely disappointed. Up to this moment she had hardly realised to what an extent she had depended on finding Sir Marcus again. London had been bleak, Edinburgh was bleaker. She was much in need of somebody with whom she could have a friendly human exchange. And, in retrospect, Sir Marcus's long cantankerous silences on the boat had diminished in importance, while his kind offer of help on the dockside stood out even more clearly.

"Ye can leave a card, if ye wish," said the clerk in a grudging tone. "Or call again, next week."

"Unfortunately I am leaving Edinburgh tomorrow."

"Aweel, there's no help for it then," said the clerk triumphantly, and returned to his previous task of opening envelopes and extracting manuscripts from them.

Dejected, and with aching legs, Val made her way back down the stone stair. It was at least a relief that Pieter and Jannie had not accompanied her here; she spared a wry grin at the idea of hoisting Jannie up the interminable flights. She had taken them out on a shopping excursion earlier in the day to buy more articles of winter wear which their great-aunts apparently thought indispensable for life at Ardnacarrig. A telegram to this effect had been dispatched to Robina Gourlay from Grosvenor Square before the ladies departed on their Mediterranean trip. The telegram contained explicit instructions about garments and the stores from which they were to be obtained—the Carsphairn sisters, it seemed, had holdings in all Edinburgh's main emporiums. Val was amused—but also irritated—by this almost military organisation of the children's affairs. It was a relief that she herself would not be exposed to much more of it; she would soon begin to find it exasperating. However she went out cheerfully enough with the children to buy the mackintoshes, broadcloth spencers, plaid alpaca dresses and trousers, and rough, warm, kerseymere garments for country wear. She also, on her own initiative, added a few more books for Pieter; if the ladies wished to scrutinise the bills when they reached Nice or Istanbul, and complain, let them do so then!

After the shopping was completed, as it snowed harder and harder, and Jannie's unreliable bladder had once again betrayed her, Val took the children back to Regent Terrace and deposited them thankfully in the care of the soft-spoken, cushionlike Robina. It was, in a way, a pity that they were not to stay here, she thought, setting off again joyously at her normal swift pace; Robina seemed prepared to lavish infinite affection on the pair. But Robina had her boarding house to run; and country air would certainly be better for the children than Edinburgh's murky reeks. Anyway, the coach was bespoken tomorrow to carry them on the last stage of their journey to Ardnacarrig.

Val herself had not intended to accompany them in the coach, but, finding that no other arrangement had been made, she perforce agreed to go along. It seemed too barbarous to despatch them on a nine- or ten-hour drive with no company but that of the unknown driver; Pieter's face of total dismay at this prospect had finally persuaded her.

Meantime, she wanted to locate a doctor, and here again Sir Marcus's absence from his office was a decided blow, since she had hoped for his expert advice; such a valetudinarian must, she thought, have all the latest information about Edinburgh medical men. Robina had proved useless in this respect; kind, vague, good-natured, and totally without intelligence, she had merely remarked in her dulcet coo, "Eh, noo, I can see little amiss wi' the wee lassie, she seems bonnie enow! Ne'er fash the doctor for a sackless errant, my dearie. Forbye, my auld Doctor McTavish is deid, a month syne, an I havenae tried oot the capabeelities of ony ither; an ill doctor's waur nor the ewking crewels!"

With which clinching brace of proverbs she had washed her hands of the matter.

How did one set about finding a doctor in Edinburgh? The town must be full of them. Nils had begun his medical training here, after all, before throwing it over to marry money. If only he or Kirstie were at hand, Val thought, not for the first time, how much easier matters would be! What could make two apparently ordinary people, devoted parents, responsible citizens, abruptly abandon their normal habits and desert their children?

Reaching the foot of the stairway, she paused a moment to refasten her collar and burrow her hands deep in her muff before venturing out again into Appin Court, where a kind of miniature snow whirlwind seemed to have worked up a violent momentum.

And then, to her surprise and delight, she heard voices outside—three voices, two of them familiar.

"Are you sure you can manage, Sir Marcus?"

"Would ye no' like an arm up, sir? Ye'll mind the stairs are unco' slippery—"

"No, no, thank you both, I can manage capitally. But come back for me at five, sharp, will you Andie?"

"Och, ay, Sir Marcus—"

Hearing these words, Val almost ran out of the doorway and came face to face with her companion of the voyage. She would hardly have known him, except by his height and bearing, for he was wrapped to the ears in ulster, muffler, and deerstalker cap. He had, apparently, just hoisted himself out of an elaborate wickerwork wheelchair, and was still being regarded with anxiety by his two attendants, as he balanced himself on a pair of sticks.

For a daunting moment, Val thought that he was not going to recognise her. He stood propped on his sticks, with what could be seen of his pale bony face above the muffler drawn into an expression of martyred politeness, as he waited in patience for her to move out of his path. And then, all of a sudden, the politeness broke up like a plaster mask, wrinkles rayed out from the brown eyes, and his features were illuminated by a smile of wholly unexpected charm and humour.

"Why, God bless me! It's Miss Montgomery! My dear child! What a totally unlooked-for pleasure!"

Absurdly she felt tears spring to her eyes as she smiled up at him. His arrival and welcome had transformed the dismal and unprofitable afternoon into a happy and successful one.

"Sir Marcus, I'm so glad I caught you! I was just going away disappointed."

"John-Jo! Andie!" Sir Marcus called. "Come back this minute!"

"What's your will, Sir Marcus?"

The attendants returned.

"Just run up the stairs, John-Jo—you'll be a deal faster than I should—and ask Mr. Hoseason to step down here a moment. Tell him to bring the English mail with him if it has come."

Val could not help being pleased that the unhelpful clerk would now see that she had, after all, met Sir Marcus. An extra trip down the stairs would do him no harm at all.

In a few minutes Hoseason appeared behind the red-headed John-Jo.

"Losh, Sir Marcus, ye didnae ought to have come awa oot while yer gout is at ye."

Sir Marcus was wearing carpet slippers, in spite of the snow.

"Tuts, man, I was doing no good at home. I might as well be in the office, seeing what's there. Has the English article not come?"

"Not yet, Sir Marcus," said Hoseason, who carried nothing with him.

"It had better come tomorrow, or I sever that connection. Aweel, Hoseason, I'll not keep you further then. I met Miss Montgomery at the stairfoot, and I am going to take her to dine."

Val opened her mouth to demur, but Sir Marcus anticipated her with an upraised hand, precariously waving his cane. "Doubtless you consider four o'clock an outlandish hour to dine, Miss Montgomery, but you must remember that we provincials keep rustic hours. At all events I'll engage to return you to your lodging safe and early."

"It wasn't that which worried me, Sir Marcus. I was only wondering if you should not be home with a basin of gruel."

"Ay, he should," said John-Jo. "But try telling himself that!"

"Do you want to drive me to an early grave?" demanded his master, climbing back into the bath chair. "Take me back to the brougham; let Miss Montgomery lead the way."

The procession wound back up the wynd to Cockburn Street, where Val and Sir Marcus were packed into the brougham and the chair was somehow fastened on at the rear. "Now drive us to the Charlotte Hotel, Andie. Its private rooms are impeccably correct," Sir Marcus told Val. "A young lady like yourself who is not afraid of crossing the Atlantic unescorted need not scruple to dine alone there with a respectable man who is old enough to be her father."

"I don't scruple at all, Sir Marcus," Val assured him. "But I can hardly accept that you are old enough to be my father—unless you begat me at a most precociously early age."

"Huts! Ye'll allow me to be acquainted with my own age, my dear lady, and we'll leave it at that! And now, tell me what you are doing in Edinburgh? I understood that you were to make a stay of some months with your relatives in London? Did they not make you welcome?"

"Well, no—it wasn't that. It's all a mystery," Val explained. "My relatives seem to have disappeared. It's a long tale, though."

"I prefer long tales. But let us keep it until we are settled at the Charlotte."

The Charlotte, as Val remembered from her earlier visit, *was* an eminently respectable hotel, and it was also plain that Sir Marcus was well known there as a person of some status in the town. They were swiftly established in a pleasant room with a fire, and a messenger was despatched to Robina Gourlay with the news that Val was dining out, but would not be late. Meanwhile no less than three waiters bustled about, laying the cloth and asking Sir Marcus's wishes.

While the waiters were in the room, Sir Marcus chatted easily and amusingly, keeping the talk to general subjects, art, literature, and public affairs. He seemed a different person from her morose companion of the voyage. Val discovered that, as she had imagined, he was both well-informed and highly intelligent. Their long, mutual silences on the boat seemed to have established them, now they met again, on the basis of old friendship; they were comfortable and relaxed together, able to tease, criticise, contradict, and argue with the utmost ferocity. How very odd this was, Val reflected, when they had next to no information as to one another's private lives. I don't even know if he is married, she thought, helping herself to another woodcock, though surely, at his age, he would be? But if so, where is his wife?

"More claret, Miss Montgomery?"

"Thank you, just a little. It is very good. But ought you to drink it, Sir Marcus, with your gout?"

"Tush!" he said. "My gout was caused, not by my own potations, but by those of my ancestors. I have no intention of mortifying myself because of their intemperate habits."

The talk rambled to travel and Val confessed her longing to visit the Near and Middle East. She was all agog at learning that Sir Marcus had made several journeys to Samarkand, Baku, Teheran, and Baghdad.

"Oh, how I envy you!" she exclaimed.

He had also, she learned, written books about his travels.

"Under what name, Sir Marcus? I have read all that I can lay my hands on about that part of the world."

"Och, I have no taste for self-advertisement. My books have come out under the pseudonym 'Viator.'"

"But I've read them!" She was delighted. "I read *The Sands of Arabia*, and also *A Voyage on the Black Sea*—it was reading those volumes that filled me with such a wish to see the places."

She questioned him eagerly about his various trips. Hearing his accounts of month-long voyages in caiques, weeks on mule or camel back, perilous ascents of craggy untrodden mountain ranges, thirst-racked passage over barren deserts, she could not help a certain amusement at the odd disparity between the man and his achievements. It seemed hardly possible to imagine this frail pernickety invalidish person—who subjected each dish, as it came, to a lengthy, suspicious scrutiny and interrogated the waiter as to its wholesomeness and antecedents—riding on a camel across the Turanian Plain, dining with sheikhs on couscous or sheep eyes. And when she thought of his total misery on board ship—why, what a mixture of improbabilities the man was!

"Your gout didn't trouble you in the desert?" she could not resist asking.

"All the time!" he said in a reproving manner. "On innumerable occasions the pain has been acute. But of course one cannot let oneself be deterred by such considerations!"

"At least your attention must have been distracted by the scenery?" she suggested demurely. But he would not permit this.

"On the contrary! I am such a wretched invalid that sometimes even the most magnificent prospect is not sufficient to divert my mind from my sufferings. When I recall the quinsy that attacked me on Mount Elbruz—"

"Shall you be returning there, do you think?" she inquired wistfully.

"Most certainly I shall. Next summer if I am spared so long. Meanwhile I am occupied in making ready the winter and spring issues of *Selkirk's*; and in putting together a volume of my verse."

Val had greatly admired the occasional verses which were scattered here and there through the travel books and said so. He was visibly pleased, and she felt their friendship had advanced another notch.

"And now, Miss Montgomery," he said, when the coffee had been brought in, and the waiters had withdrawn, "do please tell me about the untoward events in your life which have caused this—for me so delightful —change in your plans."

"Oh, Sir Marcus, I shall be glad to. It is all so inexplicable!" And, without further delay, she told him the whole story, beginning with Nils' visit to New York.

At one point during the account, when she was explaining about Nils' arrangements with the *Knuckle*, Sir Marcus stopped her for a moment with uplifted hand, to inquire, "I beg your pardon, my dear, but what, did you say, is your brother's name?"

"Hansen."

"Nils Hansen?"

"Yes."

"Ah. Pray proceed."

At the end of her tale he said, "A coincidence—but no more of one, really, than the kind which attracts two filings of similar metal to a magnet: the article from London which I was hoping my clerk would have ready for me today was a piece of reporting promised by your brother. He is a very able journalist."

"Oh—you know him?" she exclaimed.

"I have only met him once, briefly. But I have read his work in the *Morning Post*. And I understand him to be a highly reliable correspondent. That is why I was so surprised that his article was late; he has a reputation for punctuality in professional matters."

"What do you think can be the explanation for it all, Sir Marcus?"

He reflected.

"I fancy that the young man who spoke to you—Lord Orville—was probably correct in his guess. Your brother may have thought it best to disappear for a while—perhaps he has fallen foul of some highly placed and powerful individual about whom he has written in—unflattering—terms."

"But—leaving his children? *He* might do that, but it seems so unlike my sister-in-law."

"You say she is a niece of Louisa Carsphairn? She may have been relying on her aunt to take charge of the bairns."

Val thought this unlikely. "Then wouldn't she have left them with her aunts in the first place? Or at least written to them, or left word for me?"

"It seems," said Sir Marcus, "that the pair must have been obliged to leave at very short notice. Perhaps a letter went astray."

"And then," pursued Val, "what part do you suppose is played in all this by Lord Clanreydon?"

"Ah," he pondered, "yes, that is an interesting problem."

"Do you know him? Lord Clanreydon?"

"I have met him once or twice. Clever—very clever," Sir Marcus said fastidiously. "His origins, I understand, are veiled in obscurity—the colonies, I believe—and yet he has soared right to the top, both in politics and in polite circles. I understand that a substantial Whig following are canvassing him as the next prime minister."

"Do you *like* him?"

"I must confess—no. In fact," said Sir Marcus roundly, "I detest the fellow. I find something—I can only use the Scottish word *unchancy*—about him."

"Oh yes! Sinister!"

"And yet it is hard to define precisely what is wrong."

"What do you think I ought to do next?" Val asked, after a pause.

"I do not see that there is anything more you can do, my dear child, other than what you have already done. You have—very properly and commendably—arranged for the children to be cared for in more suitable conditions. With that, your responsibility ends. You say that you and your brother have always gone your separate ways—he has done nothing for you at any time; you are under no obligation to hunt him out, since he did not choose to make contact with you. And, in fact, your hunting or raising a hue and cry may be directly contrary to his interests, if he wishes to remain hidden."

An immense relief flooded through Val at hearing Sir Marcus say this, since it coincided with her own feelings. Presently she asked, "What was the article he was supposed to write for *Selkirk's Magazine?*"

"It was to have been a piece of reporting about the London murders—about the Bermondsey Beast."

"Do you think it possible," suggested Val, after pondering this information, "that, in the course of his investigations on this subject, Nils might have discovered something—something which has led to his disappearance?"

"I do not want to say yes—but it *is* possible," Sir Marcus replied. "The murders, as you know, have been a series of most revolting and atrocious crimes; mad, sadistic injuries have been inflicted on six women of a certain type—streetwalkers, not to mince matters—who were also strangled. All manner of wild rumours have been flying around about the affair: that the assassin must be a trained medical man—because of the expert nature of the injuries; that he is a person from the very highest circles of society—from bits of gossip the streetgirls themselves have let fall; that he must be a man of high intelligence and ability—in order to have escaped from the scene with such speed, as he always does, and to have committed so many identical crimes without being apprehended; that he might even be a member of Her Majesty's government—since the region in which the crimes have been committed is not so far, as the crow flies, from

Whitehall. Some theories even have it that there are two assassins working together, because on one night two murders were committed three miles apart yet within such a short space of time that it hardly seemed possible one man could have perpetrated them both. Gossip has not spared the highest in the land—even the Prince of Wales and Mr. Gladstone have been mentioned in this context, the latter because of his rash, if benevolent, propensity for attempting to reason with women of this type and bring them to a consciousness of wrongdoing. If your brother did indeed possess new evidence relating to the Bermondsey Beast, Miss Montgomery—he was certainly in possession of extremely dangerous material."

"Oh my gracious," said Val. Even to her ears it seemed a singularly inept remark.

Sir Marcus looked at her thoughtfully.

"You are very worried about your brother?"

She tried to answer honestly.

"I'm puzzled. I'm concerned. And I'm very worried about the children. Not to mention their mother, poor little thing. Where can *she* be?"

"I will put the question in a different way. Are you very fond of your brother?"

She felt something move inside her—it seemed like piled-up emotions from all the way back to her childhood. The claret that she had drunk, the warm, relaxed atmosphere, the unwonted freedom and expansiveness of their evening together all combined to give force to her answer.

"*Fond* of him? I hate him! I *hate* him! I always have!"

There was a pause, after she had spoken.

Feeling bitterly ashamed, yet immensely relieved to have got it out honestly, she sat twisting her coffee cup in its saucer.

At last Sir Marcus remarked in a meditative tone, "I did feel that there was something rather singular, you know? Here are two people vanished clean away and yet, although you took the proper steps, and indeed acted most creditably, you appeared, in a way, so matter-of-fact about it all, so calm and unconcerned. And yet it seemed plain, also, that you are a warmhearted person."

"I have always, always hated him," said Val again. "He treated me with miserable cruelty as far back as I can remember—all the time that we lived together. He was constantly tormenting me, quietly persecuting me, punishing me for faults that *he* invented, for breaking rules that *he* made. I can still hear his sneering voice, 'You've been bad again! Now I'm going to punish you.' When he went off to England with my mother, it was as if the clouds had rolled away and the sun had come out. My only fear was that he should ever come back."

Tears gathered in her eyes. She put both hands over her face.

"I felt so wicked for hating him. And when I saw him with my father, later on—in London, in Scotland, and when he came to New York this time—I tried to like him. He was so high-spirited, cheerful, friendly—I ought to have been able to like him. But I couldn't."

"It was courageous of you to make that admission," said Sir Marcus.

She wiped her eyes, blew her nose, and looked at him resolutely.

"No. I must apologise for boring on about my own affairs. It was very ill-bred and inconsiderate."

"Don't spoil it now! Pray don't distress yourself. You have been in a lonely and anxious situation, after all. What are you going to do next?"

"Well—first take the children to Ardnacarrig. There at least they'll be in good hands."

"I wouldn't just be so certain of that," said Sir Marcus cautiously.

Her heart sank.

"What do you mean?" Then she asked, "Have you been there? Do you know Kirstie's aunts?"

"Och, yes. Any time these twenty years. I own a little property between Wolf's Hope and Ravenswood, not far away, so in some sort we are neighbours. And of course Louisa and I have interests in common; we have met in Constantinople."

"You know Kirstie too?"

"I met her once or twice before she married—a fair little frightened thing, lacking sense."

"What might be unsuitable for the children at Ardnacarrig?" Val wanted to know.

"I ask myself whether you will think old Elspie a proper person with whom to leave the bairns."

"I thought she was Kirstie's old nurse!"

"Ay, she is that. But she is more. It's a complicated relationship. And I fear she may have become somewhat wayward—captious—in her old age. She has had much to try her. However I don't wish to prejudice you in advance. I hope she will take kindly to the children. Perhaps all will be well."

"What can I do if it isn't?" Val murmured, more to herself than to him.

"Why, bring them back to Edinburgh, I suppose. But Ardnacarrig is very beautiful—it is a fine place for children. Much more healthy than this dank old city."

"Sir Marcus," said Val, "forgive me for troubling you further, but that reminds me of something else I wanted to ask you. Can you recommend a good—a *really* good—doctor? I'm anxious about the little girl. I know nothing about children, but I'm sure all is not well with her. She seems some-how backward—deficient in responses."

"Humph." He pondered. "If you were staying on in town there's half a dozen I could recommend. With my own wretched health, I'm always running to one practitioner or another. But, as you say you're off in the morning to Ardnacarrig—"

"Yes?"

"Why—I can't do better than recommend my own godson, David Ramsay. He's a bright young spark of a doctor who had hardly but just started up his practice here, and was doing well enough, poor lad, when his mother took sick of the consumption. So he's e'en gone back to Wolf's Hope to be with her till the end; it won't be so long now, I fear."

"Poor boy," said Val compassionately.

Sir Marcus fell silent. She noticed a sad, withdrawn expression on his face, and forbore to disturb him. They sank into one of their old silences. But presently he roused himself, wrote an address, and gave it to her.

"There. Wolf's Hope is only a couple of hours' ride from Ardnacarrig. I'll write, myself, to Davie and ask him to call on you and examine the child."

"You are very good! I wish I could make some return for your kindness."

"Why," he said, "you can."

"Then I will, very gladly. What can I do?"

"While you are at Ardnacarrig—I expect you will be staying a few days to see the bairns settled?" She nodded. "Do you think you might find time to go and visit Davie's mother—Helen Ramsay—at Wolf's Hope? Could you do that? And give her my remembrances?"

"Of course I will," Val said. "But if she is as ill as you say—will she want to see a stranger?"

"When you know the Scottish countryside a little better you'll under-stand that one would have to be dead, not merely dying, not to enjoy a visitor from distant parts. Particularly my dear Helen!"

"Then I'll go. And I'll tell you about her when I come back to Edin-burgh."

"That will give me something to look forward to." He added in a different tone, "I would really be most grateful."

Val rose to leave.

"The gratitude is all on my side, Sir Marcus. It has been a great pleas-ure to dine with you," she said with a return to formality. "I have enjoyed this evening more than anything since I came to England."

His death's head face broke up again into its disarming smile, and he

said something, half to himself, which was to puzzle and disconcert Val for weeks to come. Could she have caught it correctly? She thought he said, "Ah, we'll make a human being of her yet!"

"And now, Andie will drive you back to Mrs. Gourlay's."

"Good night, Sir Marcus. Thank you again."

As she went down the steps, he called after her, *"Not* my remembrances. My love."

CHAPTER 10

THEY were up and away long before daylight, since Ardnacarrig lay over fifty miles from Edinburgh, and the journey, in a heavily loaded coach, would take them at least a day; possibly
longer, if it snowed and they were obliged to spend the night in Dunglass
or some other town along the way. The coach, a massive old family conveyance, seemed to be serving as carrier for all the surrounding neighbourhood, so far as Val could make out, for besides the children and herself and their belongings, its interior was crammed with stores purchased
in Edinburgh: bales of rough cloth, barrels of oil, portions of agricultural
machinery, mutton hams wrapped in cotton, wooden chests of tea, a huge
sack of salt, bales of sacking, bundles of wax candles, and packets of seed.

"There's hardly room for us," Pieter said, looking wonderingly round
the inside; and Val thought that if the horses could do fifty miles a day
pulling that load, they must be remarkable animals. However they certainly looked solid and big-boned enough. The driver, Jock Kelso, was a
taciturn, grey-headed, lean man with a bad limp, who saw to the loading
up with dour, silent efficiency, and said merely, "Ou, ay," when Robina
screeched instructions at him. "Tak' care o' the leddy an' the bairnies,
now, Jockie man! Remember they're frae the south an' they'll be grewie,

shilpit bodies; gin the snaw comes, pit up the avers and find a beild in some tavern; dinna gae yer ways i' the mirk; an' bide a wee while in some clachan for bite an' sup—I hae pit ye up a pickle victuals i' the buist—"

"Whisht, whisht, ye fashious wumman," grunted Kelso, wrapping himself in a whole series of greatcoats and plaids; he then climbed to the box without taking any more notice of Robina, or of his passengers, and cracked his whip. Ignoring this, Robina jumped up into the carriage to embrace the children once more and supply them each with a hot brick to keep their feet from freezing; then they were off.

For the first part of the journey they were all glad enough to go back to sleep, wedged in among the bales and bundles, while the coach rumbled on its way.

When dawn finally broke, and the children began to stir and rub their eyes, they had traveled a considerable distance and left Edinburgh well behind them. They were now passing through flattish country, with, on their left, occasional views of the sea behind hillocky dunes, and rolling grassy hills over to their right. This seemed to be rich farmland, with tidy hedges and prosperous-looking villages set round greens, large fields with sheep and cattle in them, plantations of trees, and dovecots in front of the big, old-fashioned farmhouses. Yesterday's snow had melted, save on the distant hilltops, and the day was clear and sunny but bitterly cold; a keen, searching wind seemed to find its way through every cranny in the ancient vehicle, and Val longed to get out and walk. But the ponderous horses maintained a trot at a pace that was just faster than the children could have managed. They did walk ahead as far and fast as they could whenever Jock stopped to breathe the horses, and in that way managed to keep from freezing. The wind came scouring at them from the sea, and the few leaves that remained on the bent, twisted, gale-worn trees were all tarnished to a curious dead-gold colour by the salt in the air.

By midday great cliffs, rising on the left, had cut off their distant view of breakers rolling in, and the road turned inland. Val had learned from Robina, though, that Ardnacarrig lay close to the sea, in its own bay, and she was glad of this for the children's sake, remembering halcyon holidays spent with her father on Long Island beaches. So at some point along their route the road must find its way back to the coast.

This coach journey was just as exhausting as the train trip had been, and Jannie was sick almost as often. But this time, at least, they could open the little front window and beg Jock to stop, at which he would grumblingly pull up, protesting that at yon gait they'd be a week on the way. Val was able to bathe Jannie's face in little icy rushing roadside brooks and make her take deep gulps of the piercing air. Pieter wanted to eat his dinner sitting by one of the streams, but the wind was too cold. They drank some of the ice-cold water in the horn cups that Robina had provided, and then jumped back into the coach to eat her oat bannocks, cheese, hard-boiled eggs wrapped in ham and breadcrumbs, and delicious biscuits which Jock, thawing a little under the influence of food, said were Tantallon cakes. He also informed them that they were now crossing the Lammermuir hills and that they had better hurry up with their eating, for there was still twenty miles to go, and soon they must leave the turnpike road and take one that was by no means so good.

"Worse than *this?*" said Val, who had suffered the ruts and potholes as philosophically as she could, but already felt bruised in every joint.

"A muckle deal waur," said Jock with gloomy satisfaction.

"And if it snows? What do we do then?" she asked, for clouds were piling up to the north.

"Gin it snaws, we must e'en sprattle on, for there's nae mair clachans twixt here an' Ardnacarrig—naught but moor and taw, rig and brae." Jock made it sound unutterably barren and dreary. "Gif it hadna been for a' this havering an' ganthering we'd be there the noo," he went on accusingly.

"Oh, well, in that case let us get going as quickly as possible."

The children were reluctant to get going. By now both were tired, after their early start; Jannie was peevish and lachrymose, while even the equable Pieter developed a whining note in his voice and asked with exasperating frequency how long it would be before they arrived.

"Oh, how can I tell?" snapped Val, and then felt ashamed of herself; she was an adult, after all, equipped with mental resources to enable her to bear discomfort and unhappiness; whereas they, poor things, with no such advantages, had mislaid their parents and lost their home, and had not the least control over what would happen to them next. Unfortunately, though, their orphaned and helpless state could not render them any more lovable in Val's eyes; she felt extremely sorry for them, but by now she was heartily sick of their company and the responsibility it incurred; she longed to be free of them.

"Aunt Valla," said Pieter presently in a small subdued voice.

"Well?"

"When shall we be going home? To our *own* home, I mean, in London, where we have all our things?" he said with quivering lip.

That one got under Val's defences. She thought of the dusty litter of straw in front of the house in Welbeck Street, the men carrying out the last of Kirstie's furniture. Really uncertain how to answer, she looked at the little pale fair-haired boy in his rough blue kerseymere coat, and he looked back at her pleadingly.

"Want Mama!" wailed Jannie, who, like a miner's canary, was always lightning-quick to pick up any hint of trouble in the atmosphere.

Val held a vague belief that the truth should be told to children at all times—but now she was faced with the question: how *much* truth can children endure? More particularly at times when they are tired, apprehensive, and under strain?

"Pieter, I don't know," she prevaricated. "Quite soon, I hope. When your father and mother come back from wherever—when they come back. But in the meantime I'm sure you'll enjoy Ardnacarrig. It's right by the sea, you know. You can play on the beach and—and sail boats and find shells. And old Elspie will look after you—I expect she'll be kind, like Robina. She looked after your mother when *she* was little."

From out of his dusky corner she could feel Pieter's eyes on her, studying her sceptically.

"Aunt Valla?"

"Yes, Pieter?"

"Where *are* Papa and Mama? Why don't they come back?"

"I don't know where they are, Pieter," she said again, helplessly. "Wasn't it careless of them to go off without leaving us their address? I expect each of them thought the other had done it. Probably your father had some writing business that he had to do in a hurry—perhaps somebody invited him to a big house a long way off, and so he had to leave, all in a rush, and he took your mother with him—"

It all sounded so plausible that she was almost believing it herself, but Pieter said flatly, "No. It didn't happen like that."

Val was stopped in her tracks. She said with caution, "How do you mean, Pieter?"

"Mama went off first, before Papa came back from America."

"She *did*?"

"Yes. I wasn't there. I was out with Mercy, getting cakes for our tea, and a man came to take Mama on a ship. When we got back, she was gone!"

"On a *ship*? Are you sure?"

"Yes," he said.

"But how do you know that? If she was gone when you got back? Did she leave a note? A message?"

"No, she didn't. She told Jannie, and Jannie told me."

"*Jannie* was there when the man came for your mother?"

"Yes, and he said Mama was to come with him on a ship," Pieter repeated.

Val studied the pair in helpless perplexity. Could she possibly believe this tale? Jannie did communicate with Pieter, she knew, but her statements and requests were mostly simple ones, concerned with her bodily needs, which her brother interpreted partly through familiarity with her sounds and gestures, partly, Val thought, from a kind of intuition. But could Jannie have framed a complicated report like that? On the other hand, Pieter could not have invented it, for he was a fundamentally truthful child and also, Val thought, somewhat unimaginative.

"Jannie?" she said gently. "Did a man really come and ask your Mama to come with him on a ship?"

But Jannie, as so often, took no notice at all; her eyes were blank, fixed on some distance that she alone could see; she was half curled up, leaning against her brother, and sucked her finger, meanwhile vigorously rubbing the thumb of the same hand against her woollen collar. The collars of all her clothes became damp and matted after each day's wear.

Val turned her attention back to Pieter.

"Well then—if your mother went off—"

"With a man, on a ship," he repeated.

"When your father came home, what did *he* do?"

Could Kirstie have *eloped*? Sailed off to Italy with some romantic lover? That sounded too improbable; too out of keeping with the quiet domestic girl who hated big parties, who had a fiercely protective love for her children and would never leave them with a stranger. But marriage to Nils must be a desperate affair—perhaps she had finally rebelled against the financial ups and downs, the contrasts of poverty at home and high society abroad, the dubious shifts and stratagems that Nils probably employed in order to keep them afloat. By the time all Kirstie's own money had been spent she must have been thoroughly disillusioned with her husband.

Just the same, Val could not believe that she would abandon her children.

Why not take them too?

But perhaps she had meant to send for them, and Nils had prevented it?

"When Papa came home, Mama sent him a letter. And a present."

A present?

"What kind of present?"

Pieter shook his head. "I don't know. It was in a box. About *so* big." He sketched a shoebox size. "Then Papa was dreadfully angry." He stopped, searching his vocabulary, which had supplied the wrong word. "Upset," he substituted. "There was a man there that day when it came."

"The same man who had gone with your Mama?"

"No. This one was called a bailiff. What's that, Aunt Valla?"

"I'm not quite sure, Pieter. A sheriff's officer, maybe?"

But Pieter did not know what that was.

"Well, then, Papa packed up our clothes, after that, and took us to the woman's house."

"Mrs. Pipkin."

"Yes. And then *you* came." He paused, and then said with hardly veiled anxiety, "Will you stay with us now till Mama and Papa come to fetch us?"

Val swallowed. She could not tell a flat lie. She said, "We'll see, Pieter. You see, we don't know how long that will be. And I have to earn my living." But the look of desperate anxiety on Pieter's face made her feel horribly guilty.

Jannie had become restless again and was flinging her small firm body from side to side, keening to herself on a high note like a seagull.

"Stop that noise, *please*, Jannie."

Jannie took no notice.

"Ask her to stop, Pieter. Shall I tell you a story?"

"Couldn't we read those books?" He looked longingly toward the bag with the books in it.

"The carriage joggles too much. You'd be sick, like Jannie."

The worsening of the road predicted by Jock had been no exaggeration; their progress had slowed down to a crawl; even so, the carriage lurched sickeningly from side to side at every turn of the wheels.

"Sing a song!" Pieter suggested. "Jannie likes that too."

Val racked her brain. What could she recall from her own childhood? Her mother had never sung to her, but Tabitha had—and her father used to come up to her room at night and sing her to sleep sometimes . . . "One more, just one more song, please, Papa!"

Slowly they came back: "Turkey in the Straw," "Yankee Doodle," "Comin' Round the Mountain," "Marching Through Georgia," "Come into the Garden, Mrs. Bond." She hummed, then sang; Pieter joined in when he recognised the song. And when they were singing Mrs. Bond, Val was amazed to notice that Jannie had apparently made some kind of contact with what they were doing, and was singing dilly-dilly-dilly to herself in a high, queer little voice, but on the right notes. It was the first intimation that she could be reached by any outside activity.

Val prolonged the singing as long as she could; then, when she ran out of songs, recited all the poems she could remember.

Meanwhile, outside, interminable heathland went past, purple-grey, brown, at last dusky, hardly visible; the road was now so rough that she hoped Jock knew what he was about and had not accidentally turned from the track and struck off across the moor. But presumably he was now in his home territory? Surely they must arrive within the next hour?

"That's nice, say it again," said Pieter sleepily.

> I know more than Apollo
> For oft, while he lies sleeping
> I hear the stars
> At mortal wars
> In the wounded welkin weeping—

"Wounded welkin weeping," he repeated, in an echo of the voice she used for recitation, and then, to Val's utter astonishment, Jannie too dreamily murmured to herself, "Ooning 'elkin 'eeping" before finally and definitively falling asleep, her head propped on her brother's chest. His own drooped over her and they lay curled together, breathing deeply and softly. Val stretched out her legs with caution and lay back, utterly exhausted, luxuriating in the silence and mental solitude. Please heaven let them sleep on till we arrive.

Her mind went back to Pieter's tale. Where *could* Kirstie have gone? Aboard Lord Clanreydon's yacht? No, that was a silly notion—obviously if she had, Lord Clanreydon would have known about it. Well then—where? Where did people go on ships? Could she have sailed round the coast to Ardnacarrig? Would they find her waiting there? It was tempting to hope so, but presumably someone would know about it—Jock, Robina Gourlay—if that had been the case?

Another very strange anomaly from Pieter's tale struck her: Pieter had said that Mercy was their only servant when the home was broken up. And he had been out with Mercy buying cakes when the "man from the ship" came and Kirstie went off. But in that case she must have gone off *leaving Jannie alone in the house?* Would Kirstie do a thing like that?

Perhaps I've got it all wrong about Kirstie, Val thought tiredly. Perhaps she had a secret life unknown to Nils. Or perhaps there *was* somebody else in the house; why do I wear out my wits trying to solve such a remote problem? Why don't I use a bit more energy on my own problems?

Her own problems, at the present time, seemed even more remote; remote as the Antipodes. In her mind's eye she recreated the pages of the letter that she had written last night to Benet from Robina's house and had posted early this morning.

"Dear Benet: Since I have been in England I have come to a very hard decision; and I am writing to release you from our engagement . . ."

But how exactly had she come to this decision? She hardly knew herself. Two weeks in New York—almost three on the boat—a week in England, less than that—and already Benet seemed immeasurably far off, completely irrelevant to her life, like some character in a novel that she had read long ago. During her days in London she had hardly given him a thought; her heart had accepted his absence with total equanimity, as if, long since, without her being aware of it, her feeling for him had quietly wound down, closed, and come to an end.

"I don't love Benet," she had discovered with astonishment, sitting on the train, traveling north. "How strange! I don't love him any more. Did I *ever* love him?"

She tried to throw her mind back into the climate of their early days: walking down Fifth Avenue, her arm in his; Benet buying her a bunch of violets; that had been a happy time, a sweet, serene time; their good future together had lain ahead like a sun-filled orderly landscape; she had felt a fondness, a respect for Benet, a happy security in his embrace. And then, unnoticed at the time, but most visible in hindsight, shadows had begun to spread over this landscape. Recurring minor, and then major, clashes of viewpoint stood about in it like withered thorn trees; and the strange thing was, thought Val, looking back, that Benet never even noticed them; he simply assumed that I would adapt my views to his; he never remotely perceived that there could be variations from his standpoint.

She had hardly realised the boundaries, the limitations of the morality within which she had proposed to pass the rest of her life, until she was away from them. But now, separated from this code and able to view it with detachment, Val shuddered at the deadly prospect of boredom and stultification which it represented; at the taboos, the areas defined as "unpleasant" "morbid" "vulgar," the people who were "our kind" and the larger number who were not. "Never talk about money, and think about it as little as possible." "Writers?" she remembered Mrs. Allerton saying. "Rather peculiar people. Of course Scott and Irving were gentlemen; but people like Melville and that Edgar Allan Poe definitely aren't; you couldn't receive them in your home—and as for Harriet Beecher Stowe—!"

Well, I have cut myself off from all that, Val thought, but what have I got instead? What do I do now? Could I live in Edinburgh and earn a living by writing?

In spite of its blackness and grimness and ferocious climate she had found the bleak northern town exhilarating; she liked its wildly jutting landscape and its wild people talking their incomprehensible language. It is a little like New York without the propriety, she thought. Though I suppose, as soon as I came to know it well, I would find that Edinburgh has its own deadly proprieties, its kirk sessions, gossip, and exclusions. As an outsider at the moment I feel free of that. But how long can one live as an outsider, without putting down some kind of roots? Well, I have one contact in Edinburgh, she thought, I have Sir Marcus; I expect that would lead to others, and others of a congenial kind . . .

She was entertaining a pleasing vision of herself as mistress of a salon, holding court among Edinburgh's poets and philosophers, established in some elegant Queen Anne house in Moray Place or India Street, when the carriage gave a particularly violent lurch. Jannie murmured plaintively in her sleep, and a bale of heavy material thudded down on to Val's feet.

"We'll no' be long now," called Jock from the front.

Peering out into the dusk, Val saw that they had dropped down from the high moor and were descending a narrow glen massed with trees that grew thick but not tall—oaks, she thought, mixed with pine or fir, but it was difficult to be sure in the bad light. A thin dusting of snow outlined the contours of the rough track. To their right, not far off, a stream tumbled downwards in a series of waterfalls; the roar was plainly audible and occasionally she caught a flash of white spray through the trees. This will be a wonderful place for the children in springtime, she thought with a shiver; it's too bad they have to see it first at such an adverse season.

Now the ground began to flatten; they had reached the foot of the glen. The road bore round to the right, skirting a stone wall behind which grew evergreens; it was plain that they were close to the grounds of a big house. They crossed a humpbacked stone bridge and passed between a pair of large but dilapidated and ivy-grown gateposts. Then followed a further half mile between the evergreens along a tolerably smooth sandy track and suddenly, making a sharp left turn, Jock drove his horses under a stone arch, and so into what seemed to be a cobbled yard, where he pulled them to a halt.

Jannie whimpered sleepily. Pieter said, "Is this the place, Aunt Valla?"

"I guess so," answered Val. Her heart sank. Not a light seemed to be showing anywhere; but Jock had climbed down from the driver's seat and was now opening the door to let them out. Then without more ado he began unloading the stores from the coach.

"Which is the way in?" said Val, shivering. They had been lucky with the weather, she supposed; their journey had not been hindered by snow; but it was bitterly cold here, even colder than it had been on the journey.

"The door? Why, yonder," Jock said, jerking his head toward a corner of the court. "Nae doubt Mistress Elspie will stir hersel' tae come oot in her ain good time," and he returned to his unloading.

"Come, children," said Val, "each bring a bundle, and let's go in."

They had just crossed the cobbled yard and reached the door when it was flung open and a tall thin woman stood outlined against a dim interior light.

"Is that you, Jockie Kelso?" she called. "What for did ye no' come to the front?"

"And carry a' the stores richt round aboot wi' my lame leg? I'm no sic a fule," Jock called back.

"Good evening," said Val, rather affronted at being ignored. "Are you Elspeth Cross? I am Miss Montgomery, the children's aunt—I hope Lady Stroma wrote you about me; and this is Pieter and this is Jannie."

"Ou, ay she wrote," said Elspie with a marked lack of enthusiasm. "Jock! Mind yerself, wi' yon barrel! Did ye bring the calico? And the cheesecloth? And the pickling salt and the tea? There's barely a pinch left i' the kist."

"Weary on ye, Elspie! Leave your havering and take the yoong leddy and the bairns in ben. Ay I brought the calico and the salt and a' the ither things—ne'er fash yourself."

But Elspie, taking no further notice of Val and the children, hurried over to satisfy herself that all the things ordered had indeed been brought.

Not best pleased at this reception, Val decided to wait no longer in the cold.

"Come along, children," she said. "We might as well go in where it's warm," and she led the way through the door and along a stone-flagged passage, which presently opened into a big kitchen. Here it was warm enough; a new iron kitchen range had been installed in the wide old chimney place, and fire glowed redly between the bars above a massive steel fender. The kitchen, like the passage, was floored with big slabs of blue slate and a huge table, scrubbed to immaculate whiteness, stood in the middle of the room. Against the walls were dressers, laden with crockery and china; hams and flitches and bunches of herbs and bundles of tallow candles hung from the ceiling. Big copper-bound tubs for washing stood upside down on a broad shelf near the door.

Seeing this comfortable orderliness, Val felt cheered.

"Look," she said to the children, "there's two little three-legged stools just right for you by the fire. Sit and warm yourselves."

They did so, looking round wonderingly; it was plain they had never been in such a place.

But at this moment Elspie erupted back into the room in a towering rage.

"The deil's in it wi' the weans!" she cried furiously at Val. "What gar'd ye let them tear the salt bag, an' half the salt rinning oot abune the stanes —and salt the terrible price it is—"

She snatched up a brush and pan and was gone again.

Val groaned inwardly. She guessed at once who the culprit was. Jannie, in between spells of openly frenetic activity, had also a truly demonic propensity for wreaking havoc while apparently sitting quietly unoccupied, vacant, and dreamy. This had already been discovered at Lady Stroma's house where, while no one was paying attention to her, she had cut about a hundred finger-sized holes with her great-aunt's embroidering scissors in a pair of brocade curtains that were waiting to be darned; and at Robina Gourlay's house, where she had spent a quiet and blissful hour mixing oatmeal and raisins in a pailful of soot, the chimney just having been swept. Jannie's tiny fingers seemed as strong as skeleton keys and her capacity for making unlikely and disastrous juxtapositions was unbounded. Val could have sworn that she had kept Jannie under close supervision during the whole journey; but there must have been a time when she was sleeping, at the start, when the child had woken and managed to prise her way through the tough sacking of the salt bag. No wonder she was so thirsty all day, Val thought, with a chuckle, as she walked out, to make amends by helping Elspie clear up.

Her assistance was received ungraciously, but she managed to make herself useful carrying the more portable of the stores into the house, and although Jock protested that it was "nae job for a young leddy" the work went on so much faster with her participation that in five minutes all the bundles were out of the carriage.

"Aweel, I'll have the cattle sorted and say good nicht to ye," said Jock briefly and led the horses off into the darkness.

"Does Jock not live here?" Val asked, reentering the kitchen.

Elspie was inspecting a dustpan full of dirty salt from the courtyard, muttering and shaking her head over it, casting angry looks at the children. She was a handsome woman, Val now had time to see: not the bowed and ancient crone that the title of Kirstie's old nurse had called up, but tall, straight, and active in all her movements, though she must be approaching her seventies. Her hair, which must once have been a bright straw-gold, still kept some of its former colour, now tarnished like the salt-bitten beech leaves, and partly hidden under a black mutch. She wore pattens, a black stuff dress under a striped apron, and a tartan screen pinned across her bosom with a large brooch containing a lock of hair. Her eyes were a blue that was faded but still clear and bright; her features, impressive and strong, might have been carved from oak, and forcibly reminded Val of somebody, some person that she had seen in the recent past—where could it have been? On the ship? In London? A portrait in the Edinburgh art gallery? Elspie's mouth was well-shaped, if puckered; her lips were set in a firm line; the skin of her face was wrinkled and weathered, and a sprinkle of short gold hairs glinted on her jaw, but she must once have possessed a beautiful pink-and-white complexion, and her hands, though roughened with work, were slender and long-fingered. She must have been a beauty when young.

If only she will take a liking to the children, Val thought. But the omens were not good.

"Jock? Nay, he's awa' to the lodge," Elspie said shortly in answer to Val's question, and then she suddenly turned with ferocity on Pieter and Jannie.

"Do ye not know better, ye thrawn, ill-deedy bairns, than to be dabbling your fingers and playing with good victuals, that cost dear, too? Have ye no' been learned better than that, nor chidden for sic ill-doings?" and before Val had realised what she intended, she had dealt each child a stinging box on the ear. Pieter went white with shock, his mouth fell open; Jannie burst into piercing wails.

"Let that be a lesson to ye that I'll no' have yon ways here!" said Elspie.

"How dare you!" exclaimed Val, springing forward furiously, and at the same moment little Pieter, with his eyes blazing in his white face, put both arms protectively round Jannie and shouted, "You mustn't ever, *ever* hit Jannie on the head! Don't you know that? When I tell Mama what you did she'll—she'll be so angry that she'll want to *kill* you!"

"Huts, tuts, what a cafuffle," said Elspie shortly. "I'll keep order in my ain kitchen. If ye need a skelp, a skelp ye'll get. Aiblins, ye'd best be off to your rooms, or I'll ne'er get the dinner on the table."

"Show us where, then," said Val, biting back angry words. She had no wish to prolong the scene, or needlessly antagonise Elspie who, after all, was going to be in sole charge of the children here. But she intended to have it out with her later.

Elspie picked up a lamp and led the way out of a different door from the one by which they had entered. They passed first along a drugget-lined passage, then through a huge cold dining room, with a table that could have seated thirty people, and blackened gold-framed portraits round its dusky walls; then into a large square stone-flagged hall with massive double doors at one end which obviously formed the main entrance. Its walls were wainscoted and adorned with antlers, crossed battle-axes, and pikes, which gleamed rustily in the soft golden light of the lamp.

A wide shallow flight of stairs, beginning opposite the double doors, climbed round three sides of the hall, ending at an almost equally large landing on the floor above. From this, passages led off in all directions. The house was much larger than Val had guessed from her brief view of its rear regions. Elspie led them some way along a passage, then opened two adjacent doors.

"Ye'll be in here, Mistress Montgomery, and the bairns alongside."

The rooms she displayed were both very large and square, with sagging floors. The box beds and old dark wooden presses they contained seemed dwarfed in the dim, freezing space.

The room assigned to Val had windows on two of its sides. In the corner between them, two steps led up to a door.

"Yon's the water closet," Elspie said curtly. "The auld laird had it pit in. Noo I'll leave ye. And I'll be setting the meal on the table directly, so dinna loiter." She set down the lamp she had brought on a chest and went out, finding her way in the dark with the confidence of many years' practice.

"A water closet!" said Val. "Fancy! Aren't we lucky. I didn't think there would be such a thing." She opened the door and discovered that this convenience had been converted from what was plainly a round turret; two arrow slits, unglazed, let in air and made the turret even colder than the bedrooms. The seat and fittings were handsomely made of porcelain and brass, and the whole was boxed in with mahogany. Through the window slits the wind keened dismally. "There you are, Jannie! I daresay you'd better use it at once."

But Jannie was wet, as usual, and shiveringly endured having her clothes changed. Val resolved that she would have fires in the bedrooms if it meant going out and chopping the wood herself; this part of the house felt as if it had not been heated for the past twenty years. An icy damp seemed to eat into one's bones.

"Aunt Valla," said Pieter nervously.

"Yes, Pieter?"

"Is that old woman the one who was Mama's nurse?"

"Yes."

"Is she always as cross as that? Is she as cross as Mrs. Pipkin?"

"I hope not, Pieter. I expect she's just tired and hasty-tempered tonight. I'll tell her that she mustn't hit Jannie. Don't worry."

He looked sceptical about the efficacy of Val's intervention, and said, "It's *us* that are tired; *she* hasn't been traveling all day in the coach."

"No but she's been busy making our beds and getting dinner ready."

"I wonder if she was cross to Mama?"

Jannie, whose reactions were never predictable, seemed taken by the size of the large icy rooms, which had a connecting door. She was dancing, skipping, whirling to and fro between the rooms like a dragonfly, with her long flaxen hair streaming behind her and her plaid alpaca dress ballooning out over her long drawers, chanting, "Dilly-dilly, dilly-dilly," in a little piping voice, shrill as a gnat; the look on her face was so intent, abstracted, almost fey, that it gave Val a strange queer chill to watch her.

"Come, Jannie," she said. "We'll go down to supper."

Jannie took no notice.

"You say it wrong," Pieter informed Val.

"How do you mean?"

"If you want her to mind you, you have to say it like this—Jannee!"

Jannie turned and came skipping towards him, trailing her sash behind her.

"Jan-nee!" Val repeated on the same high note.

Jannie gave her a wide, impish grin, then twirled round and skipped away. It was like trying to come to terms with a hummingbird or a butterfly; the contact lasted only a second, if that, then was lost again. At least she did notice me then, Val thought; that's a tiny step, but a step.

Pieter took his sister's hand, Val picked up the lamp, and they carefully found their way back to the landing and down the stairs.

Returning toward the kitchen, Val was dismayed to see that three places had been laid at one end of the table in the huge, freezing dining room. It would be like picnicking on the verge of a frozen lake.

She walked on into the kitchen.

"We'd rather eat in here, Elspie. It's much warmer—that dining room is too cold for the children. Anyway it'll save you carrying dishes through. We don't want to give you unnecessary work."

"Eat in the kitchen?" Elspie was scandalised. She drew herself up like a grenadier. "That would no' be richt, Mistress Montgomery."

"Nonsense," Val said. "It's only the children and me—we needn't stand on ceremony."

"It ill becomes *me* to speak," Elspie said grimly, "but I dinna like tae think what her leddyship would say."

"She'd say it was a very sensible notion," said Val firmly. "She's probably sitting on the sand in the desert somewhere at this minute, chewing mutton bones in her fingers with some emir."

Elspie gave a sudden crack of laughter. "Verra like! Eh, well, gang yer ain gait—I can see you're neither to hauld nor to bind." And she stood with hands on hips, watching with a sardonic expression, as Val, without more ado, carried the plates and dishes from the dining room to the kitchen table.

Jannie had resumed her airy dancing round the spacious kitchen.

"My sartie," said Elspie, watching. "She does have a look of her mither, whiles. She was a bonnie wee lassie, was Mistress Kirstie. And when will herself be coming home to Ardnacarrig?"

"Soon, we trust," said Val, lifting Jannie into a chair. "Pieter and Jannie are hoping that you can tell them lots of stories about their mother when she was little, aren't you, Pieter? Won't you sit down with us, Elspie? You haven't eaten yet, have you?"

"Na, na, that wouldna be richt," said Elspie obstinately.

"Oh, what nonsense. Anyway, you must remember that I come from America, where everybody is equal."

By a slow process of alternate bullying and cajoling, Val finally got Elspie sitting down with them and sharing the meal she had provided: soup, containing both meat and vegetables, herrings fried in oatmeal, and cranberry tart.

"You're a marvellous cook, Elspie; what do you call that soup?"

"Och, it's just the Hotchpotch; it's no' very special."

"I hope you'll give me the receipt. Wasn't it good, Pieter?"

By working hard at it, Val hoped to promote better relations between Elspie and the children. After the meal they all helped her clear away, Pieter proving quite handy.

"Ay, ay, it'll no' harm the weans to learn the ways o' the hoose," Elspie conceded. "I canna bide an idle bairn. An' dear knaws I have little help here."

"What help do you have?" Val could hardly believe there was just the one old woman in this huge place. But this, it seemed, was the case.

"Och, weel, there's Mysie, Jock's wife, up at the lodge. She lends a hand, whiles, at the spring cleaning. But she's only a poor skaterumple."

When the dishes were done Val said, "It's time the children were in bed, they've had a long day. Elspie, can you tell me where I can find kindling and coal? Pieter and Jannie come from the south, they aren't used to this cold. I want to light a fire in their bedroom, or they'll be coming down with congestion of the lungs."

Elspie's face expressed strong disapproval.

"Ye shouldna be soft with bairns! Else they'll be aye greeting and wailing for thon or the other thing and a' spoiled to death."

"A fire isn't spoiling them," said Val with the utmost firmness.

After much argument she had her way. Peat fires were lit in both rooms, and the icy chill of twenty years began slowly to thaw. The children each had a hot brick to warm their beds and were wrapped in shawls.

"Now I'll leave the lamp on the chest," said Val, "but you must go to sleep. I don't want to hear a sound from you."

She passed through the communicating door into her own room. She was dead tired and longed for her own bed, but she intended to speak to Elspie first. Nerving herself for this, reluctant to move from the tiny glow of her own fire, she stood wearily smoothing her hair, and heard the children's voices, faint, like swallows twittering under the eaves.

First an indistinguishable murmur from Jannie.

Then Pieter: "She's called Elspie. Elspie Cross. I'm afraid she may be another horrible one. Like Mrs. Pipkin. But don't worry, Jannie. I'll try to look after you."

He did not sound very confident about it though.

Another murmur came from Jannie.

"Aunt Valla? I don't *think* she's wicked. But she doesn't love us."

Jannie's murmur again.

"Perhaps Aunt Valla's a witch," Pieter said. "Witches can be partly good."

Jannie appeared to ask a question.

"I don't *know* when Mama will come," Pieter said. His voice shook—with strain, with sadness.

"Go to sleep, children!" Val called.

Dead silence followed.

She went downstairs and found Elspie sitting by the kitchen grate, mending a pile of aged towels and tablecloths; they were of the very finest woven damask but in so tattered and frail a state that every prick of the needle seemed likely to start a new rent.

"Mercy!" Val exclaimed. "Are they worth the work?"

"They are until her leddyship thinks gude to purchase some new for the hoose," replied Elspie with her sardonic smile.

Val was puzzled. Could the Carsphairn ladies be really pressed for cash? She had vaguely understood that they commanded an immense fortune which would come to Kirstie when they died; but this house hardly suggested wealth; on the contrary; all around were evidences of neglect or parsimony: upholstery brittle with age, torn curtains, cracked panelling, peeling paint, dilapidated hangings and worn flooring. Val, however, felt a certain delicacy about asking Elspie about the state of Lady Stroma's finances.

She did say, "Are you not afraid to be here alone at night, Elspie? It seems such a big place for one caretaker. Are there not valuable things here?"

Elspie sniffed her short laugh. "Ou, ay. There are pictures and stuff. But a' the folk round aboot know it's falling to bits. Castle Barebane, they call it. Forbye, what there is, her leddyship knows is safe enough. Naebody wad come pilfering here. They're unco' frightened o' Thrawn Jane."

"And who," asked Val, drily, to cover a certain inner qualm, "who is Thrawn Jane?"

"Och, she was the laird's youngest dochter twa hundred years syne. She was the youngest of five lasses, and her father hadna the siller—for times were hard then as they are noo—to give them all tochers, so Jane wasna able to marry. Syne she wished to wed a fisher laddie, as nane o' the gentry wad take her wi'out a tocher—but her father couldna thole that either. So she e'en jumpit off the tower and killed herself; she had a bairn too, some say. The daft gowks i' the clachan will have it that she's aye daikering aroond, of a night, in the long gallery upstairs, wailing for her bairn an' her lost fisher laddie. Times folk speer have I seen her? An', sin' it keeps them at a decent distance, I'll not say them nay!"

"And have you really seen her?" Val inquired with interest.

"Och, no!" said Elspie with a scornful laugh. "I'm no' one to be believing in such foolish superstitions, and me a professed member o' the kirk."

Val was relieved to hear this. Herself a strong-minded sceptic, she had no time, either, for ghosts or bogies, but there was no blinking the fact that Ardnacarrig House did lend itself with alarming ease to such notions: the wind wailed in chimneys and through cracks; all the uneven floors creaked and the shutters rattled; and the air of neglect and decay, dark panelling, smell of damp and mould, and the bitter cold of the place would incline any unwary mind to thoughts of spectres and hauntings.

"Is that why you are alone here? Will no one else live in?"

"Na, na, it's no' that, it's just her leddyship's economy." Another sniff. "Sin' her leddyship is aye off voyaging in France and Araby and dear kens where, an' disna show her nose here from one five years to the next, she sees nae reason to spend a muckle deal on the upkeep o' the place. Forbye, at best, she was aye one to skrimp, an' closefisted wi' her siller," Elspie said with a small, grim smile, breaking off a thread.

Val was aghast. "She doesn't expect you to look after those children on your own?" She looked at the old woman perturbedly. She had entertained expectations, not of a whole retinue, certainly, but at least some staff—a couple of maids—not just one old woman. Suppose Elspie were to fall ill? What would happen to the children then?

"There's Mysie's daughter Annot. She's anither silly flisk-ma-hoy, but she'll do to mind the bairns, whiles, an' maybe tak' them on an airing now and again."

Annot sounded like a hopeful ally, to Val's ear.

"Will Annot be here tomorrow?"

"Ay, aiblins I'll be fetching her," Elspie replied drily. "Nae doot she'll be eident tae see the bairns an' the leddy from London."

"Elspie, I want to talk to you about Jannie," said Val, and plunged boldly into an analysis of Jannie's peculiar difficulties and backwardness, and the dreadful time the children had had with Mrs. Pipkin.

"Jannie doesn't mean to misbehave, you see, it's not wilful naughtiness or disobedience; it's just that she hasn't learned as fast as most small children do. She doesn't seem to know about right and wrong."

Elspie's reserved expression showed what she thought of this.

"A wee bit ding or a skelp now and then is a grand help wi' yon kind o' learning for a slow bairn."

"No, no," said Val firmly. "Her mother is tremendously particular that she should not be spanked or hit, *particularly* on the head or face."

"Aye, well," said Elspie, unconvinced, "wee Kirstie was aye a douce, thowless kind of lassie herself, a thocht lacking in gumption. She'd weep buckets, gin a body flyted at her."

Val was discouraged, feeling that she had made little headway.

"Just the same, I think you should take pains to try to understand Jannie, and not be impatient with her. The unkindness of that woman in London has had a very bad effect on her, it's plain."

"Ou, ay," said Elspie sourly. "There's some lucky ones has it all laid out for 'em. 'Dinna be too hard—try to understand her—'" she mimicked. "While the lave of us e'en have to thole it oot as best we can. Naebody said 'Try to understand her' about *me*, when I first came to this cauld auld hoose, a wee thing of five, aye greeting for my mither! All I got was a skelp on the lug."

"Times have changed since then! And isn't that all the more reason why you should be patient with Jannie?" As Elspie still appeared unconvinced, Val added, "Also I've arranged for Dr. David Ramsay to come and have a look at her."

Elspie's expression relaxed.

"Ay, ay, he's a good laddie enow, an' as a doctor he's a fair marvel, folk say. I've nae need for doctors mysel'. Forbye he gave up a fine practice in

Enbra' tae come back here and care for his mither. If there's aught ails the bairn, he'll soon have her sorted to richts."

Val had an impulse to ask if Elspie knew Sir Marcus—but it did not seem very likely; and Elspie was such a dry, cross-grained character that if she did know him, she probably had a very poor opinion of him and his numerous ailments. But it was a lucky thing that he had written to Dr. Ramsay; the doctor's opinion seemed the likeliest influence to make Elspie take a more humane and less Old Testament attitude.

"Well, I'll be off to bed," Val said, stifling a yawn. "It was a long day."

"You'll no' be used to bairns either, I doot, being an unmarried leddy?" Elspie said with a shrewd and slightly malicious look. "Maybe yon'll be the first time ye had charge of any?"

Rather nettled, Val agreed that this was so. There was a considerable difference, she felt, between the attitude to be expected from an ignorant old housekeeper in the back of beyond, and an educated person who had had the benefit of growing up in the world's most modern city with a chance to read (and even to write) all the most enlightened opinions on child development and education.

However one could hardly say this to Elspie.

"Oh, I almost forgot—I have a note for you," she said suddenly, remembering it as she was about to leave the room. "An old man with a white beard came up and gave it to me just as we were about to get into the carriage. He came up and said were we going to Ardnacarrig and if so, would I please give this to Mistress Elspie Cross."

She handed over the little packet—a piece of paper folded and refolded until it was just a wad.

"My sartie!" Elspie peered at the paper suspiciously. "For me? Who can it be fra? It was no' Robina that sent it?"

"No. It was an old man with a white beard," Val repeated.

Elspie seemed so completely puzzled and mystified that Val lingered inquisitively while the note—slowly and with great caution as if it might contain explosive—was unfolded and opened out. It was lucky that Val did wait, for, at sight of the handwriting, Elspie gave a long, low, gasping cry, like someone who has been pierced to the heart, and leaned back in her chair. Her cheeks were whiter than the towel she was darning.

"Och, no, no, no!" she moaned.

"What is it?" said Val anxiously.

But Elspie only rocked to and fro, to and fro, with her apron over her head, moaning, "Och, it's too late, far an' awa too late! I canna have him noo, sic a disturbance as it would make! Forbye her leddyship wouldna care, maybe, a' taken up as she is noo wi' foreign travel. But no, no, it's too late. It's too late. I canna be fashed wi' him noo!"

She seemed so terribly distressed and preoccupied that Val began hunting through the cupboards until she found a decanter of whisky. A mouthful of this had a calming effect on Elspie and brought some colour back to her cheeks. She wiped her eyes on the apron.

"I ask your pardon, Mistress Montgomery," she said with dignity. "It was—it came on me that unexpected. And indeed it is awa' too late. I couldna change my ways now. But it did strike me to the heart, for I loved him dearly the once. And I would like fine to know how he looked. Did he—did he look well, now?"

Val racked her brain to remember some details of his appearance. She had not taken particular notice—she had only the dimmest recollection of somebody very thin—tallish—much the same build as Elspie in fact!—with white hair under a sailor's cap, a white beard, and very bright eyes.

"Yes, he looked well, I think," she said. "Brown—weather-beaten—is he a sailor?"

"And how would I be knowing? I havena laid eyes on him for over forty year! Eh me, eh me!"

She still rocked to and fro, gazing at the glow of the fire. As Val walked upstairs, she heard the murmur, repeated again and again, "Nay, nay. I canna put up wi' him now. It's awa' and awa' too late!"

Val did her best not to think about Thrawn Jane as she carried her lamp across the wide shadowy landing and along the dark passages. This is a sad house, she thought. It has been containing people's longings and frustrations for hundreds of years.

Yawning, she entered her room, where, to her relief, the fire still burned. The children were in peaceful sleep. She longed to climb into her own feather bed but first there was work to be done.

Huddled close to the fire she took up her notebook and pen. Edinburgh, the coach, the countryside, Elspie, Ardnacarrig, Thrawn Jane. *Journal of a Yankee Lass*, she wrote. Where to begin?

CHAPTER 11

WHEN Val woke next morning she jumped out of bed and dressed speedily, for the air in her bedroom was arctic; in the course of the night her fire had gone out. Washing in cold water she observed to herself that some means of taking a hot bath must be discovered in this mansion if she was to spend more than a day under its roof—and she had a gloomy presentiment that it would be necessary to stay at least a week—perhaps even longer—to make sure that Elspie was sufficiently inculcated into the correct way of looking after children so as to make her a safe guardian.

Val longed to return to Edinburgh. It was all a great nuisance.

When, clad in all her petticoats under her warmest dress, with a woollen jacket over that, she walked to the window and pulled the curtains back, a surprise awaited her. She had expected to see snow, from the white light between the draperies. What she saw instead was the sea. As they approached it from the back, Ardnacarrig House had appeared sunk in woods. But from this window there was not a tree to be seen. The window itself was half shrouded in ivy with which the whole of this side of the house appeared to be overgrown. Directly below lay a flagged terrace, half obscured with weeds. Steps led down from it to a rough lawn, which was bounded on three sides by a low-spreading azalea hedge. From a gap in the hedge on the far side, a path led across short turf to a pale crescent of sandy beach, beyond which lay the sea, inky-dark but calm, except for a white frill of waves at the edge of the sand. Looking to right and left, Val realised that the house lay on flat land in the centre of a small bay. Headlands rose steeply at either end of the half-moon of beach; to the right, a river ran out beyond a sand bar. Gulls were crying thinly, and she could hear the bleat of sheep and see a few of them feeding on the turf beyond the azalea hedge.

The morning was grey, frosty, and bleak, but at least there had been no more snow during the night. Val was filled by a sudden urge to go out and inspect this new landscape. It was a long time since she had been in the country, after all! First, though, she tiptoed to look at the children through the communicating door. They were still in profound sleep. So she pulled on her coat and fur hood, found a pair of gloves, and went softly out of the room and downstairs.

She took a different stair from the one they had come up last night, and it led to a big half-derelict room with a warped piano, some card tables, and, stacked in a corner, a tangle of rods and fishing tackle.

Two French windows led on to the terrace she had seen from above, and she tried to open one of them, but it evidently had not been used for years; it first resisted her efforts, and finally gave with a terrifying screech and such a jerk that a pane fell on to the terrace and broke. Rather dashed —though the accident was hardly her fault after all—she pulled-to the broken window behind her, crossed the terrace and lawn, then followed the path, which ran between more azalea banks, down to the beach. At the crest of its sandy slope she turned to look at the house and realised for the first time how extremely large it was. Probably a central core of seventeenth-century manor house had been "improved" in the eighteenth century, she guessed, and had then received a few more additions during the present century—all those pointed pepperpot turrets like neatly-sharpened pencils must—must they not?—have been added during the last forty years, whereas the crow-stepped gables looked very ancient indeed and were probably part of the original building.

A wall, presumably surrounding kitchen gardens, ran off to the left, and on the right were barns and outbuildings. Behind the house and gardens rose the tops of tall trees, no doubt the woods they had traversed last night. And farther back still, the ground rose sharply to purple-dark moorland, and ran out on either side to the headlands. One of these was bare and rocky, with tufts of heather; the other, much higher, rose to an awe-inspiring three-hundred-foot crag. Near the top of this crag perched a roofless ruin with crumbling battlements and shattered buttresses—no doubt the original home of the Carsphairn family before they forsook its airy height and built themselves a more comfortable and convenient residence down in the bay. Apart from the ruined castle there seemed to be no other dwelling or sign of human life in the bay, unless you counted a couple of fishing boats well out to sea.

Exhilarated by the cold salty air but somewhat discouraged by the total solitude, Val walked swiftly back to the house and let herself in through the French window. Returning to the children's room she found that Pieter had woken and managed, by blowing on its buried core, to rekindle his and Jannie's fire. Adding twigs and bits of peat, he had achieved quite a creditable blaze and was sitting by it, shrouded in a blanket, immersed in one of the storybooks Val had read him on the train, every now and then looking up to add a cautious morsel of fuel to his fire.

Val's heart warmed to the sober, sensible little boy; he did not have Jannie's touch of diabolical charm, but he was so practical, so reliable.

"Hullo there, Pieter," she said softly. "Do you want to get up? The sea's just outside."

"I know." The children's window, also, looked on to the beach. "I've seen it. I saw you out there." He did not sound particularly enthusiastic. "Wasn't it cold?"

"Yes," said Val honestly. "But there are lots of beautiful shells and all kinds of things that have been washed up in storms. Don't you want to come out and see?"

"All right. We'd better wake Jannie."

Jannie stirred drowsily. Val had already discovered that she was a very heavy sleeper, perhaps in compensation for her manic activity when awake.

"Come along Jannie—wake up!" Giving her a gentle shake Val found with dismay that Jannie had soaked both herself and her bed in the course of the night, and was lying in a dank, ammoniacal swamp.

"Oh dear, Jannie! Couldn't you have got up if you wanted to go to the bathroom? You've got the water closet right next door!"

"She's frightened of the way the wind howls in there," Pieter observed philosophically, laying more peats on his fire.

Val impatiently washed and dressed the little girl and bundled her nightclothes and bedding into a pile for later laundering. Then she led the children down, following the route she had taken before, and out on to the terrace. She was longing for them to discover *something* that they could enjoy about this place, so as to predispose them in its favour; also, she herself had such happy memories of trips to the beach with her father that she could not believe the sea would fail to please.

She was wrong, however.

"Don't like, don't like!" wailed Jannie, burying her face in the skirts of Val's coat.

"Oh, come on, Jannie, don't be a misery. Look—lovely shells. See, here's a pink one."

Jannie rudely struck away the proffered shell, and Val found herself within an ace of ignoring all her own exhortations to Elspie and giving the child a furious slap. But Pieter, accustomed to Jannie, was more successful in arousing her interest.

"Look, Jannie—sheep! Lambies!" He took her hand and pointed. Jannie's eyes followed his pointing finger to the flock feeding on the gorse-studded grass above the beach and her face lit up with pleasure and interest.

"Let's walk along to them," proposed Val.

They had gone about a hundred yards along the sand when Pieter said, "I can hear Elspie calling."

Val turned and saw that Elspie was scouring after them along the beach, running with the speed of a girl of twenty, and shouting something as she ran. Her cap strings had come undone, her pale-gold hair fell down her back in a loose knot, and when she caught up with them, breathless as she was, she burst into a torrent of commination which was so broken and disjointed that mention of individual ill-doings floated haphazardly like straws in the general denunciatory sweep.

"Broken windows—door left open for the sheep tae wander in—all that peat used—all those wet sheets, who's tae have the laundering o' them?—breakfasts getting cauld—mun I be expected to run to Wolf's Hope after ye? Och, maircy—bairns in the hoose is waur nor all the Goths, Vandals, and Pharisees pit together!"

"*I'll* wash the bedclothes," Val said irritably. "You only have to tell me where you do it. Jannie was probably upset by the journey—I'm sure she'll settle down in a day or two. And I'm sorry about the broken pane—the door was jammed—I wanted the children to see the beach—"

Elspie had her breath back. "Never *ever* walk that way!" she said, gesturing on along the sand in the direction they had taken, toward the higher headland.

She turned and beckoned them back toward the house.

"Why shouldn't we go that way?" Pieter wanted to know at once.

"Because o' the Kelpie's Flow!"

"And what," said Val peevishly, striding beside Elspie and carrying Jannie who, frustrated in her wish to examine the sheep at close quarters, had burst into dismal wails, "what in heaven's name is the Kelpie's Flow? Anything to do with Thrawn Jane? Another piece of local lore?"

"No it inna," retorted Elspie sharply. "And your joking is misplaced, Mistress Montgomery. The Kelpie's Flow is a terrible deep quicksand that has sucked down gude kens how many souls in its time. A whole patrol of dragoons went down into it in the fog in 1745."

"Well," Val said reasonably, "that's over a hundred and forty years ago —perhaps legend has exaggerated—" but she stopped, silenced by Elspie's look.

"Ne'er gae beyond that white mark on the rock face yonder," Elspie told the children, pointing back. "Ye can walk the other way, toward the burn, there's naught to fear there. But now, i'mercy's name, come your ways in ben to your porridge which is getting cauld; I've a hundred things to do wi'out chasing ower half the strand after a wheen daft young ones."

Val felt affronted at being included in this category and was not appeased by breakfast, which offered its expected aggravations: Jannie did not fancy her porridge, and Pieter asked more questions than Elspie could tolerate. The porridge came in a bowl for each person with a bowl of milk alongside for dipping the spoonfuls into singly. The children found this very odd, and outraged Elspie by asking for sugar.

A welcome interruption came with the arrival of Jock Kelso's Annot, but the first sight of the girl extinguished Val's hope of finding a useful lieutenant to Elspie in her. Kindly and cheerful Annot might be, but intelligent, no: she was a stocky, red-faced, tow-headed lass with pale-blue eyes and hardly two words to say for herself; she giggled a great deal and amply justified Elspie's description of her as a silly flisk-ma-hoy. However she gave the children a broad grin and they went with her willingly enough to "see the kye" while Val carried out her promise to Elspie and washed Jannie's soaked clothes in a bleak but serviceable laundry room where hot water was produced in a copper over a driftwood fire. After hanging the things out to dry—smiling a touch wrily at finding herself, after all her fight for emancipation, thus reduced to a traditional role—Val felt that she was entitled to some time off, and proceeded to explore the house. It was built, she discovered, in the form of a quadrangle, two sides of which were stables and sheds.

Beyond the dining room they had seen last night lay an equally large drawing room with a great open fireplace, more dark-brown panelling, and a great quantity of stuffed fish, otters, and wildcats in glass cases, the latter with ferocious snarls on their faces as if they longed to get at the fish.

Lady Stroma shows sense in preferring Constantinople, thought Val. If this place belonged to me I'd sell it or pull it down. But I suppose she isn't allowed to do that, according to the terms of some entail.

A door led from the drawing room into a library lined from floor to ceiling with mildewed calf and vellum. Mainly sermons. Someone, some previous Carsphairn, had had a decided taste for collecting sermons. Suppose at a rough guess the library contained five thousand volumes and each volume held thirty sermons . . . Val gave up the unprofitable calculation and went on, through another door, up a spiral stone stair which led to a long gallery. This, presumably the terrain of Thrawn Jane, was full of aged cracked and peeling pictures in dingy gold frames, most of them family portraits, Val guessed. No doubt the sermon-collecting ancestor was here; *everybody* was here. Over and over, in canvas after canvas, Val saw Lady Stroma's proud arched nose, her glacial eye, her thin patrician neck, her nervous taper fingers: here they grasped a sword hilt or a fowling piece, there they clasped a judicial-looking scroll, half concealed by lace ruffles. And there, too, were the gentler features of Lady Honoria, ringleted, or incongruously bewigged or crowned with a tartan bonnet. Here too—Val realised with a sudden shock of discovery—were Elspie's features. What a fool she had been! It was plain as a pikestaff that Elspie must be related—no wonder her face had seemed so familiar.

"Eh, so this is where ye've got to!" Elspie herself stood in the doorway, confirming Val's hypothesis to the full. "Doctor Ramsay's here and wishful to meet ye."

"Doctor Ramsay? That's wonderfully quick—I was afraid he might not come for days and days. Are the children still out with Annot?"

"Ay, but they'll be inbye afore long; you can have your collogue wi' the doctor while they're walking, why not?"

"I want him to examine Jannie but I can certainly do some explaining before they come back."

Dr. Ramsay was waiting in the chill, gloomy drawing room. Elspie evidently had fixed rules as to hospitality; she had provided a dish of oatcakes, two crystal glasses, and decanters of whisky and madeira. Val disliked whisky and the madeira looked old and full of sediment. She declined a drink, but the doctor helped himself to a dram of whisky.

Dr. Ramsay's appearance was a decided disappointment to Val. She did not know quite what she had expected; only that he was not it. A younger version of Sir Marcus, perhaps. But of course there was no relationship; Sir Marcus was his godfather.

He was a very odd-looking young man, slight, thin, and dapper, with pale ginger-coloured eyes, very quick and bright, rather long light-brown hair, a turned-up nose like a duck's bill, and a big mobile mouth. He also had a large disfiguring birthmark on one side of his forehead, but this did not appear to trouble him; his manner was not in the least self-conscious.

"Yes, you look exactly the way old Marcus described you," he said, regarding Val over the rim of his whisky glass.

"Oh?" Val rejoined in a quelling tone. She was dying of curiosity to hear what Sir Marcus had said, but didn't intend to demean herself by inquiring.

"A beautiful Nordic snowqueen, also an arrogant, overbearing puss."

"Oh!" She was outraged. "Arrogant? How *dare* he?"

"None of my affair," Dr. Ramsay said, briskly drinking his whisky. "Don't know so can't judge. Anyway, so long as you don't try to domineer over me, *I've* no objections; I don't dislike strong-minded women if they are intelligent with it; rather the contrary. Can't abide the silly ones."

While Val was absorbing this broadside and trying to decide what line to take, he went on, with a complete change of manner, to serious kind attention.

"Come, then, what's your worry? Cousin Marcus said you're anxious about your niece, Kirstie's younger child is it? How old is she?"

"About three." Relieved to get away from personalities, Val went carefully over her observations about Jannie's many oddnesses—her inattention, self-absorption, backwardness, flashes of fury and panic.

"Yes. I see. I'll have to look at her. They're outside with Annot? Why don't we walk out and find them?"

Val flung on a pelisse and they walked out on to the terrace. At the side of the house they found Elspie coming from the garden with a large basket of greens and potatoes.

"The bairns?" she said. "They're awa' up tae the Wolf's Crag wi' Annot; I didna ken she had it in mind to take them sae far or I'd ha' called her back." And she pointed up the steep slope toward the ruin, where three tiny figures could be seen.

"Never mind," Dr. Ramsay said. "I've no other patients this morning. We'll go after them."

"Isn't it rather dangerous up there so near the cliff's edge?" Val said.

"Och, no. Annot's got enough gumption to keep them away from the edge."

Considering how fussed Elspie had been about the quicksand, Val thought she seemed remarkably placid about the perils of the ruined tower and the possibility of falling three hundred feet over the cliff. But Dr. Ramsay took an equally tranquil view.

"Annot will fill their heads with bugaboos but she won't let them break their necks."

He set off along a path which led back through the trees on the landward side of the house but soon turned parallel with the beach and began to climb, following the course of a tiny ravine with a little brook that dashed its way from one miniature fall to another. The air was piercingly cold, the ground hard and crisp with frost, but a pale sun had come out.

"Do you know everybody in these parts?" Val asked, following him.

"Indeed I do!" He turned his head. "I was born at Ravenswood, that's about forty miles inland from here, and my father came to be minister here—at Wolf's Hope—when I was five. Of course later I went off to school and university but my parents lived here until my father died three years ago—my mother still does—so I have always come back, when I had any free time."

"Where did you go to university?" she asked, wondering if by any chance he had been one of Nils' fellow students, but he replied, "Cambridge. And then I studied medicine in Vienna."

She was impressed.

"You must find it rather dull here after that?"

"Och, well, people fall sick the same way everywhere. I believe Cousin Marcus told you about my mother?"

She nodded and said with gruff, shy constraint, "I'm very sorry. It must be dreadful for you."

"Why—thank you." He glanced at her in slight surprise.

"I'd like to come and see her if I might?"

"She'd enjoy that," he said with another sceptical glance, as if he did not expect to find a propensity for sick-visiting in Val. She said honestly, "Sir Marcus told me that your mother is a wonderful person. And I have a message to her from him."

"Ah, I see." After a moment Dr. Ramsay added, "He wanted to marry her, when they were young."

Val did not know why this piece of information came as a slight shock to her.

She said, to cover up her dismay, "I suppose somebody wouldn't allow it—like Thrawn Jane's father? Scotland seems to be full of frustrated lovers and examples of parental tyranny."

"On the contrary. My mother's story wasn't a bit like that," he corrected her. "My mother just happened to prefer my father—difficult and tiresome though he was in almost every way. But she was very fond of old Marcus too; I daresay if polyandry were allowed in Scotland she'd have been happy to marry them both. Though of course my father wouldn't have allowed that. He was a very conventional minister."

"What an extraordinary thing to say about your own mother!"

"Why? It's true. I'd not have expected you to stickle at a bit of plain speaking, Miss Montgomery? Marcus said you were a very emancipated young lady."

Sir Marcus seemed to have equipped her with a most disagreeable character, Val thought. It was really unfair, considering how warmly she felt toward him. She remained silent. After a moment, Dr. Ramsay remarked, "Why do you say that Scottish parents are tyrants? I won't deny there's a grain of truth in the assumption, but what evidence do you go on?"

"Very little, really, I suppose. I was thinking of young Lochinvar. And Kirstie and my brother. And Thrawn Jane, of course."

"You haven't heard Elspie's story?"

"No—what about her?"

"I expect you had better know it if you are going to be living here. And *she* wouldn't tell you. She was a by-blow of the auld laird, the late marquis of Stroma."

"Lady Stroma's father, do you mean?"

"Yes, he fathered quite a number of local children by all accounts. So when Elspie's mother died of a fever—her husband, a fisherman, had been drowned a couple of years before—Elspie, aged five, was adopted into the Big House and brought up there."

"With the legitimate children?" This accounted, then, for Elspie's air of breeding and the fact that her speech was less broad than that of the Kelsos.

"Well, yes and no; she didn't get sent away to school when the girls went off to Perth. But she'll have shared their occupations up to a point. Scotland is a very democratic country, Miss Montgomery," he said drily.

"Well, so far the story seems humane and liberal enough. Where's the tyranny?"

"The old laird died when Elspie was still quite young. He was full of years and drink but he had left a will and strict dispositions about his estate. There were three Carsphairn sisters, you know—the legitimate daughters—Louisa, Honoria, and Barbara—who was Kirstie's mother. Barbara was the only pretty one, she married early and luckily and died young, in India. The two elder sisters were very plain, and they hated men, it seems; they never married. Whether they hated the male sex because they didn't have any suitors, or vice versa, who can tell?"

"And Elspie?"

"Elspie, who was younger, had a suitor, but the family wouldn't let her marry him. He was a fisherman called Mungo Bucklaw, who lived in Wolf's Hope. Louisa and Honoria told Elspie that she'd been fed and housed all those years on the strict understanding that she was to become housekeeper at Ardnacarrig and remain unmarried."

"But—!"

He raised a hand.

"Elspie, being a girl of sense and spirit, said what was to stop her marrying Mungo *and* being housekeeper as well? But no, that wouldn't do, they said it would be sullying the Carsphairn blood and a shocking misalliance."

"But—!"

"In the meantime, Mungo had got tired of waiting. Some say he had a letter, allegedly in Elspie's writing, saying that it was all off. Perhaps it even *was* in her writing. Who knows what pressure was put on her? Anyway he went off to sea in a merchant ship and that's the last that was ever heard of him."

No, it isn't the last, thought Val, but she kept this thought to herself. A dreadful pang clove her heart at the thought of the thin old man standing on the black Edinburgh street sending his message to Elspie in the dark of the winter morning. How curtly, how briskly I took the paper. And then I almost forgot to give it to Elspie.

But then she thought: for all I know Mungo has been married three times in the course of the last forty years. Why only *now* does he send his message? Perhaps his third wife just died and he's looking for a comfortable billet to end his days.

After a minute she said, "What a frightful story. I *thought* Lady Stroma seemed a very overbearing sort of character."

"Oh, you have met her?"

"I wonder Elspie stays on at Ardnacarrig. I don't suppose they pay her much."

"Family loyalty. And she loves the place. It is her home, after all."

Val walked on in silence. The climb had become so steep, now they had left the trees, that they were obliged to pause for breath every few yards. How ever had Jannie been persuaded up here?

Now they could see the whole sweep of the bay, and the grey bulk of Ardnacarrig House, all gables, turrets, and chimneys, nestling among the elms and beeches of its policies, the half-wild pleasure-grounds pertaining to a Scottish melolhouse.

"Where is the village—what is it called?"

"Wolf's Hope."

"What a strange name—what does it mean?"

"Wolf's Haven, I believe—it's probably a Norse name. It lies over on the north side of this headland, beyond the castle, which is called Wolf's Crag. Have you never read *The Bride of Lammermoor?*"

"No, never, I haven't read any Scott at all—except 'Young Lochinvar,'" Val said, unabashed. "Why?"

"The castle of Wolf's Crag was the last piece of property remaining in the possession of the bankrupt master of Ravenswood."

"When was this?"

"Mid-seventeenth century."

"Even then, I daresay, it wasn't very comfortable," Val said thoughtfully, looking at the battered shell of stonework. "What was the story?"

"Ravenswood wanted to marry a girl called Lucy Ashton. But her family had a feud with his. The young couple plighted their troth; but when her parents found out, they wouldn't allow it, and married her off to someone else."

"There!" Val said triumphantly. "What did I tell you? Parental tyranny."

"That was why I wondered if you'd read it."

"So what happened?"

"Oh, she went mad and stabbed her bridegroom on the wedding night and died raving. And the bankrupt master of Ravenswood rode his horse into the Kelpie's Flow and was never seen more. So the land—what there was of it—passed to the Carsphairns, who were distant cousins, and they built the house in the bay."

Val shivered. "What a miserable tale. Even worse than Elspie's. At least her lover didn't jump into the quicksand."

"So far as we know. Have you been warned about it, by the by?" She nodded. "Look, you can see it from here." He took her arm to steady her and pointed over the shoulder of the cliff. The tide was now far out, exposing a jagged line of rocks extending outward from the foot of the cliff—Dr. Ramsay said they were called the Kelpie's Fangs—and a huge expanse of smooth, sparklingly white sand. But at the foot of the cliff and alongside the rocks a strange, curdled, dimpled patch of sand extended for about a hundred yards; when the small waves rolled in toward it, the sand heaved all over, as if, in the unknown deeps below, some great subterranean eruption were taking place.

"It's at its most dangerous now, when the tide is on the turn," Dr. Ramsay said. "But it's always fairly deadly. You've heard about the patrol of dragoons? Perfectly true story. That is why you can't walk to Wolf's Hope along the shore, which would be the shortest and most logical route. You could swim, of course, when the tide's in, but you would have to go round the end of the rocks. I do it sometimes on my horse, who is a famous swimmer."

They were nearing the castle ruins. Pieter had seen them through an archway and came running out. For once he was overflowing with excitement and high spirits.

"Aunt Valla, Aunt Val, isn't this the most awesome place? Annot says it's awesome, that's a Scots word. I'm learning Scotch."

"Yes it is awesome," Val agreed, looking up at the tottering pile, and out across the German ocean, so grey, cold, and white-capped, and down at the pale dimpled menace of the Kelpie's Flow. "Pieter, this is Doctor Ramsay, who wants to have a look at Jannie. Where is she?"

"Why does he want to look at her; she's not sick?" Pieter demanded instantly and reasonably. "There she is, just coming out with Annot."

Jannie came slowly, sucking her finger and clutching Annot's hand. She looked tired.

"Good day to you, Annot, found a new pair of bairns to tell your tales to, have you?" Dr. Ramsay said. "Well, you can run off home to your dinner now, Miss Montgomery and I will fetch them home. Is your mother still using the lotion I sent her? Has she plenty of it? That's good."

As Annot, after bobbing a curtsey, ran off down the hill, he added, "Why don't we all sit here in the moat for a few minutes? It's quite sheltered and warm."

They all settled in a sunny corner and then Dr. Ramsay began to examine Jannie, which he did with extreme care and thoroughness, cracking jokes to allay Pieter's anxiety. Jannie ignored the jokes, but she did seem to feel a rapport with the doctor and submitted trustfully enough while he peered and prodded and tapped, looked in her eyes and ears and throat, felt her glands, pressed her chest, and tried to make her repeat words after him.

"Say ah, Jannie. Say Pa. Say Pa may we all go too?"

"You don't talk to her properly," said Pieter, and explained about the intonation.

"Indeed? Thank you, Pieter, that's a great help, and most interesting."

The doctor tried again with better success and began making Jannie articulate words by the simple expedient of putting her mouth in the appropriate shape with his hands. At length she became tired and rebellious and bit his thumb quite hard.

"All right, little Miss Silence, I take your point that you have had enough for the time," he said amiably, wrapping a handkerchief round the injured member. "Here—" and he dug out a paper of treacle candies, "have a sweetie apiece. My mother always makes sure I have some of these on me when I go off on my rounds," he told Val. "Now we'll walk home, bairns; if you want to run to the foot of the hill, wait for us there, and I'll give you another piece of candy."

Pieter grabbed Jannie's hand and ran off.

"Well, what's the verdict?" Val asked anxiously.

"She's deaf."

"*Deaf?*" Val was utterly taken aback. "Not simple?"

"Simple?" he exclaimed angrily. "The child's as bright as a button. Considering the very limited amount she receives aurally from the outside world, it's amazing how far her mental development has advanced. She can hear certain sounds quite well; others not at all. But someone's obviously taken pains with her. She has a remarkably keen intelligence."

A lot of things fell into place for Val.

"So that's why—oh, what a fool I've been not to spot it myself."

He smiled. "Easier when someone else has pointed it out. Your mind was running on other lines."

"What was the cause, do you think?"

"It might have been hereditary—or she might have suffered from some middle-ear infection; or it might have been caused by a blow or an accident. Hard to say without knowing more family history. Was Kirstie ill, ever, when she was expecting Jannie?"

"I don't know. I've never met her. But I remember Nils—what a *fool* I am—saying something about a maid hitting Jannie on the head, and Kirstie being very angry. Could that have caused it?"

"Possible, or Kirstie might just have been angry because the child had the condition already."

"Can it be cured?" Val thought with painful remorse of the many times she had been impatient with Jannie's inattention.

"Helped, certainly. I'll conduct some more tests on her and find if she would benefit from an appliance."

"An ear trumpet, you mean? Oh, the poor child!"

"She might enjoy it. The old laird had one I believe—it's probably still somewhere about the house. Yes; very likely her deafness is hereditary. Also she needs speech-training to make up for all the time she's lost. I'll try to get over for half an hour every day."

"You will?—but that's unbelievably kind of you! You'll give up all that time?"

"Och, I'm not so hard-pressed at present," he said calmly. "And I'm particularly interested in deafness. Besides, she is a bright, quick little child; she ought to have her chance."

"Well—in that case—thank you! We'll be glad to accept your kindness."

And, Val thought secretly, it will enlarge my own chance of getting away from Ardnacarrig.

Certain that Dr. Ramsay was coming over every day—would she not, with an easy conscience, be able to take herself off at least as far as Edinburgh?

"I'd like you to do at least an hour a day with her too," he went on, rather dashing these plans. And he went on, "Er—Miss Montgomery?"

"Yes?"

"If I ride to Ardnacarrig every day, folk around here will certainly begin to talk, as they are very prone to do, and say that I am courting you."

"Well?" she said rather irritably. "I'm not in the least troubled by talk."

"Nor am I," he said blandly. "That was not what I was going to say."

"Oh? What was it then?"

"I merely wanted to warn you that I do not intend ever to marry," said this surprising young man. "Just in case you yourself should entertain any false ideas about my intentions."

She was really taken aback, but mustered up enough composure to say, "Please have no anxieties on that score, Doctor Ramsay," rather coldly. "As a matter of fact I am engaged to be married to a lawyer in New York." No longer true, of course, but at least it would show this odd character that she was not interested in *him*. She had once been informed by her father that some men preferred the company of their own sex to that of women—very strange!

"Oh, that's capital, then," said Dr. Ramsay. "I need have no anxieties on your score. I am sure I shall very much enjoy being friends with you— you are just the kind of quick-witted, strong-minded woman that I get on with most comfortably. *Au revoir!* I shall come over tomorrow again."

They had walked as far as the stable yard where his grey mare was tethered. He untied the mare, mounted, and rode off, waving his hat to her and the children in the most amicable way.

And what about me? Val thought rather indignantly as she slowly followed the children indoors. She had decidedly mixed feelings about young Dr. Ramsay and now wished that she had not told that lie about Benet. She wished even—a little—that she had not been so precipitate in writing to break off the engagement. She would have liked to write to Benet now, describing the scene at Ardnacarrig, making an amusing story of it. But pride forbade.

Failing Benet, she sat down and wrote a strong letter to Lady Stroma at

Nice, in which she said that it was not suitable for the children to be left at Ardnacarrig without some trained person to look after them, and she suggested that a nursery-governess be hired.

Then she added another page to the *Journal of a Yankee Lass*.

CHAPTER 12

THE realisation that she was deaf, not feeble-minded, made an astonishing, a humiliating difference in one's attitude to Jannie, Val discovered.

"Och, the poor afflicted bairn," said Elspie. "Nae wonder she paid sae little heed when a body speired her something. And now I come tae think on't, I mind fine the auld laird was deaf as an adder in his last years."

With a certain shock Val remembered that the old laird in question, Jannie's great-grandfather, was Elspie's father; that Elspie, in fact, was Jannie's unacknowledged great-aunt. No wonder she was somewhat sardonic about her half-sisters' penny-pinching ways. If I were in her place, Val thought, I wouldn't just be sardonic, I'd be spitting fire and brimstone. In fact I wouldn't *be* in her place. How dare they employ her as a housekeeper and not acknowledge her relationship?

It seemed incredible to Val that anybody in Elspie's position should not demand more of her rights from her half-sisters. Why should she be obliged to live alone in this cold, uncomfortable barrack of a house, doing the most menial tasks, scrubbing floors, digging potatoes, feeding poultry, while they took their ease in France or Turkey? True, Honoria had weak lungs; true, Louisa was probably not taking her ease but engaging in strenuous camel travel; true, Elspie appeared healthy, contented, dourly devoted to the house—but still, but still! Principles were principles.

Val suspected that Dr. Ramsay had laid down for Elspie some strong guidelines regarding her behaviour toward Jannie, for after his first visit the old woman made a definite effort to exercise patience with the child's inattention, erratic behaviour, and waywardness; occasionally, even, she showed a gleam of wintry kindness to her great-niece which it was not evident that Jannie either noticed or reciprocated. She tended to keep a nervous distance from Elspie at all times, and was almost equally wary in her attitude to Val, despite the latter's determined display of friendliness. The only person who did not change his ways toward Jannie was Pieter; the fact that her condition had been given a name made no difference to him. Jannie was Jannie, and he continued to treat her with brotherly protectiveness, mixed with a modicum of firm discipline when he thought it necessary; sometimes Jannie submitted to his authority, sometimes she rebelled against it furiously. Often, watching Pieter organise his small sister, Val was reminded of herself and Nils—but with what a difference! Pieter was both kinder and more just than his father had ever been.

Little by little Jannie displayed signs of improvement; now that the adults concerned with her knew that it was not impossible to make contact with her and were attempting to break through the barrier of her deafness, she began to make some tentative response. By degrees she became less wilful, less hysterical; and after two or three weeks at Ardnacarrig, when familiarity with her surroundings gave her a greater sense of security, less wildly incontinent, less prone to panic. But it was uphill work.

Dr. Ramsay, faithful to his word, came every day; sometimes, if he was pressed for time, he would spend a scant ten minutes with Jannie; sometimes, if the health of his patients and the state of Jannie's patience permitted, he might stay an hour or even two, working with her, steadily repeating simple vowel sounds and consonants over and over, making comic faces at Jannie and persuading her to imitate them while at the same time reproducing the sounds he made; he borrowed and brought different instruments—flute, violin, drum—to find which sounds she heard most clearly; he picked out one-finger tunes on the old broken piano, and encouraged Jock Kelso to come up to the Big House and play his bagpipes. Jannie hated the pipes at first and broke into screams of fear and dislike at the sight and sound of them, but later on she began to find them a very good joke and welcomed the approach of the "blow-pipe-bag-man."

Val, anxious in case all this extra attention to his small sister might put Pieter's nose out of joint, began giving him some simple lessons while Dr. Ramsay held his sessions with Jannie.

She had asked Ramsay if there were no local school Pieter might attend, but the answer was discouraging.

"There's only an old dame in Wolf's Hope called Luckie Mackenzie who teaches reading and writing and a bit of sewing for the girls, but I doubt Pieter is ahead of her tuition already. My father used to run the school, but the new minister comes over from Ravenswood and has his own parish and school to run, as well as ours. It was agreed, you see, that my mother should remain in the Manse until—while she lives. So, you see, Pieter is better off learning from you—if you can spare the time from your writing," he added with an ironic glance.

Dr. Ramsay had many reservations about women's entry into the world of letters. This was one of the chief grounds for dispute between him and Val, and provided material for many enjoyable and inconclusive half hours of argument. Val had told him about her career in journalism and even shown him some of her work; he was exasperatingly unimpressed and recommended that instead of writing snippets for journals—if she must write at all, for which he saw no need whatsoever—she produce something *useful:* a book of household management, perhaps, or a manual of home medicine, for which he would provide material.

"But there's far too many books written already, in my opinion," he said dampingly. Despite this divergence of views, Val and Dr. Ramsay continued excellent friends. And she continued to teach Pieter, and this added to her feeling of being hopelessly trapped; sometimes she was not far from panic.

What am I *doing* here? she would think feverishly, helping Elspie polish floors and peel potatoes (she was taking as much of the burden of housework as she could from the old woman's shoulders), teaching long division and the capitals of Europe in this freezing, crumbling, mildewy mausoleum? If I don't get myself away soon my ghost will end up keeping Thrawn Jane company in the Long Gallery.

Sometimes, on a wet afternoon, as she walked in the Long Gallery herself, she could almost imagine Thrawn Jane keeping pace with her, angry, rebellious, restlessly longing to fly away into the world.

Val had had several letters from Benet, forwarded on from the offices of *Selkirk's.* Completely refusing to accept the breaking of their engagement, he wrote calmly, kindly, affectionately.

"I understand now that you must have been suffering from an exhaustion of the nerves when you went to England," he wrote. "And indeed, after that engagement party, I am not surprised! The family all quite understand and think it an excellent plan that you should stay comfortably with your relatives for a while. As you are in Scotland, I conclude that you are with your sister-in-law's relatives there? I trust you are availing yourself of the chance to visit Scotland's historic monuments and also to inspect the many centres of *weaving, knitting,* and *homespun* industry in which Scotland abounds; our females have much to learn from Scotswomen in this respect. But I understand that Scotland is very damp; I do hope that you remember always to wear rubbers when you go out walking . . ."

Reading these lines as she walked with the children on the beach, Val glanced sardonically round the landscape. Already winter had the bay in its cold clutch; the last tarnished leaves had fallen from the deciduous trees in the policies, frost lay thicker each morning on the shaggy lawn, and took longer to melt; each day the sun rose later. The winds blew more fiercely at night while day after day high white breakers rolled into the bay.

Val resolved to lose no more time in paying her visit to Dr. Ramsay's mother. She had her promise to keep; also she still felt it might be possible to recruit some other help in the village of Wolf's Hope; surely some reliable person there might be persuaded to come and lend Elspie a hand with the children, mitigate her severities, and give Pieter a little schooling?

"How can I get to Wolf's Hope?" she asked Elspie.

"What for do ye want to go there?"

"To see it! And I promised Sir Marcus that I'd visit Mrs. Ramsay."

"Och, well, ye could walk."

"How far is it?"

"Seven mile over the headland, five along the shore."

"But one can't *go* along the shore because of the Kelpie's Flow," Val said irritably, slapping an iron on to the range; she was helping with the interminable laundering of Jannie's sheets.

"Ay, that's so; forbye ye can walk round the seaward end o' the flow when the tide's way out at the neaps."

Val, however, scouted this suggestion; she certainly was not going to trust her own judgment as to where the quicksand ended. In any case the question was academic, for the tides, just then, were at springs.

"And I don't intend to walk fourteen miles there and back, either— that's nearly five hours on foot. I'd hardly be back by dark."

Elspie agreed that this was so.

"Could I get a ride in the post cart?"

But the post cart, she found, passed Ardnacarrig at five A.M., which would mean reaching the manse at seven-thirty A.M., an unpropitious time for a social call.

"Can ye ride horseback?" said Elspie grudgingly. "I daresay ye could borrow ane o' the coach horses on a day Jock didna want it for the ploughing."

Val was not overjoyed at this suggestion, but it seemed the only answer. She *had* ridden, after a decorous fashion, with her father and occasionally with Benet in Central Park, on hired hacks, but that seemed a far cry from guiding an unfamiliar mount over fourteen miles of unknown rocky country. However she was anxious to keep her promise and write to Sir Marcus about it; she went to consult with the surly Jock, who gave her reluctant permission to take Dunkie, the brown cob.

"He's gey slow, it's true, but he winna rin awa' wi' ye, that's certain," Jock observed morosely. "I wadna trust ye wi' the mare, she's unco' wilfu' an' hot at bit—like some ithers we ken," he muttered to himself. "Ane thing, wi' Dunkie, ye canna bring him back hot an' blown, for he aye takes his ain pace—he canna thole being hurried."

So that problem was solved, though Val did not look forward to her ride. The next question was what to wear, for among her limited wardrobe nothing seemed remotely suitable.

Here, unexpectedly, Elspie proved helpful.

"There's a deal o' leddy Barbara's claes yet, i' the kist," she volunteered, measuring Val with her eye. "She was a bonnie tall lassie—she'd make twa o' Miss Kirstie—an' she went off to India an' left a' her warm things ahint. I doubt they'd no' be a bad fit for ye; forbye we might have tae take them in a wee bit."

Accompanied by Val and the delighted children she rummaged in a large damp-smelling closet in one of the many unused first-floor bedrooms where, interspersed with sour apples hung on strings to discourage the moths, were all kinds of treasures—ball gowns of a most antique cut, tight and skimpy and high-waisted; velvet mantles and swansdown cloaks of no conceivable use to anybody, which was just as well, for they were falling apart with damp and shredded at a touch. But there were more recent garments too, of a plain and serviceable nature, including a brown bombazine riding-habit which, if taken in at the sides, would do well enough, though nobody could call it flattering or fashionable wear. Val spent a day unpicking the seams and resewing them, sighing for the nimble fingers and willing kindness of Miss Chumley; she could see that no help would be forthcoming from Elspie, once she had produced the garment and some sewing materials.

Val thought it prudent to take Dunkie down on to the sands for a trial trot, accompanied by Pieter and Jannie who found this very good entertainment and demanded rides in their turn. It was soon established that Jock's assessment of Dunkie's sluggish disposition was a just one; a slow trot was all he was prepared to vouchsafe, and Val thought that riding him would be hardly faster than doing the journey on foot, though it would certainly be less tiring.

Dr. Ramsay, riding his own mare Greylag, chanced to come along the beach while they were thus engaged, and found Val leading the phlegmatic Dunkie bestridden by Jannie, who, her plaits and plaid skirts blowing, pink-cheeked and bright-eyed, crying, "Look a' me, look a' me, Pieter!" seemed for once like any normal child of her age.

"Look how well Jannie rides, Doctor Ramsay!" called Pieter, racing to meet the doctor.

"Yes, indeed, Pieter, she rides like a Cossack!"

"What's a Cossack?" Pieter demanded instantly.

Dr. Ramsay explained with his usual good-natured thoroughness; then it was Pieter's turn to ride and Jannie was set down; Dr. Ramsay wanted to draw pictures on the sand for her to identify, but she was in one of her wilful moods and danced off, whirling round and round like a dervish, singing wordless tunes at the top of her shrill gnatlike little voice.

"She's like a will-o'-the-wisp," Ramsay said, looking after the flying, twirling figure. "You'd think she could go right across the Kelpie's Flow without sinking in."

"Will-o'-the-wisp or no," said Val, "I'm taking no chances of that; I got Jock to put those big posts in"—she gestured with the hand that was not holding Dunkie's bridle—"and the children have been told they're not to go beyond them."

"You made Jock do that, did you?" Ramsay said with a quirk of the mouth that recalled Elspie's expressions. "I can see you are quite settling in at Ardnacarrig."

"What's wrong with making arrangements for the children's safety?"

"Not a thing; it was an admirable idea, though I fear you may find the midwinter tides sweep your posts away."

Val opened her mouth to say she hoped to be gone by midwinter; but after all, the children might still be here then; she remained silent. After a minute she said, "I've been reviving my horsemanship; I plan to ride over and visit your mother tomorrow or the next day, if you think she will be equal to it?"

"I'm sure she will be delighted; it's very good of you."

"I shall enjoy getting away for a day," Val admitted frankly. "I'm not used to being cooped up like this."

"No—I suppose not."

They had turned and were walking the horses across the sheep-cropped turf below the azalea hedge; Ardnacarrig House, with all its turrets and pinnacles, reared up ahead of them like some extraordinary grey geological outcrop.

"I daresay it does seem a prison to you," he said, "after spending your life in capital cities." But he sounded dispassionate, rather than sympathetic, and she was reminded that he himself must often chafe at his confined existence after former freedom in Cambridge, Vienna, and Edinburgh.

"Well, since Jannie's in no mood for learning today I'll leave you here," he said. "Greylag is as happy to go in the water as on land and while the tide's right that's my quickest way home."

"You really mean to go through the water?" Val was amazed and so was Pieter.

"Can your horse swim then, Doctor Ramsay?"

"Like a fish, laddie. She thoroughly enjoys it. We only have ten minutes in the deep water; once round the point, we take to the sand. However I don't advise you to go that way on Dunkie," he said to Val.

"My dear Davie, I shouldn't dream of it!"

"You know how to go? Over the headland you'll see two little glens ahead; you take the right-hand one, and the path down it will lead you into Wolf's Hope the quickest way; the manse lies over a bridge behind some thorn trees. Oh, by the way," he added, "a band of traveling tinklers have set up their camp in the other glen; I do not think they are to be feared, but they are rough characters and you would do better to avoid them; and warn Elspie to keep a careful eye on her poultry and make sure they are locked up at night."

"What are tinklers?" asked Pieter.

"They are a Scottish kind of gypsies; your aunt Val will tell you all about gypsies I daresay. Tinklers live by selling pots and pans and clothespegs—and love potions and charms for warts, doubtless—and a bit of horse-thieving."

"They won't break into the Big House?"

"Not a chance—too scared of Thrawn Jane."

Val smiled, and he said, "You haven't seen the lady yourself?"

"Who is Thrawn Jane?" Pieter wanted to know instantly.

"Now see what you have done," Val scolded Ramsay, who only laughed.

"I'll tell my mother to expect you at noon if it's fine—it will take you that long to flog old Dunkie over the hill," and with a wave he touched up Greylag and cantered off along the edge of the waves. Val watched apprehensively, half expecting to see horse and rider disappear under water, but they struck out to sea and soon passed out of sight, swimming strongly, round the high tumbled rocks at the foot of the headland.

Val steered the conversation away from Thrawn Jane and kept it firmly to gypsies as they returned to the house.

Next morning she started off early, having bidden up Annot Kelso for the day and impressed on her that she was to look after Jannie the whole time and never, if possible, let the child out of her sight. Annot swore that she would "see after the little lass as if the auld laird himself were on my tail" but Val had more faith in Pieter's care; Annot, except when satisfying her dramatic instincts by telling the children wild tales, was apt to go off into a dream, combing her yellow hair in front of some tarnished old glass, and forgetting her charges for half hours together; and half an hour was long enough for Jannie to get into the most fertile and unpredictable trouble if left unsupervised.

For once, the day was fine and clear; even the lethargic Dunkie seemed infected by Val's high spirits at leaving Ardnacarrig for a holiday. Unprompted by heel or crop, he broke into his lumbering trot and went rapidly enough up the zigzag cart track which led over Wolf's Crag. At the top, Val paused to breathe him, and looked back. On the beach she was pleased to observe two little figures and a larger one, with a yellow dot for its head, sitting nearby. Good, Val thought; on the beach Annot would be less tempted to wander away from her charges and fall into a dream.

Val shortened the reins and managed to thump Dunkie into a reluctant canter across the short turf on top of the headland. Presently the ground sloped away ahead, and for the first time she came in sight of Wolf's Hope village—a dozen cottages clustered at the landward end of a short curved stone pier built out on the northerly side of the headland. Threads of blue peatsmoke drifted from the chimneys. A couple of small fishing boats were moored in the shelter of the pier and Val could just distinguish the tiny, antlike figures of men busy about them. Wolf's Hope looked a well-found, tidy little anchorage and Val's heart rose at the sight of it.

Soon she came to the point where the paths diverged. Two small glens opened ahead of her with a shoulder of rock thrusting up between them and grassy tracks running down each. She took the right-hand path, which plunged down beside a rocky brook, sometimes so steeply that she found herself dizzily looking down over Dunkie's bony shoulders and in danger of sliding on to his neck. The glen bore away to the left; now she had lost sight of the village. Presently the path ran in among a stand of larches and became rather less steep, though the stream was now a nerve-racking depth below at the bottom of a young ravine; plainly there was still some way to descend. The distance from the top of the headland was much farther than Val, in her first optimism at seeing it, had supposed. Now there was another steep and slithery stretch of downhill track; Dunkie slipped and snorted, Val's thighs and shoulders ached with leaning and pulling back, and her fingers were stiff from her nervous clutch at the reins. At last the ground levelled, and she saw kail patches and drystone walls ahead.

The manse, Ramsay had said, lay to the left; soon, rounding a corner of hill, she discovered it, off by itself among thorn trees, slightly bigger and more comfortable-looking than the other houses, with a well-tended garden at the back and a few frost-pinched roses still against its walls.

All of a sudden Val found herself gripped by a paralysing shyness, a kind of dread quite alien to her usually confident nature.

What would it be like, to talk to somebody who knew that they were dying? What ever could she find to say? What could she talk about? Caught short by this anxiety, she felt she had not given the matter nearly enough thought—she had not given it any thought at all, in her childish pleasure at the fine morning and liberation from Ardnacarrig. Now she was halted by a horrified awareness of her own inadequacy. She pulled Dunkie to a halt. Dismounting, she stood leaning her back against the parapet of a small stone bridge spanning two streams that came tumbling from different directions and met at the head of the harbour. To her right, on the stone jetty below the bridge, men were stretching nets to dry in the sun. To her left, the manse door opened, and a white-capped woman stepped out, shook a mat vigorously, gave Val an inquisitive look, then went inside again and shut the door.

Dying was an unknown process to Val. She had sat by no deathbeds. Her mother's end, when it came, eight years after that parting at the dockside, had seemed so far removed in time and place that it had little reality for Val. And her father had been taken suddenly by a heart attack while he was on a visit to a publishing firm in Seattle, thousands of miles from his daughter. It had happened during a summer heat wave and the hasty funeral was over even before the news had reached Val so that, although it came as a sudden and grievous shock, his death had strangely little actuality for her; part of her mind had not even accepted it yet and she was prone, when tired and off-guard, to imagine that she saw him at street corners or coming toward her through open doors; she still half expected that a letter in the familiar writing might arrive to say that it had all been a mistake.

None of which reflections were of any help to her in the present situation.

Val shook herself, squared her shoulders, and walked over the little bridge in the direction of the manse, leading Dunkie, who followed slowly and reluctantly behind her. Tying him to a tree, she knocked on the door.

It was opened by the white-capped woman she had seen before, who gave her a pleasant smile and said, "Ye'll be Mistress Montgomery? Mrs. Ramsay's ettling to see you and asks if ye will be so kind as to step through into the conservatory."

The conservatory sounded startlingly grand—for the house was small, though pleasantly furnished and showing every sign of cultivated taste; there were books and flowers in profusion, good furniture, and many original and interesting pictures and sketches hung on the walls. Val was led through a couple of rooms and found that the conservatory was a small glass-walled and roofed extension at the back. There were ferns and geraniums in pots, two wicker chairs, a couple of small tables littered with books and papers, and a sofa, on which, covered with a shawl, Mrs. Ramsay was lying. A door and windows leading to the garden stood wide open but the little glassed-in place was warm enough, for it faced south and had the full benefit of the sun.

"Miss Montgomery—or may I call you Val, as I gather my unconventional son already does? I am absolutely delighted to see you. Forgive my not getting up to welcome you; the welcome is nonetheless warm. Tibbie, Miss Montgomery is dying of hunger and thirst after her ride."

"Ay, ay, she'll be taking some o' my diet loaf, whiles, an' a glass o' buttermilk," said Tibbie, and bustled out to fetch these articles.

"Tibbie will enjoy feeding you up on all the delicious things I can take no longer. Do sit down—there, where I can see you. Now tell me how you are liking Ardnacarrig? It must seem exceedingly strange to you after New York."

Val sat obediently, as directed, and began to talk. She felt large, clumsy, and self-conscious; shabby, too, and untidy, with her blown hair and brown bombazine. While on the surface she felt these vague discomforts, and meanwhile did her best to describe her impressions amusingly, make jokes, be entertaining, underneath she was suffering from a profound sense of shock.

For a start, the woman on the sofa was so young-looking! David Ramsay must be approaching thirty, and Val had vaguely expected that his mother would be in her sixties, but Helen Ramsay must be barely forty-five and her delicate thin face, when in repose, looked even younger. She must have married when she was hardly halfway through her teens. Her glossy sweep of chestnut-brown hair was drawn smoothly into a big loose chignon at the back of her head; Val noticed that Tibbie, when she came back with the refreshments, lovingly stroked a stray strand of this into place, as if she took more pride in it than did its owner.

Helen Ramsay was young, but she also, quite unmistakably, was dying. Val had never seen anybody who looked so desperately ill. Her beautiful brown eyes were sunk in deep pits; her cheeks were hollow; her face was transparently white as the geranium flowers behind her and her skin seemed stretched so tightly over her bones that it was a wonder her face could show such animation. Val could see plainly that the least movement exhausted her, but that she was absolutely determined not to be handicapped by her weakness. Evidence of activity lay scattered all around; while they talked, Mrs. Ramsay was at work stitching patchwork pieces over hexagonal bits of card, and two-thirds of an unusually beautiful patchwork quilt lay at the end of her couch; sketches were strewn on the floor by her—Val noticed a pencil portrait of David; a stool by the couch held more books and a piece of embroidery. Her thin, fine hands seemed to move with unerring skill, whatever she did; all the time she talked, she was setting exquisitely small stitches with the smooth speed of a lifetime's practice.

"And tell me *all* about the children. How I long to see them! But Davie thinks it would be wrong to expose them to infection—even with the doors and windows open like this, which I hope you can bear? Tibbie shall bring you a plaid if you are cold. I love the air and can never have too much."

"Perhaps next spring they could come over and visit you in the garden?" Val suggested.

"My dear, it is kind of you to suggest it, but I shan't last that long. Next spring I shall not be here," Helen said calmly. "Never mind! I choose to imagine that Heaven will be just like that valley up there"—she waved a stemlike hand at the view—"filled with all the children I would have liked to have, and the sun always shining. An endless picnic, in fact. Now, tell me more about Jannie and the way she talks. What did you say was her word for beautiful?"

"*Arla*—anything she wants, and can't have, like the clock or the crystal chandelier—or the red moon—or Elspie's bantam cock—is *arla*."

"Arla, arla," repeated Helen, savouring it. "And what else does she say?"

"She has quite a few words of her own—I suppose because she hasn't been able to learn the real ones. *Grake,* for instance, is her one verb and it does for everything—give, eat, pick up, put down; all the time she's with Pieter you can hear her commanding little voice crying 'Grake it, Pieter, grake it.' "

"And? What else?"

"She loves *noise;* sometimes she'll wake in the night and suddenly begin singing at the top of her lungs, banging two iron saucepan lids together, or thumping the poker on her brass bed head."

"I hope Elspie doesn't sleep within earshot," Helen said, laughing. "I can't imagine her being as philosophical as you about these midnight concerts."

Val did not confess that she was far from philosophical herself.

"I'm not sure yet *where* Elspie sleeps—she hasn't shown us—miles off, somewhere in the south wing."

"More about Jannie?"

"With animals, and outside things, she's completely fearless; she'll run up to bulls, Jock's farm dogs, geese, pigs, without any touch of anxiety; she's far braver than Pieter. And the creatures seem to recognise her trust; they are never hostile. But with strange people she is generally wary and timid as a wildcat. She tastes *everything*—if you let her—bark, raw potatoes, ivy leaves, pebbles on the beach; you have to watch her like a hawk or it all goes into her mouth—in amazing combinations too—onions with marmalade, porridge and pine needles, milk and grass. Although in five minutes she can reduce a room to total chaos, she's fussily tidy, too, in her own way; won't have things piled on top of one another but must put them side by side, in neat patterns."

Val went on with more ease, talking about the children, about Elspie, telling tales of their ill-assorted life together and its ups and downs.

"Oh, I can see you have your hands full," said Helen Ramsay, rocking with laughter, wiping the tears of it from her eyes, after hearing of Elspie's shoes filled with fishbones and the terrible tale of the kitchen cat's dinner. "I just wish I could see Jannie; Pieter sounds a dear little boy too; no wonder you feel you can't leave them; no wonder you love them so."

Val felt, with dreadful guilt, how far from true this was.

"I don't know that I *do* love them so," she said defensively.

"You couldn't describe Jannie like that if you didn't. Oh, how I envy you. Oh, how lucky you are! To think of living in that amazing house, and having two such interesting children to teach. But what can have happened to the parents? I cannot believe that Kirstie would have gone off and abandoned her children—when she was a child she was a loving little thing, and she had such a scrupulous sense of duty. Don't you, in your heart of hearts, believe that they must be dead?"

Seeing Val's expression, Helen added, "I am sorry if I shock you." She paused. "But you see I live so constantly with the prospect of death that it does not upset me any more."

Facing the matter honestly, Val was obliged to agree with Helen's view.

"I don't see how, if Kirstie was able to get in touch, she would not have done so by now. But suppose she is ill, somewhere? My brother might have gone off and left her," Val said with difficulty. "He is—irresponsible; I believe he might do a thing like that. He's cold-blooded."

"Like my Davie," Helen Ramsay said, sighing. "Not that Davie is irresponsible; on the contrary. He is the most caring, thoughtful creature in the world. He built me this conservatory as soon as his father died. His father would never have done such a thing; he disapproved of conservatories."

"Why?" asked Val, astonished.

"He said if God had meant us to have glass walls He would not have inspired man to build houses of stone and thatch. My husband was a very rigid-thinking man; God-fearing, of course, virtuous, but, oh dear, he was disagreeable! I loved him, but it took me twenty-five years to accept some things about him and I am afraid Davie never did. There is a very large element of his father in Davie which he does his best to keep fastened down and covered up. That is why he says he will never marry."

She looked wistfully away up the glen, as if seeing a procession of invisible grandchildren passing out of sight. Her mouth, Val noticed, was full and beautiful, contrasting strangely with the ghostlike thinness of her face.

Next moment, all laughter and animation, she was demanding news of Sir Marcus.

"Does he still suffer from his gout? And his neurasthenia and palpitations, and quinsy and spasms and tic? He is the most amazing man. Whenever he goes off on his travels he sends me beautiful things—that rug came from Kurdistan, and this robe I have on is the kind worn by Turkish women; he sent that vase and those slippers—but—he's such a wretch—write letters he will *not!* And he comes to see me less and less, which I regret bitterly—I am very much afraid that he finds it too distressing. He is terrified of being made to feel."

Val described her voyage with Sir Marcus and the evening in Edinburgh. Helen was delighted.

"Oh, you hit him off to the life. I can see why you choose to be a writer. But listen, my dear—I can see you are a little bit in love with Marcus. Don't be offended with me"—as Val, astounded and deeply upset, drew back—"after all, if *I* am not allowed to be frank, who can be? I guessed it the minute you walked in the door. You were prepared to dislike me very much, weren't you? 'She's a rival,' you were thinking, 'and not *only* a rival, but a dismal, dying invalid, and what's worse, sugar sweet with everybody so they can't even have the satisfaction of being disagreeable about her but are obliged to say how good and uncomplaining she is.' Come, confess! You expected some odious sweet little woman, her silver hair done up by a pink ribbon!"

Utterly disarmed by this, Val burst out laughing.

"How did you guess? That is *exactly* the picture I had of you."

"I knew it," Helen said with calm triumph. "And it is all because that wretch Marcus made you fall in love with him. Oh, he is a charmer, don't I know it? If I had met him at fifteen or sixteen, before I married James, I should have longed to be his wife. But James made a better husband. And truly, my dear Val, I should think twice about Marcus. He is away too selfish! A man who is still single at his age is not a good risk: far too fond of his own habits. And it is plain that you are the same."

"Am I?"

"Indeed you are! You are a *good* person; I can see that. But strongwilled; you are like my husband; when you see that something needs to be done, you do it—regardless of the inconvenience it may cause to anybody—including yourself! People won't love you for this trait—you mustn't expect that."

Am I like that? Val pondered.

Every portrait of herself that was presented to her seemed more unflattering than the last.

"No, Marcus won't do for you," concluded Helen. "Besides, he is too old. He is forty-three—two years younger than me. And this is disinterested advice I am giving you, my dear Val, for I should be glad to die knowing that some capable person would look after the dear man in his cantankerous old age."

"Upon my word," Val said laughing, "you and your son are a most discouraging pair! Davie has already warned me that I must not expect to marry *him*."

"No indeed, that would be even more disastrous. But come, don't despair. A girl as beautiful as you surely cannot help acquiring a trail of suitors wherever you go? Don't tell me you did not leave some swain pining for you in New York?"

"It's true, I was engaged to be married." Val sighed, thinking of the letter she had that morning received from Benet:

"I hope to come to England as soon as I have completed my present series of cases, in order to see you and, I trust, convince you that your change of mind was just a passing caprice, due to fatigue. I cannot believe that your feelings for me have changed so completely. I still love you as much as ever. I do hope that you are remembering to wear plenty of warm flannel underwear and losing no opportunity to sample Scottish delicacies. The *haggis* I have heard very well spoken of; also *Skink* and *Powsowdie*."

"Ah? You were engaged? Describe him!" Helen's eyes sparkled with interest.

For some reason, Val found this hard.

"He's good. He's hardworking and conscientious and capable. A lawyer."

"Oh what dull stuff. You'll have to do better than that."

But it seemed that Val was unable to paint an accurate portrait of Benet.

"I'd have to see him," Helen concluded, "before I can decide whether he's the right person for you."

"Perhaps you will. He intends to come to England and argue with me."

"I hope he comes soon, then, or I shall miss him," Helen said. "Now, you must forgive me, but I need to sleep. I tire quickly. It is annoying."

"I have exhausted you by staying too long. I should leave."

"Indeed you must not. Tibbie would be black affronted if you left before taking bite and sup—and so should I. Rest, eat, read—take any books you fancy. Here are some of my favourites. I want to talk again when I have slept a little—you have not told me near enough about New York and your life there."

Tibbie endorsed this.

"It does her gude tae hae summat new to think on, i' the lang watches o' the nicht. Bide till she wakes, an' hae anither crack wi' her. It's no' late yet, an' she'll sleep but fifteen minutes."

So Val sat in the pleasant front room, and talked to Tibbie, and ate her delicious deers' puddings and potato fritters. She wondered if Davie came home at noon, but Tibbie explained that he was "awa ower tae Ravenswood," where the minister was afflicted with a bad throat, and would not be back till late. It was plain that Tibbie was very fond of him; she had looked after him as a child, Val learned. She seemed a particularly pleasant and kindhearted woman, devoted to her mistress.

"'Tis a pity she canna see the bairns," Tibbie said sighing. "She fair longs to, but she says it's no' richt tae bring them to a house of death. My poor Miss Helen, she's no lang for this world." Unaffectedly she mopped her eyes with her apron.

Val was seized by a sudden bold notion.

Without pausing to think, she said, "When she—what will you be doing, Tibbie, after she goes? Will you stay here to look after Doctor Ramsay?"

"Na, na, he'll no' bide here, my dearie. When Miss Helen's gone, he'll be awa' back to Enbra; syne I'll pack my bags an' off tae my gude sister at Dunglass, for the new meenister has his ain housekeeper body an' disna need my sairvices. It'll grieve me sair tae leave Wolf's Hope, but ilka path has its puddle."

Val said, "If you don't want to leave these parts, would you consider coming to Ardnacarrig to help Elspie look after the children?"

Tibbie seemed somewhat taken aback at this suggestion.

"Nay, I misdoot auld Elspie'd ne'er thole sic a plan? She'd be fair scomfished that you didna think her fit tae mind the bairns by her lane."

"But if I managed to persuade her? After all, she's old, and there's only Annot Kelso to help her."

"Ay, an' yon's a puir hempie," Tibbie said reflectively. "Aweel, if ye can fleech auld Elspie into it, I'll be blythe to come—when my puir leddy's laid under."

At this point Helen called faintly from the conservatory and Tibbie sped away to her.

"What's your wish, my doo? What is it, my dawtie?" Val heard her ask. The crooning note of tenderness in Tibbie's tone brought tears to Val's eyes and made her suddenly hate herself for having conceived and broached such a coldly self-regarding plan.

"Miss Val's not gone yet?" she heard Helen anxiously inquire.

"Na, na, dinna fash yersel' my dearie. She's in ben yet. Now, bide still while I redd ye."

The door closed and Val, at random, opened one of the pile of books that Helen had pushed into her arms. It proved to be in Greek: Plato's *Symposium*. Another was Latin—Virgil's *Eclogues*. The other three were respectively Voltaire, Rousseau, and a novel by George Eliot which Val had read. She pushed the books to one side and sat with her chin on her hands, resenting the fact that she should feel guilty for having engendered a scheme which was for nobody's harm and everybody's good.

Tibbie came back. "She's braw an' redd up noo, an' will ye step back into the conservatory, she speirs? But dinna stay lang," she murmured in a lower tone, "for her hoast is at her, an' she's a wee thing spent."

Helen looked more than spent, indeed, she looked utterly depleted; two small spots of red burnt on her cheekbones, she was even paler than before, and her forehead was beaded with sweat. A recurring cough seemed as if it might shake her to pieces. She had abandoned the attempt to sew, and the materials were pushed to one side. But she caught hold of Val's hand, saying, "Don't go yet a while. Not for half an hour! Tell me about life in New York. Are they very grand there?"

Val did her best to describe the Allerton party, and way of life. But then Tibbie returned, and said commandingly, "Yon's enough, the noo. The lassie maun gang her ways before it's pit mirk. Remember she disna ken the road so well as we do."

"But you'll come again? We are to be friends?" Helen still had hold of Val's hand. "Yes, I am sure you will come; God will allow me another visit. I find he can be quite reasonable in such ways."

"Of course I will come," Val said.

"And you won't leave it too long? Next time, bring sketches of the children."

"My dear Mrs. Ramsay—"

"Helen, Helen!"

"Helen, then—I can't draw!"

"Then you must learn! *Any*body can draw—especially somebody as intelligent as you. All it takes is practice. Begin as soon as you get home. Oh, very well, Tibbie, take her away."

She blew a kiss to Val and lay back on her pillows, limp as a thread.

Val had so much to think about on her homeward journey that she rode with a loose rein, and let Dunkie choose his own way and pace, which suited him very well. She felt as if, after living on dry bread for months, she had suddenly been fed on some utterly strange, exotic delicacy; as if she had put out a hand to touch a sapling and had a current of electricity run up her arm; as if she had woken from sleep and found herself on a high mountainside, looking over a huge plain.

No wonder Sir Marcus loves her, thought poor Val; I couldn't hope that he would spare me a single thought after having known Helen Ramsay. I wonder if her husband was unkind to her? What a strange man he sounded. Can she be right, that Nils and Kirstie are dead? I am sure she has deep, wide awarenesses, far beyond my level of understanding. If I could be certain—if I had definite news that Kirstie and Nils were dead— what could I, what ought I to do about the children? I could ask Helen's advice, she thought instantly.

No wonder David Ramsay is as he is. Imagine being her son!

Again and again Val's train of thought was darkened by a suffusing sense of guilt at the vulgarity, the greedy crudeness of having looked ahead and secured Tibbie's services before her mistress was even dead. Again and again she doggedly thought, no, I was right to do it. Anybody can see that Tibbie is a person of truly sympathetic and educated feelings; and no wonder. She must have learned so much from contact with Helen. She would be a thousand times kinder to the children than old Elspie ever could—or than I ever could, Val thought ruefully.

But is Helen right in her judgment of Sir Marcus? Is he really so set in his solitary bachelor ways that he can't accommodate himself to another person?

Dunkie stumbled and Val, recalled with a guilty jerk to awareness of her surroundings, looked about her dazedly and discovered, in a sudden cold clutch of fright, that she was on unfamiliar ground. High stone cliffs rose on each side of the track. This was certainly not the way she had come.

What a *fool* I am, she thought furiously. Mooning along, thinking about myself—why didn't I have the sense to look where the horse was taking me?

Early winter dusk was gathering already; another half hour and it would be almost dark. What ought she to do? Retrace her way—if she could—to Wolf's Hope, and start again? But Elspie, and, even more, the children, would worry very much if she were as late back as that would make her; it might be better to continue on this path, which climbed quite steeply, and hope that it would soon bring her out on some height from which she could see where she had gone wrong.

Dunkie plodded on uphill. Presently, rounding a shoulder of cliff, he threw up his head violently and whinnied in surprise. Val's hand tightened nervously on the rein, for, ahead of her, completely unexpected in this wild region, she saw the flickering light of a bonfire. She could hear voices too, the yelp of a dog, a neigh from another horse. There were smells of woodsmoke, singeing fur, and frizzling fat.

Dunkie whinnied again, then shied as a lean, silent dog almost ran between his legs. A voice said sharply, "Ruffler! Here!"

Somebody called, "Who is it?"

A thin, tattered figure suddenly materialised from among the rocks at the side of the track, and a hand, grasping the rein, brought Dunkie to a halt.

Val said, "Let go of my rein, please!" in a loud clear voice, doing her best to conceal the fright and anger she felt. Who were these people? Vague memories of Scots history flashed through her head—Rob Roy, savage Highlanders, feuds, the massacre of Glencoe. She raised her crop, trying to pull the rein from the man's hand.

"Hey, lads!" he called, taking no notice of her, "this yin's a fine stoot kimmer; ou, a tasty crittery! What'll we dae wi' her?"

"Gie ower, ye daft limmer!" called somebody from the shadowy group by the fire. "'Tis the lass frae the Big Hoose—yon Lunnon lassie. Leave her gang free, ye donnart loon. She's no' the one we want."

"Aweel, aweel," said the man, sounding disappointed, "she micht gie us a bit siller, did we thrig an' sorn a bit."

"I'll give you nothing!" said Val. She wondered what thrigging and sorning were; decided she would rather not know. "Let go my bridle, if you please."

The narrow dim path seemed full of eyes and faces staring at her—men, women, children, and a few dogs; all the eyes shone with the same eldritch light, reflected from the flames of the fire. They were a wild, ragged crew, the men grasping staves, the women huddled in shawls. Val tapped Dunkie with her crop and tried to edge him past the group. The man who had taken her bridle finally, reluctantly, let go of it and stepped aside.

"Thank you," Val said haughtily. Then she noticed the face of a man who seemed remotely familiar, standing toward the rear of the group. Catching his eye she asked, "Am I on the right road for Ardnacarrig?"

The man she had addressed made no answer. In fact he moved behind another, who said, "Ou, ay. Spang on till ye see anither track on yer left hand, then ahort the brae ahint the auld cassle, an' ye'll see Ardnacarrig belaw ye—ye canna gae wrang."

"Thank you," Val said, and pushed Dunkie into his heavy trot. Soon she had left the alarming group behind her and arrived, much to her relief, at the point where the paths from the two little glens joined together. She had come by the longer way, that was all; she had forgotten to cross the bridge down at the bottom, in Wolf's Hope. And these people must—she remembered now—be the band of tinklers against whom David had warned her.

They seemed to be waiting for somebody—I wonder who? she thought, coming to the southern side of the headland, seeing with immense relief the pale, familiar curve of Ardnacarrig Bay down below, and the lights, among its trees, of the Big House. I shouldn't think many people go along that track; I suppose it must be another of their band they are expecting. I must remember to warn Elspie about locking up the poultry.

There would be much to tell Elspie, she thought, and wondered how to broach the matter of Tibbie Gordon. This would have to be done with caution and tact.

But when she got back, and had handed Dunkie over to the ministrations of the dour Jock, she found Elspie in a very queer state, upset and preoccupied, hardly waiting to greet her, but soon flitting off with some murmured excuse.

Pieter explained this, as Val spooned up a bowlful of leek broth which had been left for her on the hob.

"An old man came here this afternoon. Do you remember, Aunt Valla, the old man who came up and spoke just when we were getting into the coach to come here? I think it was the same one. The man who gave you a letter for Elspie. He came limping into the kitchen when Elspie was giving us our tea, and she jumped up, all upset. She said he was sick, and she's put him to bed."

Elspie presently reappeared and confirmed this.

"Ay, it's Mungo—it's Mungo—an' I fear he's unco' sick, puir auld carl—gey brockit an' forfoughten; he shouldna ha' come, he shouldna ha' done it! Forbye I fear he has a fever on him an' I've e'en pit him i' the hay loft where he'll no gie ony infection tae the bairns."

Val was shocked. "You shouldn't have put him there! He ought to be in a proper room with a fire."

"Aweel, I'll think on't," said Elspie. "He's fine an' comfortable the noo, an' can bide the nicht where he lies. I'll maybe fetch Doctor Ramsay tae him the morn."

Val inquired how the children's day had gone with Annot. Well enough, she gathered; they had spent the morning collecting driftwood on the sands, helped feed the poultry and carry straw to the young cattle in the afternoon, and Jannie had gone to bed, tired out, immediately after tea; Pieter had followed her as soon as he was assured of Val's safe return. For a wonder, Jannie had not fallen into the pig trough, nor got lost in the policies, nor climbed on to the peat stack and fallen off, nor eaten quantities of poisonous laurel leaves, nor had a screaming tantrum, nor any of the other endless possibilities; it sounded like a most blameless day.

"Yon Annot's no' sae skaivie, an' at least the lass is honest," Elspie said, rather belligerently. "She does well enow." Val began to feel that perhaps she had been recklessly precipitate in securing the help of Tibbie. At any rate she would keep her own counsel until the next day.

But in the dead dark middle of the night, after she had written up her journal and fallen into an exhausted slumber, Val was woken by the sound of stifled sobbing from the next room. With an irritable sigh—almost certainly Annot had allowed Jannie too many fig cakes for her tea—Val wrapped herself in a shawl, lit a candle, and went to see what was causing the trouble. She was surprised to find that for once it was not Jannie, who slept in her usual hedgehog ball, fingers jammed in her mouth, but Pieter, restless, wide-eyed, and whimpering softly. He clung with a frantic grip to Val's hands, looking past her into the corners of the room.

"What is it, Pieter? Have you a pain? What's the matter?"

"It's the ghost cradle! I can hear it rocking."

"*What?*"

"Annot told us about it. It's the ghost bairn in its cradle. It was Thrawn Jane's bairn, and whiles, when the wind blows, it wakes and cries, and whiles you hear it rocking, and whiles you hear it crying, and syne you *see* the bairn!"

He was obviously repeating Annot's words; he clung desperately to Val. "And syne it puts its cold wee hands on you, and that's when you know there's going to be a death! I don't want to hear it! I don't want to see it! I want Mama! I want my mama!" And he wept desolately, pushing his frightened face into the hollow of Val's shoulder and holding her with such a terrified grip that she felt his small fingers digging into her like staples.

If Annot Kelso had been there at that moment Val would have strangled her happily. She damned Annot from the bottom of her heart. May she burn in the pit! I'll take good care she never sets foot in the house again.

It took a great deal to upset the usually calm and reasonable Pieter, but once he was thoroughly scared, it was equally hard to calm him again.

"Listen, Pieter—that's not any ghost cradle you hear—there *aren't* such things. It's the loose latch on the door. Look, I'll wedge the door open with a piece of paper, than it can't rattle."

"No, don't—*don't!*" He clung to her even more frenziedly. "Something might come in! I don't want to see the ghostly bairn!"

Wait till I get hold of that Annot, Val thought.

"Listen, Pieter, why don't we go down to the kitchen and make ourselves some hot milk? I'm hungry again after riding all that long way yesterday, and I expect you could do with a warm drink. Then I'll wedge the door *shut* so it doesn't rattle."

"All right," he finally agreed, with a subdued hiccup. She wrapped him in a plaid and he accompanied her downstairs, keeping tight hold of her hand.

The kitchen, huge, dark, and stone-flagged, with its meal tubs swathed in cheesecloth and the dusky shapes of ham and flitches hanging overhead, was not, perhaps, the best place for somebody in the grip of ghostly terrors. But at least the range, stuffed with peat for the night, was comfortingly warm, and Val set Pieter to blowing it up while she took a copper pan and went off to fetch some milk from the pantry.

This was a small ice-cold place with broad slate shelves round three of its sides. The milk stood in big earthenware basins with the cream settling for tomorrow's porridge; a pewter skimmer lay beside, ready to draw it off. Not wishing to enrage Elspie by wasting the cream, Val set her candle on the shelf and hastily scraped off the top layer of cream that had formed, into a small pitcher. Then she dipped out two cups of milk. Having done so, she was about to take up her candle again, had stretched out her hand for it, when she was transfixed by the sight of a face outside the screened pantry window, looking in. An instant later it had gone, but she was certain that she had not been mistaken. It was a man: she had caught the flash of his eyes and seen something blue—the knot of a neckerchief—under his chin. It was the same man she had noticed among the group of tinklers on her way home the evening before. Seeing him outside the window at this hour of night was a devastating shock; she only just prevented herself from crying out. She bit her lip, stood still for a moment, then picked up the candle.

"Aunt Valla!" called Pieter nervously from the kitchen. "Why are you taking such a long time?"

"Here I come!"

"The fire's burned up nicely."

Val set the pan of milk over it.

"That's fine, Pieter—now, you watch the milk, like a hawk, and don't let it boil over while I check that all the doors are fastened."

"Why?" he asked at once. "Doesn't Elspie do that when she goes to bed?"

"She might have been a bit distracted by the old man coming—she might have forgotten."

Could it have been the old man she had seen? But no, he had a long white beard; this one was clean-shaven, and wore the blue choker that she had noticed.

Walking from door to door, she checked the fastenings. Elspie had not forgotten; all the doors were secure, the windows shut and shuttered. The stable wings had countless outside entrances of their own, but they were cut off from the main part of the house by a massive door, which was kept bolted at night. It was shut and fastened. Val returned to the kitchen and poured the warm milk into two cups.

"Let's take our drinks upstairs, shall we?"

She had built up the children's bedroom fire before they left the room, and it was glowing brightly when they returned. While Pieter, comforted by its light, sipped his drink as slowly as possible, making it last, Val succeeded in wedging the rattling door. She had also prepared a whole ramification of rational arguments in case Pieter reverted to the subject of the ghostly bairn—that ghosts were inventions of ignorant, stupid people who had too little to occupy their minds—that babies were harmless, so why should their spirits be thought baleful anyway—but, to her relief,

Pieter did not allude to it again. Hoping to distract his thoughts, she described Mrs. Ramsay's house and the village of Wolf's Hope.

"Can we go there and see the boats?" he asked.

"Yes, I daresay. Perhaps Jock would let us take out the old gig that's in the shed, and we could carry our dinner in a basket."

Soothed by this plan he seemed ready to return to bed, yawning and relaxed. But Val remembered that throttling clutch round her neck when she had first gone to him.

"Would you like to sleep in with me?" she suggested.

For a moment he seemed tempted. Then his face tightened. He said, "No, I better not. If Jannie woke and found I wasn't there she'd be frightened."

"All right. Anyway I'm just next door. I'll leave the door open. Goodnight, Pieter."

"Goodnight, Aunt Val."

Soon, listening from her own room, she heard his deep, regular breathing.

Val herself lay awake for hours, listening, straining her ears to try to catch any unwonted sound. She heard none. Where had that man gone? Why had he been there? What was he after?

And then she remembered where she had seen him before, why his face had seemed familiar. He was the man in the Tom-and-Jerry hat whom she had seen in the lobby of the Jersey Hotel.

CHAPTER 13

NEXT morning, choosing a moment when the children were out of earshot, playing in the stable yard, Val mentioned the band of tinklers to Elspie, and the fact that she had seen one of their number outside the pantry window.

Elspie took the announcement placidly enough.

"Och, ay, whiles yin or anither'll be daikerin' roond the policies, lookin' tae see what they can pick up—but there's little eneugh for the gangrels! I hae the pootry all lockit in the caveys, an' the kye lockit i' the byre. Ne'er fash yersel' aboot them, hinnie. Aiblins they may keek in the wunda tae see have we ony siller, but we havena! A'body kens the Big Hoose is a poor auld hurleyhoose, naught but Castle Barebane."

Val felt less calm about it. She somehow doubted if the intruder was after money. When the household tasks were done, she made a careful search around the outbuildings and the stable yard, through the neglected shrubberies and the big untended kitchen garden. But she could find no damage, or any sign of attempted entry. How was it possible to be certain, though? The whole place was in such a ramshackle state.

Returning, she ran into Elspie carrying a bowl of porridge toward the stable.

"May I come and visit the old man, Elspie?"

"Ay—if ye wish," Elspie agreed rather unwillingly. But Val wanted to be sure that the sick man was not last night's watcher; not that she had many doubts on that score. In fact the man in the loft was exactly as she remembered him—a lean, brown, bright-eyed weatherbeaten man with a shock of white hair, white beard, and tattoos on his forearms.

Elspie had made him comfortable enough on a bed of hay with several plaids and blankets over him. He was sleeping but woke at the sound of their feet on the ladder.

"Och, Elspie, ye shouldna ha' brocht the young lady up here!" he said, rather shocked, but Val said she wanted to see how he was getting on, and he thanked her with dignity, adding, "Forbye I'm blythe to thank ye again, mistress, for carrying my letter to Elspie. Sin' she never answered it, I made so bold as to come and pay a call on her."

"Ye camsteery limmer!" said Elspie scoldingly, but just the same it was plain that her heart had been softened by the sight of him. "Eat your sow-ans and say no more."

There did not seem to be too much the matter with him. Val thought it might have been mainly exhaustion, if he had come all the way from Edinburgh in such wintry weather. But, hearing the sound of hoofs in the yard, she said, "Here comes Doctor Ramsay. Why don't you fetch him up, Elspie? He might as well look at Mr. Bucklaw before giving Jannie her lesson."

"Ay, fegs, I'll do that," said Elspie, and climbed nimbly down. The moment she was out of earshot—"Why don't you marry Elspie, Mr. Bucklaw?" said Val impulsively. "I'm *sure* she loves you—I'm certain she does! She was terribly moved when she read your note. If *I* were you, I'd ask her right away."

Old Mungo Bucklaw burst out laughing. "Ey, ye're a canny lassie! Ye dinna let the stoor settle. Aweel, I'll no' say I havena a mind tae try!"

Elspie came back with the doctor. Val now had leisure to observe that she was unusually pink-cheeked, and had put on a very becoming mutch with goffered frills and ribbons that tied under her chin. Also she had on a clean apron over her black dress.

Dr. Ramsay gave the old man a rapid examination and asked him, "Have you traveled in hot countries?"

"Ay, I have that. I've been a sailor all my life."

"What you are suffering from is a touch of malaria. Take these pills night and morning for a few days, rest for twenty-four hours, and you should be through the worst of it."

Old Mungo received the pills gravely; Val suspected that the diagnosis came as no surprise to him. In fact she had a strong notion that he had used the attack as a ploy to weaken Elspie's defences.

She followed Ramsay back into the yard. The children were there, playing on a rope swing which Val had suspended, with the doctor's help, in the doorway of an unused shed. Pieter was pushing Jannie, who gave her little chirps of delight and commanded her brother shrilly, "More grake, Pieter! More, more grake!"

"How good the boy always is with her," Ramsay observed. Val felt a complicated, familiar pang as she watched the children playing. They reminded her continually of Nils and herself; Pieter, fair, blue-eyed, thin-faced was in appearance a small replica of his father. But in truth, how different! If Nils had been in Pieter's place he would certainly have managed somehow to oust his sister from her seat on the swing—by outright force, or by contriving an "accident" in which she fell and hurt herself, or by some form of blackmail. And he would then stay in the swing for the next hour, not for his own pleasure but merely to torment her, while she stood impotently crying or wandered forlornly off to find some other occupation. Whereas Pieter showed no impatience; he seemed to enjoy Jannie's pleasure.

However David Ramsay interrupted the swinging session by calling "Jannie! Jan-nee!" on the high note he had learned from Pieter. Directly she heard him, Jannie scrambled herself down with impetuous speed, fell, but rapidly picked herself up again, and came running, flapping her hands like fins, crying, "Crocker! Crocker!" When she reached David she attempted to climb up him, wrapping her sticklike arms round his legs.

"And how's Little Miss Silence today? Did you say all your words to your aunt Val after tea? Did you wet your bed last night? You didn't? So you stayed comfortably warm instead of waking up all wet and cold? Wasn't that better, eh?" He swung her on to his arm and said, "Where shall we have our lesson today? In the kitchen, as Elspie's in the loft? Come along—maybe we'll find a plate of snaps or gingerbread."

Val was about to follow with Pieter when she heard the sound of hoofs in the gateway, and turned to see the very unexpected sight of a stranger riding into the yard.

He was a spare, grey-haired, middle-aged gentleman with a decidedly pursed, sour cast of countenance; he was dressed in a neat brown suit, was clean-shaven, had a small buttoned-up mouth, pale-grey eyes, and wore a gold-rimmed pince-nez. He sat his horse as if he found the process of riding wholly uncongenial and greatly beneath his dignity.

"Good day, sir?" said Val, reflecting that more visitors had come to Ardnacarrig during the past twelve hours than in the previous three weeks. "Can I help you in any way?"

"I am obliged to you, ma'am," he replied, in a thin, severe voice. "Are you by any chance Miss"—he consulted a paper which he brought out from his jacket pocket, studying it shortsightedly—"Miss Valhalla Asloeg Montgomery?"

He made the name sound highly preposterous.

Val said that she was.

"In that case my errand is to you, ma'am. I will dismount, if you please," and he did so, looking about him discontentedly for someone to take charge of his horse. As nobody did, he tied it up himself to a ring on the mounting block.

"Is there some—er—private place where we can—er—hold a conversation, Miss Montgomery?"

"Certainly, sir. Pieter, will you run in and help Doctor Ramsay with Jannie's lesson while I talk to this gentleman in the library. And when Elspie comes, ask her if she can bring some refreshment—or, no, I'll do that myself," she added, reflecting that if Mungo intended proposing to Elspie on the spot, she might be in the loft for some time yet.

Collecting whisky, oatcakes, and glasses, Val put them all on a tray, and ushered the gentleman, who had been waiting with ill-concealed impatience, into the library.

He looked about him at the dusty, uncared-for place, primming up his lips, and muttered, more to himself than to Val, "Huts, tuts! I have told her ladyship, over and over, how it would be. Rack and ruin, rack and ruin!"

"What was it you wished to see me about, Mr.—?"

Val felt that the neglected state of Ardnacarrig was no affair of hers.

"M'Intyre, madam, Isaiah M'Intyre." He waved away the whisky she offered. "I have the honour to be her ladyship's man of business in Edinburgh, and I have come out here, at her behest, to put certain matters before you. And a devilish slow, inconvenient journey it has been," he added aggrievedly, "for my hired conveyance broke down at Dunglass and I was obliged to ride over on that sorry, spavined beast which I procured from a tavern."

"I am sorry you have been put to so much trouble on my account, sir," Val replied civilly. "What is this communication from her ladyship that is so urgent it could not be stated in a letter?"

"I understand that you wrote to her ladyship at Nice, giving it as your opinion that, while the Hansen children are residing at Ardnacarrig, they require some person in the capacity of a nursery governess, and requesting her to provide one."

He sounded, Val thought, as if the request had been for the children to be supplied with a resident witch doctor.

"I did write to her, yes. In my opinion it is not a suitable arrangement for the children to be here in sole charge of Elspie Cross. Firstly, she is too old; secondly, she is too short-tempered and set in her ways."

Mr. M'Intyre helped himself to a pinch of snuff from a worn tortoise-shell box. "Imphm. Ye took a good deal upon yourself, in my opinion. I conclude, by the by, that ye have no news about your brother and Mrs. Hansen, ma'am? As to the possibility of their return, or their whereabouts?"

"No I have not," said Val bluntly. "And I am beginning to fear—I'm beginning to be very much afraid—that they must have died, or suffered from some accident. It is now nearly two months that they have been gone. Of course I have said nothing to the children of such a possibility. But I cannot believe that my sister-in-law would not have been in touch long before this, if she had been able to."

"Ay. Imphm. So Lady Stroma understood. Now, I am to instruct you, Miss Montgomery, that, in the event of their parents' death, Lady Stroma is the children's legal guardian. This was a provision of Mrs. Hansen's marriage contract."

"I had guessed as much," Val agreed.

"Furthermore," Mr. M'Intyre pursued, "Lady Stroma wishes you to be fully aware that, even should the parents be presumed dead, the children stand to inherit nothing from them, nothing at all."

"That does not surprise me either," Val said.

"No?" Mr. M'Intyre's tone was as dry as the oatcakes on the plate. "And yet, to some, it might seem surprising that, during six years of married life, this young couple have managed to dissipate a fortune of some seventy-five thousand pounds."

"Seventy-five thousand?" gasped Val. "I'd no idea that my sister-in-law had half as much!"

"Indeed?" His glance expressed disbelief. "Your brother did very well for himself, ma'am, when he married Miss Christian Kinleven. However—*had* is the correct word. I am Miss Christian's attorney too and I can tell you that every penny of that money is spent. The children have nothing coming to them from their mother—not a penny. Lady Stroma wished me to make this very plain to you. If your concern for them is motivated by—ah—expectations of pecuniary advantage, Lady Stroma wishes you to understand that such hopes would be delusive."

Now, for the first time, Val understood what he was getting at, and she was very angry indeed.

Lady Stroma thought that she was a fortune hunter, a vulgar opportunist, who intended to stay around her young relatives in hopes of profit.

Without stopping to reflect that, considering the character of Nils, this point of view was hardly unreasonable, she said haughtily, "Please inform Lady Stroma that she is wholly mistaken in my motives if she thinks I expect any pecuniary reward from—from doing my duty by the children. I am sufficiently able to earn my own living and have no expectations whatever—either from Lady Stroma, or in regard to Pieter and Jannie. I am simply concerned for their welfare. The younger child is—is delicate and backward, needs special care. In my opinion Elspie—though well-meaning enough in her way—is not a suitable person. She is old, and she is hasty-tempered."

"A—a—" he raised a hand. "Just one moment, Miss Montgomery. I had not finished. Lady Stroma merely wished to be sure that you are thoroughly conversant with the position. As I said, Mrs. Hansen's own fortune is all spent. I understand that your brother had a decided propensity for gambling. And Lady Stroma wished me to express to you her attitude toward Mr. Hansen. She neither likes him nor approves of him in any way. If he is dead, she is prepared to do her duty by her wards, support them, and leave them a competence, at their majority. I need hardly say that this sum will be most carefully tied up, so that self-seeking persons will not be able to benefit from it. But if their father is alive, why then Lady Stroma is not prepared to do anything for them—anything whatsoever. Is that quite plain?"

"Very plain, Mr. M'Intyre," Val said, stifling a strong inclination to make a furious retort and sweep from the room. "Neither I nor my brother need hope to lay our hands on any portion of Lady Stroma's fortune." Her glance moved ironically round the warped woodwork and tattered leather upholstery; she missed a curious expression on the lawyer's face. "Perhaps," she went on, "I might take this opportunity of expressing my sense of obligation to Lady Stroma for permitting me to spend a few weeks in her house, rent free? As you may be aware, I had intended only to deposit the children and then return to Edinburgh."

"So I had understood, yes." His tone conveyed both considerable doubt that this had indeed been her intention, and his view that matters would have been much better had she carried it out.

"But—finding absolutely no proper provision for the poor little creatures here—I was obliged to remain and make myself responsible for them, until some suitable person should be engaged."

"Very disinterested of you, Miss Montgomery," the lawyer said, in a particularly enraging tone. "Now, I am instructed by Lady Stroma to inform you that she is prepared to undertake *no* added outlay on behalf of the children until there is definite information as to the parents' whereabouts. The children may remain here—but she will not incur the further expense of a governess. She feels that she has done her part in providing them with a home. Lady Stroma"—his glance also swept round the dismal room—"Lady Stroma has never been an—imphm—an extravagant spender —even on travel—and she has unhappy associations with her childhood at Ardnacarrig. She is not prepared to disburse more than the minimum amount required for the upkeep of this establishment."

"So I have observed."

"If *you*, Miss Montgomery, care to remain here and undertake the children's education, for the time being, Lady Stroma will, however, be prepared to provide your board and accommodation."

"Very obliging of her," said Val, whose nostrils were white with temper. "I'm sure you will agree, Mr. M'Intyre, that a handsome offer such as that can't be accepted without due consideration. I will write to you and let you know my decision."

"Very well," he said, rising. "I think we must let the matter rest there, at present, then. I may say that my opinion did not coincide with her ladyship's."

Val did not inquire as to where the difference lay. She said coolly, moving toward the door, "It seems a pity that Lady Stroma allows such a handsome property to fall into such a state of neglect."

He burst out, becoming suddenly human and indignant. "Over and over again I have made representations to her ladyship about it! But to no avail. The fact is that the estate is entailed which—as you may know— means that it cannot be sold or realised on. And for that reason the old— lady refuses to spend a penny on keeping it in good heart. She has only a life interest, you see; thereafter it passes to a different branch of the family. What condition it will be in by the time the next heir inherits, heaven only knows!" Resuming his official manner and casting a sharp glance at Val, he added, "In case you had been harbouring any misapprehensions on *that* score, Miss Montgomery, I should perhaps point out that the next heir will *not* be Mrs. Hansen's son. The entail was in the male line."

"I had harboured no such apprehension," Val rejoined shortly.

Ignoring her, Mr. M'Intyre continued, "Therefore in the regrettable— but possible, since she is only mortal like the rest of us—contingency of her ladyship's death, the estate would at once pass into other hands, and there could be no assurance of the children's continued residence here. Nor of your own."

"Thank you," said Val. "You have made the whole position abundantly clear." Acting more from an impulse to annoy than from any real wish for information, she added, "I suppose the next heir—if Lady Stroma should meet with some misfortune—is in a position to take possession immediately?"

A constrained—a somewhat harassed expression passed once more over Mr. M'Intyre's face. He replied carefully, "Not immediately, no. In fact we are not just certain as to the whereabouts of the next heir at present."

"Oh? How troublesome for you. But let us hope that Lady Stroma is spared for many years yet, and that he turns up in the meantime. By the way, Mr. M'Intyre, speaking of residence at Ardnacarrig, is it true that, by the terms of Lady Stroma's father's will, Elspie Cross can only reside here so long as she remains unmarried?"

"Ah—yes, that is so."

"Even for this family—and this country—that seems unusually barbaric?" Val remarked hotly.

He shrugged. "It may seem so, yes. Lady Stroma's father was a man of strong and eccentric character. The provision, of course, was made some fifty years ago, by my predecessor: *I* should have endeavoured to dissuade him from making such an arrangement."

"Can I offer you any luncheon, Mr. M'Intyre? I mean of course, do you think that Lady Stroma would wish you to be offered a repast?"

"I thank you, no, ma'am; it grows late; I must be getting back as fast as I can," he replied and took his leave.

Val would very much have liked to discuss this conversation with David Ramsay, but she found that he had paid only a short visit today and had departed long ago. He had, however, left her a parcel and a note: "Dear Val: My mother so much enjoyed your visit yesterday that she hopes you can come again on Friday? Do; it will please us both immensely. I found this parcel for you at the Wolf's Hope mail office; knowing that Tom Postie won't come your way again until Thursday I brought it over. Yours, David R."

The parcel was heavy and appeared to contain books. It came from Edinburgh. Suddenly oblivious of the annoying interview with the lawyer, Val tore off the wrapping paper and discovered some folded newspapers and half a dozen volumes—new, glossy, enticing, several of them titles that she had heard discussed and wished to read. There was also a short note in crabbed writing.

"My dear Miss Montgomery, Since I have not heard of your return to Edinburgh I conclude that you still remain at Ardnacarrig and trust that you are finding its air salubrious. However in case you are running short of reading matter (congenial reading matter, I mean; I do not refer to those forty thousand sermons in Louisa's library) I take the liberty of enclosing a few publications, among which I hope that you will find something to interest you. Should you wish to review them for the next issue of *Selkirk's Magazine* I shall be happy to remunerate you at our usual rates and in that case, please let me have your copy by the last day of the month! You have not yet kept your promise to write and tell me of Helen Ramsay. I very much hope that you have met by now, and I shall value your report on her. Please write soon. I recall our evening in Edinburgh with great pleasure. M.C. *Post Scriptum.* It is possible that I may need to visit your neighbourhood in order to inspect my property; in this case I shall give myself the pleasure of calling upon you."

Val's heart soared, then sank, then soared again, as she read this missive. She could see so plainly the real motive behind it. He wanted news of Helen. But still, how kind he was. He had sent her work, and congenial work too. She would expend all her talent in writing the reviews for him. And she would send him, too, a couple of the other pieces that she had written in the long silent evenings after the children had gone to bed. How glad she was that she had already visited Helen Ramsay and could write to him immediately.

She walked swiftly outside to check, before commencing, that the children were within range, and innocuously employed. They were making little gardens, with stones and sticks, dead leaves, and moss, by the carriage drive. Reassured, she turned back toward the house and encountered Elspie crossing the yard with a brow of thunder. Ignoring this portent, Val asked blithely, "Well, Elspie, how did it go? Did he propose?"

At that, Elspie's indignation burst forth.

"I'll thank ye, Mistress Montgomery, tae mind your own affairs! What Mungo Bucklaw says to me is private betwixt oorselves. It is tae be kenn't by naebody else."

"Of course—of course it's private," Val agreed with swift contrition. "All I meant was, are you going to marry him?"

"And what for do ye wish tae ken that? And how *can* I be marrying him, when it wad mean being cast oot frae my ain hame?"

"But surely," Val said, "Mungo would provide you with a home? Wouldn't you sooner be with him?"

"It's no' the same as the place where ye've drawn ilka breath of your life," Elspie said. "Forbye," she added, "gin I left Ardnacarrig, wha'd bide here tae care for the bairns?"

"Don't worry about that! I could stay on till somebody else was found," said Val, thinking of Tibbie, but not certain that this was a diplomatic time to mention her. She was right. Elspie turned on her with wrath.

"*Ye* could stay? Ye ignorant, feckless, harum-scarum, doited body? *Ye* think ye wad be able to manage here by yer lane?"

"Yes, why not?" Val was rather amazed at this broadside. "I've carefully watched how you do things. I'm sure I could feed the poultry and skim the milk and make the butter. It only takes a little intelligence."

I wonder what Lady Stroma would say to such an arrangement, she thought with an internal grin.

But Elspie's outrage at this suggestion passed all bounds.

"Ye think so? Why—ye're nae mair use than a gecking corbie or a flyting sea maw! It's aye talk, talk! But ye canna clean an ashet decently, nor singe a gigot; ye canna lay a knife straicht on the table, nor wash linen white; ye leave the cogie greasy and the carcakes burning on the griddle; och, the *hours* I hae spent setting to richts a' the things ye hae done wrong! An' forbye, thinkin' yerself so high and michty, wi' yer proud airs, aye telling how yon thing or the ither should be done! Whiles I've fair gnashit my teeth at the eeritation o't, an' the awful hirdum-dirdum that ye leave ahint ye wherever ye gae. Is it ony wonder that I'm temptit tae give the bairns a skelp, whiles? Last nicht ye took yesterday's cream frae the bowie—for what, i' the name o' goodness, what for could ye no' take what was a' ready i' the coup? An' ye left the chappin a' clarty—an' ye took the morn's oatcake tae the library that I had no' but just baked—what for could ye no' have ta'en the snaps I had set oot ready for the doctor? Ye canna even make a decent bowl of parritch! I've nae mair patience wi' ye and yer whim-whams. An' to top all, I heard ye tellin' the lawyer body that ye conseeder me ower auld an' snell tae hae charge o' the bairns! Aweel, let me tell *ye*, Mistress Montgomery, that I consider ye nae better than a silly tawpie, an' if ye were a kitchen lassie I'd turn ye awa'!"

With which parting salvo, Elspie stomped off into the dairy, leaving Val aghast, utterly astonished.

For the last week or so she had honestly believed that she and the old woman were getting on rather well; she had congratulated herself on how skilfully she was managing to fall in with Elspie's ways, while at the same time tactfully instilling a few useful precepts on how to organise the work of the house in a more rational and labour-saving manner. She had suggested, for instance, keeping all the dishes that were in daily use on one shelf, instead of distributed through a series of huge, inaccessible cupboards. She had poured all the meat drippings into one pot, and had cleaned out the half dozen dubious little individual pots previously in use. She had fetched a basket of apples into the kitchen, so that they were not obliged to make a long journey to a distant freezing outhouse every time an apple was wanted. She had offered to do some of the cooking—confident in a long and thorough tuition from old Chloe.

And this was her reward!

Certainly, it was very unfortunate that Elspie had heard herself being described as too old and bad-tempered to look after the children. Val knew that she must apologise for this and try to make amends. But how had it come about? With all her faults of obstinacy and irritability, Elspie was honest as bread, and no eavesdropper. Then Val recollected that the upper gallery of the library was reached by a door from the head of the stairs, which generally stood open; it was not impossible that Elspie, passing by on some household errand, could have caught her own name spoken. Val's heart sank. What else might the old woman have overheard?

To settle her spirits before the apology, Val sat down in the library and wrote a warm letter of thanks to Sir Marcus. She described her day at Wolf's Hope, and added, "I do not wonder that you love and admire Mrs. Ramsay. She is the most remarkable person I have ever met in my whole life. I know that she very much wishes to see you; I hope you will be able to come this way soon." Val also detailed her daily routine at Ardnacarrig, related her conversation with the lawyer, and concluded, "I did not say this to Mr. M'Intyre but since he has left I have decided that, unless some better solution soon presents itself, I believe I must remain at Ardnacarrig for the present."

The decision had made itself while she was writing.

She did not mention Mungo Bucklaw's arrival. That, after all, was Elspie's affair. She did warmly praise David Ramsay for his kindness and help with Jannie. And she mentioned the presence of the tinklers, but not the face at the window; she was now inclined to berate herself for the foolish fears of a city dweller over that and feel that she should not have been so alarmed by the incident. She must have imagined the resemblance to the man in London.

And she finished by saying that, of course, should Sir Marcus find it necessary to visit the district, she would be pleased to see him.

When the letter was done she straightened her back and went to make her apologies to Elspie, who received them dourly.

"Ou, ay, ye're well-meaning eneugh, I'll no say the contrar'. But, gude kens, ye try my patience ilka minute o' the day. What's this aboot Annot, the noo, ye've tell't her she's no' tae mind the bairnies ony mair? What gars ye *be* sae ram-stam?"

"Annot tells them frightening stories," Val said shortly. "Pieter was dreadfully upset last night. It took me a long time to quiet him down."

"And noo Annot's upset, she's fair coupit. The puir lass was greetin' sair i' the byre, an' says ye're a hard, ill-meaning wumman. What for could ye no' tell the silly hizzie juist tae hauld her tongue and keep mim?"

"She's such a chatterbox she'd never remember. I couldn't trust her."

"Ye canna trust me an' ye canna trust Annot; is there a' body i' the whole waurld that's high nebbit eneugh for ye to trust?" snapped Elspie, and took herself off to see how Mungo was getting on. She left Val very subdued.

It seemed best not to visit Mungo herself, for she was afraid that Elspie must have refused him, and he must be feeling very unhappy. Instead, Val played I spy with the children, a before-bedtime game which they usually enjoyed very much; it was also a useful means of enlarging Jannie's random vocabulary. But today, for some reason, Jannie was in a fractious mood; she would not attend but screamed like a banshee because one of the buttons on her brown holland overall was loose. Sighing with irritation Val fetched needle and thread and sewed it tight, for Jannie, if displeased with something in her surroundings, could easily keep up the screaming for a couple of hours without let, until the fault was put right.

Even when the button was sewed, Jannie did not wish to join the game; she arranged all Val's cotton reels in one of her strange, meticulous little patterns, and then abruptly knocked them all over the floor, wailing her eldritch wail; she ran about the kitchen wheeling and turning like a disturbed bat; she paid no heed to songs, rhymes, or counting games; even Pieter's tickling, which usually charmed her, now only prompted her to a shriek of "G'way, way, way!" and finally she resorted to a practice that Val was hoping she had abandoned, of sitting cross-kneed on the floor, feverishly sucking her fingers and rocking, rocking, rocking from side to side until it made one dizzy to watch her.

She resembled, Val thought, those birds that circle and cry in agitation before bad weather.

It was a relief when the children's bedtime came and they could be bathed in front of the kitchen range (a cheerful old-fashioned practice which Val was glad to adhere to in preference to using the glacial mahogany bathroom installed by the auld laird), shooed upstairs, seen through their prayers, and settled for the night.

Val's legs and back ached; by the time the children were in bed, she felt as exhausted as if six days had passed since breakfast. It was the last straw to discover that Jannie, following another of her least desirable habits, had secreted a sticky lump of cold porridge under her pillow for nighttime consumption.

Val did not wait, after this was cleared up, to go through all the events of their day with the children, as was her usual habit; she gave them each a warm but swift hug and ran downstairs, rejoicing in the prospect of the new books waiting to welcome her in the library. Soon she was lost, happily absorbed in reading, as she had not been since she left New York, making notes as she read, deaf to all around her.

Some hours went by before she woke to the realisation that the library fire had dwindled to a white mound of peat ash, and that her lamp was flickering and smoky, a sign that it was liable to run out of oil and leave her in the dark unless she went to bed at once.

She walked upstairs, sighing. The house was quiet; Elspie must have retired long ago.

As Val passed the entrance to the Long Gallery she paused, arrested by what might have been a faint, repeated sound from its shadowy farther end.

There! Creak-creak, and again, softly, creak-creak.

Val hesitated, thinking of Thrawn Jane and the ghostly cradle. It was almost certainly a swinging door or shutter, caught in some draught of air; now would be the chance to nail the myth and expose the fallacy.

But her lamp flickered again; she found herself possessed of an extremely strong disinclination to explore the far, dark, cold, silent realms of the gallery. Suppose her lamp went out? Then she would be able to discover nothing. Instead she closed the gallery door and went on, rather fast, to her own room.

All was quiet in the children's room; no repetition of last night's trouble, she thought thankfully. But when she went to inspect them, she found Pieter's eyes open—wide, dark, unwinking, fixed on her.

"What is it, Pieter? Why aren't you asleep?"

"I heard what you said this morning, Aunt Val. When you were talking to that man."

Oh heavens, she thought, not another. What now?

"What do you mean, Pieter?"

"Elspie and I were carrying pillows down for the poor man in the stable. And we went by the upstairs library door and we heard you. You said you—that you think Mama and Papa must be dead."

Val was stricken to the heart—with remorse at her own carelessness, with sorrow for the little boy.

"I'm sorry, Pieter," she said slowly. "I'm very sorry you heard that. It may not be so, you know. I didn't want you to be troubled with such thoughts."

Suddenly his face convulsed.

"It's *not* true, it's *not* true!" he cried out in a kind of anguished whisper. "I won't believe you. I hate you. You don't love us a bit. I want Mama! I want my own mama!"

She tried to comfort him but he turned from her, pushing her away with a gesture of strangely adult dignity, and lay with his face to the wall.

I am failing those children, Val thought, as slowly, tiredly, she peeled off all her layers and layers of clothes in the cold room and made herself ready for bed.

She lay awake a long time listening to the sound of Pieter's desolate sobbing.

Next morning she went to check the source of the creaking. As she had expected, it was an open window, on the seaward side of the Long Gallery. She closed it and thought no more of the matter.

CHAPTER **14**

V AL slept late the following day and woke with a guilty start into a vacuum of silence which filled her with immediate terror.

Usually the children were awake long before her and she would be roused by the murmur of their talk and thumps on the floor, and Jannie's reedlike singing. But all she heard this morning was the ever present whisper of the sea, and the creeper tapping on the window. She jumped hastily out of bed and realised that it must be very late indeed; the children had already dressed and gone. Filled with foreboding she made a hasty toilet, scrambling on her clothes and bundling up her long hair. She feared that Elspie, after the scene of yesterday evening, and further harassed by the responsibility of Mungo's presence, would be in no easy mind to cope with the children on her own. And Pieter, if he was still in last night's state of distress, might not be able to play his usual role of mediator between Elspie and his small sister.

Matters seemed all set for disaster, and Val ran down the wide stairs at headlong speed, across the freezing hall, and through the dining room to the kitchen, expecting to find heaven only knew what scene of hostility or chaos.

What she found was in almost laughable contrast to her expectations.

One of the main causes of friction every morning was Elspie's wish to get the children through their breakfast at top speed so that she had undisturbed use of the kitchen table. Jannie, a slow eater at any time, was particularly so at breakfast and would sit dreamily dipping her spoonful of porridge into her bowl of milk and then forgetting to eat it until Elspie was almost exploding with impatience and frustration. Val had several times suggested finding a small table and seating the children at it in a corner of the large room, but Elspie said that would clutter up the kitchen and was not to be thought of.

But now, apparently, it had been thought of. Jannie was placidly eating porridge at her own slow pace, sitting on her three-legged stool in front of a settle which served as a table, in a warm corner beyond the hearth. Mungo was seated nearby in a rocking chair which, the day before, and no doubt for months past, had been in an outhouse lacking a rocker. He was making a rope net and Pieter, squatting by him, was absorbedly watching the process. Silence and peace reigned. Even the tabby kitchen cat, a sure barometer for Elspie's moods, which sometimes stayed out of doors for days on end, lay at full stretch in front of the hearth, purring blissfully. And Elspie herself stood making bannocks at the big table with none of the vexed air that Val had feared; in fact she seemed positively cheerful and greeted Val as affably as if she had not called her a "silly tawpie" twelve hours before.

"I'm sorry I overslept," Val said.

"Aweel, aweel. Think naething of it. The parritch is keeping hot yonder."

"How are you today, Mr. Bucklaw?" Val asked. "You look much better."

"I thank you, mistress. Ay, my fever has cleared off finely, thanks to the doctor's medicine and Elspie's brose. So in return I'm making her a net to catch a fish for your dinner. Is the boat yet in the boathouse, Elspie, that was aye there when I was a lad about the bothy?"

"The boat?" Elspie gave a brief laugh. "Ay, an' has been this fifteen year—a' geizened an' the boards clean rottit through. There's nae boat fit for sea aboot the place, noo, an' hasna been sin' Sandie Duncan passed away."

"Then I'd best build you another," said Mungo matter-of-factly.

Pieter was amazed. "*Could* you, Mr. Bucklaw?"

"And why not, laddie? A boat's only planks nailed together."

Val wandered to the window with her bowl of porridge. The kitchen looked inshore, across the orchard, up the narrow glen. The wooded hillsides were hoary with frost and grey with mist, a melancholy sight; yet she suddenly felt hopeful. If Mungo planned to stay on at Ardnacarrig—that might entirely alter the aspect of life here! There seemed something tranquil and invincible about him, as if he let the waves of life wash past him and remained himself undisturbed.

Later in the day, discovering him in the stable yard, she tackled him straightforwardly about his plans. He stood, reflective, gazing with a measuring eye at a stack of planks that lay over joists in the coach-house roof.

"Could you really mend the boat, Mr. Bucklaw?"

"Och, ay," he said easily. "It's no' a difficult job. Seven, eight planks in the hull want renewing; the lave are sound enough. A week or two and I'll have it sorted good as new, and Pieter and I catching you a herring for your breakfast."

"You're planning to stay here, then? I'm very glad! How does Elspie feel about it?"

"Elspie is no' sae kittle and camsteerie as she makes out," he said with a grin. "It's true she's aye anxious about what will Lady Stroma say. But I've a bit put by, for I've been a saving man all my days; and if I choose to redd up the gardener's croft and pay her leddyship rent for it, I reckon she'd be sweer to pass by sic a bargain. The more so if I put in a bit work about the garden and never ask for pay! Auld Jockie will be blithe enough of a bit of help now he's so lame. Forbye, who's to tell tales to her leddyship if she's awa' stravaging around the desert on a camel?"

"Not I," agreed Val. "She can think herself lucky to get so good a tenant."

She had observed that Mungo had already mended two more of the broken chairs. Furthermore he had replaced the pane in the card room French window—a task which Elspie had been beseeching Jock to do for weeks past since the north wind whistled into the room and they were obliged to lock its door every night. Mungo had also chopped wood, fetched in enough peat from the stack to last them five days, had sharpened the kitchen knives, cleaned all the oil lamps, and had endeared himself to Pieter and Jannie by teaching the former to use a plane, and making a wooden spinning top for the latter which kept her transfixed with delight for an hour at a time.

"What about Jock, though?" Val went on. "You're sure he won't object?"

"He willna mind. He an' I were cronies, in the auld days."

"Were you born here, then, Mr. Bucklaw?"

"Nay," he said unexpectedly, "I was born in Brazil."

"*Brazil?*" How did you ever come to travel from Brazil to Ardnacarrig?"

"Och, weel, my kinsfolk came fra these parts. My great-grandfather emigrated to Brazil in 1780. Always, in my family, there was this tale we had from my father, and he from his, about my great-granny, how she went sorrowing all her days for her bits of apple trees, and the sight of the heather on the brae, and the sound of the sea on Ardnacarrig shore. So, when I was a young fellow, and footloose, I had a great curiosity tae come here and get a sight o' the place that she loved so well."

"And?"

"And I came, and I thought it a bonny spot—though I couldna find my great-granny's apple trees, nor the croft, that must have fallen down long syne."

"And?"

"And I was going off again, when I saw Elspie, spreading out the sheets to catch the sun in the bleach field."

He stopped for a moment.

"You saw Elspie?"

"Eh, she was a bonny young thing! With her hair the colour of a wedding ring, and her pink cheeks, and her blue eyes that, forbye, had sic a snap to them! An' I reckoned I'd stay here a while, gin I could earn my bread by fishing or herding sheep. And so I did."

"And?"

"An' the end of it was, I asked her would she have me."

He stopped again. His eyes often had a visionary, meditative, indwelling look, as if he glimpsed a whole pattern of large events which he observed with reverence and love but would never attempt to alter for his own ends.

"An' she wouldna have me. So I left Ardnacarrig, and I wandered over the whole waurld, but I never forgot her. I never saw another woman I could love as well. And in the end I came back."

Val had a huge feeling of sadness. If this spot is haunted, she thought, it is by the despair of thwarted lovers—Mungo, Elspie, Marcus, the Carsphairn sisters, poor Thrawn Jane and her fisher laddie. Oh, let *one* story end happily!

Gently, knowing that he would not take it amiss from her, she asked, "And will she have you now, Mungo?"

"I dinna ken," he said with simplicity. "She is thinking about it. Forbye it is enough happiness to be here, near by her."

Val felt ashamed of her own impatiences. Here she was, longing to get away, finding Elspie nothing but an impediment to her own plans. How different from Mungo, who was content to let events take their course, whose manner of loving was so pure and undemanding.

During the next few days Val observed that Mungo, by indiscernible stages, assumed a place of greater and greater importance in the household. He removed himself to the gardener's little tumble-down croft, long since left vacant, and set about putting it to rights. But his influence was to be felt even from a distance. Frictions, divergences that had hitherto invariably led to lost tempers and bad feeling now, by the mere fact of his peaceful presence, somehow sorted themselves out and became innocuous. Elspie and Val were more kindly disposed toward one another, more tolerant of each other's foibles. The children seemed to snuff in draughts of Mungo like air; Pieter learned a hundred things a day from him—knots, carpentry, the solar system, songs, geography, card games, and the names of Roman emperors. Mungo seemed to possess a boundless store of information.

"In my watches off I would aye be reading a book," he explained when Val, discovering him with a child on each knee, reciting *The Rime of the Ancient Mariner,* expressed admiration at the amount of poetry he seemed to know by heart.

Val felt that Mungo had arrived just in time to save them all from disaster.

By Friday she had not the slightest qualm about riding over again to see Helen Ramsay—an excursion which, at the beginning of the week, had seemed a pure impossibility.

"Shall you mind if I go off and leave you with Elspie and Mungo?" she asked Pieter.

"Oh, *no,*" said Pieter. "He's letting me help him mend the boat. And Jannie sits in the little cart he made her, and he sings songs to her about corn rigs and barley rigs."

Pieter had not spoken again to Val about the possibility of his parents being dead. But a clouded, unhappy air which had hung over him for a couple of days after their conversation had gradually cleared away. He seemed happy to learn from Mungo and work with him and follow Mungo's habit of taking events as they came. And Jannie had taken to Mungo as a kitten does to a tree.

"'Orny rig, 'arly rig," she repeated dreamily after Pieter, spinning her top on the kitchen table.

Val saddled Dunkie and set off with a light heart. Now that she knew the way it seemed a shorter distance over the headland. The day was grey, dull; icily, sullenly cold and foggy; each landmark loomed up at her before she expected it. Despite the bad visibility she made good time; Dunkie seemed eager to reach his destination. In a couple of hours she was crossing the bridge above the harbour. Today the village of Wolf's Hope lay completely silent, shrouded in mist; nobody moved or talked, down on the stone pier. Perhaps the boats were all at sea, invisible in the pearl-coloured distance.

Unexpectedly, David Ramsay was at the manse to greet Val. He did it gravely, with a finger on his lips, and explained in a low voice, "My mother had a bad night. She is a good deal pulled down this morning."

"Perhaps my visit would be too tiring for her?" Val said, bitterly disappointed.

"Oh, no. She has been wearying to see you. But she has just fallen into one of her little drifts of sleep, so sit down, till she wakes, and drink a cup of Tibbie's tea."

Tibbie's pleasant face was pale and heavy-eyed, but she greeted Val kindly and made much of her.

"Come in ben, by the fire, Mistress Val, for it's a gey bitter glunshie day, an' the fog is like to trickle into the very marrow of your bones."

Val drank tea and warmed herself; in a few minutes she heard Helen Ramsay's voice call faintly, "Is my girl come yet?"

"Wait till I sort ye," called Tibbie, speeding to her mistress's side, but Helen was impatient and would only suffer herself to be wrapped in a shawl and have her hair smoothed a little. Then Val was allowed in.

If Helen had looked ill on the last visit, today she had the clear stamp of death on her. Yet she smiled at Val with her dry, flaked lips, and her eyes, sunk in huge lavender-coloured sockets, were still full of light.

"It's good of you to come all this way."

"Good? I love to come."

"Have you brought drawings of the children?" Helen asked immediately.

Val had: clumsily executed sketches for which she blushed as she drew them out, but Helen said at once, "Oh, they have the very feel of childhood. There he is, pushing her on the swing. And here they are, building a little house . . . Thank you, Val! You have reminded me of something I thought I had lost for good." She studied the drawings again; Val would have relieved her of them but she held them tight. Presently she added, "You have given me something else: Marcus writes that he is coming here."

A question pierced Val: would he arrive in time? She looked down, lest by chance she transmit her thought to Helen, who was so weak today that she could only talk in short snatches. Val had come intending to ask her advice about many things: Mungo, and Elspie, and Lady Stroma's stingy offer about the children—but faced with this state of extremity she could not be so self-centred and importunate. Instead she told stories of Jannie and related her adventure with the tinklers. She tried to be entertaining, yet felt she was barely making contact with the dying woman; all that really passed between them was a warmth, a feeling of friendship. Yet perhaps no more was needed? When Helen's lids fluttered down again, after fifteen minutes or so, Val tiptoed back to the front room, where Tibbie was ironing a pile of delicate nightwear.

"She'll no' be lang, noo, my puir lamb," Tibbie said simply, wiping her eyes. "But she'll aye be as fresh as apple-florrish while I hae the care o' her."

When Helen woke again it was plain that she was too tired for more talk. She lay flat, drawing difficult breaths, her eyes half-closed, her high forehead pearled with sweat.

Sadly, Val said goodbye.

The transparent lids moved slowly up; Helen's brilliant brown eyes smiled at her.

"I have to rest," she whispered. "Such a bore! Goodbye, my dear girl. I am afraid we may not meet again. But amn't I lucky to have made such a fine new friend so late in life? Perhaps the good Lord will allow me to come back—and take a look at Wolf's Hope from time to time—for I shall certainly tell him that heaven won't be heaven for me unless I can!—and then I shall drift over to Ardnacarrig and breathe a greeting in your ear. Which will be away better than old Thrawn Jane's mumblings."

"If I'm still there," Val said smiling, trying to keep tears back.

"Oh, I believe you've taken a liking to the spot; you'll be here a while yet. And you'll keep friends with my Davie, won't you?" Helen whispered. "I know it will be back to his test tubes for that one, the minute I'm gone, but he'll be aye needing some good friends to see he keeps his clothes mended and his bills paid."

"I'll do that," Val promised.

"And my funny old Marcus—he swore he'd come and I trust him—but if he's too late—you'll give him my dear love?"

Val nodded dumbly.

"Now you be happy—with your bairnies! God gives us such amazing presents. And mostly we are aye looking at the underside of them and turning them about—and wondering what have they to do with us, instead of just plain enjoying them." Helen's whisper died from weakness. Her eyes closed. But she opened them again and smiled without speaking.

Val leaned over and kissed her cheek, then walked blindly from the room.

She murmured a goodbye to Tibbie, who said, "Ye'll no' be leaving us yet? Ye'll bide a wee while, Mistress Val?"

"I'd rather—I'd rather go," Val said. She longed to be outside, and Tibbie, understanding this, allowed her to leave. In front of the house she found David, with his own mare saddled.

"I'm coming with you," he said.

"You can't leave her!"

"Why not?" He smiled sadly. "There's nothing I can do for her that Tibbie can't do as well, or better. Anyway, she said before you came that I was to ride back with you; besides, in the state you are in you would lose your way for sure." He patted her arm in a comfortable, brotherly way, and helped her mount. "Come, don't grieve! Think how she'd scold you, if she knew, and tell you that you were wasting your time, when you ought to be enjoying the view, or listening to the birds."

"There don't seem to *be* any birds," Val pointed out. The blanketing mist had silenced the world; not a creature seemed to be stirring on the hillside as they trotted up the steep track. David exerted himself to talk, and told her about a Russian doctor called Pavlov who was conducting some unusual experiments on the physiology of digestion and stimulation of reflex responses by extranormal means. She listened apathetically at first, but presently became interested and began putting questions, arguing, and discussing. His phrase "conditioned responses" made her think of Elspie, and she told David about the arrival of Mungo, and Mr. M'Intyre the lawyer, and Elspie's problem.

David viewed it rather matter-of-factly.

"If the old body wants to marry Mungo, I don't see what's to stop her living with him in the gardener's cottage. I doubt if Lady Stroma would turn her out of there."

"But it goes deeper than that," said Val, who had been observing Elspie closely these last few days. "I think in a strange way she really feels wedded to the *house*—she has lived there alone for so long, looked after it all her life really; she has given up everything for it. And she is a Carsphairn, after all, she belongs there; she knows every corner and stair and doorknob of it blindfold. Sometimes I think I am hardly real to her—coming from so far away, such a different background—except as a kind of irritation!"

"Does Mungo seem real to her?"

"I'm sure she loves him. But I really doubt if she will allow herself to marry him."

"Maybe she will allow herself to become his mistress," David said cheerfully.

"Davie! How can you! At *their* age?"

"Oh, Val, you do make me laugh. You are such a sweet simpleton! With all your fine talk of emancipation, and city airs! What do you think folk do, who haven't the benefit of your education? Who don't—like you—know all about everything?"

She was not offended at his teasing, as she might have been a few weeks before, but said despondently, "On the contrary, I begin to think I know *nothing* about *anything*, and am the world's biggest fool."

"You can't be, or my mother would never have taken such a rare fancy to you."

They had reached the hilltop. The ruins of Wolf's Crag castle loomed like grey cobwebs in the mist to their left, but the bay below them was invisible, lost under cloud. A gull cried dolefully somewhere close at hand, reminding Val of Jannie's plaintive little songs. How long it seemed since the day they had first come up here with David, though it was only a few weeks in reality; what a lot she had learned in that time.

"Davie, tell me about the auld laird; did you ever meet him?"

"My dear girl! He died years before I was born—in his mid-nineties. He really *was* auld—a relic of the eighteenth century. Drank four bottles of claret at every meal—exercised the *droit de seigneur* over the local female population—and yet professed a gloomy hellfire religion, which justified all *he* did, but allowed no one else any latitude. The story goes that he used to beat his daughters regularly and kept them more or less locked up. And there was a younger brother with Jacobite leanings who got pushed out—or left home because he couldn't stand it—and was never heard from again."

"No wonder Lady Stroma dislikes the place. I wonder if he beat Elspie along with the legitimate daughters?"

"Perhaps not; perhaps he preferred her; it's often so."

"And then out of remorse made an unfair will, leaving them the money and tying her there for life."

"Many people try to rectify the mistakes of a lifetime in one atrocious piece of testamentary injustice."

"The worst mistake of all."

David began telling tales of death-bed repentances he had come across during his practice, and they were laughing over these as they rode into the stable yard. Where, to their amazement, they found a light traveling-carriage halted, and Sir Marcus Cusack just in the act of descending from it.

The next hours were a confusion for Val. Sir Marcus, on hearing David's report of his mother, was for climbing back into the carriage and pressing on to Wolf's Hope immediately. But the driver said it was not to be thought of. The carriage would not go over the headland; they would need to go round a longer way, by road, which was at least fifteen miles, and the horses were too tired to start off again until they had rested.

"Ye should ha' gone direct to Ravenswood, Sir Marcus, as ye planned at the outset," said Andie the driver scoldingly, "'stead o' stravaging oot here in sic a ram-stam manner."

"I know, I know, Andie. One should not give way to impulses."

David offered the loan of his mare Greylag so that Sir Marcus could ride on ahead and suggested himself following with the carriage when the horses were rested. But Sir Marcus declined with a shudder.

"My dear David, I am as anxious as can be to see your dear mother, but if I were to set out on that flea-bitten nag she would deposit me in some lochan—yes, yes, I remember her passion for water—and I should never get to Wolf's Hope. No, I must e'en put up with the results of my own foolish impatience, and wait until my beasts are rested. And the undeserved reward for that—I hope—will be two hours of Miss Montgomery's company."

David said in that case he would ride home and prepare his mother for Sir Marcus's arrival.

"Do that, David—I will be infinitely obliged to you. And bespeak me a room at the tavern, my dear lad—we shall hardly get back to Ravenswood this evening."

"I am sure that the news you are on your way will make my mother better."

David clasped Val's hand—she could only clasp his in return, speechlessly—remounted the grey, and was away up the hill again. Greylag's hoofbeats diminished and were lost in the mist.

Val was left facing Sir Marcus and found, as is often the case after building up a strong image of somebody in their absence, that the reality differed from it disconcertingly. He was both younger than she had pictured him and less handsome; more human, more weary, not such an exotic, more of a real person. She found herself oddly at a loss and fell back on offering refreshment in the house.

"Truth to tell," he said, "I would prefer a stroll. I have been sitting in the carriage all day and am cramped and jaded, rather than hungry or tired."

Remembering her own exhaustion at the end of the trip from Edinburgh, Val thought his stamina remarkable, but of course he was a seasoned traveler—and she had had the children. He wore shoes today, not slippers, she noticed. His gout must be better. Perhaps it would be kinder not to inquire after it.

"Shall we walk in the policies?" she suggested.

"No, it is too dark and damp; let us go down to the shore. Andie can go into the house and tell them that you are back."

They strolled across the lawn and down between the azalea banks. Exactly as she had in Edinburgh, Val felt that their acquaintance had ripened in the interim. Neither of them felt any need for formal preliminaries.

"You are just back from Wolf's Hope," he said. "Tell me about her."

And so Val described her visit.

Down on the hard flat white sand—for the tide was low—they walked back and forth, turning when they came to the burn, or to Jock's line of posts. To and fro, to and fro in the mist; the sea was hardly visible, though they could hear its hushed murmur; the fine icy moisture spangled Val's blond coronet of hair and the fur collar of Sir Marcus's greatcoat.

"This is like walking round the ship," she said.

"That ship! What a torture chamber! And yet I did not altogether dislike the voyage."

"Tell me about Helen's husband," Val said. "Was he like David?"

"In looks? Much more handsome. In his nature, perhaps—except that David has more of curiosity and reasonableness. Och, James was just a theologian!—a morose, bumbling, touchy, indrawn cross-grained churl of a fellow, who was forever exploring man's relationship with God while he neglected his fellow-humans. Yet she loved him—there was something childish and touching about him—he was easy hurt, though he was aye trampling on the susceptibilities of others. Without Helen to care for him, he'd have been in a bad way indeed."

"I hope she is better by the time you get there," Val said. "Should we be turning back? I do not like you to be staying here a moment longer than you need to."

She longed for him to stay and yet she had a simultaneous desperate urgency for him to be gone to the scene that waited for him.

He looked at his watch.

"A few more minutes. It is peaceful here. A kind of limbo. I have been thinking about you a great deal. I liked your essays. I shall have much to say to you about them next time we meet." He looked about and said, "I have imagined you here, walking, looking out to sea, feeling imprisoned, perhaps. How are matters going with Elspie?"

"Oh, she has been so much better since Mungo came!" Val said and described the miracle.

Sir Marcus laughed, and the laugh had its usual transforming effect on his drawn sallow face. "I was hoping that would happen when I encouraged Mungo to come to Ardnacarrig."

"*You* encouraged him? You know Mungo?"

"Och, yes, we met some years ago in the port of Piraeus. His ship was docked there, and I was taking the air on the quayside. We drifted together the way two Scots will be doing, anywhere about the world, and discovered that, besides plenty of foreign towns, we also had one small part of Scotland in common. And we cracked a couple of bottles of resinated wine (terrible bad for the kidneys) and he was telling me about how he first saw Elspie—"

"Spreading out the sheets in the bleach field!"

"So I said, why not go back and try his luck a second time? For I knew that she was still at Ardnacarrig and still single. And he said he was minded to, when he had put by just a bit more and could go to her not as a landless young rover from Brazil but as a retired second mate with money in his pocket. Well then, whiles, he was writing to me after that from different parts of the globe, and I was putting some of his descriptions of places into *Selkirk's*, for he has a fine, sharp, judgmatical way of getting the bones of a place on to paper, has old Mungo; and the result of that was, when in the end he did come back to Edinburgh and call on me, I was able to tell him that I had a publisher keen for him to write a book about his travels. So he has more to offer Elspie now than just the cash in his dorlach! But, would you believe it, the silly sumph was still not sure of his welcome and would be for writing a note first, and maybe staying away altogether, if she did not answer. I almost had to push him out on the road, before he would gather his courage. And then he was fain to walk it—like a pilgrim."

"That was one of the best deeds you ever did!"

"And so you are content enough here? You have young David to talk to, and the sea to listen to—"

"And your books to read—I haven't thanked you enough—"

"Tut! That was nothing. I am going to have some useful reviews from you. And you have heard nothing from your brother?"

"No, nothing. But, Sir Marcus—"

"Och," he said, "call me Marcus. Even David does, and he is my godson. Well?"

"In those papers you kindly sent me—there was a report of a poor unfortunate woman found killed in a London street—"

"Oh, ay, ay," he said. "One of those terrible murders—the Bermondsey Beast—I am sorry there should have been such a thing for you to come on in the papers I sent."

"It wasn't just that—but the woman! I had met her! It was—the report said that it w-was Miss L-Letty Pettigrew," Val said, shivering; "she was the actress I told you about, the friend of Nils who told me where the children were to be found. And she had been killed—in the same dreadful way."

Sir Marcus was silent for a long time, as they paced on. He looked very perturbed. At last he asked, "When did you read this?"

"Only last night. I have been reading one of your papers every day—making them last! But Sir—but Marcus, don't you think—doesn't it seem—as if there *must* be some kind of connection between—between my brother and these awful murders?"

"Perhaps. I will need to be thinking about this," he said. "Have you mentioned it to anybody else—written to anyone about it?"

"No. Nobody."

"But back in London did you at any time tell anyone that you had seen this actress?"

Val thought.

"I may have mentioned it to the waiter at my hotel—I was asking how to find the theatre—and I probably told Lady Stroma—" Had she mentioned Letty Pettigrew to Lord Clanreydon, in that curious interview? She was fairly sure she had not. But he, of course, must have known the actress—had she not intended to go with Nils on Clanreydon's yacht, on that pleasure cruise, the arrangements for which had been instrumental in bringing Val across the Atlantic? Had the cruise ever taken place? she wondered idly. What was the yacht's name—*Dragonfly*. "Cost a cool three-quarter million," she heard Nils' voice saying. "Curtains and carpets —the Prince of Wales is coming too." Had the prince actually gone? Presumably not—Val had read of his presence at a London ball in one of those same papers. "I'm fairly sure I told no one else," she said finally.

"Good . . . I most strongly advise you not to, in any correspondence, for instance."

"Do you think the police should be told—about my brother?" Val said slowly.

"Yes; I believe they should. But leave me to think about it. I am wondering if it is not too isolated for you here," he exclaimed, suddenly turning to regard her with an air of uncertainty. "Should I be bringing you and the bairns back to Edinburgh with me?"

She was amazed. "You think this place is making me morbid—that I'm letting my imagination fly away with me?"

"Och, no! But anybody who was looking for your brother—or the children—might come here."

Val shivered again, she did not know why. London, with its dark narrow streets and its sinister mysteries, seemed far enough away—a thousand times farther than Edinburgh. And why should there be any connection between the Bermondsey Beast and this remote spot? But there *was* a connection, she told herself. If Nils had known something about the crimes . . . But Nils was not here. Nonetheless, if somebody were looking for Nils—if someone thought he might be here—or even if someone thought he might have passed on information to his sister—in New York for instance—

"Come, we're wasting time, and you should be off," she said, shaking herself out of such stupid fancies. "Your horses will be rested. Besides, you must wish to speak to Mungo. Anyway—*he* is here to protect us—and sent by you! That is another thing for which I have to be thankful to you."

"Well, well," he said. "I will think it all over and be back tomorrow. I will not stop to talk to Mungo now. In the meantime I am very happy to have seen you. You are looking bonnie. Ardnacarrig has done you good. And *you* have done *me* good."

They had walked back along the azalea path and swung round through the forlorn gardens, beside the crumbling arch that led to the stable yard.

"Mungo will have his work cut out, setting all this to rights," Sir Marcus said, chuckling, glancing at the broken stonework, the overgrown, shrouding trees, the shaggy grass and untrimmed flowerbeds. "Better, maybe, he should bide in the gardener's cottage!"

"What do you—?"

"No matter. I'll tell you another time. There is Andie, looking daggers at me because he has been ready and waiting these seven minutes and I have no time for a crack with Mungo and Elspie and your bairns. Never mind. I shall be back soon enough. And you have put me in good heart, my dear girl. Thank you."

He picked up her cold hand and kissed it lightly, nodded in a placating manner at the indignant Andie, and climbed into his carriage.

Val waved, as they rattled away between the evergreens; then she strolled back into the mist-hung garden. She did not want to enter the house yet. So much had happened to her in the last few hours that she felt gasping—suffocated—as if she were drowning in some strange and unfamiliar element.

She retraced her steps to the shore, and then remembered that Sir Marcus had brought her another letter from Benet, sent care of the *Selkirk's* office. She opened it, and scanned it with only half her attention.

"Hope while you are in Scotland you are availing yourself of the opportunity to procure and read the lesser-known works of Sir Walter Scott," Benet wrote. "*Woodstock, Redgauntlet,* besides his *Life of Napoleon, Es-*

says on Ballad Poetry, Provincial Antiquities of Scotland, & Account of the Coronation of George IV are all worthy of your perusal. On no account, though, should you read the works of Burns, who, despite his national popularity, was a man of depraved tastes and sordid character. Please remember to change your stockings when you come in, as I understand that the ground in Scotland is always damp—"

Impatiently she folded the letter without reading to the end and put it in her pocket. It seemed to have no relevance to anything in her present situation.

The tide was coming in, now, as dusk fell; wave after wave rolled up, rasped and broke, not ten yards from the crisscrossing lines of prints that showed where she and Sir Marcus had walked to and fro, to and fro.

Happiness often seems a thing of the past, understood only when it is gone. But now, looking at those lines of footprints, Val thought, I was happy, walking there, and I knew it. I was full to overflowing with true feelings, beautiful, outgoing, *real* feelings. Perhaps at the very end of my life I shall look back and know that was the best hour I ever had. If that is the case, at least I knew at the time that I was in a state of blessedness; at least I made the very most of it.

She thought, I'll walk along just once more, just as far as the cliff, and then I must go in and play with the children. I have hardly seen them all day.

But they were all right, she knew; she had passed the brightly lit kitchen window and seen them inside, busy at some activity on the table, with Mungo supervising.

Walking slowly, she took a childish pleasure in following the larger line of prints and trying to match her step to it. She came to the line of cliffs, honeycombed with caves, and strolled on as far as Jock's line of posts. Here she turned to go back—and gasped with fright as a shadowy figure moved out, without making a sound, from a dark cleft at the foot of the rocks, and came rapidly toward her. She moved instinctively, to run, to flee, make her way to safety and the house with its lighted windows; but the voice stopped her.

It said: "Val! Val! Don't run off! I've been hoping you might come back. I've been waiting here all day for a chance to talk to you."

Slowly she turned, and took a few reluctant steps back toward the cliff. Cautiously the figure moved toward her; by slow degrees they approached one another until they were only a few inches apart. Val looked up into the dirty, haggard, unshaven face of her brother Nils.

CHAPTER 15

"NILS? Is it really you? Not a ghost?"

If it was not a ghost, it must be Nils. She had forgotten again how tall he was. Now, staring up at him in the gloom, she remembered how, long ago, even when they were children, he had seemed to tower over her.

He had on black, shabby clothes, and some kind of dark waterproof boat cloak over them. His lint-pale hair, long and unkempt, blew in the rising breeze.

"Hush!" he said, glancing round. "Of course it's me! Don't make a row!"

"But how did you come here?"

"On a boat—from Hull—I got them to put me ashore," he said impatiently. "Who was that man you were walking with on the beach, earlier?"

She could not help a shiver, at the thought that, while they were walking, Nils had been watching from some cranny.

"Have you been here all that time? But why didn't—"

"Who was it?" he repeated.

"Sir Marcus Cusack—but I don't—"

"The *Selkirk's Magazine* fellow? What's he doing here?" To himself he muttered, "Yes, it could have been Cusack. I saw him once, in London."

"He has left, anyway." Val was puzzled. "Why do you ask? Nils, come in! Come to the house. The children will be—"

"Wait!" he said abruptly. "Who's there? In the house?"

"Old Elspie; you know, you've met her: Kirstie's old nurse. Nils," Val said ugently, "where *is* Kirstie?"

He waited a moment before answering. Then he answered, in a low voice, flatly, "She's dead."

He seemed wholly unmoved by Kirstie's loss. She was gone, that was all, perhaps there was even a shade of relief in his tone. Freedom regained.

"*Oh . . .*"

For a moment Val had nurtured a fragile, floating wisp of hope that now, with the reappearance of Nils, normality would return. But his words struck down that hope, ground it into the earth. Indeed she had already half perceived that Nils was more removed from her than he had ever been, by some barricade of dreadfulness that she was unable to cross or comprehend.

"How—how did she die, Nils?"

"She was drowned," he said, in the same dull, dogged manner.

"*Drowned?*"

Though grievous, this did not seem quite such an appalling end as Val's worse flights of imagination had encompassed. Though, what *had* she expected? She brushed that thought aside.

Trying to disperse the formless dread from her mind, she caught his hand.

"Poor, poor Nils. I'm so sorry. What you must have been *through*. Poor little Kirstie." For a moment the frail ghost of her sister-in-law seemed to flutter past them, timid, anxious, pleading—

"*Dear Val—be kind to them? I know you will—*"

"At least," said Val, trying to draw Nils onward toward the house by the hand she held—it was ice-cold—"at least, thank goodness, the children are well. They'll be so *happy* to see you. How did you find out that we were here?"

"It was obvious, wasn't it? Where else would you be?" His tone was surly.

She realised that he was almost at the end of his strength, exhausted, probably hungry. A strange odour came from him—acid, rank; sweat and salt and tar compounded, as if he had not been able to wash for weeks past.

"Come into the house, Nils."

"Wait!" he said again sharply. "This is important! There's no one else in the house? Just you and the children and this old woman?"

"Old Mungo, possibly."

"Mungo?" he said with instant suspicion. "Who's that?"

His cold, clutching hand brought her up with a jerk.

"Mungo?" How to explain Mungo. "He's an old sailor—a long-ago sweetheart of Elspie's. He fell in love with her when she was sixteen, spreading out the sheets in the bleach field. He lives in the gardener's cottage."

"Listen." Nils spoke without paying any apparent heed to her words. "Val. Have any strangers been here lately? People from outside, foreigners?"

"No, Nils. Why?"

"Who does come to the house, from outside?"

"The postman, the doctor—Annot from the lodge—"

"Who's the doctor?" And, when she had explained, "Is that all? No one else?"

She could not fathom the reason for this interrogation and began to wonder if her brother was ill—his manner seemed so abrupt and inconsequential. He kept looking around him in a strange, staring way—at the leafless shrubs, the grey tufted grass, the ivy on the wall.

"Nils, do come along in! you must be frozen, and it's nearly dark."

"Listen!" he said again. "This is important." His grip on her wrist tightened until she gasped with pain—but still his eyes were everywhere, behind, to the side, over her shoulder; he did not look at her.

"What is it, Nils? What's the matter?"

"No one—*no one at all*—is to know that I'm here. Do you understand? Is there a side entrance to the house? Can you take me in by a way that no one will see?"

"Yes, there's the French window. But why, Nils? How can we help people knowing that you are here? Elspie will have to know—and the children, naturally—"

"No, they don't have to! It's a big house. There must be dozens of empty rooms where you could put me. You could bring me food—"

She could not see his face, for his was still looking away from her, but his voice wavered oddly. Val became more and more certain that he must be feverish, temporarily unhinged, perhaps, by the distresses that he had undergone. It seemed simplest to humour him for the moment.

"Come along, then, this way. Quietly."

It was dark enough now so that even his morbid anxieties must be allayed; there seemed no possibility that even the keenest watcher would be able to spot their approach to the house. She led him along the terrace to the French window, in across the derelict card room, and up a spiral stair in the corner turret to the first floor. There she showed him a bedroom, by the light of a candle that Elspie had left burning on the hall table.

"No, this won't do!" he whispered. "I must have a room on the sea side."

"Don't you want to be near me and the children, Nils?"

"No!"

"We'll have to go up to the attic floor, then; all the others look on to the garden or into the yard."

She thought how characteristic of Nils it was, to be so difficult and particular about his accommodation, even when he was in the last stages of fatigue.

"The attic floor would be better. Don't walk so loudly!"

They went up again, Val leading the way with the candle.

She had been in the attics two or three times on rainy days, taking the children as a diversion. They were a mazelike and surprisingly extensive series of tiny rooms under the leads, some intercommunicating, others joined by narrow passages. It was hard, on this level, to find a room looking toward the sea, for many of the small cobwebbed windows gave on to the roof, or had their view cut off by the parapet, but at last Nils found one that satisfied him, with a small round window like a porthole, looking toward the beach. The room contained a cot bed, a chair, and that was all.

"This will do," said Nils, and flung himself on the bed, which had no covers. "You can leave me. All I need is sleep."

"I'll get you some blankets."

"There's no need."

But she had left, tiptoeing down to the floor below. When she returned he was nearly asleep already. As she spread the covers over him he woke and clutched her hand.

"Don't tell anybody that I'm here—Elspie—the children—*anyone*. Do you promise?"

"Very well," said Val, but with a mental reservation that her promise held only until tomorrow morning. It would be wholly impossible—ridiculous—undignified—unethical—to hide Nils here, to keep him concealed from the other inmates of the house. What would Elspie think if she found out? And there was the whole question of Lady Stroma. She thought of Mr. M'Intyre saying, "While their father is alive, Lady Stroma is not prepared to do anything for them . . ." No doubt Lady Stroma should be informed of his reappearance. But that must be shelved until Nils was better. In common humanity, even Lady Stroma could hardly evict Nils and the children while he was in his present state.

But why should not the children have the satisfaction of knowing that their father was alive and close at hand? Particularly since the poor little things would soon have to learn of their mother's death.

"Don't you want anything to eat, Nils?" she said.

"No. I have some brandy." He drew a metal flask from his pocket, uncorked it, and drank. "That's all I want."

"Shall I leave the light?"

"No! Dark is better. Then one can't see at all. I'm going to sleep. Besides, somebody in the garden might notice the light."

He seemed, Val thought, to imagine the house surrounded by hostile watchers. She softly closed his door and carried the candle back to the upstairs hall. Then she went down to find the children playing hunt the thimble in the kitchen, with an old horn thimble lent by Elspie, watched and adjudicated over by Mungo. Elspie, looking both conscious and severe, was peeling potatoes; she wore an unaccustomed knot of slate-blue ribbon tied under her collar.

So much seemed to have happened that Val felt it must be very late. But it was not; and she presently sat down and read aloud to the children, letting the words flow from her mouth in an unheeded stream while her mind roved away into the dark; now up to the cold black attic where Nils lay lost in sleep, now over to Wolf's Hope in sad speculation about Helen —how was she? Was Sir Marcus with her? What were they saying to one another?

"You're unco' silent, Mistress Val," Mungo said presently, giving her a shrewd, kindly look, and Val answered with truth that it had been a very sad visit to Mrs. Ramsay.

"Ay, poor soul," Elspie said. "Yon Andie told us that Doctor Davie feared she'd no' last the nicht. I doubt we'll no' be seeing the doctor the morn."

"I suppose not." Val had overlooked this probability in her preoccupation with Nils; she had been planning to ask David's advice about Nils— if he would allow it, or even, perhaps, without his permission.

Oh well—she would decide what to do in the morning.

"Aunt Val," said Pieter. "Have you noticed Elspie's new ribbon? Isn't it pretty? Mr. Bucklaw gave it to her."

"It's very pretty," said Val, but Elspie, blushing, grumbled, "Och, awa', he shouldna be wasting his siller on such gear."

"And he bought me a little cart and Jannie a doll," said Pieter, exhibiting these treasures.

"Aren't you lucky? Where did all these beautiful things come from?"

"A tinkler came to the door with a tray full of toys and ribbons and combs and sewing needles. And he said, weren't there any grand ladies and gentlemen staying here who would like to buy lots of other things he had, even better, but we told him there was only you, Aunt Val, and that your clothes are awfully plain, so we didn't think you'd want any lace or ribbons."

"Na, na," remarked Elspie with grim approval, "Mistress Val has a mind abune sic whigmaleeries."

Val laughed and agreed, looking at her brown bombazine.

"Dinna talk like that, Elspie," remonstrated Mungo gently, "or you will make me think that you take no pleasure in my giftie."

"Ach, ye great silly," said Elspie, half scolding; but she gave him a soft look.

Mungo presently retired to his croft. Val longed to tell him about Nils, but held to her promise and kept silent. It was strange—the secret seemed to cut her off from them all, though it was the children's own father who lay up there in the darkness. The thought chilled her. *Why* was Nils so set on secrecy? Who did he imagine could be interested in his whereabouts? She could think of several possibilities and none were comfortable.

Next morning Val rose early and slipped up to the attic, opening the door with such care that the sleeper inside did not stir. She moved over to the bed and studied him by the meagre light from the small circular window. Seen thus, asleep, unguarded, he shocked her profoundly. He could have aged ten years since she had seen him last in New York. His face was thin to emaciation, with deep grooves chiselled in the cheeks, and a half-healed scar on the side of his jaw. The skin was a yellow, unhealthy colour, as if he had been living underground, with outbreaks of red pimples among the unshaven blond stubble of beard. His hands were oiled and grimed with dirt of long-standing, and the clothes he wore were likewise soiled and caked. His shoes were worn thin, cracked and stubbed. Glancing round to see if he had any baggage—she had not observed, last night, whether he carried anything—she noticed a sailor's canvas bag and thought, At least he will have a change of linen and we can wash those things. And he'll want food by now. I had better bring up—

She was moving toward the door when he woke and started up on one elbow with a hoarse exclamation. His eyes, blue and bloodshot, blazed at her like underwater lights.

"What are you doing?—oh, it's you! What were you doing with my bag?"

"I didn't touch it, Nils!"

"Well, don't!" He pulled himself up in the bed, propped against the end wall. Then, dragging the bag to him by its cord, he felt among its contents; a frown creased his brows. He pushed the bag aside, pulled the brandy flask from his pocket, and drank.

"Shall I bring you up some breakfast? What would you like?"

She longed to get her hands on him—to get him fed and tended and tidied up. He looked so terrible, sitting there, with all his handsomeness and charm turned to a sinister caricature. His lips, which had always been unusually red, were still so, but his mouth was turned down at the corners as if in a permanent grimace of disgust. The long yellow locks hung lank, like dirty string; the eyes seemed to have seen something so hideous that Val could not bear them; all she let herself think about was small practical measures of comfort or nourishment; she felt helpless in the presence of their dreadful awareness.

"Porridge? Shall I bring you some hot water so that you can wash up here? Have you a razor? There is a bathroom down below—believe it or not! And when you feel rested, the children can come to see you—"

"No!" The frantic intensity of his voice silenced her. He said, "Sit down. Now keep quiet. Listen. Does anybody know I'm here yet? Did you tell anyone?"

"No, not yet, I—"

"Be quiet! Are there neighbours—houses nearby—I forget?"

"No nearer than Wolf's Hope. Only the family at the lodge. And they hardly come near. They were offended because I said their daughter—"

"Hush! That's one blessing then," he muttered. "Nobody else? No one's been asking for me?"

"No." Then she recollected and said, "Some tinklers came selling stuff at the door."

"Who spoke to them?"

"Elspie. And she said there were no grand folk here."

"Good. Well, no one's to come—do you understand? Who else might come? What about that man who was here yesterday?"

"Sir Marcus?" Val remembered. "He did say he might come today."

"Send a message and tell him not to."

"But, why, Nils?" Her heart sank at this irrational order. Among all the perplexities and disappointments of the reunion with Nils, the thought of seeing Sir Marcus later, of being able to ask his advice, had been the one point of light ahead.

"You're no actor." Her brother's voice held nothing but dislike. "Anyway no woman can keep a secret. You'd be sure to give away the fact that something was up. Tell him not to come."

"But Nils—what *is* up? Why all this secrecy?"

He pulled the blankets around him and over his head. Propped against the wall with only his face visible, he looked like a ghastly monk, like a corpse wrapped in its shroud.

"It's no use telling *you* anything," he said.

The words came out of the shroud with such bitter venom that Val shivered, in the icy, dusty little room, which smelt of rotting wood. There was nothing physical to remind her, but suddenly she was back in childhood, in a wintry New York street. Nils, picking himself up after a snow battle with other boys, five against one, in which he had been ignominiously beaten, had turned with sudden fury on his small sister, who had come running just in time to witness his defeat.

"You're no good. What use are *you?"* And he knocked her down and savagely rubbed her face in the dirty snow, meting out to her the treatment he had just received himself. "But *why* do they fight you, Nils? Why aren't they friends with you?" she wept, picking herself up, stumbling along behind him. He kicked the piled snow. "Because I'm cleverer than they are. And I'm cleverer than *you,* too, and always shall be."

For a moment Val was back in that bitter windswept street; for a moment she became again the forlorn child who trailed unhappily after her brother, hoping in vain that he would ever turn and say something kind.

But I'm not that child any longer, she suddenly realised. No, and I haven't been for fifteen years. It's of no importance to me now, what Nils thinks of me. I'm grown up. I'm free. And I own the world.

She said, equably, "Now, look, Nils, I want to help you. I'm sure you need rest, and medicine, and a doctor. But I can't keep you here like—like a stowaway. The house belongs to Lady Stroma, after all; she only allows *me* to stay here because I'm looking after the children—she doesn't *like* my being here—and she will like your presence even less."

"She hates me like poison," he said indifferently.

"Still, however badly she hates you, she'd hardly want you turned out while you are ill. But it is *not* fair to Elspie to keep your presence here secret. Elspie's responsible for the place."

"Oh, rats!" Nils broke out. *"Must* you stand there, so smug and righteous, lecturing me like a schoolmarm? Like your precious Miss Chumley!"

That pierced her armour. But she said quietly, "You can't expect me to keep your secrets when you give me no reason why I should."

"I have enemies," he said sullenly. "That's reason enough—ain't it? Enemies who'd have been glad to see me drowned, like Kirstie. Maybe they think I *am* drowned. But if they knew I was here, they would come and *get* me—just as you'd go to market to pick up a cabbage."

His eyes jumped nervously past her.

A cold tremor slid down Val's spine, between her shoulder blades. And all at once it did seem the height of unfair stupidity, to stand here arguing with Nils, when he was in such a wretched state of fear and sickness and extremity.

Could he be speaking the truth about his enemies? Or were these imaginary fears—his fever talking?

"What's your plan, then? What do you want me to do?" she asked more gently.

"Hide me here a few days—till I'm rested. I had a bang on the head, back—back there." His eyes moved, seemed to look inward as at some nightmare; he paused a moment. "I get headaches—it's hard to think, sometimes. Then—when I'm better—you'll have to give me some money. Enough for a ticket to America."

"*America?* But what about the children? You couldn't take them, surely—"

"Who said I was going to? They can stay here, can't they?"

Val opened her mouth to speak, to explain, to argue—then shut it again. Time enough to discuss Lady Stroma and her conditions when he was well again, and amenable to reason. Surely a few days at Ardnacarrig would make him well. All that was needed was patience, to wait, to humour him a little.

"All right, Nils." She made her voice gentle and reasonable. "I won't tell anyone outside the house that you are here. But I must tell old Elspie. I don't think I *could* keep it from her, anyway. She'd find out by instinct."

And that means Mungo and the children will necessarily have to know as well, she thought, but did not say.

"Oh—very well," he grumbled fretfully. "But mind—that man—Cusack—is not to come. You must tell him that the children have scarlatina or some such thing. That'll keep him away."

Very probably it will, Val thought, with a wry internal smile and a sigh. She said, "All right," again, quietly, and turned to leave the room.

"I say—Val!" he called after her.

"What?"

"Be a sport and bring a fellow up some brandy, will you? I've finished what's in my flask. I don't care so much about eating just now but I could do with another nip to warm me. Do, now—will you?"

She nodded, went downstairs, and helped the children with their dressing and breakfast. Then, seizing the first opportunity afterward, she drew Elspie into the pantry.

"Elspie, there's something I have to tell you privately. I need your help. My—the children's father has come here. Last night."

"He has so?" Elspie put her hands on her hips with deliberation and looked thoughtfully at Val, who went on, "And—and I think he's in some kind of trouble. He wants to hide here for a few days—from his enemies, he says—and no one to know about it."

"Och, ay?" Elspie's tone was still the same: dry, noncommittal; she stood waiting, and her angular face expressed nothing; her mouth was compressed into a straight, sceptical line.

"And Nils has given me a piece of dreadful news: Kirstie is dead, drowned."

Val had expected an outcry of grief, or shock, but Elspie's reaction was characteristically controlled: she crossed her hands over her breast, as if to hold in pain, then nodded her head slowly, twice.

"Ay," she said presently. "I felt sairtain that must be so."

"You did, Elspie? Why?"

"Why? I reared that lass from when she was twa years old. We were as nigh as that." She cupped one hand inside the other. "When you've cared for a bairn, ye have a feeling of them with ye always, a' the lave of your life—ye know when they are in trouble, ye can sense it. Ach, I canna express what I mean! But I had thon feeling, lately, for wee Kirstie, that she was in sore trouble—and syne—all of a sudden—it was gone. I thocht: her pain's over, whate'er it was; she's no frighted ony mair, my puir Kirstie."

Elspie's gaze moved back from the distance and fixed on Val. She said, "Ye'll know what I mean, some day, maybe, when ye've bairns of your own—or gin some orra, unchancy thing were to come to Pieter or wee Jannie. Ye'd feel it, here."

Val did feel a sudden piercing pang, as she saw two tears form slowly in Elspie's faded blue eyes and run down her wrinkled cheeks, though her mouth still kept its straight, stoic line.

"I'm very sorry, Elspie," she said quietly. "I know Kirstie was like your own child."

The old woman—for a moment she truly seemed one—gave a short, loud sigh.

"Aweel, aweel! Where is your brither—is he inbye?"

"Yes," Val said. "I've put him in one of the attics—out of the way."

Elspie nodded, as if this were just what she would have expected.

"Weel—I'll tell ye this, Mistress Val. I never liked your brither, an' I never trusted him. I was sairtain he married Kirstie for her siller, though *she* was fair infatuated an' couldna see it. An' I'm sairtain he treated her hard as man ever treated wumman. Ye're a decent enough body, Mistress Val, for all your camsteery ways an' yer pigheadedness—but yon man is clean bad, richt through."

Val stood silent, accepting the stinging truth of Elspie's words.

"I know," she said, after a while. "And I know Lady Stroma would not approve of his being here, and that she feels the same way about him. I think you are right, Elspie. But he *is* the children's father, and he's starved and exhausted and ill." For a moment she thought of pointing out that Mungo had arrived in a similar manner, but felt this would not be fair. So she merely ended, "May he stay—just for a few days, just till he's better?"

"Och, ay. Who am I to say nay? He can bide. Juist for a few days. I'll come an' see him mysel', by an' by."

Val felt nervous at the thought of this visit, but it was postponed for the time by the arrival at this moment, unusually late, of Tom the postman, who brought a note from David Ramsay addressed to Val.

"My dear Val: I know you will be sorry to hear that my mother passed away during the night. Her end was peaceful: she sank into a state of unconsciousness from which she could not be roused. Marcus, Tibbie, and I were at her bedside." There followed details about the funeral arrangements for the following day, and he ended, "I know you will understand why I do not come over to give Jannie her lesson for a few days. There is much to be done. But Marcus says that, unless it is inconvenient to you, he would like to call on you this afternoon. Affectionately, D.R."

There was no time to reflect, or evolve subtleties of language. Tom Postie was drinking a cup of tea and had told her he would be back in Wolf's Hope by noon; Val scribbled down two notes, one of heartfelt condolence to David, one to Marcus which simply said, "Dear Sir Marcus, I am sorry to have to deny you, but, for reasons which I am unable to go into, I am afraid you had better not come to Ardnacarrig for the present. Yours, V.M."

Feeling as if she had severed a cord that moored her to land and sanity she handed the notes to Tom.

After he had left, Val looked for Elspie, but she had vanished, perhaps to seek comfort with Mungo, who was working down at the boathouse. The children were peacefully engaged in the card room, playing a game of house under card tables draped with old curtains which even Elspie had condemned as being beyond repair.

Val put food, and a bowl of hot water with washing equipment on a tray and bore it upstairs. She negotiated the wide shallow flight that circled the main hall without difficulty, but the narrow stair to the attic would not take the tray; she had to put it down and carry the things up separately.

The temperature in this whole region of the house was arctic; many of the windows were ill-fitting, and the wind whistled through the cracks and past the crow-stepped gables. Val, glancing out through a small window on to the leads, noticed a few flakes of snow drift by. Sir Marcus will want to get back to Edinburgh fast, if there is going to be snow here, she thought, shivering; it's as well that I told him not to come. This thought was no consolation, and neither was the behaviour of Nils when she took him in porridge, tea, hot water, and soap.

"What the devil d'you bring all that trash for?" he snarled. "Take it away! I asked for brandy, not slops!"

"You'll have to ask Elspie for brandy—if there's any in the house. It's not mine to dispense. She is coming up to see you presently."

"You *told* her?" His rage was frightening, but Val stood her ground.

"I'm not going to tell lies on your account, Nils. I won't do it. Now come on, you stink worse than a polecat. If you won't wash yourself, I shall have to wash you; you have to clean up before she comes."

Despite his furious protests she managed to get him at least partially cleaned up. He was really weak and she had to do most of the work. He was also so thin that his bones stood out like driftwood. He muttered, "So would you stink if you'd been where I've been."

"Well, where have you been, Nils? You haven't told me anything yet."

"I had no money so I worked my way here on freighters—from London to Hull, from Hull here."

"Was Kirstie on the freighter too? Was that how she came to drown?"

His eyes slid away nervously and his mouth twitched. Val said, "It can't —surely—have taken you all the time since I reached England, just making your way from London to Scotland? What happened to you?"

He ignored her question and asked one of his own. "When you were in London, did you—who did you see? You brought the children here?"

"Yes," she answered absently. She was horrified to discover that the upper part of his body was a mass of bruises and half-healed cuts. "Nils— what has been *happening* to you?"

"I fell overboard," he muttered. "In the Thames estuary. Had to swim for it. Got washed against some underwater piles. That's *enough*, now, Val, for God's sake—do leave a fellow in peace!"

"Have you any clean clothes in that bag?"

"Yes—no! Don't touch it! Hand it here, there might be a shirt—" He found one, and Val took away the rest of his clothes to wash. By the time that Elspie arrived, he was moderately clean, but the exertion of washing had tired him and he looked even more ghastly than he had before. By now he was accepting Val as matter-of-factly as if they had fallen back into their old childhood relationship—but the sight of Elspie, tall and gaunt in her black dress, white apron, and black mutch, seemed to discompose him terribly. He cowered back against the wall, and his eyes fled from side to side.

"Who's *that?*" he whispered to Val. "Don't let her near me! Has she come to curse me?"

"It's only Elspie!" said Val. "You've met her before."

Nils began to whimper. "I can't *stand* it when she looks at me so! Tell her not to. Her eyes go through me like red-hot needles. Go away—go away!" he shrieked at Elspie. "It wasn't my fault—none of it was. It wasn't my fault she died!"

Ignoring this, Elspie walked up to him and felt his head. He moaned and writhed away from her touch and hid his face in the pillow.

"Nay, he has no fever, his head's cool enow," Elspie said calmly to Val. "I doubt he's a wee thing shocked in his wits, the noo. We'll juist have tae keep him warm and quiet for two-three days an' see how he gaes. When Doctor Ramsay comes again, aiblins he can tell what's wrang. Has he eaten?"

"No, he wouldn't touch the food. He asks for brandy."

"Och, weel, there's a few bottles the auld laird left ahind him—he micht as well hae them, nae ither person cares for the stuff," Elspie said drily and left the room.

After she had gone, Nils very slowly pulled himself straight in the bed and said to Val, "Was there somebody in the room just now?"

"Of course there was! I told you—it was Elspie."

"Truly?"

"Truly."

"You see," he explained, looking round with that same sliding motion of the eyes, "sometimes I fancy things. I think I see—people. The Kindly Ones. You know who I mean? Horrible old women. Snakes in their hair. I get a glimpse of them—just behind: over my shoulder. That's why I like to sit with my back against the wall." He gave Val a haggard grin, glancing sidelong again. "And brandy's a help you see—it keeps out the cold. Helps me sleep. I don't see them when I'm asleep."

"Don't see whom?"

"The Kindly Ones."

Shivering, Val said, "I'll get you the brandy," and left him. The icy, stuffy little room was suddenly more than she could bear—it seemed filled with alien presences.

For the next four days Nils lay up in the attic. At times, after he had had a tot of brandy, he was sensible enough and did not cry out at the sight of Elspie, or address her as Alecto, or assert that there were small, threatening figures moving very fast along the wall of his room, lurking just out of his line of vision. When he was rational, Val tried hard to get him to talk, feeling sure that he needed to unburden himself; but he was singularly reticent and would only repeat the bones of his tale—"Got on a ship. Got on two ships. Came here."

At other times he would embark on long, rambling, malicious reports about people she had never heard of and never wished to meet, they sounded so unpleasant.

He slept for a good deal of the time—strangely heavy sleep—but always awoke with a start, glancing behind him and muttering, "Are they here yet? Orville says they can't follow over water but I think he's wrong—I think he's wrong!"

"What do you think is the matter with him?" Val asked Elspie.

"It micht be the drink in him. The auld laird was like that, whiles; a touch o' the deleerium treemens; but likely as not, it's juist his whole bad life has caught up wi' him," Elspie said grimly.

The children still had not been told of their father's arrival, because Nils was adamant in his refusal to see them; and while he was in his present state, seeing him would do them no good; on the contrary, it might upset them badly. It did seem as if, in some dark, unhappy way, he was reliving the whole of his life, following a random chronological pattern discernible to him alone. At times he was Val's ten-year-old brother, bullying, jealous, spiteful, domineering.

"You touched my paint box. Didn't you? You walked ahead of me, you're not allowed to! You went upstairs on the left-hand side, that's forbidden. You had two lumps of sugar—I shall punish you! You have got to be punished! Father won't, so I have to. Stand still—no, over there. Shut your eyes!"

The Val he spoke to was imaginary, but sometimes he railed and screamed at the real one.

"Go away! Get out of my sight! I can't bear you. You remind me of too much."

Then he would go off into fantasy once more.

"*You* can't come to England. Mother doesn't want you. She only wants me—she loves me best, she always will. *I* don't care if you stay in New York with Monty—he's not my real father, *my* father wasn't a hack writer, he was a gentleman. I'm nearly all Norwegian, you're only half. Mother doesn't love you at all."

Sometimes he thought that Val *was* their mother.

"Please, please dearest, don't be angry, dearest Mia! I'll stay in my room all day, I won't come down and bother your guests. You can lock me in, if you like! I won't look, I won't listen. Just so long as I know you're there. *Please*, Mia! Just so long as I'm not alone. Don't be angry with me."

Val had forgotten his pet name for their mother, which he had forbidden her ever to use, on pain of his worst punishments. It gave her a strange pang to hear it used so.

"I'm not angry," she said gently, but he was off again, assuring Mia that he would never peep through curtains, never listen at keyholes or talk to her maid, that he would not dream of being jealous of her friends, that he didn't wish to be a nuisance, or an embarrassment, but please wouldn't she come up to say good night, wouldn't she show that she loved him just a little?

A gruesome picture began to build up for Val of the life in that bijou little house in Bruton Street with the carriage and the manservant and the genteel card parties, the friends, the flowers. She could not avoid constructing a very unflattering portrait of their mother, and her various pursuits, downstairs, while Nils was relegated to his upstairs bedroom, peering through the banisters. Where he still is, Val thought, transfixed with pity. But the next minute Nils had turned on her with bitter spite, and was shouting, "You—*you*! What good are *you*? Nobody wants you! Girls are stupid lying cheats. All except for Mia! *You* couldn't even hang on to Benet Allerton—that stuffed snob—and *he* only wanted you for your money!"

"*Money?*" said Val, shaken out of the calm she usually managed to maintain with his irrationalities, "you know I haven't any money."

"Oh, you stupid stupid bitch, you're too stupid even to know *that! I* found out a couple of hours after getting to New York; went straight to Winthrop and Babcock—read Monty's will—of course you have money, only the cunning old fox left it all tied up till you're twenty-seven. Consolation for being an old maid on the shelf, eh? He didn't leave *me* any, mean old swine; what's two hundred dollars? I'm only his stepson; no, precious little Valhalla gets the lot. But Benet knew about it, you can be sure of that; those lawyers all live in each other's pockets. A dandy little nest egg, ready to hatch when the marriage is cooling down!"

Could he be right?

Winthrop and Babcock certainly were Mr. Montgomery's lawyers. And they had firmly assured Val that she had no expectations apart from the house on Twenty-third Street.

"If Benet knew about it, don't you think it rather odd that he didn't tell me?" she asked coldly. "Or—if he was such a fortune hunter—that he let me break off the engagement?"

But he hasn't allowed me to, she thought. Is that why?

"How could he tell you? He wasn't supposed to know himself! He'll be after you, never fear; pro'ly on the boat now," said Nils, refilling his glass. "Comes to Lon'on three, four times a year 'n any case—seen him on the rampage there, at Mereweather's—*gals!* Not legal business, no, no. Gals. Can't chase gals in N'York, someone might see him."

"That's ridiculous," Val said. "Benet! Of all people! You might as well suggest that father—"

Nils burst into a raucous laugh. "Old Monty? No, no, Vallie dear, I wouldn't suggest *that* para—paragon of p'fection ever went chasing gals! He couldn't! Mia always said it was a c-contradiction 'f the laws 'f nature that you were ever c-conceived! It was as much as he dared t' c-crawl into bed with her, he had no more real blood in him than C-Cleopatra's Needle."

"I don't believe a single word you are saying," Val said, at the end of her patience. She rose to leave. But the hostile teasing gaiety instantly left his face.

"Don't—don't go, sit with me a while longer, Vallie, do! Don't leave a fellow—there's a dear! I do run on, I know I do, but I won't say another word—it's only my fun, y'know!"

When she said she had to go to the children and suggested they should visit him—"No, no! For God's sake don't bring them here. They drive me wild with their noise. Can't stand little hideous voices like drills, specially the gal. Well then—if you *must* go—bring 'nother bottle 'f brandy when you come back—will you? There's a dear girl."

Val became more and more worried about him. After four days he seemed no better—worse if anything. The quantity of brandy he got through offset the benefits of rest and nourishment; and the hours he spent in solitude seemed to lower his spirits and make him yet more irrational, nervous, and prone to wild fits of malice, hostility, guilt, and despair. At times he begged Val for money for his ticket to America, assuring her that she had only to write to Winthrop and Babcock, they would advance it; at other times he let fall veiled hints about huge potential wealth of his own.

"A gold mine, a real gold mine, Vallie, eighteen carat! All we have to do is dig it carefully and we'll be set till the end of our days; just wants a little management; you wait! You'll see."

Sometimes he complained furiously about being shut away in the attic "like a servant" when, if he had his rights and certain things were known about certain people, he would be wealthy enough for a house of his own in Grosvenor Square and could thumb his nose at those two old plaster trouts who affected not to recognise him if they met him in the street.

Never once, not ever, in his ramblings, did he allude to Kirstie.

On the fourth day, as David Ramsay still had not reappeared and there had been no word from Sir Marcus, and Nils had been at his most difficult and obstreperous all day, Val, tried to the limit of endurance, decided to see what the results of getting him up would be. She felt that if he continued to lie on his bed and drink brandy, he might easily send himself into a decline from which there would be no recovery.

"Come, Nils!" she said. "There is nobody in the house. The children are down at the boathouse with Mungo watching him work on the boat. And Elspie has taken a bottle of currant cordial to Mrs. Kelso who's sick at the lodge. So come and walk in the Long Gallery for half an hour. It will do you good."

She helped him put on his threadbare black jacket, which she and Elspie had cleaned and pressed.

"Why do you always wear black, Nils?" she asked, easing it over his bony shoulders. He had never worn any other colour, even on that carefree summer holiday so long ago.

"Mourning, mourning for the best mother a fellow could hope to have," he muttered mechanically, glancing behind him. "Mourning for Mia."

The falseness and artificiality of his words discouraged Val, who said nothing more, but took his arm and helped him along the passage. The best mother? Val remembered her week-long banishment over that blue-and-black alpaca dress. If Mother was the best, she thought, heaven preserve us from the worst.

With groans and complaints, Nils allowed himself to be guided down the attic stair and along to the gallery, where he ignored the portraits of bygone Carsphairns on the inner wall, but looked fixedly out of each seaward window while slowly walking past, as if he hoped, or feared, to see a sail come over the horizon. Visibility was not good, however; snow fell steadily, and a heavy bank of cloud hung so low over the stone-grey sea that sea and sky tended to merge into a general dimness behind the fluttering, weaving snowflakes. The portraits on the inner wall wore dusk like shawls around their shoulders; only here and there could a pair of cold blue eyes be seen, gazing down at Nils and Val as they walked slowly by; here and there a fan, a wig, a scroll or sword, or mane of prancing charger was faintly discernible.

Outside, the winter afternoon was condensing into twilight. Ardnacarrig House was mute as the inside of a pyramid; the only sound to be heard was their footsteps going to and fro, to and fro. The way I walked with Sir Marcus on the beach, Val thought sombrely. Five days ago now. No letter from him. Perhaps there won't be one. Perhaps he has concluded that I don't wish to meet him again.

She longed to write him another letter, expressing sorrow for the missed meeting, expressing sympathy over Helen's death. But how could she, when so much would have to remain unwritten? She had, in fact, started one or two drafts, addressing them to the *Selkirk's* office, but, since she could not mention Nils, who was almost her whole preoccupation at the moment, they seemed wholly false, and she tore them up.

To and fro, to and fro. Nils talked, in a rambling, petulant way, of fellows in London he knew, who had said they would back his bills but then unaccountably changed their minds, of ignorant prejudiced editors, of damned encroaching tradesmen, and those two miserable old tabbies in Grosvenor Square, who would not advance Kirstie so much as a pony, though she would inherit all this one day.

"That isn't true, you know, Nils. The property is entailed; it goes in the male line."

"Well then Pieter ought to have it; or how did the old girls get their claws on it in the first place?" demanded Nils, with one of those sudden disconcerting flashes of practicality which generally seized him, Val had noticed, when money was in question, or when a malicious accusation could be levelled at some respected target.

"I don't know; perhaps Scots law is different."

But she did wonder, suddenly, if the Carsphairn ladies were in wrongful possession, and knew it; would not that account for their absentee habits, neglect, and parsimony? Were these shortcomings founded on the guilty knowledge that they were usurpers?

"I'm tired," said Nils fretfully like a child, and she was about to steer him back to his bed when the door at the far end of the gallery burst open. Noise and light streamed through and the children came clattering in, preceding Mungo, who carried a lamp.

"*There* you are, Aunt Val! We've been making a snow woman, just like the picture of Lady Christina Carsphairn! Mungo's been helping us—" Pieter began, and then his jaw dropped, his eyes opened wide, he screamed, "*Papa!*" and hurled himself joyfully toward Nils. At the same moment Jannie also screamed, equally loud, but hers was the wild, wailing cry of pure terror. She turned from Nils just as violently as Pieter had rushed toward him, and fled from the gallery. Her terrified gasping cries died away in the distance.

"Och—maircy, what's wi' the bairn?" exclaimed Mungo.

"Go after her, Mungo, can you?" said Val quickly, and he nodded and turned on his heel.

Appalled by Jannie's reaction to the sight of her father, Val stared after them, biting her lip; it was a moment before she realised that something was badly the matter with Nils. Instead of welcoming Pieter's ecstatic greeting, he was holding off the boy with one hand, staring fixedly past him, and whispering, "Keep her away, don't let her touch me! Who's that woman?"

"There isn't any woman. That was Mungo," said Val, mystified.

"Papa? Aren't you going to hug me?" demanded Pieter, abruptly transformed from a small hurtling projectile of delight into a puzzled, scared child.

Nils began slowly backing away, his eyes still on the door.

"It's no use your coming here carrying that baby!" he cried in a loud, threatening tone. "You can't get me now. You're dead! And it isn't my fault you died, damn you, it's your own! It's too late to help you—don't come whining to me now. For God's sake—*let go of my hand!*"

By now Nils had backed himself into an angle of the wall, and here he appeared to undergo some species of seizure; his breath came pantingly, foam crusted up on his lips, he let out several short but extraordinarily piercing cries and shuddered violently, as if an electric current had been passed through him. His eyes rolled upward in his head, his mouth opened, and he fell heavily to the floor.

"Wh-what's happened to Papa?" asked Pieter with chattering teeth. "Is he—is he d-dead?"

"I don't know, Pieter," said Val, kneeling by her brother, trying to control the shaking of her own hands enough to discover if he had a pulse.

"I'm frightened!" wailed Pieter.

"Hey, hey! What the devil's going on here?" demanded a familiar voice. "Mungo's downstairs with Jannie looking as if they've seen the bogeyman—what's up?" and Val turned with unutterable relief to see David Ramsay coming toward them from the other end of the gallery.

CHAPTER 16

Somehow, between them, David and Mungo succeeded in carrying the rigid body of Nils up the attic stairs and back to his bed. David listened to Val's description of the seizure and said that it sounded to him like an epileptic attack; no treatment would be necessary but that the patient should be left with loosened clothes to sleep it off.

"Oh, I am so *glad* to see you, Davie," Val kept saying. "I didn't like to send for you because I knew how sad and busy you must be, but I have been longing for you so. My brother is in such a strange state—sometimes he seems quite mad, really—at other times sensible enough. But he was so imperative that no one outside the house should know of his arrival—I haven't known *what* to do."

"My poor dear girl—you have had a time of it." David squeezed her hand sympathetically. "Well—for the moment—do nothing. I'll come back and look at your brother when he is awake—tomorrow, perhaps. At present, after a seizure of the severity you describe, he will very likely sleep four or five hours, or even longer."

"It was very frightening—he seemed to be seeing some apparition—he thought it was Kirstie," Val said, shivering. "He kept telling her that she ought to be dead."

"Perhaps it was really Thrawn Jane he saw," David suggested, only half in jest. "Who knows? After all, Thrawn Jane was Kirstie's great-great-aunt; there may have been a family resemblance."

"Let us go and find Jannie," Val said, shivering again.

Jannie was in the kitchen; Mungo sat in the rocker and she was huddled, fast asleep, in his arms, sucking her finger, the marks of tears half dried on her flushed cheeks. Pieter was there too, very subdued, reading one of his books on a stool by Mungo's knee. And Elspie was chopping cabbage on a board as if it were somebody's head under a guillotine. Mungo's usually benevolent face looked like that of an Old Testament prophet pronouncing doom on a whole generation of Baal worshippers.

Val suddenly felt an interloper there.

But Pieter came to her and held her hand tightly. David sat down in a basket chair and told Elspie about his mother's last days, while she brought him seed cake and a glass of whisky. And Jannie waking, apparently forgetful of what had caused her terror, clambered down from Mungo's knee and came, still sucking her finger, to lean against Val and be petted.

But when Pieter said, worriedly, "Where's Papa?" she began to cry again, and clung feverishly tight with both arms round Val's neck.

"It's all right, Jannie—nobody's going to hurt you," Val said. "Papa's asleep, Pieter, in one of the rooms on the top floor. It's quieter for him there. Doctor Ramsay says that he is sick, and he will sleep for hours."

Pieter repeated this reassurance to Jannie.

And Mungo said to Val and David in a low, angry tone, "It seems, by all I can gather from what the wee lassie let out when she was so frighted, that the last time she laid eyes on her father he gave her a terrible dunt on the heid; indeed, he would aye be doing it when he was displeased with her if what she says can be believed."

And how should a child her age invent such a thing? Val thought wearily. No doubt it is true.

She said, "Did your father ever hit you, Pieter?"

His face clouded. He said, "No. Papa's kind to me, mostly always, and gives me candy. I don't know why he hits Jannie. It's not fair. I'm as kind as I can be to her, to make up. And Mama's *very* kind. Aunt Val—if Papa has come—where *is* Mama? Has she come too?"

His face of hope raised to her was like a small vulnerable target.

"No, Pieter," she said steadily. "I'm sorry. Your father came here on a ship, and I'm afraid that on—on the way, your mother fell overboard and was drowned."

Pieter looked at her in silence for a long moment; then he turned and made his way blindly back to Mungo, who held him and comforted him without speaking, bending his grizzled head over the boy's fair one.

Thank God; thank God for Mungo, Val said inwardly with all her heart; where should we have been without him?

Elspie, who had paused a moment in her work, waiting to hear what Val would say, began chopping again as if she intended to cut up the board and the table too.

Before leaving, David gave Val some quiet instructions about her brother. He could have a small quantity of brandy, if that was what he craved, but not too much.

"I have a notion," David said, "from the look of his pupils, that he must have been taking laudanum. Has he any with him, do you know?"

"I've no idea," Val said, "but it is possible. Would that account for his strange turns—his seeing apparitions and talking so wildly?"

"It might well—taken in conjunction with all the brandy he has drunk. I think you should make a search among his things and, if you find any laudanum, remove it."

"Very well." Disliking the prospect of this task, she delayed his departure a moment by asking, "Sir Marcus? Is he still at Wolf's Hope?"

"No, no. He stayed only for the funeral, then went on to Ravenswood, intending to return to Edinburgh next day. Doubtless he will be there by now. I think that he was *very* disappointed not to see you again. But of course if your brother was here, I can understand why you wrote to put him off."

He paused, his foot in the stirrup, to say, "I daresay, now your brother has reappeared to take charge of the children, you yourself will be leaving Ardnacarrig soon?"

Val was astonished at how much the suggestion upset her. She said, "Oh, I don't know, Davie! How can I make any plan while Nils is in such a state?"

"Well, I will come again soon and then we can discuss it, if you like."

He rode out of the yard, Greylag picking her way dispiritedly in the snow.

Somewhat cheered by this promise, Val made her way back up the wide stairs, past the antlers and weapons; through the Long Gallery, giving a nervous glance at its far entrance, and on up the narrow flight to the attic floor.

When she entered the stuffy little room she found Nils motionless still, deep in sleep as they had left him. With great reluctance she knelt down on the floor by his canvas duffel bag and began to investigate its contents. She found the metal brandy flask, empty now. There was a shirt, handkerchiefs, and two pairs of stockings, all dirty. A notebook, pens, knife, and inkwell; some sheets of paper with notes scrawled on them in a kind of shorthand; a much-tattered, much-folded red and green theatrical print, captioned "Miss Letitia Pettigrew as Titania," which Val hurriedly refolded with trembling hands; some Lucifer matches; a razor, a morsel of soap and a candle end; small box containing snuff; and a larger, wooden box. That was all. If there were any laudanum, it must be in the wooden box. With slow and nervous care, Val levered off the tight-fitting lid. An object inside, wrapped in a dirty piece of snuff-coloured rag, occupied most of the space.

Val undid the wrappings.

After that she was concerned mainly with a desperate struggle for self-control—first, not to scream aloud, secondly, not to vomit. For what lay in front of her on the dark-smeared cloth—grey, wrinkled, cold, leaden, horrible—was a small severed human hand.

One if its fingers still wore a wedding ring.

Bluebeard, Val thought confusedly. Scheherezade. She kept calm and told a story every night. No, that was heads, not hands.

Her own hands were shaking so much that it was difficult to rewrap the horrible object. Along with it was a phial, presumably containing laudanum drops. She wrapped a handkerchief round both things, ran downstairs, flung on a cloak, let herself out by the French window, and walked rapidly down to the snowy beach. The tide was far out; the stretch of wet sand it had left exposed was a bleak grey, reflecting the colour of the sky.

Val walked rapidly along to Jock's line of posts. Beyond them the Kelpie's Flow rippled slightly, heaved and sighed, like porridge just below boiling point. Val drew back her arm and hurled both objects as far as she could into the middle of the dimpled, vibrating space; then waited and watched. In a moment both the small dark things had disappeared from sight, sucked into the sand.

It was lucky for Nils, she thought, turning, that he didn't walk into the quicksand, hiding in the cliff cave along at this end of the beach. But I suppose he knew about it, I suppose Kirstie will have told him—when they came here—before they were married.

She imagined them, young and lighthearted, running along the sand, exploring the caves, laughing as they tossed stones into the quicksand, climbing the terrifying goat track that led straight up from the rocks to Wolf's Crag castle. Kirstie didn't know that one day, her hand . . . If Kirstie was drowned, what was her hand doing in that box?

Val walked along the beach as if the furies were after her; the snow stung her face and she welcomed its cold bite; she breathed huge gulps of the piercing air and rubbed her hands violently on the snowy grass; anything to expunge the smell and feel and thought of what Nils had carried about with him.

To and fro along the beach; a jerky tune wandered through her head, to which her feet automatically kept time; vaguely she identified it as one of those she had danced to at the Allertons' ball—something called the "King Pippin Polka." *Tum te tum te tum.* The foolish music, the chandeliers, muslins, smell of floor polish and gardenias, the snobbish chatter of the Allertons and their friends came back to her with a mad irrelevance. That evening seemed in another century. There I was, she thought, dancing over that huge expanse of polished floor with my yellow ribbons flying out behind; there I was making polite conversation with Mr. Dexter about the Bermondsey Beast, and all the time Nils was waiting for me on the doorstep in Twenty-third Street. And all the time that hand was waiting for *him.* But where did it all start? To and fro, to and fro. With that goodbye on the quay, Mother in her black velvet and green muff? It's a good thing I'm not still engaged to Benet, at all events, she thought; he'd never put up with hands in people's luggage. But of course Nils thinks that Benet is a fortune hunter. And Nils ought to know, being a fortune hunter himself *par excellence;* first you marry, then you chop their hands off. I'm hysterical, she thought, I must stop thinking these thoughts, which do not help at all. I must pull myself together and go back to the house, to kind blessed Mungo and sane, tough, fair-minded Elspie.

What would *they* say if I told them about the hand?

She simply could not imagine. Perhaps Scots take such things more matter-of-factly? They have a tradition of battles and border raids, feuds and murders and mutilations, not too far in their past.

But she knew she was not going to mention this horror to them.

Back in the kitchen Elspie was distracting Pieter, who showed a tendency to nervous harping on his father's illness, by tales of smugglers and their doings.

"Och, yes, there were plenty around here! Every drop of brandy the auld laird drank was run over from France; he ne'er paid a penny of duty. The exciseman used to come roond fra Wolf's Hope, but he ne'er caught them; they used to bring it along the underground way from the cliff foot—"

"Underground way?" Pieter cried, eyes sparkling. "Can we see it? Is it still there?"

"Fegs, I daresay it is, but no one's set foot in it this fifty year; it comes oot in the auld part o' the hoose; there's a hidden entrance i' the ingle that's in the little cheese room. But ye dinna want to go in there; it's a' dark and dirty and cobwebby—"

Pieter's fears seemed as likely to be aroused by this as by thoughts of his father's seizure; Val soon made an excuse to take the children off to bed. Pieter, when he had Val alone, wanted to ask her questions about his mother's death. But she could tell him nothing. She could not bear to think of Kirstie's death. Had she been killed like those others—the street-woman? *How* had she died?

Val had to stay with the children longer than usual before they would settle; Pieter was nervous and tearful, Jannie prone to hysteria, reverting to all her former troublesome ways.

Val herself lay awake for hours, and when she did sleep, it was to such horrible dreams that she was glad to wake, though she did so with an aching head, and a feeling as if no night had passed, as if the new day were but a dreadful continuation of the old one.

She leaned out of the window. It was black dark still, but she could feel the snow brushing her face. Not a sound was to be heard, except the distant murmur of the sea.

"How happy we were before Nils came," she thought, brushing her heavy fair hair. "Just Mungo and Elspie, just the children and me. Why was I so discontented here? Why do I never learn?"

Downstairs it was a faint pleasure to find that Tom the postman had brought a letter for her in Sir Marcus's handwriting. Val opened it quickly, wishing with all her heart that the writer were present in the flesh.

But the contents were dismaying.

He wrote briefly and simply of his sorrow at Helen's death—"I will speak more of this at a later time"—and his disappointment at not seeing Val again. "But doubtless you were right in forbidding me to come," he wrote. "In my sad spirits I might heedlessly have blurted out more than you wished to hear. (Such babes are we all at heart.) And I imagine you had the best and strongest reasons for prohibiting my visit.

"Since my return to the city I have had the pleasure of a meeting with your friend Mr. Benet Allerton, who yesterday called on me to inquire your direction. I have not yet given it to him, being uncertain of your wishes in this matter, but he is very urgent to see you. Shall I tell him where to find you? He and his mother and sisters are, I understand, staying at the Caledonia Hotel. I thought him a most estimable young man and—need I say it—I have every sympathy for his evident desire to be reunited with you."

A note from Benet was also enclosed. Val eyed it as if it might, when opened, emit a poisonous gas.

"Is Tom Postie still here?" she asked, when she had swiftly digested its contents.

"Och, no!" said Elspie. "He was awa' back to Wolf's Hope as if the dragoons were after him, before the bents are a' blocked over wi' snaw. 'Tis like tae be a dooms heavy fa'—the whaups are awa' inland, an' that's a sure sign. Tom says he mightna be this way again for three-four days, gin the tracks are covered deep."

Val was dismayed at this news. She wanted to write to Benet at once and tell him not to come—what disastrous concatenation of chances had brought him to Scotland *now*, of all possible times? All she could hope was that he and his womenfolk (sisters, Sir Marcus had written, but he had only one; who could the other be?) would tire of waiting in wintry Edinburgh and return to London, and thence to New York. But her hope was not strong; Benet was dogged and persistent to an extreme degree when in pursuit of some desired object. If he had come all this way to see her, he was not likely to be put off.

She read again the little note that Sir Marcus had enclosed. It was somewhat curt and dictatorial. "My dear Val: Please make arrangements to see me. It is an absurd piece of childishness not to send your address. You must allow that I have the right to see you and discuss this matter. If it is concern for your brother's children that is holding you back—and if you persist in this quixotic wish to look after them—though I see no reason why you should, since your brother never lifted a finger for you—then why not bring them back to New York where they can be cared for in a proper manner? If the parents still have not reappeared by the time we are married, we can adopt them legally; or, Mother and Delia can look after them in Washington Square." Val gulped at this, thinking of the drawn curtains, and all Mrs. Allerton's bric-a-brac; bare and shabby Ardnacarrig might be, wintry and bleak, but at least there was no chance of the children growing up into helpless stuffed stupidity there, like poor Delia.

"I suppose there will be some money coming to them from their mother's family?" wrote Benet, and Val thought of Nils, saying, "Of course old Benet knew about your money; all those lawyers live in each other's pockets."

Could Nils have been right? About the money, about Benet's knowledge of it? "I've a talent for finding things out about people," Nils had said, and she could see that he had; suspecting the worst about people, he then proceeded to hunt for it and profitably find it.

Val had a sudden grotesque vision of the world seen in his terms: Benet, a calculating fortune hunter; their father, an impotent, Puritanical prig; David Ramsay, warped into an oddity by excessive devotion to his mother; Elspie, wedded by old grudges to a mouldering house; Sir Marcus, a valetudinarian egoist, incapable of real love—the Carsphairn ladies, loveless misers—

Is nobody truly good, truly disinterested? she wondered, and then thought, Don't be a fool, look at Mungo, look at Helen Ramsay. (But is Mungo really truthful, what do I know about him? Only what he has told us.) No, she thought, Nils has a view of the world that is distorted by his own sickness; I think he is really mad; his horrible occupation of searching out people's secret faults, making money from the ugly irrational side of their behaviour, has tipped his own mind over into unreason. He always had a streak of it.

She remembered an occasion when she had been standing by him at the window, watching the approach of the muffin man, bell in hand, tray on head, along Twenty-third Street. When the man was in front of their house, Nils had flung open the window and deliberately tossed down Val's cherished pot of geraniums which hit the tray of muffins and smashed, scattering earth, cakes, flowers, and shards of pot all over the snowy sidewalk. When punished by their father, Nils had merely said, "I thought it would be a lark to stop little Miss Greedyguzzle from having a muffin for once. She's too fat!" "But you like muffins as well," Mr. Montgomery said, utterly baffled by his stepson's spiteful perversity. "Not so much as seeing that pot smash on the tray!" Nils said, and took his punishment with indifference. "*Why* do you break my things?" Val wept on another occasion when he cracked her ivory thimble in the nutcrackers. "Why, you little simpleton? I'll tell you why. Because, once a thing is broken, *no one*, not you, not Father, not the president himself, can do anything about it. It's gone, for good and all!"

Rousing herself from this unprofitable reverie, Val went to see how the children were occupied, before nerving herself to interview her brother.

She found Mungo crossing the yard, carrying a pot of tar.

"The bairns? They're fine," he said. "They're down to the boathouse, a' set to watch me paint the boat. Pieter's boring holes in a wee bit of wood, an' Jannie's playing wi' the shavings. Never fret about them, Mistress Val. They can bide with me for an hour or two. You try and get your brither out for a bit walk; he needs air to blow the horrors out of his mind."

"How should we manage without you, Mungo?" said Val gratefully, and went up to the attic; her task could be postponed no longer.

He was still sleeping when she went in, but she shut the door with a deliberate bang, and then walked across to the bedside and slightly shook his shoulder. He opened bloodshot eyes and looked at her sensibly and recognisingly. He was wax-pale, but his breathing and pulse appeared normal.

"Nils," she said without preamble. "Why did you have Kirstie's hand in your box?"

He stared at her in silence for a long moment, during which she had time to think, Perhaps he is really raving mad. Perhaps he will cut my throat with that razor, slash me, disembowel me—he is trying to make up some lie—perhaps he will just never speak again?

"I might have known you'd pry, you bitch," he said at last in a low voice. "Anyway—how did you know it was Kirstie's?"

"Whose else could it be?"

"It might have been Let— No, it is Kirstie's," he said.

"How—?"

"He sent it to me."

"*Who* sent it to you?" asked Val, utterly staggered.

"Nuggie Reydon. That was what I found when I got back home."

"*Oh*—" Val drew a long, appalled breath. "You mean that man—Lord Clanreydon? Did *he* kill Kirstie?"

"Of course!" Nils answered wearily. "Kirstie always a stupid little trusting idiot, who'd believe any tale, who couldn't say boo to a goose. I think they got her on board the *Dragonfly* with some story of my being there, ill —why she should believe such stuff!" he grumbled discontentedly. "I don't know—perhaps they just took her by force. I got back to find the—the hand, and a message that I'd better come, if I wanted to find her alive. It wasn't true—she was already drowned. The hand was just to get *me* there."

"So you went—what happened? Where was the *Dragonfly*?"

"At Tilbury. I went—didn't know what she might be giving away. Nuggie wanted my articles—I hadn't got them with me," Nils answered disjointedly. Obviously he could hardly bear to recall that occasion. "He told me then that Kirstie was dead. They all came round me—his sailors—he has an Arab crew. Picked 'em up at Port Said. They don't even speak English; just do as he tells 'em. There was a fight; but I got away. Jumped over the side." He added in a self-congratulatory tone which Val found both ludicrous and painful, "I've had experience in getting away."

"But Nils—for God's sake—what is all this *about*? *Why* did they do— that—to Kirstie? Poor, *poor* little Kirstie who probably never hurt a fly—it's like a horrible nightmare—" Val, weeping, burst out. "That man—that Clanreydon—what *is* he?"

"Oh, hadn't you guessed?" Nils drawled coolly, looking at her under his white lashes. "That's rather slow of you, my dear Valla. You're usually such a clever gal at discovering things about people. He's the Bermondsey Beast."

"Lord Clanreydon? You must be joking?"

But part of her did believe him.

"Hardly a joke," said Nils. And indeed, he had grown even paler.

"But he's a member of Parliament! He's going to be a cabinet minister!"

"Oh yes—he's a clever fellow. However even cabinet ministers have their quirks—like the rest of us. And that makes an excellent reason why he don't want the news getting round. No one can deny he's got a good brain, though—as good as they come."

The appalling thing was, Val thought, that Nils really did seem to admire Clanreydon.

She began to see a great deal.

"You found that out," she said slowly. "You have evidence about it— enough to prove your case?"

"Yes." He lay back against the wall, among his blankets, with a faint, gratified smile. "I nosed around quietly—oh, for several years now. Put two and two together. Watched Nuggie—when he didn't know I was at it. For a long time I suspected there was more to him than met the eye, don't you know." He burst out again. "But think of it! Think of being able to stand up and make a speech in the House, about free trade, or home rule, and all the time hold *that* tucked away inside you—it's like living two lives instead of only one!"

His eyes shone with fanatical admiration—almost awe.

"What a nerve the fellow has! Of course he's mad—mad as a March hare—but, just the same, he's a genius! You should have heard his speech on fiscal policy—they said there'd been nothing like it since Pitt! And then —when he's off duty, as it were—out he goes, into the dark."

Val shuddered.

Nils went on—now that he had got started, he seemed to enjoy talking about Clanreydon—"I found out where he came from. His parents were Irish, both convicted murderers, deported to Van Diemen's Land in 1853; they escaped and turned bushrangers. His father was called the Tasmanian Devil. His mother had poisoned her first husband, in County Cork. Nuggie ran off from them and went to Hobart and got himself adopted by a clergyman who put him through school; he repaid the man by stealing his savings and taking off to Queensland, where he did well—Oh, I've traced him right along!"

"But why didn't you go to the police?"

He made no reply. Val answered herself.

"You were in financial difficulties—you thought you'd squeeze some money out of him—so you threatened him."

"And he threatened me back!" Nils burst out angrily. "The fool! He ought to know me better than that. I'd got my articles all written—ready—I showed him a page or two—"

"But couldn't you see that a man like that—who had done those things" —she gulped, remembering the newspaper reports—"who had everything to lose—would stop at nothing to keep you quiet?"

"But I was his *friend*." Nils sounded pathetic, really injured. Has he no moral sense at all? Val thought amazedly. "He might have known he could trust me—we've known each other so long. But I've diddled him anyway." Nils ended on a triumphant note. "I got off his cursed yacht—swam ashore. Had to lie low, of course—couldn't go to my usual haunts. He'd have been after me. But he ain't likely to come here."

"Nils, you have *got* to inform the police about all this. If you don't—I shall."

"But then I shall lose all my advantage over him—it's worth half a million at the very least. You might at least wait till he's paid up," Nils said injuredly.

She saw that he was quite beyond reason and rose to go downstairs, determined to take action about it herself. She would write to Sir Marcus and give the letter to Tom the postman as soon as he made his way back over the snowy hill—

Nils cried, "Val, don't leave a fellow! There's someone standing over in that corner, I swear. If I turn my head I shall see her. Don't leave me here alone in this horrible little room."

"Do you want to come down and walk on the terrace, then?" she said reluctantly.

"All right—so long as the children ain't about."

She helped him downstairs and walked with him on the snowy flagstones, though she found it hard to endure his company. Even the sight of him filled her with such horror that she felt almost physically sick; he seemed imbued with a dreadful contagion which must affect anyone who came near him. She was glad to keep the children away from him. They, luckily, were still with Mungo in the boathouse, and she insisted on Nils returning to his room before they came in.

When they did, they were serene and cheerful.

"Mungo has a little fire in the boathouse, Aunt Val," Pieter told her. "An' he heats up the tar an' paints it on the boat, and I help him. But there's an awful lot more to do."

It was fortunate, Val thought, that the boathouse was so far from the house—down a steep, slippery, laurel-girt path by the streamside. By good management, another confrontation between Nils and his children could be avoided at least for some time.

Two uneasy days went by. No further snow fell—but what had fallen still lay on the ground, hardened into an icy crust. The sun seemed to have withdrawn permanently; a freezing fog hung low, filling every cranny, creeping under doors, making it impossible to see across the stable yard.

Nils made but slow progress, although Val persuaded him into the open air as much as she could. He complained furiously about being deprived of his laudanum drops and constantly accused Val of being too stingy to give him his passage money to America.

"If I'd known you were going to be so cursed clutch-fisted I'd have borrowed it from Letty along with the twenty pounds she lent me to get here," he grumbled. "She's a good gal—a regular trump. She'd ha' raised it somehow. She knows I'd pay her back—I'd send it to her from America. Poor little Let—she'll miss me like the devil."

"But Nils—didn't you know—" Val was so startled that the words escaped her before she had reflected. "Letty's dead!"

He stopped and gaped at her—they were walking on the snowy beach—as if her words made no sense. Then he said peevishly, "What can *you* know about it? I mean Letty Pettigrew."

"I know; I met her. She told me where the children were lodged. But she's dead, Nils; she was killed by—by the Bermondsey Beast. Like the others. It was in the papers."

At that, Nils showed the first signs of compassion she had ever seen in him; he began to swear, helplessly, childishly, and then, turning away from her, buried his face in his hands and sobbed. After a minute, though, whirling round on her, he cried out, "But that means he knows—"

"Knows what?"

"Where I am! He's sure to have got it out of Letty—don't you see—you've got to give me the money to get away!"

"Oh Nils, don't be so foolish. How could you possibly travel in your present condition? God knows I have no wish to keep you here. But you are too weak. And I have only ten pounds until I get paid for some of my work—"

Besides, she was going on to say, you have a public duty to give evidence.

But Nils was not paying any attention to her. He was staring over her shoulder, out to sea, with his mouth open, and a stunned, almost stupid expression on his face, incredulity and resignation mixed.

Oh dear God; now what is it he thinks he sees? Val wondered, in alarm and impatience; if he takes a notion to see the Kelpie down here and falls into a fit on the beach, how shall I ever get him back to the house?

But then her ears caught the creak of rowlocks and she turned in astonishment to see the dark outline of a dinghy which came looming out of the fog, quite close in, rowing toward the shore.

"That's not Mungo? Benet can't have come by boat—" she exclaimed, and then broke off.

A couple of the seven or eight men aboard now jumped out into shallow water and dragged the boat up on to the beach. Another man, wrapped in a dark boat cloak, then stepped out and walked toward Nils, who remained rooted, staring, speechless, as if his will were paralysed. Then he began to back slowly up the beach.

Val, too, watching, huddling her plaid tightly round her, was fascinated by the almost dreamlike quality of the scene—this scene which, in a way, she felt she had brought on Nils by forcing him to come out of the house. And, in a way, he did not seem altogether terrified, but almost relieved—as if, knowing that this moment must come, he was glad to have the waiting over. As if he were glad to see his friend—for Lord Clanreydon it was, who came crunching over the snow toward them, until he stood about six paces away from Nils.

The rowers had followed quietly behind, and now spread into a rough circle round the pair; they were swarthy, dark-eyed, dark-bearded men; Lord Clanreydon gave them a quiet order in a guttural language and they closed their circle slightly; Val noticed, almost with disbelief, that they had pistols through their belts.

"Well, my dear Nils! I have caught up with you again," Clanreydon said calmly. "You seem surprised to see me here? Did you not expect it?"

His strange wide-set eyes were fixed on Nils; of Val, he took no notice at all, and she remained silent, looking at her brother, who still said nothing.

The two men were of similar build, though Nils was half a head taller, and, seeing them together Val began to feel that there was a queer resemblance between them, the sort of shadowy mirror likeness that sometimes draws two people together, and is then fostered by proximity, like the similarities between married persons. They stood in an aura of their own, formed from their reacting energies—hate, perhaps, rivalry—admiration, perhaps, love. Each man seemed curiously burnished by the other's presence.

"Didn't you appreciate, my dear fellow," Clanreydon said, smiling almost affectionately at Nils, "that I was bound to follow you here?"

And Nils smiled back; he answered quite calmly, with an almost teasing note of gaiety, "But what about your pleasure cruise to Patmos and Izmir? What about all your guests? Won't they be disappointed?"

"Oh, that cruise was a bore. I have given up the notion. Who wants to be out of town for two months? I came up the coast instead—a fitting-out trip. The minute my people here told me that you had arrived—"

People? Val wondered. Then, glancing away, she saw two more groups, at either end of the beach—men wearing plaids, and carrying cudgels, the tinklers. He commands a whole army, Val thought vaguely; why hadn't I thought of that? He is a man of high administrative ability.

"So, *this* time, dear boy," Clanreydon went on, "produce the papers, will you? Very agile and plucky, your sporting jump over the side, but I can't be fobbed off twice; where are the papers?"

"Why should you think they would be here?" rejoined Nils carelessly.

"Because I know you, dear boy, as well as—or shall we say a deal better than I know my own mother! You would never be parted from those articles. They are here."

"Well, they ain't!" retorted Nils with febrile impudence. "I posted them off to *Selkirk's*. Or to the *Knuckle*."

Clanreydon shook his head. "That won't wash, my dear friend. Now, look about you—I have these men with me who are both obedient and discreet; as well as several more on the yacht. You can't get away from here; the tinklers guard the paths. We know you have posted off nothing. I want you to come with me on the ship—and, just to ensure that the whole scurrilous, trouble-making business does not start up once more, I want the papers too. Otherwise, my men are quite capable of taking that house apart stone by stone, I promise you."

"Take it apart, then!" Nils rejoined unperturbedly. "It ain't my house. I don't care! But the papers are not there. Val will tell you the same—I had no papers on me when I arrived here."

And it's true, he doesn't care, thought Val in a rage. He cares nothing for the house—or the children—or anybody but himself.

Clanreydon glanced her way for the first time.

"Miss Montgomery—such a helpful, energetic lady—" the pale eyes swept her with dislike. "I'm afraid I couldn't believe even her endorsement of what you say, dear boy."

"Nils—for God's sake—" said Val urgently. "*Give* him the papers, if you have them, if that will make him go—"

"Ah, I'm afraid that wouldn't answer, quite; no, I need both Nils *and* the papers. And, I am sorry to say, *you*, my dear lady as well—"

Now, for the first time, Val began to appreciate the deadly danger implicit in this extraordinary scene.

She glanced out to sea. There, dimly visible through the fog which kept clearing and then thickening again, was the outline of a yacht, the *Dragonfly* presumably, which had cost its owner a cool three-quarter million with curtains and carpets.

They were caught in a trap, here, in Ardnacarrig Bay, Nils, and herself —and what about Elspie, Mungo, and the children? Or anybody who happened to interfere with Clanreydon's intentions?

"We will go up to the house," Clanreydon said, "and your sister will help us locate the papers."

"No she won't!" said Nils.

Clanreydon compressed his lips. At his first arrival, at his first cool remark, Val had felt the same shock of dislike as on their two previous encounters, but, as well, she had come up against a barrier of incredulity. *Could* this quiet-spoken suave individual be what Nils asserted he was—a hideous murderer who dismembered women in dark by-streets? Or could Nils be holding an invented threat over his head, which, in the perilous world of politics, might do just as much damage as if the story were true?

But at the continued defiance of Nils a red spark of anger began to burn in Clanreydon's eyes and Val realised, with a cold prickle of fear, that she did, in fact, believe him capable of any savagery.

At that moment the sound of cantering hoofs made them all turn their heads. To Val, the interruption came as no relief; on the contrary, she drew a breath of desperate apprehension. For she knew who the rider must be, and she could see no possible good outcome from his arrival.

"Hollo!" said David Ramsay, cheerfully riding up to the group on his dripping mare. "Here's a crowd, here's company! I saw the ship as I came round the point. Ah, you have your brother out-of-doors, that's capital," he said to Val. "The air will do him more good than all that moping indoors. How do you do, sir?" he said to Clanreydon. "You, I assume, are the owner of that fine ship out there. She is a deal handsomer, I may say, than any craft that usually sail our waters! But don't I know you?" he went on, a faintly puzzled expression flitting over his face. "You seem so familiar— your face—have we met in Cambridge or—"

Clanreydon shot him, quite calmly, at six-foot range. He fell instantly, pitching off his mare into the snow. The mare whinnied, reared, and bolted. Val screamed, and rushed forward to David, who was lying on his back. And Nils, taking advantage of the second's confusion, bolted for the azalea hedge and disappeared behind it. Several shots were fired after him but none hit him. Half a dozen sailors started in pursuit but he easily outdistanced them. He could run like the wind.

Clanreydon let out one sharp expletive, then drew a long breath, deliberately reining in his anger, and proceeded to reload his pistol.

"That was a very stupid thing to do," he remarked sourly. "My men will only treat him the more roughly when they catch him—which they are bound to do."

Val ignored this. She had dropped on her knees in the snow beside Ramsay and was frantically doubling her plaid into a bandage.

"Where does it hurt, Davie? Where did the bullet go? You're bleeding— let me tie this—"

"Nothing you can do—my dear girl—too bad—shan't get back to the lab now—" and he coughed blood and died.

For a moment Val could not believe it.

"Davie!"

But he was gone. She sprang to her feet, with tears pouring down her cheeks. Clanreydon, clicking shut the magazine of his pistol, calmly met her blazing look.

"Don't do anything stupid, my dear lady—I could shoot you, you know, just as easily," he remarked. And the look he gave her suggested that he would relish doing so. He is just calculating, she thought, whether I am more use to him alive.

"Why did you do that?" she said, shaking from head to foot with rage and terror.

"Why—to make you understand that I am in earnest," he said. "Come— we will go to the house and I will demonstrate to you how my men intend to conduct the search for those papers."

One of the men jerked her roughly along the path.

"Don't you think, if I knew where the papers were, I would have told you?" she shouted to Lord Clanreydon. "Why should I protect him? How much more harm do you have to do?"

She twisted her head to look back at the snowy beach where David's body lay; the mare had returned and stood beside it with hanging head.

By the time she was pushed into the house, Clanreydon's men were at work; they did not seem to be searching, but simply engaged in systematic destruction—shredding, splitting, hacking, ripping, tearing, stamping, smashing.

Val felt sick with rage, and terror. What if the children came in—or Elspie?

Elspie erupted in at this moment, from the back regions, wild-eyed.

"Whit the deil's goin' on here?" she screamed like a virago. "Who are a' these blackavised scoondrels makin' sic a collieshangie?"

Val said quickly, lest Elspie should draw down more violence on herself, "They are looking for my brother, Elspie, and some papers he has got. Do you know where he went?"

"Ay, I do," said Elspie grimly. "He cam' rinning to me, saying his foes was after him, an' askit me whaur he could hide; an' I showed him the way into the undergroond passage that leads tae the cliffside—but gin I'd knawed what was to follow I'd ha' seen him in hell first—they could ha' wheepit him with plew stilts for a' I cared. *Stop that!*" she shouted at the men. "Stop till I get my hands on ye, ye ill-deedy raskills!"

"Elspie, hush, don't provoke them for God's sake!" Val muttered in terror. "That man *killed* Doctor Ramsay; he just shot him dead, down on the beach."

Elspie stopped at that, shocked, silenced in mid-protest; her mouth dropped open.

Clanreydon said, "You showed Hansen an underground passage? Take those two men to its entrance. And don't try to mislead them or they will kill you."

Oh God, thought Val, looking after them. She had not the least vestige of sympathy for her brother at that moment; but still—to be trapped like a rat, in an underground tunnel—

"Aunt Val?" said Pieter's puzzled voice. "What are all these men doing —why are they spoiling Elspie's kitchen?"

Val turned to see the children walk in from the yard: Pieter struggling under the weight of a toy sledge, Jannie dragging a wheeled wooden horse behind her.

"Ah, yes," Clanreydon said, into the sudden silence that fell. "Hansen's children. I had forgotten about them, temporarily. I expect they will be the best lever of all, to ensure his cooperation."

Jannie burst into wails of terror at the scene of desolation.

"Don't like—don't like!" she sobbed.

"Don't come in here, children—run, run away!" Val had burst out, but it was too late.

Clanreydon snapped out another order, and two men, picking up Pieter and Jannie as if they weighed nothing, carried them, kicking and screaming, out of the room.

Val rushed in pursuit. But one of the men tripped her so that she fell headlong, and by the time she had picked herself up, the way through the dining room had been blocked by the huge table which had been turned on its side by two men, who were hacking it with axes. Val had to run back through the stable yard and all round the house. She saw the men carrying Pieter and Jannie far ahead of her, halfway to the beach. Clanreydon was with them. They had far too great a start for her to catch up, but still she raced after them screaming, "Stop! Bring them back! Stop!" No one took any notice.

By the time she had reached the azalea hedge the children were in the boat, which had been dragged back to the sea's edge. Clanreydon stepped in and the boat was pushed off; the two men began rowing. Val could hear the children's thin, crying voices. She ran to the water's edge and stood up to her ankles crying, "Bring them back!"

"Ah—Miss Montgomery!" Clanreydon called to her, across the widening gap of water. "I shall be sending back for you—presently. In the meantime, I strongly advise you to persuade your brother to come out of hiding —if he wants to see his children again, that is."

The oars dipped, the boat moved on. She heard Pieter's voice, desperate, crying, "Aunt Val!" and Jannie's high-pitched screaming—an incessant, piercing, hardly human note. The boat went farther and farther away. Beyond it, in the fog, wavered the outline of the ship, all white, like a ghost ship. This *must* be a nightmare, Val thought.

Then something horrible happened; something that she could not have invented in a nightmare. Jannie's screaming mounted to a new pitch of frenzy and abruptly stopped. Half an instant before this, Val had seen the boat lurch violently as something—a heavy something—was flung from it into the sea. The splash, then silence.

Val said aloud, disbelievingly, "They've thrown her in the sea. They threw Jannie into the sea."

She started wading out but realised, instantly, that she could not swim in that bitter sea, in her heavy layers of petticoats and skirt.

But—but—there was Greylag—David's mare who loved to go in the water—standing disconsolately with hanging head, not far from where his body still lay on the sand. Running like a thing possessed, Val flew to the mare, who snorted and threw up her head nervously. Val somehow scrambled on to her back, sitting astride. The stirrups were all wrong. No time to change them. Greylag snorted again, in fright; she was not used to being ridden by a woman. But Val drove her into the sea, sobbing, "Find Jannie, please, Greylag, find Jannie—"

Obeying the urgency of Val's voice and hands, the mare walked into the water and soon began to swim, in the direction taken by the boat, which had now disappeared.

Val had never ridden a swimming horse before and found it frightening; she clung desperately to the pommel. Her trailing skirts were soon drenched, her feet and legs numb with cold; she felt unbalanced and thought, suppose something frightens the mare so that she swerves and I slip off? No use thinking about that.

But most of her attention was taken by the desperate necessity of finding Jannie—soon—immediately, *now*; her eyes raked the green water, she combed the heaving sides of the waves for a wisp of flaxen hair, a strip of floating tartan—

"Jannie, *Jannie*," she called hoarsely. No cry, no answer at all. The mare swam to and fro—but how long could she go on? How could Val tell where the child had gone in? And that had been five minutes ago now—seven—ten—twelve.

It was hopeless.

Jannie had gone. Already she was far below, deep down under all this heaving green water. She was gone.

Val began to cry, bowed forward over the pommel in utter despair. She made no resistance when two men rowed to her in the ship's dinghy, and dragged her off the horse's back into the boat, where she crouched, dripping, sobbing, with her hands over her face, utterly broken down by all that had happened.

The boat returned to the yacht, where Val was unceremoniously hauled on board.

Lord Clanreydon, standing on deck, gazing at the shore through a telescope, looked at her with disgust. He said, "I do hope your brother turns up *soon*, Miss Montgomery. I cannot tell you how much I dislike these kind of scenes. I find them quite abhorrent. But I expect my men will discover your brother quite quickly. If they do not—well, I need hardly remind you what happened to your sister-in-law."

"I don't know where my brother is," Val said.

He shrugged and turned his back on her, calling something to the men, who hustled Val over the deck, and down a companionway. She was in a carpeted passageway; then she was pushed into a cabin and the door was slammed on her; she heard a key turn in the lock.

The cabin seemed pitch-dark at first, for dusk was closing in. Val lay prone on the floor where she had been flung, exhausted with sobbing and despair. Presently her eyes became a little accustomed to the dimness. She lifted her head and could see a porthole's faint circle of light. Pulling herself up she found the upright of a bunk and a folded blanket—then almost cried out as her groping hand touched something warm that moved.

A small whisper said, "Aunt Val? Is that you?"

"Pieter!"

He was huddled at the back of the bunk. She pushed her arms round him and pressed her cheek against his. She could feel that he was shaking badly; tears coursed down his face. Presently he gulped out, "Th-they th-threw Jannie in the s-sea—"

"I know, Pieter, I saw it. I know. I know."

"He said, 'One of them will be enough, we don't want that bawling brat—' Jannie was screaming and screaming because she was frightened, she had been all the way—so—so they just threw her in. Like a rotten potato. Her arms went up. She just sank."

"Oh, God," Val muttered.

She knelt by the bunk, holding Pieter. A long time passed. Neither of them said anything. Val thought, What can be happening on the shore? Have they found Nils? What did they do to Elspie? And the house? Did they find Mungo? Why does nobody come back on board?

The ship was very silent.

Val thought about little Jannie, with her bright wits and her terrible problems, which she was learning to solve. And about David Ramsay. She thought about Kirstie, also, floating, sinking somewhere in that vastness of water. Almost certainly Pieter was thinking these things too.

She thought, I ought to talk to him, distract him. His whole past life has been torn from him in tatters; he ought to have some kind of future to aim at.

"Why does everybody have to *die?*" he cried suddenly in anguish. Val could not answer. All she could do was hold him and murmur from time to time, "There, there, Pieter. There, there, my lamb."

Presently, kneeling by Pieter, she slept a little, and he did too.

They were roused by the increased pitching of the yacht. More wind was getting up; even down here they could hear it wail in the rigging. Timbers groaned, cables creaked, metal clinked. But still the ship seemed strangely quiet.

Then Pieter's voice said, "Aunt Val?"

"Yes, Pieter?"

"I think I can hear someone at the door."

CHAPTER 17

T HE door moved gently, inch by inch. Val's mouth was dry. She tried to swallow but could not. Pieter gripped her hand so tight that she could feel the bones of his. Neither of them said anything. The door opened a thread wider, so that they could see light from the lamp in the passage outside. And it was not a bearded Arab face that they saw in the opening, but Mungo's—lined, anxious, his finger at his lips.

"Mungo!"

"Whisht, lassie! Not a sound. Ye have Pieter in there too? That's fine. Come out quick, the pair of you."

They were after him before he had finished speaking.

In case he intended seeking farther for Jannie, Val caught his arm, as they climbed the companion stair, and murmured in his ear, "Mungo—Jannie's dead. They killed her."

"I know," he said. "I know." His face was bleak, set like rock, and he said no more, while they crept along the deck to where a black dinghy was made fast at the stern on a long rope. The yacht was silent and seemed deserted. Brass lamps burned here and there.

Mungo pulled on the rope and they climbed into the boat; Val went first, then turned to receive Pieter from Mungo, who came last. He untied the boat and cautiously pushed off from the stern of the yacht, then sculled with one oar over the boat's gunwale until they came abreast of *Dragonfly*'s anchor cable, which he cut, sawing through it with a knife.

"Cutting them adrift?" breathed Val, amazed at Mungo.

"Ay." She could not see his face but his whisper, just audible, sounded as stern as a judge pronouncing sentence. "The tide's making. In half an hour they'll be driven on to the Kelpie's Fangs and the world will be rid of that man, please God. Folk that could kill a defenceless man and a wee bairn do not deserve to live."

By now they had made the circuit of the ship. Mungo cut the other mooring rope, and then pulled away rapidly. The sea was much rougher now; his boat rode bouncily over big choppy waves that cut and crossed each other in the cross-currents of the bay. Overhead the sky was beginning to clear; white drifts of cloud scudded sideways, giving glimpses of stars; a full moon showed, ghostly, for a moment, then was lost in cloud again. The cold wind bit; Val, in her soaked clothes, shivered, and said, "Let me row with you, Mungo. I do know how, and if I don't I shall freeze to death."

"Ay, if ye wish."

"Where are we going?"

"To Wolf's Hope, to give the alarm, in case there are any of yon blagyards left."

Val found she had to concentrate to keep in time with Mungo's stroke; they rowed in silence for a while. Pieter, who had been wrapped by Mungo in an old boat cloak, was curled up on the bottom boards and seemed almost asleep.

Val said, "How did you know where to find us?"

"I climbed aboard an' went looking till I found a door that was locked," Mungo said simply. "Probably the good Lord was helping me—yours was only the third I tried."

"But if you'd met somebody—one of the men—Lord Clanreydon?"

"I'd ha' fought them. But I didna. There's only two-three left aboard."

"But how did you know to come to the ship?"

"Elspie told me that. One o' the sailors had told her yon man had ye on the ship. And he'd said to her, 'Best hurry up and show us where yon ska-terumple is that we're seeking, for our master is no' a patient man, he'll hae ye spitted against the door gin the callant isna found soon.' An' he told her what had been done to the wee lassie."

Mungo fell silent. Val wondered what Elspie had replied to the sailor and, as if guessing her thought, Mungo presently went on, "I knowed that Elspie was a powerful, fremit, deep-thinking woman, with an uncommon strength in her for good or evil. But I ne'er guessed at the power that was in her till I saw her after she heard that."

"What happened?"

"Ye mind Elspie had shown your brither the way through the smugglers' tunnel, thinking that would give him a bit start on them, and then he could climb up the cliff path and so away."

"Yes. Did they go after him?"

"Ay. When she saw how they were smashing a' the furniture, she took them an' showed them the entrance to the passage. 'But ye'd best gae cannily,' said she, 'for he has ta'en a crossbow from the hoose, an' he'll shoot ye if ye follow through the tunnel. Best if ane or twa follow, but slowly, keeping well back, an' the lave o' ye gang saftly roond by the shore, through the posts, to the cave mouth in the cliff, so as to take him where he'll no' expect it; then ye can kepp him like the rat he is,' she telled them."

Val shivered.

"Did they catch him?"

"No, no, he'd got clear awa' by then—she allowed him time for that."

"So the men found nothing?"

"They found a shortcut to Eternal Fire," said Mungo grimly. "For Elspie'd neglectit to tell them about the Kelpie's Flow. A' that gaed along the shore walked into it, every man o' them, for the fog was that thick, by there, that none o' them could see what happened to the ithers."

"Oh my God," whispered Val incredulously, "you mean they are all *dead?*"

"Ay, they are. Elspie followed to the edge of the shore, and there she waited, an' syne the fog lifted, but not a man was to be seen."

"What about the ones who went through the tunnel?"

"They came out the far entrance and found naebody, so they went daikering about; twa o' them went into the quicksand also. So there was only twa left, and they in a fair puzzle what had come to the lave o' them. After an hour or so, a light flashed on the yacht, a signal, maybe, for them to go back on board, for Elspie an' I, watching, saw them jump in their dinghy and start rowing."

"Where were you, Mungo?"

"Elspie was on shore; I was in my boat, already halfway to the yacht. Maybe they have reached her, by now; or maybe they had a longer trip than they reckoned for."

"Where is Elspie?"

"I tried to get her to come in the boat with me. 'Yon man will be fell angered when he finds what's come to his crew an' his ship. Gin he swims to land he'll be dangerous,' I said. 'Ye'd best be awa' from the hoose.' But she wouldna. 'My place is here, Mungo my lad,' she said. 'Maybe he'll want to burn the place doon, but he shan't if I can stop him. Come back as soon as ye've gie'n the alarm at Wolf's Hope and left Mistress Val and the bairn in safekeeping. An' if ye dinna come back, knaw that ye take my love and respect wi' ye, for you're a good man, Mungo Bucklaw, and I like you fine, and gin we come through this trouble, I'll be pleased to wed ye if ye still wish it.'"

"Oh, Mungo," said Val, greatly touched that he had told her this, "I'm very happy for you. And it's only what you deserve. You're the one who's come out best in all this—you saved me and Pieter, and you've told no lies and done no harm. I'm glad you never met that horrible man."

In fact she had a shrewd suspicion that Elspie had deliberately kept Mungo out of the business, only summoning him when the worst was over; and very sensible too, thought Val. "It was just a mercy that you had been working so hard on your boat, and got it finished."

By now, due to hard rowing through the steep, black-and-silver seas, they had almost rounded the point, and had passed the long saw-toothed beak of rocks known as the Kelpie's Fangs. The moon had floated from behind the cloud-wrack and the night was becoming piercingly clear, frosty, and cold; above them the snow-covered headland stood up like a wedding cake, with Wolf's Crag castle ruins a dark pinnacle on its very tip. Ardnacarrig Bay was out of sight; only occasionally the lights of the *Dragonfly* glimmered into sight for a moment and then were lost again behind the rocks.

"What will happen to the ship, Mungo?"

"It would be a miracle if they saved it now," he said. "Once the tide pull carries it inside yon point, even if they start the engine, they could hardly win out again."

Both of them fell silent. Val wondered where Nils had got to, what had become of him. She hoped that she would never see him again and marvelled at Elspie's fairness in allowing him time to get away, after the trouble he had brought on everybody. She also wondered, though she was glad that Elspie had said yes to Mungo at last, if he might not be a little daunted at what he was taking on. Somebody who, in cold, stern, retribution for two deaths, could, without a qualm, send seven or eight men into quicksand, was a frightening force to reckon with. No: three deaths; there was Kirstie too. And the rape of the house probably counted high in Elspie's tally.

But it was true that Mungo, with equally inflexible judgment, had been prepared to despatch *Dragonfly* and her owner to the Kelpie's Fangs. Perhaps, after all, they were a well-matched pair. They were, Val thought, like the vengeance of nature: slow, inexorable, and devastating.

Just the same—

"Mungo," she said, when they were past the point. A line of snow-covered beach now shone to their left. About a mile ahead, two or three dim lights showed where Wolf's Hope lay.

"What is it, lassie?"

"I'd like to go back to Elspie. Would you put me ashore? I can walk over the headland from here, it will only take an hour. I hate to think of her alone in that wrecked house. And just in case—oh, I don't know—in case my brother turned up again, or one of the men from the boat survived—"

It was a virtue of Mungo's that he seldom argued. He took his own way when he felt it right; otherwise, anyone could have theirs.

"I'd suggest that *you* go back and I go on," Val added, "but I don't think I could row all that way. And the people at Wolf's Hope will pay more heed to you. You should tell them about the tinklers too."

"I doubt the tinklers will have taken themselves off when they saw the yacht gone," said Mungo. He set course for the beach. "Aweel, gang your ways, lassie; I'm no' saying you're wrong. Mind yerself, now."

She looked down at Pieter, who was sleeping peacefully.

"I'll come over to Wolf's Hope for him tomorrow. Maybe Tibbie will take him in. Goodnight, Mungo. You go carefully too."

She squeezed his hand, then jumped on to the beach, sinking ankle-deep in freezing foam—but what was the difference, she was soaked altogether, by now—and set off walking at a fast pace toward the snow-covered saddle of headland which now lay to her right. It was easy to find a track, which the snowfall had outlined on the hillside. At one time, presumably when Wolf's Crag castle was inhabited by Carsphairn ancestors, this must have been their quickest route to the shore, and a well-defined path had been trodden, probably over hundreds of years. It zig-zagged up the hill, snowy, slippery, and steep, but not dangerous, and Val struggled up at a fair speed, pausing on the hairpin turns for breath. It was during one of these pauses that she had another glimpse of the *Dragonfly*; listing over, now, at an odd angle, the yacht was drifting broadside on, closer and closer to the frill of white which outlined the reef. Though she loathed Clanreydon and wished him no good, Val could not suppress a shiver at the thought of the boat's helpless predicament.

And then, when she could no longer see the ship, she heard its death rattle—a grinding crunch, the sound of a nutshell splintered to fragments between huge nutcrackers.

At last she reached the top of the hill, and paused again, getting her breath back. She was close by the castle, now, and could see the whole sweep of the bay. No ship was in it.

The first time I came here, she thought, was with David Ramsay, when he did those tests on Jannie. Now both of them are dead: that odd, kind, intelligent, thwarted man, and little Jannie whose mother loved her with such desperate hope and devotion. *"Be good to her. I know you will."* I wasn't always kind to her; often I was impatient; often I wished to be rid of the burden. Oh David, oh Jannie. An irrepressible sob burst up in her; she leaned against the castle wall and wept without restraint.

I must go down to Elspie, she thought presently, wiping her eyes. In the moonlight, now bright as midday, she could see the house, pinnacled among its trees. It looked peaceful enough. The level of her sorrow began to sink, like a tide, and simple grief was replaced by a strangeness, a wholly unfamiliar mystery, loss of identity, anonymity. Who am I, what is Val? Am I really here, or shall I wake and find myself in Twenty-third Street and all this a dream? How did I ever come to be here? I must go down or I shall freeze to death, what am I doing, loitering on the cold hill side?

But she could not move. She was afraid to go down—the bay looked so secretive, in its silence and calm. The ship had gone, who was left? What had become of Nils?

As she thought this, a hand gripped her arm. She turned and saw Nils, who must have walked out of the castle ruins. He looked like a wild man, with pale floating hair and staring eyes; he clutched at her, and said, earnestly, "Will it be all right to go back, now? I saw the ship founder on the rocks. Have you come to tell me that it's safe?"

In her high-strung state, Val had been horribly startled at his first touch, and barely repressed a shriek. When she saw that it was only Nils, a terrible depression overcame her. Why does *he* have to reappear to plague us? she thought bitterly; why did it have to be Davie, so kind, so useful to the human race, who was killed? How easily could Nils have been spared. And how like him now to be concerned only for his own safety; not a question about the children, or Elspie; he might be the only person in the world. And what am I going to do about him?

"I don't know if it's safe, Nils," she answered shortly. "I came from the other direction."

"Oh." He looked disappointed. "Perhaps you had better go down first and see if the coast is clear. If it is, then you could come back and help me with my box."

"Box?"

"Yes." He laughed a little ruefully. "You see, I've done rather a tiresome thing. I've dislocated my arm, pulling the box up the cliff. I ought to have left a long time ago—Elspie gave me some money—but I couldn't carry the box any farther. That's why it's so lucky that you came along when you did."

"What are you talking about, Nils?"

"Come in here."

With a jerk of the head he beckoned her inside the castle keep. This was circular in form, mostly just a shell of wall, with a few remaining little cell-like rooms backed against it. Two or three entrances led outward, here and there, to the snowy cliff top.

"Here," said Nils, and led the way to one of the cell rooms, into which the moon shone. Val, following, noticed that he carried his left arm awkwardly. She looked into the cell and saw that it contained a black, japanned box of the sort in which lawyers keep wills and deeds.

"I'd got it hidden in a cave, down there at the bottom of the cliff," Nils explained, giving the box an affectionate kick, as if it were his favourite child. "So it was quite convenient for me when I came out of the smugglers' tunnel. In fact, when I first came to Ardnacarrig, my plan had been to get into the house that way. Kirstie showed it to me once. But I couldn't find it! And I was afraid of falling into the quicksand. So that was why I called out to you on the beach. But I left the box in the cave; turned out to be a good thing I had. Only then, climbing up the cliff with it, I wrenched my arm so badly that I could hardly stand the pain. And then the fog began to lift so that I had to wait for hours and hours in a tiny cave half way up, no bigger than a dog kennel. I've had a wretched time of it."

All this was delivered so artlessly that Val could only marvel at him. He had climbed the cliff, by a path little better than a goat track, carrying the heavy box. He had risked death and wrenched his arm out of its socket. He's like a dung beetle, she thought, rolling his horrible ball of muck around—for the box must contain all his papers and articles—and now he wants me to carry it back to Ardnacarrig.

She tried the box, which had a black ring handle on its lid; she could hardly shift it off the ground.

"Good God, Nils, you brought this all the way from London?"

"Letty had it for me in her lodgings," he said. "How do you think we can get it to the house? Perhaps we could tie a rope and lower it down the cliff?"

"I'm not taking it anywhere, Nils. And you had better stay here till I see what has happened down there."

She had no intention of telling him about the fate of Clanreydon's men, or about Jannie—he was plainly in a very abnormal state.

"I'll come back in an hour or two," she began. But he was not paying attention; he had wandered out of a door hole that led toward the cliff top. He was muttering, "Yes, I think a rope would be best. When you come back—bring one, would you? Two or three hundred feet. And a bottle of brandy—"

She had started away when she heard him give an extraordinary, hoarse cry—like somebody who suddenly sees the ground gape under his feet.

She turned, expecting to see that he had fallen, but he was on the cliff top, staring down.

"What is it, Nils?"

"He's climbing up!" Nils muttered. He backed away, pointing downward.

Full of dread, Val moved toward the edge—which was not sheer, but a series of angled slopes becoming progressively steeper. Even from six feet back it was possible to look down and see a man who now appeared pulling his way, partly with his hands, partly with a spiked stick that he carried.

He came toward them up the final slope.

"Throw something at him, Val!" whimpered Nils. "I can't stand him coming *now*; there's nowhere to hide the box. It ain't fair!"

Nils had backed as far as the castle wall; his face worked as if he were going to burst into tears. Val wondered if he would have another epileptic attack. She herself experienced almost the same feeling of dread as she watched Clanreydon approach. Was the man indestructible? She could not run but must simply watch him as he came slowly toward them. He limped badly; his clothes were soaked; his face was fixed in a grimace of pain or disgust.

"So this is where you got to," he said when he was within speaking distance of Nils.

"Why can't you leave me alone?" burst out Nils petulantly like a quarrelsome child. "Why must you follow me everywhere?"

"Why—my dear fellow? Because I'm so *fond* of you, of course. Hell's teeth, how I love you!" answered Clanreydon, grinding it out between his own teeth. "Whither thou goest, I will go; and where thou lodgest, I will lodge. You aren't free of me yet, Hansen. If you are round my neck—God help you! I am going to be round yours."

"What have I done? All I wanted was a little friendship—a little financial aid."

The two men were now staring at one another as intently as if each were looking into a mirror. And in a way they are, thought Val, watching them. They had forgotten her; were ignoring her as if she did not exist, absorbed in an extraordinary kind of silent dialogue, as if each sought to enter and possess the other. They do love each other—in a horrible way, she thought. Each has a map of the other in his mind.

"Friendship? Due to you I've lost my ship; my crew have vanished, God knows where; the last two men I saw sink in a quicksand as they tried to scramble ashore, and I would have sunk in it myself if I hadn't been thrown on the rocks; my leg is badly hurt; I'm stuck on a freezing mountain top; and you say you want *friendship*? How could anybody be friends with you?"

"How could anybody but you? We *are* friends. I know you—you know me."

And suddenly Nils smiled at him with a kind of childlike trust; his face crinkled like a small boy's in the brilliant white light. He said, "Do you remember how the blood ran out in a pool shaped like a rose—and she had dropped a tinsel rose, it lay just on the edge, in the dust, and the smell of old dirty bricks was sweeter than a hayfield in the hot summer night? And the angles of the little mean houses were like a pack of playing cards just about to tumble down, and in the distance a man was playing on a hurdy-gurdy."

"Be quiet! I remember nothing—*nothing!*"

"That was one! And another time there was a smell of hot fried pies and lamplight coming from the Three Cocks Inn; she was laughing as you cut her throat and the laughing turned to a choke, and the choke to a gurgle—"

"*Will you be silent?*" The other man took an awkward, painful step toward Nils, and now Val saw that the stick he held was one of the kind with a sword contained in it; he had pulled out the sword and it shone like a crack of white light.

Merciful heaven, she thought; I should not be witnessing this; any person who sees these two together like this must be due to die; neither of them could afford to let me survive. I ought to try to steal off; escape while they are absorbed in one another. But she could not; Nils now stood in the doorway of the castle, and Clanreydon barred the way past the wall, along the cliff edge; on the other side a buttress ran out, and part of the cliff had crumbled away, so there was no way by.

At sight of Clanreydon's sword Nils, unexpectedly, began to giggle as if he were drunk and sang out suddenly in a clear tenor voice that brought a whole cascade of childhood memories tumbling about Val's ears,

> *"A frog he would a wooing ride*
> *With sword and buckler at his side—"*

"Be quiet, you fool!" said Clanreydon and lunged at him with the sword; but Nils took a step to the side and escaped easily enough.

"Old Froggie Reydon! Do you remember waltzing all the way along Stamford Street and down Rose Alley to the cockpit? And there we picked up a gal called Winnie Ginger?"

Clanreydon lunged again, grimly intent although his face was screwed up with the pain caused by his hurt leg; and this time he managed to stab Nils in the side.

"Hey, damn it, that hurt!" exclaimed Nils in a voice of astonishment and outrage; suddenly whirling on his heel, using his good arm as a club, he brought his fist round and caught Clanreydon a powerful glancing blow on the side of his head, which he was not expecting; it caught him off balance and toppled him over. He was up next minute, swearing under his breath, and darted a swift thrust forward, to avoid which Nils took a hasty step back. Now Clanreydon was in the doorway and Nils retreating toward the cliff edge.

"Mind out, Nils!" Val tried to call, but her voice had died, as in a nightmare; no sound came out.

And did she really want him to win? She hardly knew.

"Winnie Ginger; she was a rum 'un," Nils went on in a meditative tone, as if the sea were not tumbling behind him, three hundred feet down. "She carried a canary about with her in a cage—remember? You took a fancy to her and once we all three went to Lowestoft—remember? There were lots of scrapes I'd never have got into but for you, old Nuggie."

Clanreydon made another lunge, but now Nils had picked up the stick which had formed the casing of Clanreydon's sword, and with it he struck the blade aside. In doing so he slipped, however, and Clanreydon, thrusting in the blade again like lightning, ran it through Nils' shoulder.

Nils gave a loud, angry yell of pain.

"I say, you know, that ain't fair!" he roared. "One fellow with a sword and t'other only with a stick, that's devilish unequal! You shouldn't treat your pal like that."

"I'm not your pal, damn you!"

"Then I ain't yours," said Nils, who was now a frightening sight, with blood streaming down him in two places and his hair tousled like a berserk

Viking. He swung the stick up in both hands and, gasping with the pain it gave his wrenched arm, brought it violently down on Clanreydon's wrist, knocking the sword out of his hand. Both men were panting heavily, swearing, and slipping about in the snow; if it had not been terrifying, the scene would have been grotesquely funny.

Clanreydon reached for the sword again, but Nils kicked it away, and it slid over the frosted snow—reached the beginning of a slope—accelerated —and disappeared over the cliff. But in kicking out, Nils had lost his balance and fell headlong, rolling over on to his stomach. Clanreydon dropped on him and savagely gripped his neck, sitting astride his back. Val did not see how Nils would be able to escape from this grip, but, striking wildly sideways with his right arm, he must have landed a blow on Clanreydon's hurt leg, for Clanreydon screamed shrilly, and suddenly the two men were rolling over and over, kicking, grappling, biting, punching, and trying to gouge out one another's eyes.

"Mind!" shouted Val, to which of them she was not clear; perhaps to both. But her warning came too late and in any case went unheeded. They began to roll faster, and were now sliding as well as rolling, still both, apparently, so absorbed in the fight that neither had a thought to spare for their situation. Locked like lovers in a last embrace they plunged down the slope, seemed to pause a moment, caught on a projection at the point where the cliff became vertical, and then both of them shot out of sight.

Val waited with clenched fists pressed against her breastbone for some terrible sound—some scream or shout or crash like that of the ship breaking on the rocks, but she could hear nothing; only the rumbling sigh of the sea below, as if the waves were relieved to wash over the jagged human passions that had disturbed their peace.

After a while, Val screwed up enough courage to creep to the edge and look over. The tide had reached the foot of the cliff; waves chopped and slapped at the rock, sending up great white plumes of spray. Farther out, in the moon-silvered sea, black fragments of the *Dragonfly* drifted and tossed. But of the two men who had fallen over the cliff, there was nothing to be seen. And whatever secrets they had shared must now remain locked between them till Judgment Day.

After a while Val crawled back up the slope to the castle. Using the last of her strength she dragged the black japanned box out of its hiding place. When she had pulled it as far as the slope it began moving of its own accord; it slid faster and faster until it reached the projection, balanced a moment, then somersaulted on, and followed its owner into the sea.

CHAPTER 18

Val walked down the snowy hillside to Ardnacarrig House. Not a light showed, not a soul was to be seen in meadow, orchard, or garden. Val tried the main door, but it was locked. However when she walked round to the terrace she found the French window broken, and she was able to get in that way.

The house was all dark and silent. A dread began to fill her. What terrors might it contain?

Grateful for the moonlight that lay in lozenges here and there across the bare floors, she picked her way through the wreckage to a little room off the kitchen passage where candles and lamps were kept. She found a small brass hand lamp which, by some miracle, had survived the general destruction and lit it. Then, somewhat braver for its moving pool of golden shadowy light, she went on into the devastated kitchen.

"Elspie?" Val called softly, and then, louder, "Elspie?"

The silent house listened and waited with her for an answer, but none came.

That was the moment when Val reached true despair. Lamp in hand, she wandered through the ravaged rooms: the library, where the shelves gaped empty and a huge heap of torn paper, crumbling calf, and vellum filled the middle of the room; the dining room, with its great table hacked and splintered, the chairs backless and legless; up the stairs, whose banister hung in a broken swag; through bedrooms with disembowelled beds where sheets and curtains lay ripped and trampled on the floor; through the Long Gallery where the pictures were thrown down and panels hacked in a vain search for secret cupboards; what had Thrawn Jane thought about that?

"Elspie?" Val called, again and again. Sometimes she sank down in misery—on a step, on a window seat—but always she rose up and wandered on. The house reproached her in many voices: rooms where the children had played, chairs they had used as adjuncts for building houses, now smashed; floors that Val had rebelliously swept or polished under Elspie's ironic eye, now covered with rubble and debris; objects the children had used as toys, now in fragments; here a glass from which David Ramsay had drunk whisky, there Elspie's cherished chopping board, broken; pieces of furniture that Mungo had mended, smashed again; towels and curtains that Elspie had preserved by infinitely slow and patient darning, torn to shreds; valuables that Elspie had grimly defended from the children, now wrecked beyond repair.

What would the Carsphairn ladies think now, if they came back to Ardnacarrig?

And *I* brought all this trouble here, thought Val; if I had kept the children with me in London, all this mad violence would have been unloosed elsewhere.

But that was an unprofitable train of thought; and in any case, whatever she had done, Nils might still have fled to Ardnacarrig as a refuge, dragging crime and death behind him like a slug's trail of slime.

"Elspie!" she called again, loudly, despairingly. If Elspie were not here, how could she, Val, ever bring herself to face Mungo again? A series of horrible images came into her mind: Elspie thrown down the well, hanging from some rafter in the barn, pinned to a door by a crossbow arrow. There were all the outhouses to be searched yet, and the farm buildings, and the moon was near setting. Val was filled with dread at the prospect of the long search, and yet she could not rest. Her own room, and that of the children, had suffered some of the worst damage, as being in evident occupation; she could not bear the sight of the children's beds, ripped and smashed; wearily she wandered downstairs again.

Now she realised that, in fact, to this day, she did not know exactly where Elspie's own bedroom lay. In the mornings, Elspie had always been up first, and at night, she generally retired after everyone else. But just occasionally, if Val had stayed up late writing, she remembered seeing

Elspie departing for bed, candle in hand, in the direction of the stable wing.

Val made her way through the green baize door and along the silent stone passages. Beyond the dairy there was another heavy door, and beyond that, a flight of stone stairs. At the top of these, Val found a narrow, uncarpeted passage with a row of doors on either side. It was cold, bare, and dusty, suggesting stable boys and scullery maids, the lowest and least-regarded fry in the domestic hierarchy. Two or three of the doors stood open: Val looked in; the tiny damp rooms were empty, unfurnished, and smelt of dry rot. The moon shone on bare boards and crumbling plaster. Evidently the wreckers had looked into a room or two here and given up. And so they had missed Elspie's room, for, at the end of the passage, Val found it: furnished with a bed, a chest, and a jug and basin.

And, kneeling against the bed, with her head on her arms, Elspie herself, fast asleep.

At first Val thought in terror that she was dead. But then she saw the thin chest move in a breath; and, laying her hand on Elspie's shoulder, found it warm. The old woman was wearing a flannel nightgown, with a plaid thrown over her shoulders; her long hair hung down her back in a careful plait, glinting a little in the lamplight.

"Elspie!" Val said softly.

"Ay, what is it—what is it?"

As Elspie stirred, and woke, and struggled to rise, Val looked round the tiny, prim, icy room, thinking, There can't be a smaller one in the whole house. Why did she choose to stay *here*, when she might have slept in any of the master bedrooms? Was it fear that the ladies might come back unexpectedly and catch her out of her place? Or inverted pride? But—at least her room has survived the wreckage.

"It's only me—Val," she said gently, and, taking Elspie's arm, helped her up.

Elspie looked rather wildly around.

"Where's Mungo? He's no' hurt? And Pieter?"

"No, no—don't worry—they've gone in the boat to Wolf's Hope to give the alarm. But I thought I'd come back—"

"Eh!" said Elspie, on a note of satisfaction. "For a moment ye had me frichted! But gin they're at Wolf's Hope they'll be safe eneugh."

She did not thank Val for returning. But there was a certain dry approval in her expression.

"At least," said Val, "things seem quiet enough here? Everybody's gone."

"Ay. Ye'll likely have heard from Mungo aboot the ones that went into the Kelpie's Flow?"

"Yes. And Mungo cut the yacht loose; and she was wrecked on the point. And"—Val's voice wavered as she thought of the horrible scene on the cliff—"my brother and Lord Clanreydon are both dead."

"An' that's as weel," said Elspie matter-of-factly, "for an iller pair o' wanchancie scoondrels ne'er trod groond." She did not inquire how they had died, and Val did not go into detail, nor pretend sorrow. Instead she said, "Elspie, I'm grieved to the heart about your house. I think of it as yours—you are the only one who has loved it and cared for it all these years. If I and the children hadn't come here—"

But Elspie, as usual, was remarkably detached about it.

"Och, dinna greet about sic a trifle as that," she said. "The good book says we maurna bow down tae idols o' wood an' stone. Forbye the hoose itself still stands—an' whit's a few bit tables and curtains? Gin Lady Stroma is sae fashed she dismeeses me, Mungo an' I will marry an' live in a wee croft."

"It would be very unfair if Lady Stroma dismissed you—it certainly wasn't your fault. But all your household things that you loved and kept so carefully—I can't bear to see it in such a state."

"Ach, ye silly tawpie! *Things* arena that important. It's wee Jannie ye should be greetin' for, an' Davie Ramsay, an' my puir Kirstie that I dinna doot was hurried oot o' her life wi' carking an' trouble. 'Tis them ye should mourn."

"I am; I do," said Val, and fell silent. Elspie looked at her and said, "Would ye like tae sleep in here, the nicht? The lave o' the hoose is no' juist very comfortable the way things are at present. Tomorrow's morn we'll set to worrk an' pit a' to richts."

"Yes, I'd like to sleep here," said Val, "if you don't mind having me."

"There's a few bit covers i' the awmry. I'll spraid mysel' a pallet on the floor; I've sleepit there mony an' mony a time when I was a lassie."

But Val would not hear of this, and insisted on Elspie getting into bed while she made herself up a bed on the boards. And there she slept, not too well, for she was assailed by strange fierce dreams and terrors, while beside her Elspie lay motionless and lightly breathing, in a slumber as untroubled as that of a child.

Next morning Val felt stiff, aching, racked with tiredness, and with the painful throat and difficulty in swallowing that were probably precursive warnings of a heavy cold. Small wonder, she thought, after riding through the sea, rowing in the bitter night, walking in the snow, all in the same soaking wet clothes. But her feeling of ill-health was the least of her troubles; the day seemed wretched in every way. Inspected by daylight, the devastation of the house filled her with wild rage and grief; while the deaths of David and Jannie ached intolerably in her heart. The thought of Pieter, too, troubled her deeply; how was he going to bear the loss of his sister?

"Ach, he'll just have to," said Elspie, raking ashes and lighting the range. "Childer bear trouble easier than grown folk, whiles; they're easier distractit. An' syne he'll gae to school, an' a' the things he learns will put wee Jannie oot o' his mind."

Val supposed this to be true. Pieter, like the rest of them, would have to find some way of meeting his loss. And the next thing to do was always the best—as Elspie was demonstrating. Val took a broom and swept the spilt meal and broken pottery out into the yard; presently they had some porridge made, and were eating it in an almost cheerful atmosphere of improvisation. At last Val felt herself on equal terms with Elspie; their concerns, plans, and satisfactions were the same; they both rejoiced equally over a whole barrel of oatmeal found unbroken behind a door, and the discovery that none of the poultry had been taken by a fox despite the fact that they had been turned out of their hen run; the cattle were unharmed, also. But it was unfortunate that they had no cash, for Elspie had lent her last ten pounds to Nils, who had taken it over the cliff with him.

"I'll write to Sir Marcus," Val was saying. "He promised he'd take some of my articles and I'm sure he'll pay up promptly when he hears what's happened—" when there came a loud trampling of horses in the yard.

Elspie paled.

"It's no' those hellicats comin' back?" she gasped.

"No, it's a carriage—drawn by four horses—who can it possibly be?"

Val's heart leaped—then sank again. For who, of all people, should step out of the carriage, looking about him with an air of puzzled gloom at his extraordinary surroundings, but Benet Allerton; and he then turned to help a lady descend: Mrs. Allerton.

"Oh, no!" muttered Val.

"Dod save us, it's a leddy!" exclaimed Elspie with equal dismay. "Was there e'er a like time for sic a one tae come calling!"

She turned and surveyed her ravaged kitchen. "Aweel, the fire's lit, but that's a' ye can say. I doot if we've sae much as a dram o' whisky or a hale tea cake ben the hoose."

Two more ladies stepped out of the carriage—Delia, and Charlotte Warren, who both looked wonderingly around and then proceeded to pick their way across the courtyard through the snow.

"Losh, losh," grumbled Elspie, making for the door, "of a' the times folk choose tae come steeking their nebs in, yon's the waurst."

But Val was still watching the carriage and now observed a tall, thin, well-wrapped form walk round from the far side: Sir Marcus, who stood talking to Benet for a moment and then strolled with him across the yard in the rear of the ladies.

"Oh, the wretch!" thought Val. "How *could* he? How could he bring them, without giving me warning? Oh, what a monster!" But nonetheless, at sight of him, her heart had bounded up so high that, just for a moment, she forgot her many troubles, and how far from well she felt.

She started to walk across the kitchen, and heard Elspie saying, as dourly as only Elspie could, "I'm afeered it's no' juist very convenient tae receive callers at praisent—we're in a wee bit o' a clamjamfry. Hech, Sir Marcus, is that you?"

Val walked out into the yard and said composedly, "Benet; how do you do? Mrs. Allerton—Delia—Miss Warren—how pleasant to see you. But, I'm afraid, as Elspie says, we are in a pickle here, not really in a position to offer you hospitality. However—come in and see for yourselves."

It was worth it, she thought, it would almost have been worth all the agony—no, no, not the deaths of Davie and Jannie, never that—to see the faces of the Allerton ladies as they gazed in utter stupefaction and horror about the havoc in the dining room and library. Val went on politely, "Of course the house is not always like this—as Sir Marcus will corroborate. But we had—burglars—yesterday, and they left the place as you see."

"My dear Valla—*burglars?*" Benet said in his most weighty legal manner. "Are you joking? It looks as if a tribe of Goths or Vandals had been through the house. Is this the result of some Scottish—ah—feud? Was anybody injured?"

"No, I'm not joking." Val felt suddenly very weary. "And, yes, several people were injured. Killed, in fact." She looked up at Sir Marcus, who was standing beside her, his eyes fixed very intently on her face. "David Ramsay was killed," she said in a low voice, "and—and Jannie. It was Lord Clanreydon who came here. In pursuit of my brother, over the Bermondsey murder articles, you know. And Clanreydon told his men to wreck the house." The alert, lined face of Sir Marcus expressed perfect comprehension, but Benet exclaimed, "You mean Lord Clanreydon the politician? You must be mistaken! What extraordinary cock-and-bull tale is this? I can understand your brother being involved in such scandalous goings on—he did strike me as an adventurer, I am sorry to say—but Clanreydon! Why, I've met the man. In London, at the Inns of Court! Why, it's too ridiculous!"

"Yes, it's too ridiculous," said Val, and fainted, feeling very much ashamed of herself as the floor came up to hit her.

When she recovered, she found herself in the library, lying on a sofa which moulted flock and horsehair. The Allerton ladies were clucking over her solicitously and very ineffectually. "We must get her out of here *instantly*," she heard Mrs. Allerton say.

Val propped herself on one elbow and croaked out a request for Elspie.

"Here I am, my doo; I ran an' borrowed a dram for ye from Mysie Kelso; an' no harm conseedering a' they've had from the Hoose; no' but what it's as weel they were a' sick wi' the influeenza an' nane o' them around when thon villains were here. Let that slip down yer throat, noo, my dearie, an' lie back easy."

The dram helped her throat considerably. It was plain that while Val had been unconscious a certain amount of explanation had taken place between Elspie and the men. Val heard, vaguely, from a distance, discussions between Benet and Sir Marcus as to the proper legal steps to be taken, the need for informing Lady Stroma, and the doubtful possibility of redress. Val closed her eyes. She was not interested.

Benet, seizing a chance when the others were upstairs inspecting more of the damage, came into the library—how well she recalled his loud, ponderous, assertive tread—but he had put on weight, surely? she thought, opening her eyes to look at him. He pulled up a broken chair and sat down by her chaise longue.

"My dear Valla. I deeply regret that you have suffered from these unfortunate alarms. But I hope it will have been a demonstration to you of the unwisdom of your course. I need hardly say that if you had remained in New York, none of this would have happened."

"No, it wouldn't would it," agreed Val, shutting her eyes again. "And I should never have seen Ardnacarrig, or met Elspie and Mungo and the Ramsays. Have you been to see David Ramsay's body, Benet? It's out in the grange, on a trestle. Elspie and I brought it up from the beach."

"My dear Valla, death is hardly a subject for levity."

"No levity was intended," she said coldly. "Elspie would take your visit as a mark of respect."

"To return to my main theme," he went on, ignoring this, "I hope you now see the advisability of returning to New York without delay. My mother and Delia and Charlotte (who has come with us for her health) will be glad to give you their escort; we can wait another week, by which time you should be sufficiently recovered to travel. Once you are away from here it will be easier to put all this behind you; you can forget these people."

"Never in my life," she said. "Which I owe to them—among other things."

"You are still upset, I am aware," he pronounced. "Believe me, you owe these people nothing. What have they ever done for you?"

She stared at him.

"Mungo saved me from that man's ship! He rowed out in the middle of the night—risking being shot—and got me out of the cabin where I had been locked in—"

"*What?*"

Benet's composure totally left him. Evidently this part of the tale was new to him.

Val explained.

"Clanreydon had taken me and Pieter—as hostages for Nils and his papers. He—he had thrown Jannie overboard—"

"You were on his *yacht?*" Benet repeated as if he could hardly believe his ears. "*Unchaperoned?* You spent the night there?"

"Well, part of it at any rate." She studied his face with curiosity, almost sympathetically. It was evident that for him she was now suddenly and permanently devalued. Poor man, thought Val with detachment, and tried to find an image for his dismay. It was like, she decided, it was like choosing the biggest shining strawberry from the dish and then having the misfortune to drop it in a cowpat.

"Benet," she said tiredly, "I am sorry if you came here hoping to resume our engagement. But I must tell you again once and for all that we should not suit. Our—our modes of thinking are too unlike. I accepted you, when I did, for the wrong reasons. I was lonely—you seemed so strong and kind and reliable—but we should have been wretchedly ill-matched. I am sorry."

"My dear Valla—I am sorry too. But perhaps, after all, you are right. Since we have been apart, I believe—I believe our ways of looking at things *have* insensibly diverged."

"Yes, that is it," she agreed, smiling. "You are so good at finding the *mot juste*, Benet! Our ways of looking at things have diverged."

"However, my mother's escort is still at your service should you wish to accompany her."

"That is extremely kind of your mother, but I could not possibly go off abandoning my poor friends here in such straits."

"Well—if you are certain—" He looked suddenly younger, unhappy, troubled, and a little ashamed of himself. "I am sorry to leave you like this. But I will disturb you no further. I most sincerely wish you well."

"Yes, do go away, Benet." She shut her eyes again, knowing that she had behaved badly but too tired to care. Then something occurred to her; she opened her eyes and called, "Benet?"

"Yes?" he said, turning.

"Could you send Miss Warren to me a moment, if you please?"

"Miss Warren?" He sounded startled.

"If you please," she repeated.

A few minutes later she heard soft footsteps and saw Charlotte Warren creep into the room looking big-eyed and apprehensive, despite a ravishingly pretty traveling costume of oyster velvet with swansdown trimmings.

"Miss Warren," said Val, "I have an apology to make to you. Last time we met I was wretchedly rude and unkind to you—I was feeling rather unhappy at the time but that is no excuse—and, since we are not likely to be meeting again—since I am not returning to New York at present—I wanted to ask your forgiveness."

"Forgiveness?" repeated Charlotte, looking totally puzzled—though also, suddenly, hopeful—"I don't understand you, Miss Montgomery? I don't recall the occasion."

"But I recall it," said Val, "and I have felt bad about it ever since. Goodbye, Miss Warren. Enjoy your journey."

She closed her eyes again as Charlotte, still puzzled, tiptoed from the room.

A longish time passed, during which Val fell into a doze. She heard, at a distance, voices, footsteps, the slam of doors, the clatter of wheels and horses' hoofs. They've all gone, she thought tiredly; none of the others came to say goodbye. I must get up and help Elspie. But her back ached badly.

A tear trickled from under her lids.

And then she heard footsteps: quick, too heavy for Elspie. A hand was laid over hers.

She opened her eyes.

"They've gone," said Sir Marcus. "I sent them off in my carriage. I am sorry you had to be troubled with them, my dear—but the poor young man was so anxious to see you—and I feared my letter to you had miscarried—so I thought they might as well come with me. I understand that you have sent Mr. Allerton about his business? Are you sure that was wise?"

"The wisest thing I ever did," Val said from her heart.

"Well," he said, "I cannot pretend that I am not delighted. Och, Val, my dear, I believe you know my feelings for you? I was *that* cast down when I had your letter bidding me not to come back here—I believed that it was your kind way of letting me know that there could be no hope for me. But now I understand that it was because your brother had concealed himself here I cannot forbear to try my luck—"

He suddenly came to a dead stop. His usual air of sardonic composure had completely deserted him. He looked defenceless, vulnerable—rather like Benet, she thought, touched and amused, under the joy that was flooding her. Speechlessly, he held out his hand. Without a word, she laid hers in it.

He stooped and kissed her. "My dear, I am the happiest man in Lammermuir. And the most undeserving! It was not I who rescued you from the ship, or sent those villains into the quicksand, or pushed Clanreydon over the cliff. Indeed, I would hardly know how to set about such business. But nonetheless, I hope I shall know how to make you happy."

"Why, it is so easy," Val said, smiling at him. "Next time you go to Baku or the Aral Sea, just equip me with a camel and take me along!"

"That I will! But still, I don't deserve you. Or so Helen said."

"Helen . . ." Val looked away from him and drew a long, sad breath. "I don't know how—after loving *her*—you can see anything in *me*—"

"*She* could," he said. "When I spoke to her about you, she said, 'Why, Marcus my dear, you are really in love at last! And, although you don't deserve her a bit, that girl will be the salvation of you. Mind you don't let her slip through your fingers, now!' Och, I was in such terror when that lawyer-laddie came to call on me (although I did wonder how you had come to love such a ponderous kind of a public-speaking fellow)—I thought I had lost you for good and all! So I decided to bring him straight here and learn my fate at once."

"How did you get here so early? You never came from Edinburgh today?"

"No, no," he said. "We spent the night in my house at Ravenswood—where I am going to take you back, shortly. Just for a wee visit," he added hastily as he saw her look of protest. "Mungo has brought back Tibbie Gordon, from Wolf's Hope, and some other folk are coming presently to help with the clearing up, so you need not feel you are deserting them. And Pieter can come with us, if you wish."

She clasped his hand tightly, thinking about Jannie, and, as if guessing her thought, he said, "My dear—I know you cannot help grieving about the poor little child. And it was a dreadful thing—it is right that you should. But do not take it *too* hard; for Davie had told me that she might have had more wrong with her than just the ear trouble, poor bairn. She might not have lived to grow up."

"Oh, *poor* little Jannie." Val covered her face with her hands.

"Try not to cry," he said. "Listen—I have another piece of news. I'll not pretend that my main wish in coming here was not to see *you*. But I also had business with Mungo."

"With Mungo? About his book?"

"No. I have various legal acquaintances who have been undertaking research for me, on Mungo's behalf, over some considerable period of time, and I came to announce to him in person the results of their labours—in fact," he said, "the long and the short of it now is that Mungo's direct descent from Andrew Bucklaw Carsphairn is now established beyond question, and I came to tell him that he is the Master of Ardnacarrig."

Val gasped.

"*Mungo* is? Not the Stroma ladies?"

"No, their claim was only valid—as they are well aware—if no descendants of the other line, the male line, were still alive."

"Who was Andrew Bucklaw Carsphairn?"

"He was the auld laird's younger brother. Lady Stroma's uncle."

"The one with Jacobite tendencies who left home. I *see*," she said slowly. "And Mungo is—"

"His great-grandson."

"Did he never guess?"

"Mungo is a remarkable person. He did not greatly care. It was I, who became interested in the name Bucklaw, who began to inquire and to ferret out people's histories and write to correspondents in South America. But, now that he is assured of his claim, he will take his responsibilities with the utmost seriousness and will make an admirable laird. I am certain of that."

"Oh, I am too! This is wonderful news! And I don't imagine the Carsphairn ladies will be very upset—perhaps they may even be relieved to have it all settled? And Mungo will marry Elspie—oh, please bring them here—I can't wait to see them—or, no, help me up, Marcus, let's go to them," exclaimed Val, scrambling off the sofa.

"Carefully, my dearest girl. You are as pale as a gean flower; you should have a dram of birk wine with a pinch of ipecacuanha, or some sulfate of zinc—"

"Yes, yes," she said, taking his arm lovingly, "all in good time—but now let's just go and congratulate Mungo and Elspie."

She walked haltingly, leaning on his arm, as far as the kitchen door, and there paused. It was open. Inside, at the kitchen table, Tibbie was carefully sorting through a big wicker basket of broken crockery, putting the few uninjured pieces to one side.

Elspie sat in the rocker holding Pieter tightly; his arms were round her neck. And Mungo, standing in the front of the range, read from the Bible:

"They slay the widow and the stranger and murder the fatherless. . . .

"But judgment shall return unto righteousness: and all the upright in heart shall follow it.

"Unless the Lord had been my help, my soul had almost dwelt in silence.

"But the Lord is my defence; and my God is the rock of my refuge."

He closed the book and stood with his head bowed for a moment, then, looking up and seeing Val and Marcus, came forward to welcome them in with grave friendliness, as befitted the master of the house.

ABOUT THE AUTHOR

JOAN AIKEN has published nearly thirty-five books for adults and children alike.

The daughter of the poet Conrad Aiken and the sister of two professional writers, she began writing at the age of five, because, as she says, "Writing is just the family trade."

Ms. Aiken lives in Sussex, England, and in New York City, where she is currently at work on a play for children.